Acknowledgements

Many people have assisted the creation of this story. Feichang ganxie ni to my editors Kathryn Robyn and Mike Zhang, my coach Larry Brooks and my readers Harriet, Helen, Barbara, Judy, Linda and Marty. Special thanks to Linda Price for cover design.

To my patient and supportive husband Bruce

Prologue

Over dessert, a charming miniature flan with tiny blueberries and praline crumbs, she suddenly remembers something. Out of her purse, she produces a card and lays it on the table.

"What's this?" the man asks.

"That's what I'd like to know," the woman says.

Seeing she's serious, he pulls reading glasses out of an inside pocket and holds the card up to the candle lantern.

"Where did you get this?" he asks, returning it to her.

She puts it back into her purse and clicks it closed. "Odd things have been happening lately. Like this card. I was coming in late the other night, and a man calls out my name from a parked car in the rain. He says, 'Your safety is our concern,' hands this to me, and drives away."

"Well, I have to tell you," he replies, "I'm in a line of work that, uh, well, hmmm ..." he pauses and looks at her carefully before continuing. "This is what I do; I solve problems like this. Exactly like this. And that is odd, too; wouldn't you say?"

Contents

CHAPTER 1
Scooter Guys

August 29

At quitting time, Mai Martin goes down the hall to the other office. Ms. HAN and Dandan are still there. "You guys working late today?" she asks.

Average height back home in the United States, she's suddenly tall next to her diminutive Chinese colleagues. Straight, dark eyebrows frame round eyes, an elegant nose rests over full lips, and a small chin masks intensity beneath the calm exterior. When she was younger, her wavy hair was what they called strawberry blonde. Now closer to forty than thirty, she's become an indistinct brunette. Soon after arriving, she visited the campus hotel beauty shop to make a change.

"No, I'm going now. You are leaving?"

Dandan Xiaojie and Mai go downstairs to the bicycles. They ride together for a ways, but at last Dandan turns and goes toward the West Gate where she's meeting a friend for dinner. Mai continues straight toward the *hutong* neighborhood. They've been working on the streets around her neighborhood for the past couple of weeks. She'll leave in the morning one way, just to be blocked on the way back by barricades and a big ditch where there used to be a street.

As she approaches the intersection at the back end of the primary school, she sees a black Dongfeng SUV like the one parked near her office yesterday. It's off to the side, between two apartment buildings. She stops and thinks, reaching for her cell phone, pretending to talk, looking for an alternate route. Turning right where she usually goes straight, she travels the short distance to the next cross street and sees a guy on a motor scooter, lounging on the corner and talking on his cell. As she turns left, to her dismay, he pulls out behind her. Just beyond, she sees the Dongfeng rounding the corner.

Ahead is the second Southwest Gate checkpoint, one block inside campus, manned by two young guards during the day. Instead of turning onto her street, she passes the guards and looks toward the last checkpoint at the Southwest Gate. The bicycle repair shop on the corner has a small group of loungers sitting around playing cards. People are busy coming and going through the gate. Mai stops a second and looks over her shoulder. The guy on the motor scooter passes her and turns right outside the gate. She can't see the Dongfeng. Suddenly it pulls around a parked car and is heading at her.

She passes the guards and turns left onto the avenue. While the SUV is stopped at the car gate, she slips into the bike lane. At the end of the street, near the newsstand, she stops to look again. The Dongfeng passes her and makes a left onto the big boulevard, Chengfu Road. Just as she is about to turn around and head back onto campus, the motor scooter guy returns, two of them now.

Turning left at the corner where the regular fruit peddler has a truck, she heads into the small amount of traffic coming at her in the bike lane. Just as the motor scooter guys start to overtake, she cuts into the parking lot of a strip mall directly behind her LiNai apartment. Dodging pedestrians and cars, she makes it to the front of the building housing a massage clinic, just as she sees the motor scooters circle around and come back in her direction. Rushing past the private guard sitting on the entry porch, she finds her phone and calls Ron.

August 26

When Ronald ZHAO learned about the ballet tickets, he thought it would be a good way to treat his mother, perhaps make her happy about moving to Beijing from Hong Kong. Finding a place to park in the rain wasn't easy, but then nothing was easy here. The pay was pretty good, and the cost of living in Beijing was better than Hong Kong. At least he got more apartment for his money.

Ballet tickets to see *Carmen* at the Tian Qiao Theatre had been distributed throughout Beijing to Foreign Experts only, and Mai Martin was seated next to him at the program. They hit it off and agreed to meet the next night.

August 29

A massage clinic is on the ground floor at the back of the six-story building next to a craft store. Mai sits on the stairs going up to the Korean coffee house on the second floor. From here, she can clearly see the parking lot in front where the two motor scooter guys are waiting. In a few minutes, the black Dongfeng drives slowly past her view. She gets up and looks out to see it pull into a parking place. She goes back to sitting on the stairs. She's stuck in here, trapped, only one way in or out.

"*Wei, nihao*, Ron," says Mai. "When can you get here?"

"*Weishenme*? It's only five-thirty."

"If you left right now, when could you get here?"

"Probably not until seven. Are you okay? Something's the matter!"

"Yeah, I'm being followed by two guys on scooters and the black Dongfeng SUV."

"Where are you?"

"I'm at the massage clinic. I came here 'cause there are a lot of people around. I don't think they'll come in here after me."

"Stay there, I'll come get you."

"I'm going to try to get to my apartment. I'm so close."

A middle-aged man approaches her—the private security guard who is usually sitting outside at the top of the steps. He says something like "*Ni buneng ba zixingche fangzai zher,*" you can't park your bicycle here, gesturing to where she dropped it on the steps.

She takes his arm and points to the two guys waiting in the parking lot, who stand up when they see her. The guard notices them now. She won't let go of his arm, dragging him over to where her bike rests, keeping the *shifu* between her and the scooter guys. She keeps looking around over her shoulder. He gets the idea: she's afraid.

The guard nods to Mai and pats her hand reassuringly while extricating himself from her grasp. He swaggers toward the scooter guys and starts talking loudly. Mai jumps on her bike and pedals as fast as she can in the fading light through the parking of the next mini-mall. At last, she turns left into the gated parking of the new apartments behind LiNai, where she integrates with a stream of pedestrians and bicycles heading toward the south pedestrian gate onto campus.

Cutting through the back of the parking area, Mai passes through the gate. She leaves the scooters and SUV behind, threading through the busy foot traffic, zigzagging through the *hutong*. When she turns through the gate at her apartment, the black Dongfeng is parked in front.

Her heart is pounding, and tears start steaming behind her eyes. She rides her bike into the shed. *Don't panic!* Bright lights shine on the road between her and the LiNai entrance. Two men are in the guard shack playing cards. Mai walks up to the open door and starts talking, part Mandarin part English.

"*Nihao, keyi bang wo hui jia ma*? [Hi, can you help me get into my apartment?] I lost my key." Mai makes like a key fitting into a lock with her fingers, smiling and talking non-stop. The men politely listen but have no idea what she's talking about. Somehow, she pulls one of them up to his feet and drags him across the road like a human shield. He goes along with this for a few feet, she's so beautiful and a favorite of the men. Mai keeps wheedling and smiling. Once she's past the Dongfeng, she says, "*Xiexie*," and flees into the entrance and up the five flights of stairs to her apartment, leaving the guard scratching his head and looking into the front seat of the Dongfeng, recognizing the campus security insignia hanging from the rear-view mirror.

Once she's inside, having double-locked the gate and door, she runs to the bedroom and slams that door. Not feeling safe yet, she retreats to the sun porch and crouches in the gloom. Mai hunts for her phone. A text from Ron says, "B ther soon."

She texts back: *Im @ apt brng din.*

August 27

The night after the ballet concert, Ronald ZHAO waited in front of her LiNai Apartment and texted her. She locked her door and walked past the surveillance cameras in the stairwell.

On shift in the next building over, Maj. TANG Xiaobei, Battalion Commander, Beijing University Security Office and Lt. Col. GUAN Qinchen, from Harbin, were monitoring the video feeds. "Do we know where she's going?" asked GUAN.

Maj. TANG reviewed the notebook from the previous shift and reached for his phone to call JGTS YANG Cai at the computer lab.

"Cai, she's leaving. Do we know where she's going?" asked TANG.

A pause while the tech specialist checked the email log. Maj. TANG and Lt. GUAN waited until they saw the Subject emerge from the entrance and get into a black Buick Park Avenue.

"Grab that license number," hissed GUAN.

Finally JGTS YANG Cai got back to him. "She got an email from a guy named Ronald ZHAO today, saying to call him."

The Park Avenue slowly turned through the big gate and disappeared from their view.

"I just sent you a license number. Trace it. Get back to me ASAP," said TANG.

While the Beijing University Security Office scrambled, Ron drove Mai to a restaurant which was a big step up from the family eateries in her neighborhood. They watched the sun drop like a volcanic fireball through a wavering mirage of smog into the black, Beijing skyline from the top of a tall building in the Silicon Valley neighborhood near the university. The wine was French, and the food was exquisite, an endless-seeming stream of little dishes of shellfish and wild vegetables garnished with slivers of ginger and toasted seeds, little cakes of pressed rice or puffy pastry buns with green onions, some meat things she nibbled slightly with a sweet glaze and hot peppers. And more wine which blurred the anxiety she had been feeling recently.

Lights winked on all over the city. The *fuwuyuan* lighted a candle lantern on their table. In the warm light, her face looked like an Italian painting, and he told her so.

She gave him her best Mona Lisa smile. She thought he looked handsome in a black-knit shirt and silvery gray jacket, and she told him so, picking a white carnation out of the table decoration and stuffing it into his lapel pocket. She felt less lonely, and he felt more lovely.

Suddenly remembering, she said, "I'm in way over my head, Ron, Things are happening I don't understand. Can you help me?"

Her brown eyes were wide, and he felt himself falling into them. Ordinary caution was distracted. His skeptic's mind was a little drunk. She intrigued him the first time he saw her, and this second meeting only added more mystery.

"You came to the right guy! This is my specialty," he declared. He reached across the table and grasped her hand. She didn't pull it away. "So, tell me about these *odd things.*"

August 29

By the time Ronald ZHAO arrives, Mai has showered and changed into shorts and a tee-shirt. She starts a load of wash in the little washer in the bathroom and plugs in the rice cooker. Cleaning house, setting things straight, helps her sort out the today's disturbing events. *Who is chasing me? Here on campus and off. Am I safe now? Is my apartment safe? Where's Rick and why can't I call or email him?* She looks through the apartment for things she could use as defensive weapons: hammer, kitchen knife, an ex-acto art blade goes into her purse.

She's listening to a San Diego internet jazz station on *Pépe* and checking her email. She sees a message from her husband, Rick, when she hears a knock on the door.

August 29   To: Mai   From: Rick

Subject: Skype Soon?

I'm at Joe's house and had fun at the San Berdoo show. Be leaving Monday morning to home on Amtrak and will be there 5:30AM on Tuesday, so we can Skype Wednesday August 31 morning or evening. Raleigh meet was fun too. Chat Wednesday morning.

The heavy, old doors rattle and clang as she unlocks both the door and iron gate. Standing in the dim entry, backlit from the sitting room, she holds the doors open for Ron to enter.

"You made it here safely," he says, and then holds a finger to his mouth, carrying take-out bags of Chinese food in one hand and a gadget bag over his other shoulder. Neither talks. He hands her the food and immediately turns on the radio frequency (RF) signal detector, bug sniffer, and sweeps for listening devices, turning up the volume on *Pépe*. "They put the microphone back in the same place in the entry," he says. He removes it and drops it into his bag. "Okay, Mai, come here."

In the stairwell, he shows her where they've drilled and twined wires around her internet cable. "When you come in, look here. They seem to be creatures of habit; used the same place. Your walls are solid concrete, so all the wires have to be on the outside, where we can see them."

Using a flashlight, he follows the wire trail to a transformer box out in the landing near the electric box and phone jack. A tool gadget opens up to a screw driver and wire cutters. He removes the box and brings all the wire and paraphernalia into her apartment. Mai finds a shopping bag for him, and he fills it with the spy junk.

"What's that?" she asks, her black hair, fluffy from the shower, surrounds her pale face. *Yuanfen* joins with memory and budding tendrils form. Breath vibrates, and millions of atoms begin dancing in an ageless pattern.

"Signal booster. Their listening post must be outside the normal range of their microphone transmitter."

While he's busy with the bugs, she sets out dishes and things for dinner. The electric tea kettle is hot, and she makes a pot of tea. She wants to feel better now that he is here, but is still upset from the afternoon. Looking out the windows, she doesn't see the black Dongfeng. Everything looks normal in the street below.

The freedom she felt when she first arrived here at Beijing University, free from the depressing American economy and the depressing state of her marriage, the freedom to find adventure in the world, the freedom to seize control of her destiny, now that feeling is taking on political overtones she hadn't expected.

She turns toward Ron, looking good in a Chinese-tailored shirt and black trousers. He has a lot of black, glossy hair which he mousses up and styles himself. Compared to her husband, the geek, Ron looks like a GQ model, an obsessed metrosexual man groomed down to manicure. Rick is a natural man, happiest dressed in button-down, short-sleeved shirt and jeans, his blond hair curling over his ears, in need of a trim, but he can't be bothered. And then there's the uncomfortable fact that she only learned this past summer that he's been working for Homeland Security since 9/11. Lying to her for ten years! How could she have missed that?

Over *jiaozi* and *chaomien*, rice, and beer, Ron asks, "Tell me about today. Leave nothing out."

"I saw the black Dongfeng on the way home, but I managed to elude it. Some guys on motor scooters, too. I followed your suggestion. I stopped when I first saw it and pretended to get a call. I changed my usual route and slowed them down at the gate. The massage clinic is just around the corner, so I went in there and waited. Here's the license number," she says, showing him where she wrote it on a grocery receipt.

"What happened then, did they leave?"

"They parked in the mini plaza outside the building, a couple spaces down, but I could see them. The scooter guys parked in a space directly opposite and waited. That's when I called you."

Mai gets up and disappears into the bathroom, returning with her arms loaded with wet things from the washer. "Help me?" Neither Ron's mother nor wife ever asked him to help hang up the laundry. Without waiting for his reply, Mai turns toward the sun porch and continues her story. "The private security guard told me I couldn't leave my bike lying on the steps. Somehow, I got him to hassle the scooter guys. That allowed me to cut behind them and get back on campus at the pedestrian gate."

Ron springs to follow her to the sun porch and help clip sheets over lines stretched in front of the broiling hot windows. "Why are the clothes lines so high here, Mai?"

From behind, she gets a good look at Ron's backside.

Coming here and taking a job at the university, she had accepted there would be risks. And she's still willing to pursue her China adventure, especially for the risk and the clarity she's getting about Rick and what happened to their marriage. The first disillusionment.

"Good question. I usually have to drag a chair in here to reach this end. Thanks for helping, Ron."

"Mai, genius method to escape but so dangerous to run from them. You're not afraid?"

"You bet I was afraid. And then, when I got to LiNai, the

Dongfeng was parked right in front!"

Mai reaches clean sheets from the armoire, and they tuck in the heavy, cotton damask bottom sheet over the firm, Chinese mattress in the office, where Ron has been sleeping for a few days.

"Do you work out? At a gym?" she asks.

He's never helped with housework in his life. Doing it with Mai is a novelty and an intimate privilege, seeing her in an unguarded, domestic moment makes her seem more vulnerable and feminine to him, and she seemed to need his help.

"I practice martial arts at my kung fu club," he answers.

Mai continues with the story. "I ran the bike into the darkest part of the bike shed. There were two guards in the shack playing cards. I got one of them to come with me across the road. Once past the Dongfeng, I ran up the stairs."

Pulling on the fresh duvet cover is more challenging, finding the ties hidden inside the deep corners.

"More clever methods. You are fearless and smart. Wery good, wery good, *haode ha-ha.*"

"Do you see the Dongfeng now?" he asks, getting up to find a slim report cover in his duffel. "Here's some info on car licenses." He opens it to a spreadsheet that folds out. Every car he'd observed on the street near her apartment last Sunday, the time of day, location, and other details are organized neatly.

She bends her head over it, admiring his thoroughness and feeling a little better now she has eaten. "It was a black Dongfeng. And no, it's not down there now. Look, here, it's on your list!" she says, comparing the number on the receipt with an entry on the spreadsheet. "Now we're done with housework," she says with a smile, "want another beer?" She retrieves a bottle from the fridge. Mai pours them each a small glass painted with cherry blossoms or fall leaves.

Ron says, "The ownership registration is 'Not assigned, PRC motor pool Beijing University'; pretty obvious. I want you to start writing down the license numbers of suspicious vehicles, okay? He produces a tiny notebook out of his pocket and slides it across the vinyl table cloth to her. "Here, use this."

Behind the spreadsheet is a TSC contract. "We need to talk about business for a minute. I want you to hire us to work for you. That allows me to do a better job. Please look this over and complete it with your signature." He turns the folder around and lays a pen down next to her glass.

After a couple minutes, Mai flips to the end of the document and signs her name. "Do you need a deposit?"

"Yeah, that would be great. I can trim it down, give you a friend discount, but they still want 50 thousand yuan to get started," says Ron. The way the firm wants them to get a signed contract jars Ron's sense of correctness. The Chinese way is more vague—and never talk about money.

What's that in dollars?" asks Mai. Talking about contracts is natural to her; it's the American way—get it in writing.

"Around eight thousand dollars, depending on the rate of exchange on any given day," answers Ron.

August 28

Commander GAO was enjoying his weekend. Although he got called on Saturday at his in-laws', it was just an update on the Martin investigation and didn't require him to go into the office. Cai ran the ID on the car that picked her up and found a surprising contact: Mr. Ronald ZHAO from Hong Kong, retired police commissioner, relocated to Beijing, and currently working for a private firm, TSC Security Consultants Ltd. *Interesting*, he thought.

Lt. GUAN and Maj. TANG were running the operation, keeping 24–7 surveillance on the woman. Lt. GUAN set up a listening post at her office and at her apartment. He thought he could intercept her at one of several identified locations she passed almost daily. The whole thing disgusted GAO, but he had witnessed worse. At least he tipped her off before Lt. GUAN's net was in place. She could call his mobile ... and he would do what? Warn her? Of what? He sighed and turned the shower onto hot and forgot about the mess for a few minutes.

Sunday, after breakfast, his wife got onto Skype with their son at college in Nanjing while the Commander retreated into his nook in the spare bedroom, checking his emails. The vibrating mobile phone interrupted, "*Wei ...* Commander GAO here, *dui, dui ... ZHAO Xiansheng!*"

"This is Ronald ZHAO. I'm a friend of Mai Martin."

"I see," GAO leaned back into the deluxe executive office chair he and his son dragged up to their apartment from his office, one arm folded across his chest propping up the elbow of the hand holding the phone. "Do you play basketball?" he asked, eyeing his gym bag and ball sitting on the washing machine in the next nook.

"I'm fair ..." replied ZHAO.

"Join me for a game this morning at Beijing University?" asked Commander GAO.

"I could."

"*Hao*, go to the Main Gate and call me."

Most of the men and the few women in the security bureau were regular exercisers. Sr. Col. GAO Bu, Deputy Division Commander and First Bureau Office Director of the Beijing University Security Office, tried to keep in shape with some strenuous, aerobic activity every weekend. The Harbin Chief could use a workout, he observed wryly to himself, and lay off the booze and cigarettes. He looks like hell. That Lt. GUAN, though, is really fit. The guy must work out in his sleep. From across the yard, he saw Ronald ZHAO's black Park Avenue pull up and park. A younger man, about 45-years-old, tall, 180cm or 5' 11", and slim, approached the court.

"ZHAO?"

"*Dui*, Commander GAO?"

They shook hands and exchanged ritual greetings, bowing and exchanging cards with both hands, the Chinese way. ZHAO unzipped his windbreaker and tossed it in a pile by the basket post.

"Mrs. Martin is in grave danger." Commander GAO gave ZHAO a pointed look. "You have your mobile handy? Tell her to stay in her apartment until our game is finished."

ZHAO raised his eyebrows in a surprised way while he fished the phone out of his jacket pocket. "*Nihao*, Mai? ... Ronald.... *Dui*, I'm here at Beijing University. ... Where are you right now?... Shopping, really, *zhende*! Where?... Farmers market ..." ZHAO looked at the Commander briefly. "I want you to stay there until I can pick you up.... No, don't go out and don't go back to your apartment.... Please, I want you to stay there. Can you get a cup of tea or coffee or something?... I couldn't be more serious. DO NOT LEAVE THAT PLACE. Have I made myself clear? I will be there shortly.... I'll text you. Bye-bye, *dui, dui*, don't worry, I'm here, I'm here, Okay? Okay."

Commander GAO shot the ball at ZHAO hard, "21?"

ZHAO bounced it a few times and shot, *"Haode."*

Bouncing the ball off the rim, GAO jumped, tapped it in and took a free throw. ZHAO was patient and waited for GAO to start talking. He'd gotten his attention.

"I have your ID sheet on my desk." He gestured to the building behind them a couple blocks away, on the other side of the stadium, bamboo park, and VIP parking. "My office is up there. Third floor, fifth window from the right." He turned and resumed the game.

"You work at TSC Security Consultants Ltd., started nine months ago, moved to Beijing from Hong Kong with your mother. Left your divorced wife and son in Hong Kong where you were a police commissioner. Total years of service only nineteen, from 1991 to 2010, six of those years before repatriation. You hold a third-degree red belt in martial arts."

Commander GAO stopped talking and took a shot, missed. Ron caught the bounce, made a point, and trotted around to the free-shot line. "One thing I want to know," continued GAO, "how did you and Martin Taitai meet? Is she a client of TSC?"

The Commander kept a few points ahead of ZHAO without much effort. He let the younger man get a point or two, and then took the lead away.

"No, not client. We are friends. We met at a Foreign Expert event at the Tian Qiao Theatre."

ZHAO waited until Commander GAO was ready to continue with his story. Steadily, Ron made his points. He didn't have to win.

The Commander wanted to probe farther about the connection

between Martin Taitai, Mrs. Martin, and Ronald ZHAO, but let it go. "This game is very unofficial, you know," said GAO at last. "Don't often get to play like this anymore. You have my mobile. I have yours. Don't call unless it's an emergency." He shot the ball over to ZHAO and took a position near the basket. "I shouldn't even be playing with you this morning."

"So why are you, *weishenme?*"

"She's a Beijing University employee. Her security is my responsibility. But there are others who ..." He grabbed the rebound and trotted around ZHAO to take his final shot.

Commander GAO walked over to the gym bag on the ground, retrieved a towel, and mopped his neck. The two men faced each other only a few centimeters apart; GAO said in a low voice, "I'm glad she has a professional to help her. I'm counting on you. Don't screw up." GAO dropped the towel into the bag and zipped it. ZHAO accompanied him to his car, bouncing the ball, and tossed it into the trunk. "Good game, ZHAO. Good luck."

***

The atrium at the Lan Yuan Shopping Center was full of people coming and going. A florist shop displayed buckets of lilies, snapdragons, chrysanthemums, sunflowers, *Anthurium,* and dahlias. Across the way was a shop selling eyeglass frames and another with university memorabilia and clothing. Disturbed by Ron ZHAO's call, Mai slowly climbed the stairs and leaned over the second-floor mezzanine, watching the streams of people going in and out. *Ron ZHAO is here somewhere?* She expectantly watched the doors as if she would see his figure appear any minute. She sighed and walked up to the third floor and sat at a tiny table outside the student canteen where she could watch the stairs and the doors below. She pulled the phone out of her purse, laid it on the table, and waited.

Finally it rang. "I'm parked next to the Bank of China. Can you come to the car?" Ron asked.

When she arrived, he stuffed her bike into the trunk and stowed the groceries in the back seat. They threaded their way through the packed mob of bicycles, cars, and people on the one street that wasn't torn up by the construction.

"I've been with Commander GAO, the man who gave you his card," he said.

"Really! Who is he?"

"He's *dalaoban*, Mai, he runs the campus security. He's the guy who's been messing with your computer and all the things you told me about last night."

Ron looked at her. She looks glamorous in the daylight, wearing big sunglasses and a little straw hat that focuses attention on her lips, painted bright pink. "But ... what? ..." she stammered.

"Yeah, I know, seems a little strange to me too. The guy who is spying on you is also helping you," said Ron. He found a place to park near the entrance of her apartment where the building will shade the car. He turned to look at her, resting his long arms along the back of the seat and the steering wheel.

She removed her sunglasses, and he saw lines of tension around her intense eyes. Her dark brows were pulled down in a frown. She impulsively reached for his hand, "Please help me, Ron. I'm scared."

Slowly, he glanced around the street. He saw the bicycle shed directly opposite the entrance to her apartment. A small white car was parked near the trash barrels at the west end. More cars were parked in the shade of the building on their side. Ordinary people were going back and forth. Nothing looked out of place.

"Open the glove box and find a pad of paper in there. You see a pen, too?" he asked. Dutifully she dug around in the immaculate compartment. "Write these down for me," he said and read off the license plate numbers of the cars he could see.

"This is probably as good a place for us to talk as any; the best, really. I want you to be very alert to your surroundings. Commander GAO says you are in grave danger." Ron ZHAO stopped for a second and waited for Mai to digest this. She nodded and he continued. "The *local* security guys are on your side, so it seems, but there are others— probably from outside the campus—who seem not to be. He was very vague. Had to be, I guess. I have to run these license numbers and do more surveillance myself before I can tell you the whole story. This is China, Mai, not the US," he looked at her sternly and wondered what she had gotten into, this American woman. She acted innocent, but she's in it up to her chin ...

Mai sat there frozen. Finally, Ron said, "Okay, we're going to get out now. I'm going to get your bike out of the trunk and put it here near the entrance where you can get to it quickly. Can you get the groceries?" Mai gulped and nodded. Ron ZHAO carried a small bag over his shoulder and helped her with one of the grocery bags upstairs. As they climbed, he put his finger to his lips and pointed at some things on the way up. He noticed every detail of the stairwell. Once inside her apartment, he sat her down in the living room, and quietly and carefully looked around. He took a small gadget out of his bag, which he fiddled with while touring the rooms. At last, he took her by the hand and pulled her into the bedroom, closing the door behind them, and then out into the sun porch, closing that door too.

"Your apartment is bugged," he said. "Only one microphone in the entry. Two cameras, at least, are in the stairwell. I'm going to take care of something. Stay here."

Mai listened as Ron ZHAO opened her front door and left her apartment for a few seconds. She thought she heard a crash like the sound of broken glass. He returned to the sun porch and said, "I just broke the light at the top of your stairwell and in front of your apartment door."

"That light at my door didn't work anyway," she said, finding her voice. "Are there cameras in my apartment? How did they get here?"

"These old doors are easy to jimmy for a pro. When you are at home, I want you keep your iron gate locked on the inside, okay? That old gate makes a lot of noise. If anyone is trying to break in, you'll hear it. Call me. Okay?"

Her eyes were big as saucers, and her heart was pounding in her chest. "Break in here?" she asked incredulously.

"Maybe you should go back to California. Have you thought about that?" asked Ron.

"No, I haven't. Go back now? You mean, quit my job? I've got five more months on my contract! Wow," she put her hands up to her face; it's hot, and she felt dizzy. The sun porch was broiling. Suddenly her knees buckled, and she lost it. Ron caught her by one arm and half-walked half-carried her into the bedroom, laid her on the bed, and then left the room again.

He came back a little later, sat on the edge of the bed, and stroked her face with a damp cloth. "Here's some tea." She looked at the cup of hot jasmine tea he offered. "Just set it there," she gestured to a little table next to the bed and sat up, resting her head on her knees.

Ron switched on the AC and television, turning up the volume. "I removed the bug and searched all over for a camera. Odd, but I don't think there is one in here. So we can talk, for now, with this on. When you're at work, there's nothing stopping them from coming back in here and bugging you again."

"Just like with my computer. I got it cleaned, and it's probably bugged again."

"You want to tell me why these guys are so interested in a beautiful lady from California?"

"Well," she started doubtfully. "I'm not so sure myself. I call them *The Dage.*" They share a moment of levity when she sees him smirk. *He gets the joke*! "But yeah, besides being *Red Chinese*—which says it all to most Americans—what's the motive? There is none." *This wouldn't have to do with Rick, would it?*

"They don't go to this trouble for no reason, Mai. Think!" demanded Ron.

She reached for the tea and sat there staring at him, "I wish I knew. You know everything. Last spring, it was about the website; this summer, I had that weird hack attack when I was in Sebastopol. Since then, nothing, and it's been really nice. No blackouts. Just a few little things, but *this*! Omigod!" She took a gulp of tea and stared morosely at the dark armoire across the room.

"I'm going downstairs to take care of the bugs in the hallway and look around. I'll be back in a few minutes." He looked down at her intently while standing.

"I'm okay; just hurry back."

***

Walking around the building, he made more notes about the cars he saw. They obviously knew about him. Somehow they had gotten his ID, probably from his license plate form yesterday. He tried to imagine how they could have seen it and decided there must be a camera across the street near the bicycle shed, angled at the front of her building. The range on the cameras in the stairs was only a few hundred meters. He paced it out to the farthest distance and looked around. He's standing near another apartment building; it's six stories high, older, and made of brick, with a bicycle shed across the way. He concealed a tiny camera in the palm of his hand, capturing images all up and down the road. He thought they're probably in there with their receivers right now, and one of these cars was probably theirs. He had a bright idea.

"Mai, let's go to your office. Leave your phone here."

"*Weishenme*? Why?" she asked.

Ron removed the battery and left the mess on the desk next to *Pépe* her netbook.

Once back in the car, he felt more relaxed. She's safe in his car. She's exposed out there.

"You can be located by your phone GPS through the SIGINT towers, capturing and relaying your mobile signal."

He circled around the streets that lead to her building. She sat quietly, not talking. He stopped to write a few things in his notebook, slowly proceeded down the street, and stopped to draw a map of an intersection. After an hour at least, he parked in the library lot under the bauhinia trees.

Once in her office, he solemnly scoured the room. Out of her office phone, he removed a tiny wireless microphone, and put it in his pocket.

"That's done," he announced. "Tell me about the people you know on this floor."

Mai spoke for the first time since they left her apartment. "The office across the hall is vacant. The next one has young researchers going in and out. I don't know any of them. The next office is Ms. HAN and Dandan's, from our department. Next to that are two more offices of research students. I don't know any of them. Then there's the stairs; next is the server farm for the building. And then there's the bathroom. Way at the end is a suite of offices for the Carbon Institute. I met the director once. Coming down the other side of the hall are a few more offices of the Carbon Institute. I know a French girl working in one of them; Danielle is her name. I think there's another office, which is a different department, but I don't know them. They have a sign on the door, Global something. The next office is next to mine. The woman doesn't speak much English. She manages a big database."

"How about offices on the second floor?"

"They have locked laboratories on both sides of the stairs. I've never been in there. At the top of the stairs is the office of a young man, Xiaozhong, post-doc, working at the Carbon Institute, and his office mate I don't know."

"And the first floor?" Ron asked.

"More locked laboratories. I don't know anyone down there."

Ron opened her door quietly and peeked out into the hall. The vacant office across from hers was suspicious. The door was new with a peep hole. All the other doors had frosted glass set into solid wood. He studied the floor and around the door jamb. For a vacant office, it's getting some traffic, the dust was disturbed where feet had walked and the door handle was polished and clean.

"They have agents here, possibly in the office across from yours. I don't think anyone is there today. Over the weekend, you aren't usually in your office, are you?" he asked as he gently closed the door. The old door handle was loose in his hand and didn't latch properly. He sat in one of the several chairs around the empty conference table. She had an electric teapot on one end and a can of tea.

"No, not every weekend, but sometimes I'm here; can I make you some tea?" she asked, suddenly hungry. "I have some snacks in the cupboard."

"I want you to keep your door closed and locked all day. Don't let anyone in your office unless they're a co-worker, understand?" giving her a stern look.

He got up as if looking for something in particular. "You have music?"

"Ron, a car's down there!" she said. Suddenly her throat tightened, and she remembered: *Oh yeah, they're after me. But why? Why are they after me?* She unplugged the headphones from her computer and clicked onto an online music player to mask their conversation.

Ron turned up the volume, and looked down at the bicycles, and then over to the west behind the library. Sure enough, a black Dongfeng SUV where there wasn't one a few minutes ago.

Ron's car was parked to the east of the only way in or out of the building. The Dongfeng was to the west. He produced a small pair of binoculars from the gadget bag. "Write this down," he said, reading off a list of numbers.

He turned to Mai, "We have to wait here until it gets dark; and then we can go. Where are those snacks?"

Sitting in her office as the light fades, they quietly talked. She told Ron about her husband's *hobby:* playing with the Iranian government website. And about the covert meetings in Colorado, Maryland, and North Carolina. She called him a tech nerd.

"Rick quit the tech industry after the dot-com bust. For a long time, he was bored by his usual interests. He had some stock in a tiny biotech startup that paid off when it went public. The first indication was when he bought a Farsi phrase book. And on a couple of occasions, he would comment on a news story on television by saying, *'Oh that happened a couple weeks ago!'* Finally, he told me that he had been hacking into the official Iranian website, mainly looking for images and pages showing missiles in various stages of development, nuclear plants, stuff like that ... and sanctioned activity of American corporations. He gets together with his political nerd friends and they share their findings. He's gone on one of those trips now.

"In November of last year, North Korean agents came to our hometown of Sebastopol to photograph him. But he didn't tell me until much later, not until I had been here in Beijing for several months. *They* probably got some pictures of *me*, too."

"Well, that puts everything in focus ... dangerously in focus," he said. "What do you know about those meetings? Or what he's found out?"

"Nothing!"

"He's found nothing, or you know nothing?"

She looked at him evenly for a moment. *Is this an interrogation?* But what could she do? She had to trust someone. "I don't *know* anything. By the time he tells me, it's already on CNN or BBC. They're a bunch of paranoid neocons—"

Ron got up and looked out the open window. The night air was still warm from the day. Little puffs of air rustled the tired leaves on the magnolia tree outside the window. Down below it's already black. "Let's go."

He took her hand, and they noiselessly crept down the stairs, hugging the wall on the first floor. Large shrubs on both sides of the glass entrance door obscured the SUV. He figured, if he can't see them, it means they can't see either. They crept along, staying close to the building, letting the juniper trees hide their heat print, just in case the Dage was watching with infrared. The summer's hot pavement and walls will screw that up anyway, he rationalized. At the end of the building, Ron peered around the last tree. He felt for the binoculars and tried to see any movement from the other end. One minute, two minutes, five minutes. At last, he saw two shadows separate from the gloom and turn into the building.

***

Ron grabbed her hand, and they dashed for the Buick.

"I want you to stay with me tonight," he said, quietly backing onto the road, turning east and switching on the headlights.

"I have to be at work tomorrow, and I have language class at eight o'clock," she said.

He drove around the campus, not talking, just thinking, considering the options. "Okay, I'll stay here … in your spare room," he added giving her a quick look. "I want to check your apartment again for bugs, anyway."

Ron ZHAO stayed the night at Mai's apartment in the guest bedroom, which was her office. Next morning at the bank, Mai withdrew cash for the deposit, five thousand yuan, the equivalent of $800, and Ron drove her the few blocks to language class.

"I want you to be really careful today. I'll be back later tonight. I'll text you when."

"Okay, I'll be careful. I know, I know, take a different route every day. Look for suspicious cars or a van, probably a van … some way they can just grab me right off the street. I'll just stay away from cars and streets. The campus is pretty safe that way," said Mai, sounding more confident than she felt.

"Not just that. Don't go out at night and don't go out by yourself." He gave her a stern look as they waited at a red light. "Ambush points are near your office. Where that SUV was parked is one. If you see something suspicious, stop and pretend you are getting a phone call, turn around and go a different direction," warned Ron.

She nodded in agreement.

"Here, use this," he said, giving her the RF signal detector. She tucked it into an oversize bag with her language notes.

Ron drove all the way into the cul-de-sac behind the hotel where the language school was located. He pulled her bike out of his trunk and watched as she parked it and disappeared into the building, waving at him over her shoulder.

He slowly backed around and returned to Sanlitun in Chaoyang where his mother was waiting. "Hi Mama, I'm on my way back now…. Okay, okay, *dui, dui,* bye-bye."

Ron's mother wanted him to bring her fancy, boxed sandwiches from la Boulangerie Francais in Wudaokuo. After stopping there and while driving back to Sanlitun, Ron called Alan Spires, TSC's legal eagle.

"I'm coming in late today," started Ron.

"Wish I were you, mate," bantered Spires.

"Been with a new client all weekend," continued Ron.

"Even better for you."

"I need to get their signature on a standard contract tonight. Can you do it, *laoren*, old man?" challenged Ron. "Where's the boss? I need to clear this job as urgent."

"Urgent, you say! Just how urgent, Ronald? Our boss is in Pakistan."

"*Weishemne?*"

"Something about old family business and opening another branch there," gossiped Spires.

"When can you send me the contract?" asked Ron.

"I'll courier it as soon as possible, mate. Look for it before 4PM," confirmed Spires.

Ron entered his flat with a gym bag in one hand and a shopping bag from the French bakery in the other.

"Here, Mama, the sandwiches. I have to get to work," said Ron loudly to the empty kitchen, before retreating into his apartment to get dressed.

When he emerged, in cream colored linen trousers, short-sleeved Italian knit shirt with sleeveless V-necked vest and his black hair slicked back with gel, his mother was waiting to pounce on him in the kitchen. She has opened the crystal clear sandwich boxes and arranged them on a platter with a pot of tea.

"I am just taking this to the dining room for you, Ronnie. Where have you been all weekend? Working?" asked Mama.

Ron kissed the top of her head, took the tray and led her into the dining room. On the west side of the building, it was cool in the hot morning. Below them was the busy city.

"Look at this," he said, removing two business cards from his wallet, placing Sr. Col. GAO and Mai Martin's cards on the polished table top.

"Who are these people?" asked Mama suspiciously.

"Friday, I met this woman, Mai Martin, at the ballet with you. Saturday, I took her to dinner in Haidian. Sunday, I called Commander GAO, just to help because she said "odd" things were happening. Indeed, odd things are. He and I played basketball at Beijing University. This man, GAO, head of the Beijing University security office," continued Ron, between bites of egg-salad sandwiches on white bread, perfectly trimmed of crust into diagonal quarters. "The Commander warned me that she is in grave danger."

"Zhenda," said Mama, greatly interested in Ron's story, examining the cards, one and then the next, over and over.

"She's a new client. I have to get to the office to get a contract for her to sign tonight," explained Ron, selecting an immaculate section of tuna on rye, also trimmed.

"You go there again, tonight?" asked Mama.

"Dui, Mama, until our services are no longer needed," continued Ron.

"What services, Ronnie?" Mama wanted to know, skeptical about what services her son provided the big, American woman.

August 30

The Dage

Tuesday, August 30, the Bureau Meeting starts at 08:00.

The conference room in the Main Building has all the trappings of the grand Soviet days after the end of WWII. In 1949, when MAO Zedong's People's Liberation Army defeated the Kuomintang (KMT), the Soviet Union offered an alliance with the newly formed nation. By 1960, relations between the two titans of communism turned on the interpretation of Marxism in regard to peaceful coexistence with the West. MAO called peaceful coexistence revisionist.

Red velvet curtains hanging at the tall windows are old and threadbare. Some of the curtain hardware is missing. GAO's personal assistant, Sgt. WANG, brings in hot water for the members, as is customary to drink in Beijing—plain, without tea. The men sit in their usual positions around one end of the long table. Copies of the reports are stacked to one side.

Commander GAO quietly greets his group. They have high-level–classification clearance, allowing them to work unimpeded on projects needing the greatest confidentiality. Many times at Beijing University, they interface with all levels of security agencies, providing services ranging from protection for China's and other country's heads of state to crowd control and to industrial and academic espionage. Never dull.

GAO Bu is in the prime of his career at fifty years old. Although he is Office Director of the university security section, his military rank is Senior Colonel and Deputy Division Commander in First Bureau, overseeing six subordinate sites, including the Beijing Military Region TRB 66407 and TRB 61786 units tasked with decryption, encryption, and information security functions.

He progressed gradually through the ten-year plans of the young nation's history. People learned to trust him, and he earned their confidence over the tumultuous years, forging important relations with several co-existing branches of security departments within the PLA and the Beijing Police Department's Municipal Public Security Bureau (BMPSB). Today, GAO wears a tan fatigue jacket over a black tee-shirt, a discrete, gold, party pin in the coat lapel. His bland Han features, high Mongol cheekbones, flat face, and black eyes reveal no clue. His broad shoulders and short, powerful legs evoke images of a modern-day terracotta warrior.

"Let's hear it," starts Commander GAO, looking at Sgt. WANG.

A poised, slender man about forty-years-old stands up and begins,

Monday August 29 07:35: ZHAO drives the Subject to the bank on campus and language school in Wudaokou.
10:05: The Subject returns to campus.
10:20: The Subject arrives at her office and removes the audio/video feed.
11:45: The Subject lunches with co-workers at the staff canteen.
17:45: The Subject leaves the office with co-worker Dandan Xiaojie, traveling the west route.

Sgt. WANG indicates the route on an enlarged map of the campus, "Here is what we call the west route. Near the west gate road, Dandan Xiaojie left her. The subject Martin proceeded straight ahead toward the primary school. We were located here and here." WANG indicates where the university Dongfeng SUV and the guards on scooters were hidden.

"At this intersection, we attempted an intercept. She turned here, like this; we had a scooter here. Instead of turning left toward her apartment, she went out through the southwest gate checkpoints. The Dongfeng and scooters played tag team with her; she turned left onto *Chengfu Road*. She turned into this parking area here at the shopping center. Here she left her bicycle and entered this building. All this took about 20 minutes, 18:05."

He resumes reading the report:

At 18:30: The Subject exits the FuLuShou Building in the company of an unknown man who identifies himself to the guards on scooters as the parking lot guard. The subject returns by bicycle to her apartment through the south pedestrian gate, arriving at the LiNai Apartments at 18:40. The Subject enters the LiNai Apartments. The surveillance equipment had been replaced in the stairs and in her apartment. She does not remove it at this time.

At 19:40: Ronald ZHAO arrives. Shortly after that, our equipment goes dead.

Sgt. WANG concludes the events of the previous day and sits.

Commander GAO rubs his chin thoughtfully. "Maj. TANG, is there anything you want to add?"

"No sir."

"Lt. GUAN, how about you? Is this typical for one of your operations?" Commander GAO inquires.

Lt. Col. GUAN Qinchen, Deputy Regiment Commander from Harbin, dressed in the same brown trousers, camouflage tee shirt, and Harbin Institute windbreaker every day, turns his head to address him. "We adhere to basic rules: We only choose opportunities when the Subject is alone. We are patient. She will make a mistake, and we will be ready. We will pick her up and take her to the interrogation cell."

"What happens then?" the Commander wants to know.

August 23

Commander GAO remembered the way Lt. GUAN first came to the Beijing Security Office. Sgt. WANG had set up a video conference with the Harbin Chief DIANGTI after their failure to hack into the Meiguoren's husband's email server while Mai was in California.

"*Nihao,* Chief," began GAO.

"*Nihao*, Commander GAO, it has been a long time since we last spoke. How is your family?"

"They are well, and yours, *ni ne?*"

"Quite well, *xiexie*, and do you have good news for me today?"

"Unfortunately, we have failed to obtain the information we both desire. The attack was repulsed," admitted GAO.

"Did you launch another attack?"

"We are prepared with a new infection, but ..." GAO paused, "the Subject removed our network backdoor and other necessary programs, rendering our new attack vehicle useless."

Both men were silent for some long seconds.

"Perhaps we should send some of our programmers to assist," the Harbin Chief suggested after a moment. Commander GAO was not sure if he was being sarcastic, threatening, or helpful.

"Of course, we would welcome your assistance," he replied.

"Please have your office make the usual arrangements."

The video connection abruptly ended.

***

By helicopter, the travel distance between the two facilities was under one hour. Sgt. WANG sent Maj. TANG to the heliport to escort the programmers. Maj. TANG returned with two men carrying small flight bags, identified as LAO Zengjin, Senior-Grade Technical

Specialist (SGTS); and Lt. Col. GUAN Qinchen, Deputy Regiment Commander. At 17:30, Lt. Col. LIU Fengshou, Deputy Brigade Commander, joined them in the conference room. During the briefing, the men listened attentively to JGTS YANG Cai's account of their attempted cyber-attack and the Americans' counter measures. Soon SGTS LAO and JGTS YANG were huddled over the printouts.

Commander GAO turned his attention to the second man, Lt. GUAN. This man was less interested in the cyber conversation. Instead, he poured over the stack of profiles and reports in Mrs. Martin's dossier. Lt. GUAN is not the nerd type, GAO decided. He's athletic looking, dressed in brown trousers, camouflage tee shirt, and Harbin Institute windbreaker. Definitely not a programmer.

Cai and LAO disappeared into the computer lab. GAO ordered dinner from the canteen. "Do you have any questions about the Subject?" he asked looking pointedly at the new man.

"Yes, I have several. First, do you have a surveillance schedule on her?"

Lt. LIU spoke up. "We have been using a variety of methods. Through her computer calendar, we're able to track her appointments and when she goes off campus. The Beijing Police Department has a man who tails her on the few times she goes out of the university jurisdiction. I think you have Capt. LI's briefing notes under your left hand, there....Dui, those are the Beijing Police Department notes.... We have a random schedule for her movements on campus. I think the completed schedules for the past several weeks are attached to her profile.... There, at the back."

Lt. GUAN examined the reports for a few minutes while the commander's men exchanged glances. Maj. TANG walked around the table to sit next to Lt. GUAN. He gave the new man a slight smile. They looked evenly at each other. The man's eyes were black and expressionless. His narrow face, accentuated by high cheekbones, turned back to the report in front of him.

Maj. TANG reached for a report at random from the pile and shot it across the table to Lt. LIU and pulled another one out, the Harbin Report. He had read it at least a half dozen times, but this time he was looking for something he might have missed. The men passed the time quietly studying.

GAO turned around in his chair and looked out the long window toward the lawn in front of the building. The grass stretched a long distance—past rows of campus buildings, the Law School, the Business School, the School of Public Policy, one after the next, all the way down to the Main Gate and the tall buildings of the Business Park beyond. Lights winked here and there in the tall buildings. The smoggy sunset colored the western sky bright pink, orange, and cerulean blue. Long rays of the setting sun bounced off the modern glass facade of the Hualian shopping center to the east. He looked at his mobile and got up to turn on the lights.

GAO passed two young women from the canteen arriving with covered dishes and a big thermos of hot water on a cart on the way down to the second level to the computer room to check on the progress there.

"Well?" he asked. Cai and LAO were side by side at a console. They looked up at GAO briefly and returned to their work.

"Nothing to report, sir," responded Cai. LAO, blank-faced, seemed to concur.

"Dinner is in the conference room," said GAO, and then turned to exit, returning to the others.

The programmers *qua* hackers attempted to make the connection manually by duplicating the Subject's FTP login using data from their copious collections, but when they tried to make the surrogate connection, they were repulsed. Something had changed—a password?—or perhaps the US server in Santa Rosa had become vigilant to this port? SGTS LAO concluded they had tried every reasonable alternative. Returning to the conference room, the young men glumly ate their dinners. At 23:00, the helicopter returned to Harbin with programmer SGTS LAO, but the other agent, Lt. GUAN, remained behind.

"I want to see the Subject's habitats. Will you drive me, Maj. TANG?" asked GUAN.

Commander GAO sent everyone home and turned out the lights. He could hear their footsteps down the stairs ahead of him.

The rest of the night, Maj. TANG drove Lt. GUAN around the campus, showing him the Subject's, Mai Martin's, apartment and office neighborhoods. At each location, Lt. GUAN got out and did his own fact-finding, poking his head into dark doorways and behind and beneath shrubbery. His gum-soled boots made no sound as he climbed the stairs to her fifth-floor apartment, checking each floor for details, making notes in a small book. On some floors, the lights automatically came on, responding to a motion sensor, and on some floors, the lights were not working. Her apartment door was in a recessed alcove, the light above it was out. Her neighbor's door was immediately adjacent. The solid wooden doors all had peep holes and were protected by sturdy iron gates on the outside, fitted into the deep door jamb and fastened with a keyed deadbolt lock.

At her office building, both men went up to the third floor. The main doors on the ground floor were open. On the second floor, the doors to laboratories to left and right were fastened with bicycle locks through the door handles as well as with digital security pads, the same as on the first floor. The iron gate at the top of the stairs on Mai's third floor was left open. Some students were in one of the labs working late. Opposite her office was a vacant one with a new solid door with a peep hole. Lt. GUAN told Maj. TANG to requisition it. Later, Maj. TANG dropped him off at LiHua, the campus guest house, leaving him at the reception desk to check in.

***

In the morning, Commander GAO picked up Lt. GUAN on his way to the office.

"*Xiexie* for your hospitality, Commander GAO."

"*Bukeqi,* Lt. GUAN. Did you have a chance to get some of the breakfast buffet?" inquired GAO.

"*Dui*, it was very satisfactory, *xiexie*."

"What are your orders for the investigation, if you don't mind telling me?" GAO continued.

Lt. GUAN searched the older man's inscrutable face before returning his own passionless gaze to the road in front of them. "The Harbin Chief's orders are clear. If the programmers aren't successful, we will develop an operation that will bring the husband to Beijing."

Commander GAO slowly negotiated the one traffic signal at the busiest intersection on campus; at that early hour, it's crowded with students on bikes traveling every which way. He was not a talkative man, yet this last bit of information left him speechless. Creating an incident on his campus ... with one of Beijing University's employees! He gathered his breath and measured his tone to ask, "What would that situation be?"

"I prefer if you would discuss the details with the Harbin Director," answered GUAN, settling into a taciturn silence as GAO parks in the VIP lot. In a few minutes, Commander GAO was in his office where he could safely close the door, letting out a low wheeze.

Sgt. WANG was at his door with a cup of coffee. "Come in," he growled. "Shut the door." WANG looked alarmed. The Commander waved at a chair: "Sit." Sgt. WANG complied without hesitation. "Before we schedule another video conference with Harbin, tell me, what the hell is going on here?"

Sgt. WANG had made some assessments. "It seems that Lt. GUAN is taking over the investigation. He's been giving Maj. TANG orders all night, making him drive around until two in the morning. We're now requisitioning the empty office across the hall from Martin Taitai for more immediate surveillance or something. JGTS YANG Cai hasn't come in yet this morning. Lt. LIU is in the conference room with Maj. TANG and Lt. GUAN working up some kind of plan. Didn't he tell you?"

"No! He said I had to hear it from the Harbin Chief! What do *you* know? Do you know what the hell *else* is going on in my office that I don't know?" Commander GAO was almost hoarse with rage.

"Well, you won't believe it, but we already have a video call scheduled for 08:30, boss," WANG added weakly, feeling ill.

Things were spinning out of control fast. The Harbin Institute had inserted themselves into the middle of their investigation and it looked like they had the clout—the *guanxi*—to run it, whether GAO liked it or not. Both men looked at their phones.

"That's in ten minutes," GAO said. "Okay, give me a little time.

I'll be there. I want everyone present who is in the building. Now get. And show Lt. GUAN every courtesy. We will make effort to cooperate, clear?"

Sgt. WANG suddenly felt better and color slowly started returning to his pale face. He closed the door with a soft click, and GAO spun his chair around, looking down into the little oasis, the bamboo blowing like green feathers in the soft morning air.

The view from his office looks north over the top of the VIP parking and down into a small park recently refurbished with a huge, grotesque rock and lots of bamboo. When he isn't tethered to his desk, he likes to take a break and sit on one of the benches down there and meditate. He can pretend just as well by closing his eyes. After years of secret practice, he is adept at shutting out the world and connecting with the oneness that guides his life, gives him direction, and sustains him.

At 08:15, Maj. TANG and Lt. GUAN were sitting together in the conference room, on one side of the big table. Lt. LIU and Sgt. WANG sit on the other side. Maj. TANG gave his boss a solemn nod as Commander GAO entered the room and took his place at the head, facing the video screen. The Harbin Chief's office flashed into view, and the Director walked in and sat opposite them. A little red flag sat on one corner of the desk. A framed picture of the Chinese space launch hung behind his head; some other pictures of men shaking hands, fighter jets, the usual stuff.

"*Zao shang hao*, Commander GAO," said Harbin Division Chief and Director of ISRI and NIC, Ninth Bureau, DIANGTI.

"*Hen hao*, Chief, *ni ne?*" responded Sr. Col. GAO Bu, Deputy Division Commander, First Bureau Office Director, Beijing University Security Office.

"*Bu hao*, GAO. I am very unhappy with the failures of your office!" The words were harsh, sliding out of his mouth like oil, the corners turned down in a slight sneer.

"*Duibuqi*, Chief, it has been a source of extreme anxiety for us that our software attack was repulsed and continued efforts have been fruitless," apologized Commander GAO. His words were carefully chosen and uttered with humility, but inside he seethed.

The men were frozen in their seats.

"Lt. GUAN told me your office has been very accommodating. *Xiexie* for your cooperation."

GAO nodded his head but said nothing.

"Now, it's time for Plan B. We would have liked to gather more information. That is not possible now," Chief DIANGTI paused and sneered again before continuing, "Our North Korean partners are eager to take advantage of his wife's presence at Beijing University. She will lure him here. Lt. GUAN is expert at arranging the right kind of incentive. I expect you will continue to provide him with all the assistance he requires. He will be reporting to me daily."

"I see, Director, you can count on us one hundred percent. We will not disappoint."

"Yes, I am sure of that, GAO. We have worked together before, and I am confident we will make a good team."

The video feed suddenly ended.

"So, Lt. GUAN, would you please brief us on Plan B?" asked Commander GAO. He hoped the sarcasm could not be detected.

The rest of the morning, they went over details and strategies until a tentative plan was outlined: Lt. GUAN and Maj. TANG would surveil Mai Martin, intercept her on campus, and take her to an interrogation room in a remote administration building. Lt. GUAN was thorough and precise, taking no unnecessary risks. He assigned tasks around the table. One by one, the men left with their new assignments, until only Commander GAO and Lt. GUAN were left.

As a Red Guard during the Cultural Revolution, Commander GAO had destroyed antiquities at Beijing University and elsewhere. Guilt and anger over being manipulated by MAO when he was younger and impressionable ... like Lt. GUAN ... simmered after the fresh rebuke from Chief DIANGTI, a non-ranking, *political*, not PLA, officer below him in rank, but nevertheless a highly placed party operative.

August 30

While the Bureau Meeting continues, the Commander's thoughts return to the current problem. Being on a need-to-know basis is getting under his skin. On the exterior, GAO's placid, unexpressive countenance is flawless. He extends every professional courtesy to Lt. GUAN, lending him his office's resources, their vehicles, personnel, and equipment. On the interior, it's another story. He's been in touch with his *dalaoban*, Maj. Gen. HUANG, who referred the matter to his *laoban*, Gen. MENG Junjie. First Bureau Chief MENG had been in touch with Sr. Col. CHEN Yibo, Ninth Bureau Chief about the investigation. HUANG got back to GAO and said, "Wait and see. Be patient. Be deep. Be sudden in your action. Terminate this investigation as soon as possible." Commander GAO is jerked back to the now when Lt. GUAN begins speaking again.

"We will persuade the Subject to contact her husband and implore him to come to Beijing as soon as possible."

There it is, thinks GAO. As soon as possible. It will be

concluded soon. One way or another.

"Why this method? Why not simply ask her to come in for questioning?" asks Commander GAO.

This time, Lt. GUAN is stumped. He never questions the methods or motives of his superiors. The line of authority is clear in his world. The only senior authority is his direct supervisor, Chief DIANGTI Yong of the Ninth Bureau and Director of the Harbin Institute. Lt. GUAN is Deputy Regiment Commander in Chief DIANGTI's division. He only has to cooperate with GAO. He doesn't have to follow orders.

"I'm not privy to the motive of the methods used in this investigation. My orders are clear: to obtain the target for interrogation and induce the husband to come to Beijing, keep witnesses to a minimum, and protect the chain of command from the Ninth Bureau Section Chief." DIANGTI told him he wanted no connection to the investigation. That's why GUAN was there. If something should go horribly wrong, DIANGTI wanted no trail to him. Stick it to old GAO.

***

The campus public works department is tearing up the main road in Mai's *hutong* neighborhood, which extends past the local shopping street at Lan Yuan Shopping Center, down to the Senior Center and primary school, where it flooded this summer during a typhoon event.

Once she crosses onto the campus proper, it's easy for her to avoid cars. Only near her building does she have to merge onto a road. She rides around the library complex next to the soccer field. A different car is parked where the Dongfeng was yesterday. She makes a note of the license plate, going around to the other side where a low hedge divides a bumpy driveway from the old library parking. She parks her bike, enters the building, and goes up the stairs. Once inside, she checks the office for bugs and throws the tiny device she discovers, smaller than a watch battery, out the window into the bushes below. She texts Ron the license number. All morning she sees the car down there: it's a dark blue university sedan, Maj. TANG's Camry.

At lunch, she leaves with Ms. HAN and Dandan to go to the canteen, like she did yesterday. All through the meal, she looks around; suddenly, everyone looks suspicious. Walking back to her building, Mai falls behind the two women who are busy talking about something.

She's been thinking about her husband, Rick. He's on his way home from covert meetings, but she's not sure where he is or how she could contact him. He's off doing his thing. She's not worried about him, and he's not worried about her, obviously.

Back in her office, she locks the door, pulls the shade across the big window and lies down on a row of chairs under the AC for a nap, falling asleep for a few minutes. She awakes with a jerk at someone knocking on the door.

"Who's there?" she asks.

"It's HAN."

She unlocks and opens the door, and her department supervisor enters. "What can I do for you? Have you got another article for me?" asks Mai.

"Here are three articles for correction. If you could have them done by end of day?"

"There should be no problem."

Ms. HAN leaves the draft articles on the conference table, and Mai locks herself in again. Walking to the computer and booting up, she turns back to the table and the three articles for the Beijing University Newsletter. They send this magazine out by the hundreds to university libraries around the world, and especially in the US. She looks at the headlines of each article. One is "Low Carbon Energy University Alliance with California Institute of Technology." Another is "The First Master's Degree Program in Hydraulic Engineering in Tibet." Using a red pen, she starts scanning.

At quitting time, Mai cuts through the library breezeway. It's terraced with a fountain and broad steps in all directions, full of students and no cars. Through the busy shopping area and construction zone to the apartment, she goes without incident.

Slipping down a deserted side alley beside the *hutong*, she is only a couple blocks from her apartment. She follows where others have gone, her dusty, blue bicycle rolling over a big pile of dirt and rubble where a path was worn from earlier in the day. Turning behind a row of *siheyuan* houses, she sees a blue construction barricade blocking the end of the path. No one seems to be around. Immediately, she's cautious, alert and fearful. She stops and looks around for an alternate route. Pushing her bike along another narrow, common walkway, she looks into the small yards at potted plants and climbing bean vines.

Beyond the last *siheyuan* house Mai spies a black Dongfeng. It appears to be the same one ID'd in Ron's spreadsheet. The rear door opens. Mai sees a husky man with a military look, buzz haircut, and camo tee-shirt, step out. *Who is this guy? What does he want with me?* Not hesitating a second, she pushes her bicycle at him and runs the other way. The clunky bike tangles his feet for a crucial few seconds, giving her a head start.

Passing an open doorway with laundry hanging on either side,

Mai knows better than to try to hide in one of the *siheyuan*. They would give her up in a second. The maze of walkways and shacks conceals her, but not for long. Glimpsing traffic, Mai runs into the clog of cars picking up students from the primary school. She turns to look.

Cutting across the construction zone, Mai enters the shopping center from the back side. She darts into the bank. Breathlessly, she takes a number and sits with a half dozen other customers waiting their turn, punching Ron's cell number.

"*Wei*, Mai, where are you?" asks Ron.

"God, Ron, I just had to run for my life. I'm here sitting in the bank. What do I do?"

"Even if I left work right now, I wouldn't get there until 18:30—it's rush hour!" he says.

"18:30? What time is that?"

"6:30"

"Call that GAO guy and do something. Maybe he has an idea. Bye."

Next, she calls her neighbor, the cab driver, "*Nihao*, Robert."

"*Nihao*, Martin. Do you need a cab?"

"*Dui, keyi xiànzài jie wo ma?*" [Can you pick me up now?]

"Where you go?"

"Can you get me at the Lan Yuan Shopping Mall? ... How long will it take you?... Okay, I'll wait half an hour. Pick me up in front of China Postal."

***

Commander GAO still sits at his desk at 17:30, finishing a call from Lt. LIU. The officer gives him a quick update on the progress of the Martin investigation. After she eludes them in the *hutong* neighborhood, they locate her in the shopping center and are waiting nearby for her to leave the bank. "Okay, LIU, are we done? I have another call." Looking down at his phone, he sees it's from ZHAO. "What now, ZHAO?" asks Commander GAO.

"Call it off, Commander. Don't tell me running through the *hutong* and chasing a woman is *your* plan! This has got to stop!"

"You're not Police Commissioner here, ZHAO," retorts GAO.

"She asked me to call you. She doesn't know where to go or what to do. You want to protect her? Then help her!" says Ron.

"You don't know the people involved, ZHAO!"

"I know the North Koreans are involved—how does that make you feel? You're a decent guy. Do you want to help them? Are you trying to abduct her? What *are* you guys doing?" asks Ron.

"I'll call you back." Commander GAO snaps the phone closed and fumes in his chair.

Next Ron calls Mai, "Where are you now?"

"I'm still at the bank. In five minutes, I'm leaving and walking down the mall to the department store. I can leave by a rear exit across the alley from China Postal. Robert is waiting for me in front of the post office. He'll drive me to meet you. Where are you?"

"I'm on the way."

"Did you talk to the Commander?" asks Mai.

"Yes. Tell the *shifu* to take you to the Jade Market. I'll call you in a few minutes. Now go," says Ron.

Only one street is open. Road construction has closed the main road on the other end of the shopping center, where Mai is headed, through dinnertime crowds of students on bicycles, peddlers on their little carts, electric bicycles, and scooters, cars, and pedestrians.

The men in the Dongfeng watch Mai leave the bank and walk to the end of the mall. They've got her phone ping on their tracker. They see her enter a store but don't see her walk straight through to the other side.

Looking carefully out the back door, she doesn't see anything suspicious. Quickly, she moves around to the front of the post office where Robert's cab waits. After she closes the door, he's pulling into the constant stream of cars and people when she sees the black Dongfeng coming toward them and ducks under the dash. "Go to the Jade Market, Robert, hurry, *zouba!"* [let's go!]

After a few minutes, Commander GAO's men see she is on the move and start to follow her phone blip on the GPS tracker. At the South Gate, they call the Commander.

"Contact BPD. She left campus and is headed east on Chengfu Road."

"Do you see what kind of vehicle she is in?" asks GAO.

"No, we don't see her at all. She entered the department store and went through to the post office side, where someone picked her up, and we lost track of her ping. Was it ZHAO you think?" asks LIU.

"With this kind of lead, I think it's best we let her go for now. She always comes back. Leave someone at her apartment and come back to the office now," orders the Commander.

Maj. TANG parks in the VIP lot behind the main building. Lieutenants LIU and GUAN get out of the Dongfeng without conversation. Upstairs, sitting around the conference table, they are hungry and annoyed. Every day, the Subject slips through their fingers.

Commander GAO says, "I discussed this with the Harbin Chief. We decided to stop the investigation for now. Lt. GUAN, check out of the guest house tonight and return to Harbin. The Chief is arranging transport for you. Maj. TANG, will you drive Lt. GUAN to the LiHua Hotel?" The two men rise and leave without saying another word.

To Lt. LIU, GAO says, "Go home, take a shower, and get some rest. Tomorrow is another day. Try to forget about this operation for a few hours. You will be fresh in the morning, and we will discuss it at that time."

Commander GAO stands and steps to the tall windows overlooking the campus. The sun throws its last golden rays at the tall buildings around the quad, the whole sky lit in a quickly changing palette of gold to mauve, orange to gray.

***

The Jade Market is across the street from the Fourth Ring Road Expressway, in a six-story warehouse on a boulevard which dead ends at the Main Gate of Beijing University. Zhongguancun Donglu Street has three lanes in each direction lined with office buildings, apartments and shops on both sides. It passes through a neighborhood they call the Beijing Silicon Valley.

The traffic is crushing at this time of night. Commuter buses creep in and out of the traffic lanes, swarms of people empty from the buildings, beginning their long commutes home for the night. Only a few kilometers from campus, it takes Robert twenty-five minutes to get there from the campus shopping center. Ron is waiting for Mai in the funky parking lot surrounded by peddlers hawking faux jade artifacts and phony brass trinkets when she arrives.

"*Nihao*, Mai. Do you want to go inside and look around?" he asks. "We need to kill some time until Commander GAO calls."

In the lobby of the market, they walk around a monolithic, carved dragon and thread their way through cases of jade and pearl jewelry to get to the really good stuff farther into the maze. Inside the large building are little shops filled with every kind of stone, carved and displayed on stands, resembling fish or food or fruit, figures or mountains; the colored veins suggesting flowers or clouds, snow or water.

Ron finds a ceramics shop where the proprietors make them specially scented tea. Ron selects a mug for his mother. Mai picks out a darling mug with a crouching tiger on the lid and a hidden dragon with tiny teeth ingeniously fitted inside the tea strainer for herself.

"You know what this means, Mai?" asks Ron, playing with the mug.

"That movie, *Crouching Tiger Hidden Dragon?*" she says examining the amazingly small teeth and wondering how it was made.

"Also an old Chinese proverb about the mysterious, hidden talents that lie beneath the surface of a person."

She's thinking, *I trusted Rick, he's my husband, of course I trusted him. Because of my stupidity, I believed him. And now, the North Koreans are after me. And he's out of town on one of his meetings somewhere.*

She remembers getting emails from him last spring.

May 14 To: Mai   From: Rick

Subject: NK

There were North Korean guys at the gas station photographing me last November. Think they are still really pissed too. I'm sending you something you should know.

May 15 To: Mai   From: Rick

No Subject

I'm not worried about this happening in the US but sure will worry about this while out of the country. NK is tight with Iran and do some of their dirty work as they are much more experienced about this sort of stuff. I sure wouldn't want to end up in Iran as they will like my head on a pike.
I have the passport application but not sent in yet.

Mai looked at the Skype link. Good, Rick was online. She video called him.

"Hi, I see you're awake."

"Yeah, you too."

"It's more secure to talk like this than to email me, Rick. What are you *thinking?"*

"I guess that was careless of me. But the Chinese probably already know."

Skype was sold to Microcon shortly after Mai moved to Beijing, and a clone entity was established called TEDSkype, which redirects communications to a site that looks the same as the original—same logo and everything. The VOI technology is impervious to hacking, but not to the license to run all communications through sophisticated search engines to extract information on users, to identify who is using forbidden words, and more.

"Why would they know?" Mai asked.

"We just think so," answered Rick.

"Why were the North Koreans in Sebastopol?"

"I can't tell you, Mai. But I can tell you this, they were here looking for me and got some pictures off before they left. We tracked them to where they went back over the border to Mexico. Probably down to Venezuela or over to Barbados."

"What else are you not telling me?"

"Remember when that Wikileaks scandal broke last year?"

Mai nodded *yes* into the video camera. Rick sat in their familiar living room with the reading light casting harsh contours on his face and chest.

"The Iranians found out about something I did to them on their website. They're really mad at me now because they thought it was their guys. I think some of their internet boys got tortured or disappeared. I haven't been able to get into their site again ... until lately. At least I don't have to worry about you in Beijing, where there's a policeman on every corner."

Mai turned the startling information over in her head. *The North Koreans were in Sebastopol, looking for Rick.* What did they have to do with the Iranians anyway?

May 16   To: Rick   From: Mai
No Subject

What does Iran do for North Korea?

May 16   To: Mai   From: Rick
No Subject

They make small mini subs and weapons. Nuclear stuff too.

"I'm hungry," Mai announces flatly.

"Where would you like to eat?"

"Somewhere they won't watch us. Whoever they are. Who are they, Ron?"

Ron pays a few *mao* to the *laoren*, old man, watching his car, maybe half a yuan. The last color of sunset disappears between buildings in the distance. Smoggy dusk obscures all features.

The dark city is full of life. The Park Avenue noses into the flow of traffic. Mai pulls the visor down to look at her face in the lighted mirror, applying dark pink lipstick and pressing her lips together. She runs her fingers through her hair and snaps the visor closed. She's wearing a thin silk cardigan, unbuttoned at the neck, and black trousers. A silk scarf tied loosely at the neck obscures the fullness of her breasts.

Watching her out of the corner of his eye, he wonders if it is modesty or if she's playing him. He couldn't be sure. Although Commander GAO didn't promise anything, Ron feels relatively safe from watchful eyes tonight. Just having her with him is safer. Every day and every night, they have been together, since they met at the ballet. When they aren't together, she's in his thoughts. Sitting at his desk in the office, while driving or eating lunch with his mother, she's in his thoughts. He wonders if she's safe. And why she's being watched. He considers the idea she could be someone besides who she says she is. Puzzles, bits of pieces fit together but don't relate to the rest.

And the fantasies. He imagines her with him, holding her, kissing her. And the way he feels, wanting her, wanting her naked beside him, wanting to be inside her, and then scolding himself for being unprofessional. He tries banishing the thoughts, but they float around pale and vague, sweet and beckoning until he's thinking about her again.

Unfulfilled desires form into her face, her hands, her throat, her lips, joining with the *yuanfen*, finding the breath of life, rising from his unconscious mind, filtering through his every day actions.

"Do you like Cantonese?"

"Yes, I think so, *dui*."

Mai turns to face him. Reflecting on the past several days, she's astonished to realize he's been with her every day since they met, sleeping every night in the guest bedroom. Lying in bed in the morning, she hears him rise early and shower. Every morning, they sit across from each other at the heavy, red-lacquered wooden dining table, drinking tea and eating Chinese porridge for breakfast. Every evening he returns, carrying bags of takeout, and removes all the spy gear from the stairs and her apartment.

During the day, she can't forget about the crazy events. She tries concentrating on work, yet constantly broods over everything, reviewing every hour of every day. Ron suddenly enters her mind. She remembers his solid profile in the dark at the theater and his spontaneous chivalry. He's the only thing she can count on now. Looking at that same profile in the dark car, strong and confident, his eyes smile at her. His lips are saying something, flashing her a toothy smile.

The scarf slips from around her neck, her nipples are soft bumps in the dark, and he imagines the sweet softness of her cleavage in the glow of the passing street lights and neon signs.

"Here we are," he says.

The bright red-and-gold exterior of the restaurant with two big, stone lions flanking the door, cheers her. Ron speaks a few words to the *fuwuyuan*, who leads them to a private room, dims the lights, and leaves them alone, returning quickly with tea and *mi jiu*. The table is huge, it seats eight, and the dinner is perfect. Ron enjoys watching Mai expertly wield chopsticks. Explaining every dish, the ingredients and method of preparation and how the seafood is flown in daily from Guangdong Province, he teaches her about Cantonese cuisine and culture.

Finally, they get some privacy where they can relax for a few hours. Thoughts about the day fade while the warm, rice wine heats her face and neck.

"Mrs. Martin, you are the most beautiful client at TSC, like an American movie star," he says.

Mai peeks at him over the wineglass, but says nothing.

Sometime between the first course, *xiangchun doufu,* and the last course, *danhuang ju nanqua,* they know. The looks between them are long and intense. Conversation trails off just to start again. Under the table, he captures one of her feet between his. She doesn't resist. Steadily gazing at each other, her mouth slightly open, barely breathing. His chest is tight, the sound of the ocean rises in his ears. Reaching under the table, he squeezes her thigh just above the knee. The wave of pleasure almost chokes him, she opens wide her eyes. He looks deeply into the dark pools.

"I'll get the car and pick you up in fifteen minutes," he says.

Paying the bill on the way out, Ron breathes in the night air. Looking up, he takes in the starless Beijing sky, reflecting black purple and orange light from low misty clouds. Brisk walking helps clear his head a little.

Seeing her waiting for him at the curb, he feels a spasm in his loins. Somehow, he drives back to the quiet and dark *hutong* neighborhood near her apartment. He still hasn't gotten Commander GAO's call. What's taking so long? Prowling through the maze of *siheyuans*, he finds a place to park where he can see in all directions. They sit quietly in the car until he's satisfied it is safe. He gets out and walks around to her side and opens both her door and the back door. The new car smell hugs the cushions in the cool back seat, where he makes a pillow for her to lie on out of his jacket.

His fingers touch her soft hair and pull it away from her perfect face. Holding her head, he bends close to her lips; they touch—eager kisses, nibbling, cutting, probing—from the face to the eyes and the closed eyelids, burying kisses in her hair and breathing kisses into her ears. She grasps him around his slim waist and pulls him closer.

Two hearts that beat as one don't know Chinese or American. Seeking gratification of deep need crosses all cultural divides East or West. A wave of *chi* or *yuanfen*, she doesn't know or care which, roars in her ears and heats moist skin. She hides her face deep in his neck, black hair mingling.

"Kisses in the Moonlight" drifts through her mind, twining the tendrils of desire in frosty mist. She had fantasized about kisses in the moonlight with Ron, wanted to know the sweet surrender to her inflamed desire, just didn't imagine it in the back seat of a Park Avenue.

"Not here!" she gasps.

"Where?"

"*Hui jia*, my apartment."

"We have to wait," he says, "GAO should be calling any minute now."

Sitting up in the dark, back seat, he in one corner, she in the other, they stare at each other's shadowed faces. A slight film of condensation forms on the windows. He draws a line in the glass, wondering if he crossed the line with a client. She pulls the sweater down over her breasts, pale in the Beijing moonlight, wondering if she let things go too far.

Ron's mobile interrupts the silence. At last, the Commander's call.

"*Wei ... xiexie*, I'll tell her. *Da, da, zaijian.*" Turning toward Mai in dark profile, backlit by the window, Ron says, "Commander GAO says you can go home. He's called off the so-called investigation for now. They've removed all the spy gear from your apartment."

Mai's relieved, flushed and confused for a moment. "*Zouba, hui jia,*" she says, committed to following her instincts and stop worrying. "Let's go then."

He fastens his belt and opens the car door a crack, listening to the night sounds in the *hutong*. They get back in the front seat, and he drives straight to her apartment, shifts the car into park, rolls up the windows and turns off the ignition. In the quiet, he drops his hand onto the console near her seat. She covers it with hers. They stare at each other in the dark.

Running away from their problems at home seems foolish, but not as foolish as hoping for love to appear. But they want to feel something again, and the spirit of *tan* whispers to them in the dark, promising something sweet.

Before getting out, Ron powers off his smartphone and conceals it in the glove box.

On the way up the stairs, Ron notices where gear has recently been removed. Leading the way, Mai isn't thinking, she's feeling hot and sexy, excited and confused.

She lets him overtake her in the dim, sitting room, stopping in the middle of the room where they are outlined by lights from the business park. He clasps her to him from behind. She thrills to the feeling of his strong arms encircling her waist, feeling his breath on her neck, smelling his sandalwood scent.

Mai crosses her arms, pulling the loose shirt off over her head and dropping it onto the cool, polished floor. She twists in his embrace to face him.

Ron ducks his head into her cleavage, while Mai unfastens her brassiere from behind. In a burst, her breasts break free assertively. Fumbling hurriedly, he unbuttons his shirt, his fingers, usually nimble and dexterous, tremble with eagerness.

Mai drags Ron into the bedroom, pulling him willingly by the hand. The AC whispers in the coolness of the room, contrasting with their urgent heat. *Chi* condenses in vaporous droplets inhaled by the lovers. It goes to their heads like a drug. They're dizzy with desire, *tan*.

He pulls her pants down as she crawls across the silk brocade duvet. She lets him capture her and impose his will, directing his passion at her pleasure.

"Do you have a condom?" she asks.

"No, do you?"

Mai thinks, *Oh God, this almost went too far.*

Ron's thinks he might have one in the car.

Slipping on shoes, he walks down to the Park Avenue and looks in the glove box. *Meiyou.* He grasps his smartphone and checks it for messages. A text from his boss: meeting tomorrow 9AM. The glow from her open door through the black, patterned gate beacons him. Inside, Mai, wrapped in a blue chrysanthemum-flowered robe is making white tea and thinks it smells like alfalfa grass hay. She turns when she hears the gate clang shut.

"*Meiyou*, I don't have any," he says, wondering if this is how Americans have sex. Like with a prostitute? Remembering the message from his boss, he asks, "I think I should go. You don't need me for your bodyguard tonight, Mai. Are you okay to stay here tonight without me?" Struggling against conflicting priorities, he explains, "Tomorrow I have to be at the office for a 9AM meeting with my boss."

"Can you stay a few more minutes, *qing*?" asks Mai, holding out a small cup of tea. He sinks into her favorite, upholstered armchair, the one facing the view of Wudaokou. "Thanks, for everything ... and thanks for coming up tonight ..." she starts, sitting on his lap and snuggling back into his arms.

"I want to see you again," he says, sliding his free hand under her robe.

"Call me?" she asks, holding her hand in a simulated phone calling gesture against her face and smiling into his eyes.

Driving back to Sanlitun that night, Ronald ZHAO pushes himself to drive the seventeen kilometers home. This has been a most unusual *assignment*. Most of their clients are celebrities or important people in government; sometimes, it's a spouse in the middle of a contentious divorce. He can't think of another client like Mai Martin. *Maybe someday I'll understand what this was all about. Can I trust the Commander that it's over?*

August 31

In the morning, Mai sits up in bed. It feels strange not hearing Ron rustling around. Taking a mug of tea into her office, she logs on and checks her emails.

August 31   To: Mai   From: Rick
Subject: I'm Home.

Skype me.

"Hi, are you there?" asks Mai. Finally able to talk to Rick. The video screen is black, but the audio is working.

"Yeah, I'm here. Great trip, but I'm glad to be back. That was a long time to be gone. At LA's Union Station, they were making a movie. I'll send you pictures."

"Hey, Rick, crazy stuff has been going on here," interrupts Mai.

"Crazy, how crazy?"

"More than crazy, I'm scared. I've hired a security firm to protect me."

"What's that all about?" asks Rick.

"It probably has to do with you."

"No shit! Are they trying to get you? In Beijing?"

"Since Sunday, they've tried every day. This guy, Ronald ZHAO, he's a guy from TSC Security, he's been great. Every day he checks my apartment for bugs. I do it at my office now, I know how. They have guys in the office across the hall from mine spying on me, and in the apartment building next to mine."

"Geez, Mai, what for? What did you do this time?" asks Rick.

"Nothing, Rick. NOTHING!! Another guy who runs the security office at the university tipped me off a couple days before all this started to happen. It's really complicated. This guy, according to Ron ZHAO, is the same guy who's been spying on me, but now he's my friend."

"I want you to come home. Come home, Mai," says Rick.

"Well, it's stopped now. This university guy, Commander GAO, called last night and tells me I can go home to my apartment, they removed all the spy gear, called the whole thing off."

"What are you going to do?" asks Rick.

"I want to stay and finish my contract."

The next morning, Mai walks the short mile or so to the office. The past couple of weeks she's seen freshmen appearing on campus, opening bank accounts, and buying phone service in large numbers; it's shocking to the locals trying to go about their business. Lines of brand new bicycles appear outside buildings that have been empty all summer. Squads of incoming students, dressed in camouflage fatigues, march around campus. It's part of freshman orientation. Soon classes begin. At the front door to her office building, she sees her old, blue bike.

The Dage

Commander GAO rises earlier than usual and feels great. Giving his wife a kiss on the way out the door, he drives to the stadium dressed for running and does several laps with early-rising students. Heading into the showers, he's almost singing. Sgt. WANG has coffee ready and waiting when he arrives at the office. Maj. TANG, Lt. LIU, and JGTS YANG Cai take their places around the big table. Each one receives a calm and cool evaluation. Commander GAO smiles, "*Zao shang hao* [Good morning], *gentlemen*."

"*Zao shang hao*, boss," they return.

"Let's get this started. Sgt. WANG!"

Copies of Incident Report 2011082-0829 are already at each man's place.

"The events of the past several days are fresh in our minds. This is the right time to review our performance and draw conclusions. Let's start with a statement of the investigation: what was the purpose or objective? Sgt. WANG?"

The Commander's number-one aide launches in. "The Beijing Security Office was cooperating with the Harbin Institute to obtain more data about the Subject and her husband, who lives in California. This investigation was prompted by automatic database searches of the Subject, prompted by her repeated internet-use violations. A connection was discovered in a covert database linking the Subject and her husband with the North Korean Department of Surveillance. The Harbin group first tried to gain data about the husband through the Subject's internet connection. When this failed, the plan was amended to pick up the Subject in a covert manner, seclude her in an interrogation cell on campus, and induce her to get her husband to come here to Beijing, where he could be more conveniently questioned than in the US."

GAO nods and then asks, "What was the nature of the Korean intelligence that needed corroboration from the American? Lt. LIU?"

Lt. LIU, who had supervised the technological surveillance, answers, "Cables revealed in the Wikileaks scandal named her husband, Rick Martin, as the perpetrator of a zero day exploit he committed while spying on the Iranian intranet for the US Government. The Iranians have offered a bounty of 120 thousand US dollars for the man."

"You have seen these cables yourself, not just a rumor?" continues GAO.

"*Dui*, Laoban, we searched the Wikileaks database and discovered those communications."

Commander GAO turns to Maj. TANG, "Tell me about the street operation. You were working closely with Lt. GUAN."

"We were unable to intercept the Subject for interrogation. Why? First, she keeps avoiding us. We can't obtain her alone or near the car. Our own protocol prevents us from entering a building or traveling upstairs in pursuit of a Subject. Why? Returning with the Subject without attracting attention is difficult if too far from the transport vehicle. Getting a struggling or sedated Subject downstairs requires too many people. The main tenet of the procedure is secrecy. No one should witness an interception. Our main tool is surprise. An unprepared Subject is easy to obtain without attracting attention. Why is this important? Agent GUAN told me many times that the Subject is never released or found. They simply 'vanish,'" concludes TANG.

"Why is that, Major?" GAO wants to know.

Maj. TANG scratches his ear suddenly, distracted by the question, "That is something I never understood. What was the point of some of these escapades?" He pauses a moment, thinking, before continuing, "I got the impression that the future unfolding of the investigation would depend on what happened next with her husband coming. I was not privy to what lengths he was prepared to go in order to persuade the Martins about cooperating. What I mean is, I was concerned about the safety of the Subject, Martin Taitai, and I was getting progressively concerned about the persistence of the Lieutenant from Ninth Bureau."

Lt. LIU speaks up, "After several attempts, the Subject, Martin Taitai, is no longer unaware. To the contrary, she had become hyper-vigilant and hired protection. Ronald ZHAO has performed many valuable services for her, including identifying spy equipment and removing it. That aspect alone is enough to scuttle the operation, since her disappearance, even for a day, would be noticed and perhaps documented by ZHAO's firm, TSC."

Commander GAO asks, his tone the teacher, *laoshi*, more than the inquisitor, "And what was the purpose of this investigation of our employee, the Subject?" The Commander glances around the scuffed conference table at the squad. That old table has witnessed many intrigues and conflicts and still exudes elegance and power despite its current, worn condition. He persists, "Besides the database searching, I mean, what needs in-person questioning of Martin Xiansheng?"

Cai says, "It's about the Wikileaks story."

"*Haode*, but what about it?" asks the Commander throwing the question back.

"The bounty," says LIU, realizing.

"Right, the bounty! That starts to sound like money and corruption, revealing motives and causation for these crimes. For these several reasons, the investigation is halted," GAO continues. He takes a gulp of coffee before continuing. "I question Harbin's overzealous cooperation with North Korea. Their cooperation conflicts with our operational priorities: to protect the members of Beijing University. I also have concerns about recent leaks on Weibo."

Sgt. WANG passes around a brief on a recent scandal involving a high-ranking general who made public remarks about several, previously secret, spy convictions.

Commander GAO continues, "I am more concerned about Chinese compromising our own country's security through unauthorized activity with North Korea than with chasing a woman around this campus who hasn't done anything ... that we've been able to determine. Whereas, we might have secret agreements with North Korea, we also have agreements with the United States regarding the treatment and safety of American nationals. Over these past several weeks, our Beijing office's own investigation has turned up *no evidence* of her being a spy. Conclusion: the investigation is suspended for now. For this next period, we will continue to monitor the Subject, as her computer continues to trigger our protocols, but we will not attempt to contact her or harass her in any way. Clear?"

With another serious look around the room, Commander GAO satisfies himself that his men are in agreement with the conclusion. He assigns JGTS YANG Cai to keep internet surveillance at a high level on the Subject, as much to protect her as to monitor her. He also assigns investigations to Maj. TANG and Lt. LIU on Harbin and North Korean activities in Beijing.

***

August 31   To: Mai Martin   From: Ronald ZHAO
No Subject

Go to Hong Kong and Pakistan for business. Wanting to see you.

August 31   To: Ronald ZHAO   From: Mai Martin
Re: No Subject

Hurry back ☺

September 1   To: Rick   From: Mai
Subject: help me?

There is an article in Sun News about military guys talking about secrets, which is blocked for me. What do you think, could you cut and paste the article into the body of an email and

send to me? I am doing some research BTW. Here's the link:
http://news.Sun.com/news/section?pz=1&cf
    I got "noticed" for clicking on this. I'm still dogged by the
Dage all day—little things they are blocking now

September 1   To: Rick   From: Mai

Subject: got it?

    I sent you a link an hour ago, but wonder if the Dage are
delaying it. Have you received yet?

Later that night, Rick sends her the article about an
embarrassing moment when a Major General, in unrehearsed remarks
in front of cadets and the press, revealed several infamous cases of
spying in China, which had previously been secret.

CHAPTER 2
Rick zai Zhongguo!
Rick Comes to China!

March 2011

Mai's initial interview had been with Ms. ZHANG Hong, Director of the Media Communications Office; Ms. HAN, the department's supervisor, and a man from the UK teaching in the English Department.

Ms. ZHANG asked Mai, "How you translate the sample we sent you? You say you are not fluent in Mandarin. Did someone help you?"

"I ran it through two translation programs. Then I checked each character for all the possible meanings. Once I got the idea, I rewrote it from scratch. Was that satisfactory?"

"We have our staff that will do the translations," said Ms. ZHANG.

Mai interjected, "I write freelance for magazines in the US. This won't be a conflict, will it? Can I work on my own projects if I'm caught up on my work for you?"

"What are these publications, Martin *Taitai?*"

"Here, I brought you a few you can see." Mai spread several slick, shiny art magazines on the conference table, where the others crowded around to look.

Following the interview, Ms. ZHANG took her next door to meet the rest of the staff. Mai and Yunling had been communicating by email in the weeks leading to her arrival. The two women liked each other the instant they met.

Yunling looked up at Mai shyly from under dark, feathery bangs. Her sweet, sad, pixie face, framed by long, dark, shoulder-length shagged hair, smiled, and Mai thrust out her hand, "*Nihao.*"

In return, the younger woman limply offered her small hand with its pale fingers and perfect rosebud nails. "Delighted," she whispered.

The Media Communications Office was split between two buildings on campus. Ms. ZHANG and Yunling worked in the International Building surrounded by antique gardens and lotus ponds. Mai parked and locked her bike in the row of bikes already there at the Mingqiang Building where she was assigned an office on the same floor as Ms. HAN and Dandan *Xiaojie.*

The fragrant odor of magnolia *denudata,* or Yulan magnolia, rested delicately above the sidewalk littered with spent petals, already passed its prime bloom, pushing tips of leaves. Looking up at the fresh green, the most unexpected anxiety wafted in with the fragrance. *Spring is hurrying by,* she thought, *April next week. Don't miss it! Savor every breath as if it's the last spring on earth.*

That spring, news articles about the earthquake and tsunami in Japan said the radiation from the disaster drifting over Beijing was harmless. Levels were below the average 1:100,000 annual exposure levels. *And what does that mean,* she wondered? The National Nuclear Emergency Coordination Committee said no protective measures were needed.

At the university and in chat rooms online, everyone's internet was behaving oddly. Everyone had a theory about it. What Mai didn't appreciate is it's her connection to SpeedLog.net that was malfunctioning—and not because of electromagnetic-field disturbance from earthquake aftershocks. Mai was unaware that the campus security bureau—which she calls The Dage, meaning Big Brother in Mandarin—was redirecting her to a fake result on the SpeedLog.net diagnostic and giving her random speeds.

September 1

Mai spends the day researching news stories online for Ms. ZHANG and sends the tenth media report to her, Ms. Han, and Yunling, triggering a violation from an automated filter that catches her media reports, registering each one as an incident.

Since Mai Martin's arrival in February, almost from the very start, she has violated internet-use policy at her job at Beijing University. Whereas some of the violations are typical for her department, others triggered responses from the campus security office. Searching the internet for stories about Beijing University is a normal function of the Media Communications Office where she works. Her personal projects, art videos and website, had attracted a barrage of countermeasures, rendering her work almost unusable.

In Mai's case, the frequency and number of her violations started triggering Incident Reports. An intercept-related information (IRI) tracking bot was injected manually and her internet connectivity would be shut down for twenty-four to forty-eight hours, keeping her internet account running during the week so as to not interfere in her job, and shutting her down over a weekend. Every time she went online, an alert would be delivered from her computer, and a Logic Bomb Surveillance Protocol (LBSP) would activate, which conducted a live-stream search.

Dandan Xiaojie followed her out of the building one afternoon.

"Martin, how is it, your internet now?"

"*Nihao*, Dandan, it seems to be fine. Thanks ... *xiexie.* "

They stood near the bikes a few minutes, visiting. Mai unlocked hers and straightened to face the younger woman.

"Martin, this also happened to me, what you say happened to you."

"When was that?"

"Last year when I was making the internet research for Yunling."

"What did *you* do to trigger that ... whatever it was?" asked Mai.

"I don't remember. I was working on the media report like you. I am glad not to be doing that research now you are here. Remember, Martin, if something happens ..." Dandan paused, searching Mai's face for clues, "don't expect anyone will help."

Dandan turned suddenly to greet Ms. HAN, coming out the double glass doors opposite the bike rack.

Incident Report 20110901

TRIGGER ACTIVITY: MEDIA REPORT 9/1

    17—Subject violates normal-use criteria: uses
SunSystems search to access keyword-excluded media.
9/1
    Security Response Activity:
    17—Response: Automatic keyword search Layer 7 Tier
III: IP identifier unit
Keyword search data collected in live stream search
Tabulation violations pushes alert

But there was another trigger too. An ultra-secret consequence of the Layer 7 filter activation opened a covert database in another office some 700 kilometers away in Harbin. The highlighted file held images of Mai and Rick Martin taken by North Korean agents in Sebastopol, California, months before her arrival in Beijing. Her presence at the university was a matter of intense interest to someone; whether it was a matter of national security was yet to be determined.

November 2010

Three months earlier, Mai had attended an overnight trip to a job fair at UC Berkeley, carpooling with alumnae from Sebastopol. It brought some interesting and unexpected prospects.

During the same weekend, back home in Sebastopol, Mai's husband, Rick was coming out of the Texaco with his usual morning coffee. Pumping gas at the pump right in front of the door was a short guy with black hair under a ball cap pulled down low. Something about him made Rick take a closer look at how he was leaning on the driver's side door—his hand resting on a small camera set on the roof of the rental car, pointing right at him.

Rick ducked into his Explorer and chewed on the coffee cup, driving around town with the North Koreans in his rearview mirror. He cursed himself for not having a camera with him, just when he needed it. *At least Mai's not here.* He ditched them at the freeway onramp and got home from the other direction. He contacted his Homeland Security group, DHS104, immediately. Then went outside to scan the neighborhood and have a cigarette.

None too soon. He saw a car pulling over under apple trees in front of the house, dropping Mai off in the driveway. He hastily ground the stub and shredded the filter.

"Hi, sweetheart, welcome back! Have a good trip?" Rick asked Mai, slipping his arm around her waist in a gentle squeeze as he took her travel bag with the other.

"Yes, but I'm really tired. Can we go out for dinner? I'm too bushed to cook," Mai answered, too exhausted even to hug him back. She headed straight into the shower while he bounded upstairs to check his email ... again.

Thinking that they were out there somewhere in the dark, Rick replied, "I'd rather stay in with you. I'll call for a pizza." He imagined they probably had night vision goggles and heat sensors and everything. And he wondered why he was getting her into the middle of this.

When they'd met in college in the 1990s, he was a math major/political science minor and she was studying art and Chinese. Tall and lanky back then, with broad, straight shoulders and a shock of white blonde hair over friendly blue eyes, he'd smiled warmly as soon as she sat next to him in the lecture hall for Political Geography.

***

Curled up on the sofa, munching pizza, Mai took a deep breath and started, "I found a couple of leads for jobs overseas."

"Where overseas?"

"China."

"You want to go to China, Mai?" asked Rick.

"I used to want to go badly, remember? When I was in college, studying Asian culture and poetry. I think I still have my old grammar books," she answered.

Mai rose and went into the kitchen to get a bottle of Hopmonk Tavern ale and a couple glasses. The full harvest moon, rising through the notch in the hills to the east, caught her eye out the window over the sink. Coming back into the room, she set her load down on the low table. The shower had refreshed her. She pulled the long strands of wavy, light brown hair, once the color of red gold, into a loose French braid, wisps of hair curl where they escaped.

"They're looking for a native English speaker who can work in media communications, you know, public relations, for Beijing University. They publish some magazines and brochures. They also want someone with web-development skills."

"Don't you have to speak Chinese to get the job?" asked Rick.

"I can't speak Chinese, but I can write HTML. It's worth a shot."

Rick poured her a spot of ale and they clicked glasses. "Might be a good idea ... there aren't any jobs around here. How long would you be gone?"

September 5

Although Ron tells her about Commander GAO's assurance the investigation has been suspended, it's hard to stop thinking about the past days' events. Yet, friends email. Life continues.

September 5   To: Mai Martin   From: Yunling
Subject: Palace Museum

Not see you so long. Join me. The ancient Chinese porcelain is beautiful. I will see about getting some time off during the week to go, and I will let you know. Do you have a day of week or morning or afternoon better?

September 5   To: Yunling   From: Mai Martin

Subject: Re: Palace Museum

Afternoon is better for me.

September 5   To: Yunling   From: Mai Martin

Subject: Re: Palace Museum

I have made an appt with ZHANG. I will ask her for an afternoon off this week. I'll get back to you when I find out.

September 5   To: Yunling   From: Mai Martin

Subject: Re: Palace Museum

We can go with ZHANG's blessing! Tues, Thurs or Fri afternoon works for me. What is best for you?

September 6   To: Mai Martin   From: Yunling

Subject: Re: Palace Museum

Friday afternoon is better for me, is it ok for you? We can go there after lunch. Palace museum will close at 5PM. We only can enter it from the South Gate in the Tiananmen Square.

September 6   To: Mai Martin   From: Ronald ZHAO

Subject: more travel

Go to Hong Kong be back next week

September 7   To: Yunling   From: Mai Martin

Subject: Re: Palace Museum

Okay, Friday September 9, when should we leave? Are we going by di tie? [subway]

September 7   To: Mai Martin   From: Yunling

Subject: Re: Palace Museum

Okay, I will see you Friday 1PM at West Gate

Conducting daily live-time searches on Mai's email and internet activity, JGTS YANG Cai finds she's going off campus with friends on Friday to Tian'anmen. Beijing Police Department is notified for surveillance.

September 15

The National Security Administration, under the Homeland Security umbrella, picked up a mini-trend on Rick's visa application matched against his DHS ID during automatic meta-data sweeps. It isn't long before Rick gets an official inquiry.

September 15   To: Rick Martin   From: DHS 104
Subject: Passport

ENCRYPTED: We see you have visa app to China. Why is that?

September 16   To: DHS 104   From: Rick Martin
Subject: Re: Passport

ENCRYPTED: Vacation to see wife

September 20   To: Rick Martin   From: DHS 104
Subject: Re: Passport

ENCRYPTED: Does this have anything to do with incident last fall with NK?

September 21   To: DHS 104   From: Rick Martin
Subject: Re: Passport

ENCRYPTED: Maybe

September 22   To: Rick Martin   From: DHS 104

Subject: Re: Passport

      ENCRYPTED: Collect as much data as possible on North Korea. Looking for someone with a new perspective

September 30

Mai completes and sends her Media Report #12 9/30/2011.

Incident Report 20110930

TRIGGER ACTIVITY: MEDIA REPORT 9/30

    20—Subject violates accepted–use criteria: uses SunSystems search to access keyword–excluded media. 9/30

SECURITY RESPONSE ACTIVITY:

    20—Response: Automatic keyword search Layer 7 Tier III: IP identifier unit
Keyword searches are collected in a live–stream search
Tabulation of violations pushes alert

September 30   To: Mai   From: BU Network Admin

Subject: Guard Against Fraudulent E-Mail Notification

    Dear Campus E-Mail Users, Hello!
    Recently, the Network Center Beijing University, found that it was fake e-mail system administrator, to send e-mail scams to cheat the user's mailbox password. E-mail scams in English or Chinese, the message requires the user to reply or click on a link address (such as Beijing University Home address http://www.Beijing University.edu.cn), please do not be fooled, do not make any reply or click! Otherwise, it may cause your system has been infected, or your network account, bank account numbers and other important personal information was stolen, and cheaters out with your account to send a large number of

malicious deception content with spam, directly or indirectly, to bring you great loss.

In this regard, Beijing University Network Center solemnly declare:

1, we will not e-mail inquiry form, grant or confirm any campus application ID and password and other private information, not to compose a message in English to send similar notices.

2, the network center, and e-mail will contain details such as telephone customer service contact information.

Network Center solemnly remind you encounter a similar message, please do not disclose important personal information, be vigilant and guard against Internet fraud!

Please keep your login password, ensure that your password has some complexity, do not use simple passwords; If possible, please change your password regularly.

Hereby tips. Thank you for your attention and cooperation!

Beijing University Network Center
Customer Service Department
Address: Room 212 Main Building,
Beijing University

October 1

The first weekend of the national holiday, everyone Mai knew was going somewhere for the week. Yunling went to her hometown to visit her grandfather. Dr. Rebecca and Wassily visited Harbin by train and stayed at hostels. Dr. Summerlake visited friends in Seoul.

Mai stays in town and spends a blissful afternoon at the square near the Mingqing office. She sits in the hazy autumn sunshine and draws the grotesque rock, bits of bamboo in the background, and wispy clouds indicated by a few lines, thinking about Rick. *He'll be here soon.* *Yuanfen* threads weave a curtain between them, an unspoken, invisible effect. Over time, part of the curtain is filmy and vague. She can just make him out in the hazy distance. Sometimes the curtain is heavy and coarse. The charcoal pencil scribbles in the round, dark recesses of the rock while Mai bitterly chews on the taste of rejection, brooding about

Rick's attachment to Homeland Security, her rival.

Of course, DHS is the reason for the distance between us. They turned him into one of them. Chasing imaginary enemies on the internet.

One day, it's warm and sunny; the next, cool and hazy. Casual summer dress and lifestyle is over; fall is blowing yellow leaves onto the dark, green mondo grass by her office. The gingkoes are the first to color. In the warm afternoons, she packs a folding chair, and her art stuff, and pedals around campus, looking for another scene to paint. Something with trees in rows with a road or sidewalk feature. *Kind of impressionistic,* she thinks, *Van Gogh-esque, or maybe French-looking.* She tries to improve her Chinese brush technique, adding color.

It's like a moment of stillness before an earthquake. Or quiet before a typhoon. She feels suspended in the air, surrounded by dancing golden motes, ignoring or forgetting, suppressing or hiding the approaching conflict.

Since suspending the Martin investigation, Commander GAO's office has been busy combating a heavy cyber-attack during the holiday on the university network server. Some users had their passwords stolen and became victims of internet extortion through computer infections. The Harbin Institute informs them the source is Hong Kong. Although Commander GAO wants JGTS YANG Cai to keep watch over Mai's internet activity, he's working overtime on the hacking problem and misses Rick's email about his visit.

Mai's money transfer arrives, and she needs to get 15 thousand yuan to TSC, and that starts her thinking about Ron. She hasn't seen him since the night he drove away, when the Commander called off the investigation. That was more than a month ago. Listening to music, she hears a tune by the Eurhythmics: *Was it just another love affair?*

For his part, Ron ZHAO has thrown himself into work since coming back from business travel with his boss. Mai Martin needs to pay the balance of the deposit, and the bookkeeper keeps bothering Ron to get the rest of his hours in and close the account. The words of a new hit song by Adele keep running through his head: *Whenever I'm alone with you, you make me feel young again.*

October 4   To: Mai   From: Ron
No Subject

Hello Mai, are you busy on 10/1 holiday? If you are in town would you like to get together? I have motorcycle, want to take ride?

Kismet. She does, and Ron picks her up in a 1957 vintage Russian M72 bike with a sidecar. She hadn't seen anything like it before. People in the neighborhood stare at them as she climbs into the little compartment. He hands her a modern helmet and tucks a blanket around her legs. She thinks, *Ron looks dashing,* dressed in blue denim jeans and a black leather jacket, a white turtle-necked tee shirt underneath.

"You're going to want this," he says, producing a woman's leather jacket out of a side compartment.

Merging onto the freeway heading west, there's not much traffic. The holiday has emptied the big city. While everyone crowds into airports and train stations to visit notable sites, Ron flies under overpasses in search of the less-visited, charming neighborhoods in the far reaches of Beijing Province. The villages here still look much like they did before the modern era, with cobblestone lanes winding around hillsides perched next to lakes bobbing with boats.

The sun is over their shoulder, lighting up the Western Hills. Ron exits the big highway. Looking at her beside him in the sidecar, Mai flashes him a big, *movie star* smile. He can't see her face well behind the helmet, but he can feel the warmth growing in his chest. They ride along next to a big canal, a man-made feature of the land and testimony to the advanced technology possessed by the ancient Chinese people. On the other side is a communal farm; stands dot the lane selling eggs and pears. His legs need a stretch, so he stops at one.

"What a good idea to come out here on a ride, Ron," Mai says, ducking out of the helmet. He offers his hand to help haul her out of the seat. A brief flash of electricity passes between their fingers.

"Ouch!" she says, looking at his smiling face, warm eyes with little crinkles at the corners. "I brought that 15 thousand yuan with me I owe TSC," she adds.

"Good, we can now afford pears," he teases. "These pears are the best, do you want some?" he asks. They're lined up in perfect rows with boxes of Chinese dates or *Ziziphus* jujube, and baskets of fresh eggs. The Pyrus *x bretschneideri* is not to be confused with the more common Asian pear. The Chinese white pear is a regional specialty, a natural hybrid species, native to northern China near Beijing. It's very juicy with light flesh and shaped like a European pear, refreshing and juicy with low sugar content.

Leaning back on the seat of his bike, stretching his long legs and munching on a juicy fruit, he recalls the last night in the back seat of his car—how she wrapped her arms around him, and the feeling of his skin against hers in the moonlight.

Standing with the sun in her face, feeling its warmth, she remembers their last night together, too—lying in the back of the Buick Park Avenue while he played around with her sweater and brassiere, finally getting his mouth onto her nipples and sucking hard on them.

"Who runs these fruit stands?" she wants to know.

"Peasants from the commune farm over there," says Ron, gesturing to a large area of fields dotted with buildings on the other side of the canal. "They can make money now."

Mai's attention drifts to the bucolic scene on the other side of the road. Standing a meter apart, Ron fights an urge to grasp her around her waist.

"This ancient canal was built to bring water to the palace gardens, even ultimately to Beijing University. You know, the university is built on the grounds of the Summer Palace residence of the last several emperors."

"*Dui*, I knew that. But I didn't know where the water came from. On campus, the canals are lined with concrete. The carved stone balustrade is beautiful, and the way the willow trees hang over the still water ... I've photographed it many times."

"There's a village near here on a lake. We can stop there for lunch if you like," he offers, thinking about a hostel he knows with a beautifully terraced garden and rooms to rent.

"Great, I'm going to be seriously hungry soon," she agrees, finishing the pear and gently blotting her mouth with the back of her hand. Resetting her helmet, she clambers back into the sidecar, and they hit the road again, encircling the lake for a mile or two before he turns onto a bumpy dirt road.

A refurbished farm house with red lanterns hanging in front sits cheerfully at the end of the long driveway. "Western Lily Hostel" is printed in gold letters below the Chinese name across its front. Foregoing the indoor dining room filled with guests, Ron chooses a table on the terrace where they can see a glimmer of water through the trees and enjoy the privacy.

He orders some dishes special to the region and a bottle of beer with two glasses.

"How long have you had the motorcycle, Ron? I thought you just moved here."

"I bought it for myself to celebrate my birthday this year—my first birthday without being around my family … my son and ex-wife, I mean."

"Well, Happy Birthday, Ron," Mai says, raising her glass in a toast. "And which birthday would that be?"

"Well, I'm forty-five, and here's to you, the most beautiful client at TCS … and you are?"

"Thirty-nine…. It's been really quiet around the apartment without you," she ventures, looking at him over the rim of the glass. She sets it on the table and resumes studying his face, his high cheekbones and almond shaped eyes. Playing basketball and motorcycling this summer tanned his smooth skin. She sees light lines around his eyes where he squints in the sun.

"I've been able to get a lot done at the office now that I'm not flying all over Asia or driving out to the suburbs every day," he counters delicately, pouring more beer into the little glasses. "And my mother is happy to have me around to fuss over."

"I bet; how is she?" asks Mai.

"She's always complaining about this and that. Getting used to Beijing and making friends will take time. Nothing is as good as it is in Hong Kong. And she wants me to get married again to a nice Chinese girl—from *Hong Kong*."

"Nothing wrong with that, Ron," Mai adds.

Reaching across the table and taking one of her hands, "Nothing, except I'm not interested in any girls from Hong Kong." He pauses and looks long into her intense, brown eyes. "We can get a room here for the afternoon …"

The narrow room has two long windows at the far end, overlooking the terrace and garden down to the lake. The bathroom is newly refurbished with white tile walls and floor, all new fixtures: pedestal sink, Western-style toilet and bathtub. The hard Chinese bed takes up most of the room. The *fuwuyuan* brings extra towels and a silk duvet, leaving them alone at last. He starts with her shoes, removing them, and then the motorcycle jacket, hanging it over the back of one of the chairs near the window. He hangs his jacket on the other chair before sitting down and pulling off his boots. Not talking, just looking at each other quietly and savoring the first time. He pulls the shirt off over his head, and she sees his smooth chest and narrow waist. Ripping the belt out of the loops, he climbs onto the bed in his jeans.

Obediently, she holds her arms over her head while he pulls her sweater off and then her brassiere. Kissing her slowly from ears down her neck to her breasts. He cups them in his hands and tries squeezing them into his mouth. Lying back on the cotton damask pillows and silk brocade duvet, Mai deliriously surrenders to his gentle passion.

October 8

On Saturday, Mai brings her camera downtown to where her language class has relocated. She wants to get pictures of the colorful street life in the upscale neighborhood. Early risers are lined up at the breakfast cafes and stands. Pancake—or Beijing pizza—at Tu Jia Jiang Xiang Bing.

Steamed buns—*baozi*—come with a variety of fillings—*zheshi shenme xianr de baozi?* Her teacher, *Laoshi,* happens to walk into the picture frame. *Her* favorite filling is *nai huang bao*—steamed creamy custard bun from 7-Eleven.

After class Mai texts Ron: "*Im dun, where 2 meet?*" Her language class is not far from Ron's flat.

He replies: "@ *Dong sta @ Ginz mall newsp stand @ exit 10:15.*"

On the short walk from the school, Mai passes through a crooked alley lined with small shops opening for the day, two fruit sellers across the way from each other vie for customers. Expensive apartment buildings loom up behind the shops—"mistress apartments," her teacher calls them. Once on the boulevard, Mai turns toward the main street. Fashionable boutiques entice her with mannequins draped and booted and belted. A small mob of young agents in suits and ties hang out in front of an apartment rental office. The big Ginza mall sits on the corner with valet and VIP parking under the broad marquee.

Mai spots him waiting at the newspaper stand. *What kind of police commissioner was he? Did he wear a uniform or a suit?* "Nihao, Ron!"

Engrossed in an article about international gangs, Ron doesn't see her until she's right there. "Mai! You look fantastic!"

Wearing jeans and a bright, persimmon orange Chinese jacket, she shines like a golden flame in his eyes. "Did you take the *di tie?*" asks Mai.

"Yeah, sometimes I like to get around the city without dragging that big car with me everywhere. It's a hassle having a car in Beijing. Want a cup of coffee?" he asks.

In the basement of the mall, they find a bakery selling all kinds of fresh-baked goodies. Where they sit, drinking cappuccino and nibbling, they can talk while people-watching.

Outside, the day is faintly sunny and pleasant to wander through the streets. Ron wants to buy something for her at one of the cute boutiques, so she lets him pick out a camel sweater in silk-cashmere blend attached to a short chiffon skirt, and stretch faux-suede coffee-colored pants. He won't let her see the price, but she imagines it's a lot.

Standing on the broad street lined with boxwood and geraniums and carrying shopping bags of boxes, Ron hails a cab. *"Women qu yishu 798"* [Take us to art district 798].

"Where are we going now?" asks Mai, stowed in among the bags.

"Have you been to the art district?" asks Ron, settling his arm across the back of the seat and planting a big kiss on her lips.

"Yes, I love it. I was there during Dragon Boat Festival with Dr. Rebecca and Yunling," she says, kissing him back on the ear.

"Who are these people, Mai? Your friends?"

"Would you like to meet my friends, ZHAO *Xiansheng*?"

"Not really, I'm just fascinated—you have Chinese friends?"

"Dui, dear. I'm friendly. That's me. Students, colleagues, or co-workers. Maybe I should have a party and you can meet them."

"Dui, tangzi" [sweetie], followed by more necking before Ron directs the *shifu* to take them to the north entrance with fewer cars. The art district was originally built by Bauhaus-inspired engineers for Beijing North China Wireless Joint Equipment Factory in the 1950s and is one of the few places outside of Germany to display this distinctive architectural style. The factory became obsolete and declined, until the 1990s, when it

was decommissioned and reinvented as an art district. The *shifu* drops them off near an old steam locomotive exhibited with an array of new Porsches, music blaring "Watermelon Man."

The first gallery they visit is showing two artists. One paints sumptuous traditional *huahua*-style lotuses in every season and stage of growth or decay. The other one paints small, oil canvases from the beach in Los Angeles. Mai is instantly homesick and buys the artists' book. Inside another gallery, Tibetan monks lie or sit on a raised stage and painstakingly make a sand-painting mandala, scraping metal funnels to jiggle colored pigments out the narrow mouth, grain by grain, into an intricate pattern.

As they come around the corner, a narrow lane opens into a wide brick plaza entirely taken over by cast wolves in various attitudes, circling a central victim. Turning into another lane, they encounter a gallery reception. Tall baskets of red and yellow flowers entwined with intricate ribbons line the front of the brick factory façade, ample glass windows beacon with glimpses of beautiful people inside holding champagne flutes.

"Let's go in here, Ron," urges Mai.

"Oh, we're not invited," he objects.

"Doesn't matter, I bet they'll let us in. You look like a rich Chinese who wants to buy art. *Zouba!* Let's go!"

Once past the young tough in a tuxedo at the door, the room opens up with high clerestory windows in the ceiling above steel beam rafters. Mai stashes her shopping bags behind a catering table with a long white tablecloth.

"I see someone I know," says Ron, gesturing with a nod of his head toward a tall, talkative Anglo with a large watch and jade cufflinks winking from under an ivory-colored silk jacket. A petite, Chinese girl hangs on his arm. "He's a TSC client."

"Well, let's go talk with him," says Mai, steering Ron toward the back of the room where she can see something of the paintings behind the fashionable crowd.

"I'll be, it's Ronald ZHAO," starts the big man with a heavy British accent.

"Nihao, Alan, this is Mai Martin, she's also a client of TSC."

"Alan Spires, ma'am," he says bowing over her proffered hand. "Attorney and art connoisseur." Turning to Ron he says, "You should go out more, ZHAO and get a life that's not work-related."

"Like you?" counters Ron.

"Ha, ha; got me. Here I am, networking ... or trolling ... for new clients among these trendy and mostly Chinese nouveau riche."

Alan and his friend Annie, Ron, and Mai stand with their backs to the depressing and tortured paintings to people-watch. Wealthy men with their wives sit at small café tables near the entrance. The ones with their mistresses stand near the bar in the back.

The party looks like it's just starting when Ron and Mai make their excuses and then walk a few blocks out of the district to find someplace to eat. At a Buddhist, vegetarian restaurant, Ron expertly orders for her: a towering salad with skewered, grilled tofu sausages, a spicy curry–type soup with pumpkin and dates, and finishing with fruit and jasmine tea.

Outside again, the buildings are dark gray shapes with lighted window squares and black trees. The moon is almost full, lighting the Beijing skyline. Warm light reflecting off large patches of silver-edged clouds hanging low in the gray sky combines with the amber streetlights to expose people out in the night, black shapes on foot or on bicycle.

"I'm sending you home now, to your LiNai apartment."

"Aren't you coming with me?" she asks, as they slowly walk toward a busy boulevard where they can find a taxi.

"I promised my mother I would take her to an orchid show at the botanical gardens tomorrow."

***

October 8   To: Mai   From: Rick
Subject: Call Your Morning Today

The travel agent guy called and this is what they came up with. Have to call him back. Dates they gave me are okay? They gave me these dates ... Good price! That I can afford ... Leaving SF Oct 30 and returning Nov 16 ...

October 8   To: Rick   From: Mai
Subject: Re: Call Your Morning Today

Are you really coming? I guess those days are ok. I'll check with ZHANG.

All spring and summer, Mai's invitation to her husband Rick sat on the back of his mind, going nowhere. Things at Homeland Security kept him occupied. Mai kept him updated. He could go a long time like that. Now, after all these months begging him to come, Mai suddenly feels ambivalent. She doesn't want him to come after all. What should she tell him? *Stall.*

October 9   **To: Rick**   **From: Mai**

Subject: Re: Call Your Morning Today

ZHANG says we will be busy with Newsletter deadline first week in November.

Starting in October, the campus internet service provider—BeijingUniversity.net—requires signing in with a password twice; the first time doesn't always take. Mai supposes it's a security measure to guard against the machine brute-force attacks on their system. The university server is slow and inconvenient, and probably spies on her, but she can't find the other telecom office. She's stuck with them for now.

On the first day back to work after the long holiday, tired, golden brown leaves drop one by one off the smooth, white-barked branches of the magnolia outside her office window, leaving fuzzy buds of next year's flowers on their tips. Some leaves are still green, showing burnt, brown edges where the sap withers away. Birds ate all the coral-red fruit that hung in bunches along the branches all summer. A magpie dressed in a black and white tuxedo flew onto the window ledge and looked into her office.

It's getting cold and foggy … or is it smoggy? … heavy mist almost like rain smothers a melodious Chinese flute, floating over brown, spent lotus foliage. Workers chip bricks from a demolition project adjacent to the road and sewer improvement projects running concurrently near her apartment.

The day after the full moon, her computer crashes. The black screen's error message tells her: if she hasn't seen this before, she can try automatic reinstall. It seems to work. Then another message appears: "Windows has detected an IP address conflict. Another computer on this network has the same IP address as this computer. Contact your network administrator for help resolving this issue. More details are available in the Windows system Event Log." But they aren't. The log is empty.

The same day, her cell phone dies. Still under warranty, they send it back to the factory.

October 14   **To: Rick**   **From: DHS 104**
No Subject

ENCRYPTED: Confirm travel plans for Oct 30 to Nov 16. Schedule briefing meeting before you go. Attached confidential report. For your eyes only.

October 15   **To: Mai From: Rick**
Subject: Got It!

Got passport back with Chinese visa inside:
11 Oct 2011 to 11 Oct 2012
60 days at a time.

The sun is shining no brighter than the moon through thick clouds of mist and haze. In the still air, tiny—almost microscopic—bugs mass in a frenzy of last-minute life. Soon the night frosts will steal in, preparing the way for winter.

October 16

October 16   **To: Rick**   **From: Mai**
Subject: Re: Got It!

Btw I'm worried about your trip. Aren't you?

Rick clicks on Mai's account on his Skype page, and soon the video of her apartment flashes.

"Hi, sweetie," Rick says.

"Hi, Rick, aren't you worried about the North Koreans getting you here?" asks Mai.

"I'm going to be there on a job for Homeland Security."

"Oh." *So that's why he's coming.* "No!"

"Yeah, so not to worry! There'll be Homeland Security guys from the Beijing Field Office to keep an eye on everything. Don't worry. This is a great opportunity for us to get more intel on them."

After the connection terminates, Mai remembers an argument she and Rick had on Skype in May.

After spending an hour and a half struggling with the internet, trying to upload new files to her website server in California, Mai had abandoned her personal project for the night, turning instead to Skype and some consolation from Rick.

The blue screen popped into black and then a still shot of Rick in front of his laptop, in tee-shirt and lounging in the big, reclining, executive chair in his office.

"Nihao, Rick," started Mai, "can you see me?"

"You're up late," said Rick, "This video display is crap. Turn off the video, and let's just talk."

"God, I've been hammered trying to work on my website," started Mai.

"What's the matter with your code?"

"Nothing's the matter, that's the problem. It's everything. Nothing is working right."

"Calm down, you probably forgot a *div*," offered Rick lamely, referring to the commonest mistake of web designers writing their own code.

"Div? I've checked and checked. I've written to every tech-help person I can think of. Nothing."

"Have you talked to Desiree?"

"She's busy."

"Too bad for you."

"Like hell, thanks for nothing. More nothing."

"Calm down, Mai. Maybe you should go to bed."

"Ms. HAN asked me again when you were coming."

"Yeah, well, I don't have my legal birth certificate. I told you, I have to get a copy from the state before I can apply for the visa."

"That was like a month ago. Don't you want to come here?"

"Not really, Mai; this is your adventure, remember? Not mine."

"You're an idiot!"

She had clicked on disconnect and stared at the blue screen for a minute before resting her head on her arms, over the keyboard. She remembered regretting mouthing off to him at the time. That was before he confessed to working for Homeland Security and involving her with North Korean agents, something about a stunt Rick played on the Iranians. It was unreal, like out of a novel.

***

Mai finishes her thirteenth Media Report and sends it 10/17/2011.

CHAPTER 3
Radiant Star

October 2011

Harbin: the Dage of Dages

The temperatures have been dropping since September. Today the weather is almost the same in Beijing as it is in Harbin, foggy-smoggy, high of 70 F or 25 C, dipping to 47 tonight or 8. Tomorrow will be sunny.

The Harbin Director, Chief DIANGTI, thumbs through the reports on his desk and shoves them to one side, staring out the dirty window in the Soviet-style building onto the barren campus below.

In Korea, when the old man goes, things will be different DIANGTI thinks, and he's well-placed to benefit from the ensuing wars between the generals. The ruler's kid will be swept aside in the power grab. Another strong man will emerge. Who will it be? He muses, twirling a pen through his fingers. He's been funneling resources through his network to certain accounts, leading to certain strong men. He'll be rewarded. Or he'll have to be dealt with. Either way, he has the connections they want.

What does that clown GAO think? Shutting down the Martin investigation when he was close to grabbing the woman and forcing her husband to come to Beijing. He'll show the Commander who runs things at Beijing U. Those idiots have no clue. It's brazen, hacking into the university accounts, but GAO deserves it ... and the North Koreans are insatiable. The elite are getting a little crazy with all the money, he thinks, kind of like that Kaddafi clan—cases of French champagne and the abducted women and boys, kind of sick. But, he only provides the network. He's not involved in the actual procurement of the luxury goods they crave. What a racket. And the people freezing and starving in the dark. It gives him the creeps if he thought about it, but he rarely exercises his conscience. He rarely exercises! Ha ha! Only with his young mistresses, ha ha! It makes him laugh.

October 17

Incident Report 20111017

TRIGGER ACTIVITY: MEDIA REPORT 10/17

21—Subject violates accepted-use criteria: uses SunSystems search to access keyword-excluded media. 10/17

SECURITY RESPONSE ACTIVITY:

21—Response: Automatic keyword search Layer 7 Tier III: IP identifier unit
Keyword searches are collected in a live-stream search
Tabulation of violations pushes alert

Monday afternoon, October 17, JGTS YANG Cai bursts into Commander GAO's office, "I've got some big news on the Martin woman's husband, boss!"

"*Haode*, so tell me," says GAO.

"He has his visa and tickets to Beijing."

"Zhende? Who else is in the office right now?"

"Want me to round everyone up?" Cai asks.

"Dui, I'll meet you in the conference room in fifteen minutes," finishes GAO, glancing at his phone while Cai hurries out.

The first person Cai sees is Sgt. WANG, walking toward him in the corridor, hunched over a stack of reports. "The Commander says *meeting in the conference room in fifteen minutes*."

The office Lt. LIU shares with Maj. TANG is around the corner from the elaborate marble stairs. Cai knocks briefly before opening the door. "Martin *Xiansheng* is coming," he announces as he sticks his head in the door.

"When?" asks LIU, looking around his computer monitor at JGTS YANG Cai in the doorway.

"October 30, we have thirteen days. Where's Maj. TANG?"

"He's out in the field."

"Can you call him? Tell him the Commander wants us in the conference room in fifteen … uh … ten minutes?"

***

Commander GAO looks around the conference table. "Where's Maj. TANG?"

"He's coming," says WANG.

"Cai, why don't you start the briefing with the new information?" asks GAO.

"We just finished filtering and checking the Martin woman's internet history this afternoon. Martin *Xiansheng* has obtained his visa and has made plane reservations to arrive in Beijing October 30, leaving November 16." With that, Cai sits down.

Commander GAO notices everyone sitting up with attention. The door opens. Maj. TANG enters and takes a seat.

"*Duibuqi, wo chidaole* [Sorry, I'm late], what did I miss?" he asks.

Sgt. WANG abridges the report. "The Martin woman's husband is arriving here on October 30, that's in just thirteen days."

The Commander pulls on his chin, resting his elbow on the corner of the table. The men digest the information quietly, waiting for their boss to speak first. "Cai, what's the status of the network hacking?" asks GAO.

"We've been running diagnostics every day. Fresh outbreaks erupt on a cycle we are trying to interpret. Our guys have been working constantly, servicing the victims. Their computers need cleaning and resetting. All this takes hours and hours of our resources."

"How many victims do you estimate?" asks GAO.

"We figure 2 percent of the network users were breached. That makes about 2,000, but only 500 have come into the office for help. The rest either resorted to self-remedies or paid the ransom. If you figure 500 are capable of fixing the problem themselves, that leaves an estimated one thousand users paying 200Y each—or 200,000 yuan total. That's just the individuals. Numerous university bank accounts were also attacked. The extent of the raid on these ancillary ports is not known at this time."

"What have you done to contain the infection?" GAO wants to know.

"The Internet Office sent out a notice to users. I can go into the criteria for the selection now if you want," offers Cai.

"That's all right. I want to know the current status of the containment."

"The daily frequency of infected users coming into the office has dropped significantly. We've reduced the number of programmers assigned to that duty and are confident we will solve the riddle of the infection cycle soon.... Just one thing."

"What's that, Cai?"

"It bothers me that Harbin is so sure that the source is Hong Kong, and the Hong Kong people are adamant that the origin is somewhere else. They haven't tracked that string to any of their servers or nodes—reminds me of that old cyber-attack rumor...."

"Thank you, Cai," says GAO, silently thinking while the men quietly check their messages and text.

"What do you think about the Harbin Institute returning and reopening the Martin investigation?" GAO asks the men.

No one speaks.

"Lt. LIU, what are your thoughts?" asks GAO pointedly.

"I suppose we're obligated to inform them."

"Yes. I plan to contact the Harbin Chief tomorrow."

Lt. LIU continues cautiously, "It seems to me, they're interested in the husband and not the wife. The husband is not our concern, but Martin Taitai is our employee, and she has not shown evidence of being involved in her husband's cyber-spying activities."

Commander GAO gravely nods in assent. "Maj. TANG, what are your views?"

"Agent GUAN is very professional, but he has no scruples about what he does. He follows orders well. From what he told me during his last visit, he's been involved in some things that would make me lose sleep at night."

"Have you finished the reports I ordered at the last Bureau

Meeting?" asks GAO, trying not to think about his own Red Guard days. Whether GUAN is just loyal to a fault or ideologically self-righteous, if he's a good man, his regret will be the same. If he's not ... well, that's what's worrying GAO.

Lt. LIU glances at Maj. TANG and speaks first. "I have compiled a few pages on the Harbin activities."

TANG adds, "I haven't found much on the North Koreans here in Beijing. I welcome ideas."

"I want you two and Cai to get together in the next couple days and finish your fact-gathering. Cai has interesting ways to get information, which is not generally available," he grins at Cai, whose face turns red. "In addition, I want a Profile on Rick Martin. Let's reconvene this meeting on Thursday the ... what is it, WANG?"

"The twentieth, sir."

"Okay, here, the 20th at 08:00."

The men drift out, full of tension and excitement at the turn of events.

***

Downstairs in the parking lot, sitting in his car, Commander GAO lets out a deep sigh. He puts the key into the ignition but doesn't start the car. Looking north over the tops of parked cars and a tall hedge of bamboo on the edge of his refuge park, he instantly drops into a meditative state.

It's almost dark when he reaches for his mobile and calls Ron ZHAO.

"*Wei, nihao*, Commander GAO," answers Ron, sitting in his

corner office, overlooking the Beijing skyline.

"*Wan shang hao, ZHAO*," replies GAO. "I've got some information for Martin Taitai. Can you relay it to her for me?"

"Certainly, Commander, what is it?"

"Today, we found Martin Taitai's emails about her husband's visit on the 30th." All the air in the room disappears; Ron feels like he's suffocating. "Why is he coming now, ZHAO?"

"It's just a visit to see his wife." Ron straightens the pens and pencils on his desk while he waits for the Commander's reply.

"We can benefit each other by sharing information. You will recall, we've shared important facts with you, which has aided in the security of your client Martin Taitai," says GAO.

Taking his time to answer, ZHAO breathes slowly, controlling his anger at Mai, "Doubtless, your interventions have been key to the well-being of Martin Taitai."

One part of Ron's brain kicks in and carries the conversation, while another part reels with the news. She hadn't told him! They'd been together so many times, and she'd said nothing. In fact, they avoided discussing him at all. When they were together, all he thought about was her. He thought she felt the same ... At least, that's what she led him to believe.

"There's more I want to know from your client. Can we arrange a meeting?"

"I'll ask her. Will you be home this evening? I'll call you."

He barely finishes hanging up with the Commander before his speed dial rings Mai's cell.

"Hi Ron, what's up?" she asks.

"I'm in your part of town," he lies. "Want to get together?"

"Anything special, or do you want to show up with take-out like the old days?" she asks gaily. "I have rice in the cooker if you want to bring something to go with."

"Yeah, that sounds perfect. I'll be there in a bit." He hangs up and broods, looking at the twinkling lights of the city. That's a fib, but she's been dishonest with him, and he's angry and confused. Taking his time, driving to Wudaokou at the peak of rush hour, he feels some satisfaction making her wait for him.

***

After the last dumpling is devoured, and she's in the kitchenette cleaning up, he tries relaxing in the comfortable, worn armchair with upholstery like rhinoceros hide. Mai opens a second beer and pours some into his glass as she sits in the armchair opposite.

"I got a call from Commander GAO today," he starts.

"You don't say. What does GAO want now?" asks Mai.

"He has some important information for you he wants me to relay." Ron holds back, savoring the moment, looking at her intently over the top of his glass, taking a big gulp. He thinks she looks adorable, curled up in the big chair, a little high from the beer and flirting at him with those round eyes.

"They just found the emails from your husband about his visit on the 30th. Commander GAO wants a meeting with you tomorrow morning." For some reason, his throat contracts, and he strains to get out the last few words, almost choking him. Finished speaking, his mouth compresses into a sardonic smile. His breath passes in a thin stream through his nostrils, in and out.

Her eyes widen, and she plays nervously with the collar of her shirt, "I should have told you." *Ron looks so fierce!*

"Yes, you should have, Mai!" barks Ron hoarsely. The hurt in his voice stabs like a knife, and she can't look at his face. "Why didn't you tell me, Mai?" gradually recovering objectivity with his voice.

Again her weakness and stupidity eroded the happiness she had found. Afraid to tell him about Rick, thinking she could go another few days or a week. Before Homeland Security barges in and takes over.

"I'm afraid of what might happen when Rick gets here. These past days are treasured memories I'll never forget."

"You talk like it's over," he says.

"We'll finally get to see the players."

She's thinking, *Pretty soon I won't have to lie. It's all coming out.* She says, "I know I haven't been honest with you about Rick. He's involved in some things I wish I could tell you."

She's been living a fantasy, here comes the reality check.

"There's more you're not telling?" Ron grunts and retreats into the studio where he boots up his laptop while he checks his phone for messages. He remembers he said he'd call GAO back.

"Hey, Mai," he calls from the studio. When she doesn't come, he gets up and goes looking for her. She's in the kitchenette setting out the things for breakfast: Hong cha, Nestle creamer, Chinese porridge.

"The Commander wants a meeting tomorrow at 8AM," he says. "He wants to know why your husband is coming. And I'd like to know the same thing."

He can smell the scent of her shampoo as he stands behind her in the doorway. They stand together but not touching for several minutes looking down into the hutong. A car horn honks in the street, muffled through the closed window.

Sighing, Ron reaches for his mobile. "Commander, *wei, nihao*, ZHAO ... What time and where? Martin Taitai agrees to meet with you ... tomorrow? ... eight AM?"

It's cold in her fifth-floor, cement apartment. The city won't turn on the heat for two more weeks. Ron and Mai snuggle under layers of duvets, the heat of their bodies pooling in the center of the bed where they lie, embracing and whispering to each other into the late hours of the night.

"Do you love *him*?"

"Yes," she confesses.

Ron makes a muffled moan into the pillow and holds her closer.

"Are you working for Homeland Security, too?"

"No, no, no! I'm not involved in Rick's work. This is really complicated. Honestly, I don't know what the right thing to do is," she whispers, putting her hot mouth over his ear.

Ron grunts and rolls over and off the bed. He steps into the house slippers Mai had bought for him and shuffles into the studio bedroom.

Mai awakes before dawn—there's only a faint hint of light showing in the sky to the east between the business park buildings—putting details into their places and outlining the options. She's wanted to know who was behind those attacks in August that sent her running through the hutong. Now she'll be front row and center.

October 18

Ron and Mai take the back way through the VIP parking. The young guard checks their names against his list and tells them how to find Commander GAO's office. They climb the three flights of stone stairs. On each floor, Mai sees poster-sized, framed photographs from the university's long and sometimes violent history. Not that any of the violence would be pictured here. *These* pictures are all proud achievements. Sgt. WANG greets them at the top of the stairs.

"*Nihao*, I am Sgt. WANG, Commander GAO's assistant," he says, bowing slightly.

"*Nihao*, Ronald ZHAO here; this is Martin Taitai," says Ron.

Mai nods politely but says nothing.

Sgt. WANG leads them to a small conference room next to the Commander's office. The walls are plain; the oval table is set with lidded cups of hot water in front of four empty chairs. The only feature is a window with a view down to the parking lot and the bamboo grove beyond.

The door opens, and Commander GAO walks in. Mai immediately recognizes him as the man in the drizzle who offered his card to her, today dressed in a camel jacket over a black crew-neck shirt. His bland Han face looks her directly in the eye before he drops his gaze with a small bow. "Martin Taitai, I am Commander GAO. Please sit, and you, ZHAO Xiansheng."

"We came as you requested. What can we do for you?" asks ZHAO.

Mai toys with the cup of hot water, removing the lid, taking a sip, and re-covering it.

"You will recall, we suspended the investigation of Martin Taitai last month. Our research indicated she has not seriously violated any protocol here at the university. However. In the course of internet searches, we have found much information about her husband, Rick Martin." The Commander sits quietly and looks impassively across the round table at Mai.

At the mention of Rick, Mai's dark eyes flicker to the Commander's face and back to the cup.

Ron gives her a steady gaze of assurance, but she's looking down.

"Why is your husband coming here, Martin Taitai?" asks GAO.

Ron translates for her. "Tell him it's just a visit. Nothing special."

"Does your husband work for Homeland Security, Martin Taitai?"

"No, *bu dui*, do I call you Commander?" Mai gives him a smile for the first time, and takes the conversation away from Homeland Security. Rick told her to keep his involvement between themselves, even though she knows lying to GAO now makes her complicit. *How long can I get away with pretending I don't know?* Conflicted. Her loyalty to Rick and her country wins out, and she lies.

"Commander is fine, Martin Taitai. We are aware that North Korean agents visited your hometown last November, and we have photographs of you and your husband."

Holding her cards close to her chest, Mai plays poker with the Commander, playing the innocent wife. *What's the worst thing that could happen*, she muses. *They would just send me home. They don't imprison Americans, surely. Still, I like living here, and I don't want to leave. Not yet.*

Mai is not aware of the dozens of American businessmen in detention for non-payment of wages ... or bribes, depending on whose account you hear. She slips her hand under the table and grips Ron's. "That's crazy, Commander, I don't know what you're talking about."

Commander GAO's mouth curves sideways into a sneer of disdain, "As you wish, Martin Taitai, but we have evidence that says otherwise. Unless, you can explain ..." He slides open a report cover and spreads photos across the table. Ron and Mai stare at the clandestine images for the first time: a picture of Rick standing next to the back door of their house, another one of him at the Texaco, and two of Mai. One taken in Sebastopol with her old, earth-mother look, and one, taken from her own computer, from a department outing at Phoenix Hills, with her new Chinese look.

"For a while, we thought you were a spy. Your husband, though, is involved with internet spying on Iran. We know this. I'm sure you do, too. So why continue lying about it. It makes it worse for you, Martin Taitai!"

"Is what he does dangerous, Commander GAO?" asks Mai through ZHAO.

"It could be very dangerous for him to come here, Martin Taitai. And for you. Our government does not take kindly to spies. As yours does not, of course," warns GAO, bluffing a little, since no American has ever been arrested for spying that he can think of, in contrast to the almost monthly stories about Chinese nationals being arrested in the US for industrial espionage.

"Of course."

Looking over the frothy bamboo foliage toward hazy north campus, Mai considers the options. There's no stopping Rick now he's sponsored by Homeland Security. Instead of that reassuring her, she aches for the loss of him to the huge organization. He loves Homeland

Security; he doesn't love her. Not if he's willing to use her as an excuse to insert the paranoid agency into her happy life in China. *Still, I'm an American ... and he's my husband.*

"What if he came to your office, voluntarily, to answer questions?" offers Mai. "And who would be in on the meeting?"

After a considerable pause, GAO responds, "There would be your husband, Rick Martin; myself; my top staff, Sgt. WANG, Lt. LIU and Maj. TANG; the Harbin Institute Director Chief DIANGTI, perhaps some people with him, and a translator. Ronald ZHAO could be present," answers GAO.

"Can you give us a couple of days to consider this?" asks Mai.

"I will consult my colleagues and contact you through ZHAO Xiansheng by the end of the week."

After a few more ritual comments, the brief conference concludes. Commander GAO returns to his office, Mai goes to work, and Ron drives east to Sanlitun into the bright new day.

***

In the main conference room, the empty video display of the Harbin Chief DIANGTI's desk greets Commander GAO. Sgt. WANG follows with a cup of coffee for his boss and one for himself. They sit quietly for a few minutes until Chief DIANGTI walks into the view and greets them.

"Zao shang hao, Commander GAO."

"Hen hao, ni ne, Chief DIANGTI?" replies GAO in polite greeting.

"Wo hai hao a," DIANGTI replies, completing the pleasantries.

"We are reopening the Martin investigation," says GAO, jumping right in.

"*Weishenme?*" asks the Harbin Chief, wondering if there are new developments.

"We have recent information that Martin Xiansheng is coming to Beijing."

"Ah! This is just what we wanted. When?"

"Are you interested in continuing with the investigation?"

"Certainly."

"Our objective in this case is to protect Martin Taitai, our employee, and prevent harm to her and to the university. We have no evidence she's involved in her husband's cyber-spying activities. What is *your* objective?" asks GAO, trying to take a firmer position this go round.

"At this time, our interest is to interrogate Martin Xiansheng, to corroborate the facts we have," answers DIANGTI.

"I think we can get Martin Xiansheng to cooperate—by bringing him to the Bureau for questioning. I will notify you when we have confirmed his arrival date."

This time, Commander GAO terminates the video chat.

The Commander and Sgt. WANG finish their coffee, looking at each other with satisfaction.

***

Downtown, Ron plows through a stack of papers. He can think better about how to handle the Martin case if his desk is clear of clutter. The past weeks, before the National Holiday, he'd been in and out of airports and hotels and conference meetings and expensive meals, traveling with his boss. During their layover in Hong Kong, they both visited their families for several days before flying on to Taiwan for another week of meetings and lavish meals. Ron loved seeing his son, but he's exhausted, buried in work and not thinking about Mai. The bookkeeper reminded him for his billable hours. As a partner at TSC, he brings the organization nearly twenty years of police procedure and organization and the potential of hundreds of clients. One of his responsibilities, besides servicing the clients, is training new agents. He promised them a training manual by year's end in addition to supervising the branches.

Now that the Martin account is reopened, he wants to put all that aside and concentrate on Mai's case. His phone rings with a text from her: "can i call u?"

"*Nihao*, Mai," greets Ron.

"*Wei, nihao.*"

"What do you need?" asks Ron.

"We never got a chance to debrief after this morning's chat with Commander GAO."

"There's much to discuss. And what about your husband? Is he a client now?"

"Yes, no, does that make a problem for you?"

"Not for me, Mai; my work at TSC is strictly business. We'll need a new contract and get another deposit. When do you want to meet?" Ron asks, thinking about what the Australian bookkeeper had said to him: If you're going to be handling this project of yours with your girlfriend as a job, we need more money … and a new contract.

"Tonight, okay?"

"Always okay, Mai. Take-out or go out?"

"Let's do sushi and go back to the apartment," she suggests.

"Sounds good. I'll text you when I leave the office."

Ron picks her up and drives to Koreatown on the edge of Wudaokou, serving the students attending the many universities in the area. He parks, and they walk with the constant flow of pedestrians, bicycles, and peddlers crowding the sidewalks in the busy commercial center. Mai leads the way through bollards separating the 20-story development on the corner from the lower-rent vendors behind it. They walk through a series of plazas under a red arch that says in Chinese 欢迎来到韩国城 "Welcome to Koreatown." Zigzagging past dress shops, hair salons, and a pet store, she turns into a deserted-looking area behind the buildings. Tucked away in the back, they find a restaurant with two jade lions flanking the glass doors the size of German shepherd dogs. Getting there early, they choose a corner booth. Along one long side of this room is a sushi prep kitchen behind a counter with several chefs. *If they are Chinese or Korean, it's impossible to tell*, she thinks, *but definitely not Japanese.*

Over maguro sushi—tuna—and California roll—faux crab and avocado—Mai and Ron share details of their day, sitting side by side on the cushioned bench, watching the chefs from across the room. "Do you want to talk business?" he asks her.

"Yes. When we're in the apartment, there's only one thing I want to do," giving him a meaningful look, taking his hand under the table and sliding it between her legs.

Sitting in a public place like this restaurant, hiding his groping hand under the tablecloth approaches a private erotic moment that pushes Ron to the edge of his comfort zone.

"Okay, I'll try," he says, retrieving his hand and pulling papers out of his jacket pocket. "Here's the new contract. See Rick's name and yours. The rest of it is the same. Back here is where you sign. When he arrives, we want his signature too, and photocopies of his passport."

The *fuwuyuan* brings a glass of plum wine for Mai and a beer for Ron. She sips the delicious, cool, sweet liquor, swirling the goblet and watching the heavy, gold liquid make rivulets on the inside of the glass. It's hard lying to Ron. The stakes are getting higher. The US government is involved. *It's not fair to Ron, not to tell him.* But she's not ready to show all her cards.

"What about money?" she asks, always the American.

"We need another 20 thousand yuan to add his name, and another 20 thousand to reactivate the account. I have to hand in my hours to the bookkeeper before the end of the month. They'll send you a bill for the last job."

"Tell me again what that is in dollars," asks Mai.

Ron accesses a converter app in his iPhone. "The total amount is 40 thousand yuan or … $6,436."

"Okay," she responds, signing the back page. "I'll tell Rick to send some money. Is there anything else?"

"I thought you handled yourself well this morning with GAO."

"Ha, thanks, *xiexie*. What did you think of those pictures?"

"I couldn't believe they were *you*. Where did they get that one with your black hair?"

"They must have pulled the JPEG out of my computer, one of the many times they got in there to look around. That's me and my supervisor Ms. HAN at Phoenix Hills. Do you know where that is?"

"No, never heard of it."

"It's out there where we went on your motorcycle." Mai reaches for Ron's hand across the table through the clutter of a dozen sushi dishes. "Our first date."

Ron's phone vibrates, "It's Commander GAO … *Wei, nihao* … Basketball on Saturday? I'll be there…. *Shenme shihou?"* Ron replaces the phone in his jacket after confirming the time. "GAO wants another game. On Saturday."

"Tell him I would like to attend the meeting."

"I understand your investment, but we need to think about the best strategy."

"I can't see myself waiting in the car. Would *you* be okay with that?" asks Mai, pouring the last drop of wine into her glass.

"I guess not. But top of my list is protecting *you.* However I can best do that will determine where each of us is situated," states Ron unequivocally. "This is what I do, Mai. Let me choose our tactical positions."

Mai looks at him over the rim of her glass as she sips. One last maneuver. "The room will be full of Commander GAO's men; I'm starting to trust them. But Rick doesn't know them from Adam."

By now, all the tables are filled with young students, mostly Asian, but a few Europeans and Americans arrive before they finish and leave. Out of the black sky, the wind whirls, blowing gold and brown leaves across the wide boulevard. In the cold night, the two lovers press closely together as they walk. He turns on the heater in the Park Avenue, leans over, and gives her a long kiss.

"This is crazy what we're doing, Mai," he whispers.

"Shhh, don't talk," is all she can say.

October 20

The Dage Report

The campus security team meets in the conference room in the afternoon on Thursday, October 20. Sgt. WANG has provided each man with a copy of the Incident Report.

"What have we learned?" GAO asks no one in particular.

Maj. TANG speaks first, "I didn't find much on North Korean activities in Beijing. Everything we heard turned out to be a rumor or we were blocked from getting more information. There is a fair amount of information out there on the internet about North Korean activities in general, which we reviewed before this meeting. Noteworthy is something about crystal meth—or *ice*—traffic coming from North Korea through Jilin and the Korean Autonomous Prefecture. They call it *bingdu* in Korean." He distributes his written report.

JGTS YANG Cai is the first to speak. "The Harbin Institute has been *active*, we are certain, but we don't have much in the report besides these seemingly unrelated topics. I'm still wondering about the cyber-attack rumors and what role Harbin has played. SunSystems, the American firm, pinpointed a location in Harbin."

Maj. TANG continues the report, "As background, it's noteworthy there's a large People's Liberation Army division in Harbin, one of the military area commands besides Beijing. There doesn't appear to be a main connection between the Harbin region and Russia for distribution of *bingdu* to the Western countries. The connection most likely goes from Changchun to Manzhouli via the railroad," he concludes, taking a swallow of water.

Commander GAO turns to his lieutenant.

"Our Rick Martin Profile is very weak," offers Lt. LIU. "We only have data from his visa application and a few things online..." He passes out copies of Rick's file.

Commander GAO says, "I met with Ronald ZHAO and Martin Taitai Tuesday. Under direct questioning, she denied knowledge of her husband's covert activities. They offered to have Martin Xiansheng meet here, voluntarily, to answer questions.

"While I was video conferencing with Harbin Chief DIANGTI, I made it clear: we will help them while protecting our employee, Martin Taitai. They'll be making their own plans, and I don't expect them to tell us what they are. I want you to work up a couple scenarios. Try to think of contingencies and worst-case outcomes," continues GAO.

Sgt. WANG glares at the men, leaning on the table with both arms. "The worst scenario would be an embarrassing incident that puts the university or our country in a bad light. The repercussions would be huge and personal: if a dramatic incident like an abduction or murder occurs on our campus involving the Martins, we will all be fired ... or worse."

"Sgt. WANG is right," says GAO. "Our Office is responsible for the safety of all persons on this campus. If we plan an interrogation and things go wrong, everyone will point fingers at us. We won't be fit to work security at a garbage heap!"

"High government officials come here ... officials of other countries come here ... it's not just a matter of a couple of Americans," reiterates Sgt. WANG, frowning. He stares at a bigger-than-life painting of the Beijing University President shaking hands with the People's Republic of China President, which hangs at one end of the enormous conference room.

The men are aware of the seriousness of the situation. "I don't trust that the Harbin guys won't try something more drastic than simply asking Martin Xiansheng questions," worries TANG.

"Like what, Maj. TANG?" asks GAO.

"Like taking Martin, before we get to him, and giving him to the North Koreans," TANG answers frankly, "for the bounty."

"I have the same concern," adds LIU.

"What about the North Koreans themselves? Should we expect them to be in the background?" asks GAO.

"Everything points to that possibility. They operate in the background throughout the country and act with impunity. Every time they commit a crime against our citizens, they get away with it," grumbles Cai.

"Okay, work out your scenarios, men, and strategies for an effective response ... as if your lives and the lives of the Martins depend on it! I want a Bureau Meeting Monday morning to review your plans."

Commander GAO leaves the men still sitting around the big table, discussing the new problem.

***

Back in his office, Commander GAO closes the door and looks for Police Capt. LI's number in his cell phone.

"*Wei, nihao*, Commander GAO," answers LI.

"Is this a good time to talk?" asks GAO.

"Good as any. What can I do for you?" asks LI.

"Remember that case we were investigating, about the American woman Martin?"

"*Dui*," says LI.

"We're reopening the case. I need to get you in for a briefing," says GAO.

"*Zhende, weishenme?*

"The woman's husband is coming to Beijing next week. She was never the target. Her husband is the one wanted by the Harbin Institute, Ninth Bureau, for questioning, something about his internet activities for the US," explains GAO.

"I see," says LI. "And this concerns the BPD how?"

"It's the North Koreans. They're the ones who want him."

"Whoa! *Zhende*! Here in Beijing?" LI is interested now.

"We have to cooperate; you know how that is. So I'm arranging a meeting at the university Main Building. We'll get Martin Xiansheng to come in and answer some questions," says GAO.

"*Haode* … I'm still waiting to hear how this involves the BPD," continues LI.

"There's probability the Harbin people will try to deliver him to the North Koreans who are working as mercenary agents for another country. Iran. If they can't do it here at the university, then they'll try it in the city," answers GAO.

"Ah, makes sense."

"Can you join me for a game of basketball Saturday morning?" asks GAO.

"*Shenme shihou?*" What time?

October 22

The poplars are turning gold. Mai tries to capture it *en plein air*. She takes her easel, tubes of paint, and brushes that she had shipped from California, to the end of her street. There she sets up to paint an avenue of trees at the Southwest Gate, while Ron meets Commander GAO at the basketball court.

After rain, last night's temperatures dipped into the thirties. It's freezing, sitting in the street and painting, but she doesn't feel anything. One part of her blocks in the darks and lights, the big shapes of the sky, the foliage and the street. Another part of her obsesses over Rick and Ron and the Commander ... and what is going to happen once Rick arrives ... putting Rick in the hot seat in the same room with GAO, drawing out the DPRK with Embassy people on the alert, forcing a confrontation and controlling the outcome through location and timing. Making the Koreans react is better than being the one reacting. *Strike first and all that.*

ZHAO pulls into a space near the courts and sees Commander GAO shooting baskets with another, younger man—tall and athletic looking. The buzz-cut hair and muscular build of the new man suggests he's probably in the security business, too.

"Hey, *nihao*," calls ZHAO as he trots onto the court and gets in place for a rotation.

"*Nihao*. This is Capt. LI of the Beijing Police Department, Sanlitun Division in Chaoyang. I've been filling him in on some details."

The men greet each other with a nod, and Capt. LI bounces the ball to him. The three shoot baskets in rotation for a few minutes, getting warmed up in the frigid morning air. The two younger men wait for the Commander to begin talking.

"So here's the situation. We're expecting the Harbin Institute to send some agents to participate in an interrogation of Martin Xiansheng. Although we believe North Koreans will be nearby, watching and waiting, we don't think they will try anything until after the interview. Too much is at stake to rush a situation when our meeting offers a measured and planned ambush opportunity. We're developing some scenarios on this, which we'll present at a briefing on Monday morning. I'd like the two of you to be there."

Commander GAO jumps for a shot, lands, and turns to look at the two men. ZHAO and Capt. LI gravely nod in agreement. LI grabs the ball and runs up to make a point.

"Your client Martin Taitai is a good observer, ZHAO," says LI, trotting back to the free throw line.

"*Weishenme*? Why do you say that?" he asks.

"She spotted me a couple of times. The BPD has been working with the university to surveil the Martin woman when she's off campus," says LI, taking the shot.

"You're easy to spot, LI—how tall *are* you?" Ron asks, passing the ball back to the Captain at the free-throw line.

"188 centimeters." Six, two.

Ron takes the rebound and makes a point.

"So, LI," says GAO, "Martin Xiansheng will come into the office for some questions. We are very committed to the safety of Martin Taitai. She's an employee of the university and an American citizen. Nothing has turned up in our investigation implicating her in spy activity. Everyone in my department is in agreement," confides GAO.

"Well, Martin Taitai will be happy to hear this," says Ron, making his second point. He bounces the ball over to Capt. LI.

"Martin Xiansheng is a different matter," adds GAO, pressing

Captain LI with the ball. The men play back and forth for a few minutes while Commander GAO decides how much to say.

"We need to meet with him, ask questions, and form our opinion as to his threat level. Right now we have very little information, except what has been supplied by the North Koreans." The Commander gets the ball and makes a basket.

"This sounds ominous, Commander. I should advise my client to cancel his travel plans," says Ron, standing near the basket, facing the Commander, waiting to block his shot, brows drawn down in a vee.

"If your client, Martin Xiansheng, is concerned for his safety, the best thing for him is to remain in the US," agrees GAO, making the shot easily. The two younger men jump toward the ball. Capt. LI grabs the rebound, trots around ZHAO, and shoots for a point. "So tell me again why he is coming? And don't give me that bullshit he's having a vacation to see his wife."

"Why don't you tell me?" Ron asks, letting Capt. LI and Commander GAO score against him.

"The North Koreans are determined to get Martin Xiansheng to come to Beijing, where they can get close to him. If they have to use Martin Taitai to get him to come, they will. They're working with the Harbin Institute, Ninth Bureau, on this. Honestly, I don't know why Harbin is involved, but they are, and I am committed to cooperating at this time. The meeting here will give us an opportunity to question him, but he'll also have an opportunity to question us. Valuable information can be obtained this way, which now is hidden." Commander GAO finishes dribbling the ball and makes his free shot ... misses.

ZHAO takes it and gets the rebound and trots to the free-throw line. The men continue shooting baskets for several more minutes, reflecting on the Commander's comments.

GAO continues, "Why would Martin Xiansheng walk into a trap like that unless he was prepared in some way, perhaps backed by his government for a covert reason we don't know? Perhaps he's engineered this to create a situation of his own, using his wife's position here. Do you think she's *innocent* of knowledge of her husband's work for Homeland Security, spying on Iran?"

"That's what Martin Taitai tells me, and I believe her. She wants to attend the meeting with Martin Xiansheng and we need assurances for their safety if you want them to come," says ZHAO.

"Come to the briefing on Monday. Help us develop the plans, and you can give your input for his protection … and for hers. Don't forget for a minute that the North Koreans are watching and looking for an opening if they are not satisfied with the interview. That's where you come in, Capt. LI." Commander GAO bounces the ball to LI who dribbles around ZHAO to make a layup, but also misses.

"They might avoid action on campus, but the city is another story. We need BPD to work with us on a contingency plan for after the interview, anticipating their actions," finishes GAO. He towels off as the men stand in a sweaty clump, concluding their game.

"Good meeting you, LI. See you Monday … *shenme shihou*?"

"Can you make it at 08:00?"

"No problem, *mei wenti*."

***

Cleaning the brushes and packing the gear takes several minutes. The wet canvas board Mai sets gingerly into the bike's basket and pedals back to the apartment. Ron's Park Avenue is already there.

Climbing the stairs behind him, she says, "It's almost lunch time. Want to go out for something or do you want tuna sandwiches, Western style?"

"I'd *love* tuna sandwiches Western style, as long as you're making them, Mai," Ron answers.

"Well, what happened?" she wants to know, unlocking the big iron gate and door. Ron rests his gym bag on the little washing machine in the bathroom and follows her into the living room.

Ron says, "There was another guy there—Capt. LI from the Beijing Police Department. He's been following you when you go off campus. Have you noticed a giant guy with a shaved haircut?"

"Yes, looks like he works out a lot?"

"That's him. He thinks you're a good observer, thinks you spotted him a couple times," says Ron.

"Yes, once in the *ditie* with my friends, another time on bicycle. He carries a flat bag over his shoulder."

"That's a listening device," explains Ron.

"Ah."

"Can I take a shower?" he asks. She nods and turns toward the little refrigerator in the corner of the sitting room.

Mai toasts buns in the electric wok while listening to Ron in the shower singing a Chinese pop tune with which she is unfamiliar. Open-faced sandwiches topped with a slice of tomato greet Ron, along with pickled cucumber and onion and a pot of fresh jasmine tea. Ron emerges later in a natural colored shirt with Chinese styling around the collar under a quilted vest and jeans. Her wet painting leans against the back of the table. It's a scene on campus with golden-yellow fall leaves on big trees lining a street with an iron railing cutting across the picture. Small figures on bicycles are indicated with a few dabs of color. It has a very strong smell of turpentine and linseed oil that he is not used to smelling. The sandwiches are delicious: crispy-crunchy and soft-squishy at the same time.

She joins him at the table. For a minute, she thinks about Rick and imagines him with Ron in the same room.

"Did I see a little cloud pass over your sunshine, Mai?"

"No, not really," she lies. "You were telling me about your basketball game ..."

"*Hao*," he says, pouring tea. "That picture of yours is really colorful. I like it, but what is that smell?"

"Don't you love it?" she answers. "I love the smell of oil paints!"

Ron grunts. "Commander GAO tells me they're committed to your protection. They don't think you're a spy. Your husband, they're not sure about. We speculated about Rick and why he wants to come. Is there something you haven't told me, Mai?"

The toasted bun, smeared with Kewpie mayonnaise, spicy, five-spice tuna, and a slice of red ripe tomato, salt and pepper, always reminded her of home, as she savors the crisp and soft textures and salty, spicy, rich flavors for a second. "Rick is going to be here on an assignment for Homeland Security. He *does* work for them. I told you before, remember?"

The night they waited in her dark office last August, she had told him about Rick's covert life. She called it a *hobby*.

"So why is he a client? Isn't he covered by your government? I don't think the contract covers espionage. I shouldn't be at that meeting

Mai. The contract will have to be nullified.

"You're going to abandon us? Just like that?!" Mai wanted control and a firewall but not this.

"Not abandon you, Mai; your old contract is still viable. But Rick will have to rely on your embassy for his protection. I'll drive you there and wait in the parking lot. Rick is on his own inside. If what you say is true—then there will be embassy people looking after him in Beijing. But you might want to keep your distance."

"The embassy is a good point I hadn't thought of. But I don't want to be shut out. I'm always getting shut out. I think we should get Rick in on this conversation. It's time you guys met." Mai was thinking fast to preserve equilibrium. She just had to make an adjustment, that's all.

"*Haode*, that's a good idea. Can you Skype him now?"

"No, he'll be asleep. We can Skype later tonight." She gets up from the table and plops into her favorite armchair, pulling the robe around her and staring at the floor. The heater in the office keeps the apartment warm, but they still have to wear jackets over their clothes for a few more weeks until the heat gets turned on.

"Are you okay?" he asks.

"Yeah, I guess, I'm just … Oh I don't know … I should just go home, and then all this will go away. No, that's not right." Mai shakes her head. "I used to think that I could run to Rick and he would save me, be strong for me, and stand between me and the bad world. That's not true any longer," she looks into Ron's concerned, handsome face. "He hasn't been there for me for a long time. He's in love with Homeland Security. That's all he thinks about. Not even my safety means anything to him except as an opportunity to further his work." She looks bitterly out the window toward the hazy Science Park in the near distance in Wudaokou.

Ron adds, "These people will pursue Rick, no matter where you or he goes. They were in your town once already." She nods her head.

"Here, I have help. I have you," she says, "I have the Commander *and* I have the Beijing Police Department." She waits for Ron to consider those facts before continuing.

"More tea," he says.

Mai switches on the electric tea kettle and fusses with the little glass tea pot in the kitchenette. She glances through the open door at him sitting in the big chair, wearing the house slippers she bought for him. Her Cantonese cop. Bringing the tea things in and pouring him a cup, she says, "You can go to the office or visit with your mom for a while. Come back later tonight and we'll Skype with Rick."

"*Shenme shihou?*"

"I usually Skype in the evening around eight-thirty or nine o'clock." He puts his things into the gym bag and gets ready to leave. "I'll bring takeout if you like, or we can go out. Text me. Bye-bye."

***

Later, Wudaokou lures them to the bustle of its commercial neighborhoods. Ron texts Mai: "im her" and waits downstairs for her to join him. They walk amid the crowds of students and workers, busses, cars and bicycles coming and going. Ducking in and out of food stalls and cramped eateries, they finally settle on Korean again, behind the big theatre.

Coming in later, they have to hunt for a parking place.

Something doesn't seem right to Ron. He can't put his finger on it. "Wait a minute, *deng yixia*, Mai," he says, putting a hand on her arm. At last, he notices a shabby van. "I can't see the license plate on that white Honda Odyssey parked opposite your apartment entrance. I want to drive up and let you out; go upstairs and wait for me."

The interior of the van is dark, but he sees the shapes of two men sitting in the front seat, too dark to see their features. Mai gets out, and he slowly motors toward the car gate where the streetlight casts a bright light on the back of the van. He rolls down the window and quickly takes a picture of the plate, turns the corner, and parks in the hutong alley. When he walks back around to the entrance, the van is gone.

In the apartment, Mai is already booted up and waiting for him. Ron powers on his camera and displays the image taken in the street.

"Look," says Ron, dialing his mobile.

"*Wei, nihao*, ZHAO," greets Commander GAO, "What can I do for you?"

"*Wanshang hao*, Commander," replies ZHAO, "I've got a plate I want you to run. A van parked in front of Martin Taitai's apartment looks out of place."

When he gives Commander GAO the sequence, GAO says, "That's not a Beijing number. Be expecting a call back from someone from my team tonight with the ID. *Zaijian*."

Mai's already talking with Rick on Skype. "Hey, good morning!"

"Morning ... or evening to you, Mai. How did your day go?"

"I went painting this morning: fall colors, street scene. My whole apartment smells like turpentine. Hey, Ronald ZHAO is here and wants to meet you on Skype." She turns the computer around in front of Ron.

"Greetings Martin Xiansheng," starts Ron. "I'm Ronald ZHAO, the security consultant your wife has retained."

"Hi there, Ron, glad to have you. What's this all about, anyway? Can you tell me?" asks Rick.

"I had an informal meeting today with Commander GAO from the campus security and Capt. LI from the Beijing Police Department. There'll be another meeting Monday morning that Mai and I will attend."

"What's this about … North Koreans, Mai tells me?" asks Rick.

"They're here. I think I spotted them in a van parked in front of her apartment tonight. We're running the plate," answers Ron.

"I see. Am I walking into an ambush? Or worse—is Mai in trouble there?"

"Those are good questions, Rick. The Beijing people don't believe Mai is a spy and are prepared to protect her. They are less supportive of you. They want to ask you some questions and determine whether you pose a threat to them."

"I could cancel my trip. Sounds like it's a bad idea, my coming there," says Rick.

"Don't come, Rick!" interrupts Mai, agreeing with his suggestion.

Ron responds, "You could, definitely. But it's been pointed out that this problem won't disappear just because you stay in California. They can use Mai as a lever to get you to come anytime. I think that's what was going on in August."

"Why did they stop?" asks Rick.

"Honestly, your wife is too hard to catch. She was very vigilant. I did my best to prepare her, and she managed to elude them a few times. At last, it became imprudent to continue. They needed secrecy, and too many people knew what was happening. The Beijing Commander called it off. The faction pressing for her pursuit lost favor. They didn't have any proof she was a threat." Ron pauses, letting Rick think before adding, "You were out of town—she had no way to contact you."

"Yeah, I'm sorry about that. Mai, are you there?"

"Yeah, Rick, I'm here."

"I'm sorry, honey, I got you into this mess."

Did he just apologize to me? Mai wonders startled. "So, don't come. Stay in the US ..."

"This guy, ZHAO, he's done a great job. Thanks," says Rick.

Mai and Ron sit side by side in front of the computer in the dim light of the office. She arranges the desk lamp to light their faces so Rick can see them better.

"So tell me why Mai shouldn't just come home and leave all this behind?" Rick thinks he sees something pass between them, but then, they've been through a lot. He shouldn't be reading too much into a video screen.

"Commander GAO pointed out that this is going to follow you wherever you go, Rick. Anywhere Mai goes, she can be tracked, and they'll try it again ... try getting you to come out where they can pick you up. Here, you have me. You have the Beijing University Office and the BPD ready to help. This is our turf; we have resources." Ron pauses. "The decision is yours."

"No, the decision is Mai's. What do you say, Mai? I got you into all this, and I never asked you. Now I'm asking, do you want to come home and take your chances here, or do you want me to come there and take them on in Beijing?" asks Rick.

Just then Ron's phone rings. As he gets up and walks into the hall, Mai replies to Rick.

"Well, I don't agree with ZHAO and the Commander. I think the North Koreans are just interested in you. There's another option: you can take the trail in another direction, away from here."

"I've talked to my guys, Mai, I've got contacts at the US Embassy. I don't know what you've already told ZHAO about me. Where is he, anyway?"

"He's out in the hall taking a phone call. Probably about the van's ID."

"So, keep this between us, Mai, don't tell him, okay?"

"What if things go haywire, Rick? What do you mean 'assignment?' I only just found out about your little side job with Homeland Security! I don't even know what you do for them for God's sake," she hisses into the monitor just as Ron returns.

Mai remembers when Rick first told her about his work for Homeland Security. In Sebastopol last summer, while she was visiting stateside over summer break, she and Rick were relaxing with their laptops open, enjoying the wireless connection in the house—not like her apartment with Ethernet cable strung everywhere. She opened her FTP file archive, pulled out the source file, made a few changes, and transferred that up. About twenty minutes later, she's ready to upload another file. Oddly, the connection was dead. She tried it again. And again. She shut down, rebooted, and tried again. *It's happening again! And I'm not even in China! Really strange.* That was when Commander GAO's team was attacking her server to gain access to Rick's emails.

With the internet connection down, they had to look at each other and talk.

She put her netbook away with a bad feeling and asked, "Hey, now we're in the same hemisphere, would you tell me about this North Korean story of yours?

"I should have told you sooner, but I was under a restriction on talking about it."

"What do you mean, *restriction?*" asked Mai. She stretched out on the tan, plush couch, a dull brocade floral pillow scrunched under her neck and another under her knees. At 9PM, the sky showed tarnished teal behind the western mountains, glimpsed through bay windows behind Rick, casting a pearly aura around the back of his blonde head. She reached up and turned on the lamp, his face taking on the appearance of a glowing Caravaggio angel.

"It means, Mai, I can't talk to you about these things. For a while, anyway. Most things are okay to talk about after six months. Some things I'll never be able to." He took a long draught from a bottle of Hopmonk ale.

"So tell me one thing."

"I can tell you about the virus the Iranians got dropped by crawler into their nuclear plant by the Israelis," he says over his shoulder from the kitchen, getting another bottle out of the refrigerator.

"And for how long has this been going on? Since 9/11?"

Rick's voice brings her back to the now.

"We'll have more to talk about after your meeting on Monday. Let's Skype your Monday night, my morning," concludes Rick, and the connection clicks off.

The internet radio comes back on. They're playing Adele, "*You make me feel like love again ...*" Ron stands in the hall looking at her. She turns to look back at him.

"Well, that went well, I guess," she ventures. "Who was that on the phone?"

"The van is registered to a Chinese firm that does a lot of business importing electronic devices from South Korea: Radiant Star Co, with headquarters in Seoul, Republic of Korea."

"I'll bet," says Mai.

October 30

The sky was gray with a slight stinging drizzle fighting Mai through Wudaokou to the Shangchang to get some American breakfast cereal and instant coffee for Rick. Later in the afternoon, the wind had blown all the rain elsewhere, when Robert drives Mai to Capital Airport to meet his flight.

"I wait for you. Take you back, Martin Taitai. You text me, I come here, same place."

"*Xiexie*, Robert," Mai says, climbing out of the taxi in front of the arrival gates. Checking inside that Rick's flight is on time, she waits outside Customs with a hundred people holding signs, meeting travelers or family. Trying to disguise herself, she covers her hair with a scarf and turns the collar up on her coat. Standing near a big column, she surveys the crowd. *They could be here ... watching,* she worries. Commander GAO assures her it's doubtful they will do anything before the interview Tuesday, but there are so many people coming and going....

Travelers start trickling through the exit. She turns her attention to watching for Rick. Two young men, dressed like security guards and standing near her, don't attract notice. When she waves to Rick, she doesn't see them following her.

"Hi sweetie," he says, grabbing her around the waist.

She stands on tiptoe to kiss him. "I have to call the cab driver."

Robert pulls over to the curb. Rick lifts the small carry-on bag into the trunk. "Robert, this is my husband, Rick. *Zhe shi wode laogong.*"

"Oh, wery good, wery good, wery tall husband, Martin Taitai."

Compared to the diminutive cabdriver, Rick looks gigantic. His powerful build and white-blond hair attracts stares, but he's too tired to notice. The young security guards standing at the curb notice him, though, as Robert navigates into the stream of cars, matching Rick to images on their mobiles.

Riding back to the city, Mai gives him a mobile phone. "This is yours while you're here." Rick looks heavier, but otherwise the same. "Have you gained weight?"

"Yeah, how do I look?" he asks.

"China blue eyes, blonde hair, strong arms—you look as good to me as always," she says.

"You look terrific! That hair! Wow, I'm still surprised looking at you. You look so Chinese!"

She laughs, and they chatter all the way back. It's dark when Robert pulls up in front of the LiNai Apartments. Rick travels light with a small carry-on bag he totes up the five flights of stairs.

"So this is where I live," Mai says as she struggles with the gate key in the dark. "Are you tired? Do you want to crash or what?"

Rick has to duck to get through the doorway. Mai flips the hall light on and locks the doors behind them. "Hey, this is nice, Mai ... but cold, don't you have heat here?"

"Put your bag in there," she gestures to the office while powering on *Pépe*. She hands him the bug sniffer. "Ron dropped this off. Do you know how to use it?"

Rick solemnly scans the rooms while Mai boots up, not finding anything.

"Do you want to check your email? It's warmer in here," she says, raising the thermostat with the remote. "They'll be turning the heat on soon, they say. Until then, we have to make do with this space heater."

She takes a liter bottle of Tsingtao beer from the compact refrigerator in the corner of the sitting room and pours some for herself into a glass decorated with fall leaves and carries the bottle to Rick. Scattered on the glass desktop is the debris of a transcontinental flight. Mai sets the bottle down next to a crumpled pack of cigarettes. He's busy scanning his email.

"What's this?" she asks, flicking the package across the room with her finger.

Rick looks up at her, "Sorry, Mai, I had a couple cigarettes."

"You promised you had quit," she starts, hurt.

"Sorry," he says and turns back to his online correspondence, so she leaves him again.

She looks through her closet and picks out what she wants to wear in the morning. The clothes hanging on the sun porch are dry; she unpins them and puts them away. Wrapped in her fleece robe, sitting in her favorite chair with the view of the night cityscape, she texts Ron: "we're home," then calls to her husband, "Rick, are you done? Come out here and talk."

His hulking form fills the doorway as he ducks again and drops into the other armchair. "Take off your shoes; people wear house slippers on these cold stone tile floors." She slides a pair of large, men's house slippers across to him. "These are the biggest I could find. Do they fit?"

"Almost," he says grinning at Mai and looking down at his heels hanging off the end of the soles.

"If you're not too tired, I want to talk."

"Okay."

"Well, what's the plan with you and Homeland Security? Do you already have a meeting set?"

"I'm going to the embassy tomorrow. Seeing the Homeland Security Director at eleven o'clock. I'll know more then. How do I get there?"

"I want to go with you."

"No way, Mai."

"Why not? Aren't I involved? Don't I get to know what you and Homeland Security are doing?" Just then Mai's phone rings; it's Ron texting: "whn? tak?"

October 31

Facing the morning in her favorite chair, color steals through the still-black foliage of the hutong, turning pink to salmon to dark orange where the sun reveals its brilliant red golds. She makes a strong cup of tea and waits for Rick to wake.

Robert the cabdriver takes Rick and Mai to the American Embassy. The car entrance for passenger drop-off is patrolled by PLA soldiers. For at least a hundred meters, they protect the area with bollards.

"Here is US Embassy, Martin Xiansheng," says Robert. Two guards approach the cab and say something. "I no wait for you here. They make me go. You get cab to Beijing University, okay, Martin Taitai?"

"Sure, fine," says Rick. Mai peels off some eighty *kuai*—another word for yuan—all small bills, "Bye-bye." They exit the cab and cross the wide expanse, while guards wave Robert back onto the busy boulevard.

Inside at the information desk, Rick is told to wait for Homeland Security USCIS Beijing Field Office (BFO) Director Lawrence Wright. He doesn't wait long. Within minutes, the director comes himself.

Extending his hand to Rick, "Lawrence Wright. Been looking forward to meeting you Mr. Martin. And this is ...?" He stares at Mai, taking in her fierce glance.

Wright is shorter than Rick, built tough and looks fit in his suit and tie; blinking at Rick past bushy eyebrows, his most notable feature is a completely bald head. He finished his undergraduate work at Brown University and received his law degree from UCLA in the early 1980s. He was transferred to this field office from the Bangkok headquarters two years previously, before the new Chinese American Ambassador arrived.

They shake hands, "This is my wife, Mai, and she's determined to be part of the team here. You don't mind she sits in on the briefing?" asks Rick.

"It's extremely awkward, Mr. Martin. There are many things that are outside your wife's clearance. I'm so sorry you came down here for naught," Wright replies. He regards her through squinted eyes.

"How about at the end of your meeting?" suggests Mai, keeping cool while smoldering. "Give me a five-minute summary? Can you do that?" flashing a big smile. *He looks familiar!*

Leaving Mai in the lobby, Rick follows Wright into the maze of hallways and cubicles, back to the corner offices of Homeland Security. They rent space in the embassy and are co-located in the building with the Executive Office of the Ambassador and various other offices housed there. "Want coffee or anything?" asks Wright as they pass the cafeteria.

"Yeah, sure, coffee," answers Rick, surprised to see a Starbucks concession.

"I've got some things to show you in my office. We've been tracking the two North Korean agents that were in Sebastopol last November. We think they're in China now—last known location was Harbin."

Wright pays for the coffees, and they continue to his office.

"Where's Harbin?"

"Northeast of here, near the Koreas. You been studying that packet we sent you?"

"Yeah."

The office is chilly like Mai's apartment. An electric heater struggles to keep the temperature up.

"What's with the heat here? Mai says they're going to 'turn the heat on soon.'"

"Free radiant heat all over Beijing, but they turn it on mid-November and turn it off mid-March. All winter you see these smokestacks belching noxious clouds all over town. So here's the packet for your stay." Wright slides a report cover across the desk. Inside are the same images taken in Sebastopol of him and Mai that Commander Gao has.

"These two guys are going to be your backup while you're here," continues Wright, pulling two more pictures out. "This guy here, Ed Poole, is a veteran from the Bangkok office, like me. I've worked with him many times. This other guy, Frank Choy, is from our Honolulu Field Office. They're both fluent in Mandarin. This is your first time out of the country?"

"Yeah, that's right. First time. I've been sitting on my can digging into the Iranian's systems from there."

"I read your profile. That was a real stunt you played on them. I guess you geeks have some value. What makes you think you can handle yourself in the field?"

"I've had some training. What's the plan?"

"We're filling some gaps in our intelligence on how the Korean spy agency works. It's a gift, your attraction of these Korean agents." Wright pulls two more images out of the pile. "They are KIM Yong-Kyung and KIM Sang-Bo. In Asia the last name is first and the first name is last."

Rick bends his head to look carefully at the pictures. He doesn't recognize them. "Are you sure these are the guys?"

"Yeah, pretty sure. So, we're expecting to see these agents in the background when you are going for the interview tomorrow. Keep your eyes peeled."

"What about Ed Poole and Frank Choy?"

"They'll be around, but you're not likely to see them. Now. Explain to me about TSC security and your wife."

"Well, she retained these guys for protection last August when I was gone and she was being cyber-attacked and stalked. I didn't believe her at first. It seemed fantastical to me that they would try something in China. I thought she was safe from all this."

"You guessed wrong, Martin. So, she just opened the phone book and picked out their name?"

"I don't know. I'll find out."

Wright pauses to make a note in his palm gadget. "I'm having our office send you by encrypted email our file on TSC. They're heavyweights, Martin. Your wife got the best. Their new guy, ZHAO, is from Hong Kong. We could use some more info here."

"I'll find out what I can."

"Do you have a phone yet?"

"Mai gave me this one," Rick says showing it to Wright. "I haven't used it yet. It's all in Chinese."

"You'll get used to it. They work the same way. Here, I'll copy Ed Poole and Frank Choy's numbers into your address book for you. What's your number, do you know?"

"I wrote it on tape and put it on the back," Rick turns the little gadget over and shows Wright.

"Good idea."

"You're going to be wearing a wire. A new design we want to test."

"Fine."

"Remove your jacket and shirt," says Wright.

"What?" objects Rick.

"I need to hide the device in your shirt. Off."

Wright searches Rick's shirt for a suitable inside seam, cutting a slice, inserting something the size of a sunflower seed and closing the cut with fabric glue.

"Your wife going to be a problem?" asks Wright, holding the shirt and then the jacket for Rick to dress.

"What do you mean?"

"Is she going to blow the operation?"

"Blow it? She set it up. Drop it. Mai's okay," insists Rick.

The meeting goes on; they finish their planning. Wright buzzes to send Mrs. Martin back. Mai checks her mobile at the reception desk. A staffer accompanies her to Wright's department. The receptionist, a slender Chinese woman, stares at Mai from behind feathery bangs until Wright waves her into his office and motions for her to sit at a conference table next to Rick.

"Do you drink tea, Mrs. Martin?"

"Yes, I love tea."

"Shall I make some for you?" asks Wright.

Instead of sitting, Mai turns to look at the bric-a-brac decorations in Wright's office. She finds an elaborate tea set, well-loved and used, and a cupboard of choice teas. The glass teapot is just like hers. The electric teapot is full of water. Wright switches it on and examines the tea selection. "Which one would you like, Mrs. Martin?"

"Let me see," she says. Standing next to him, Mai asks, "Haven't we met, Mr. Wright?"

Wright sprinkles some Kuan Yin Cha into the strainer and pours in the hot water. "I'm sure I would remember meeting a charming woman such as you," he oozes. Mai's not convinced. While the tea steeps and the men are still sorting through things on the table, she continues to look around Wright's office. On the corner of his desk is a small volume of Chinese poetry by ZHENG Min.

"Mr. Wright, you're a poetry lover. Look." Mai reaches into her Bernini bag and pulls out the same slim volume, *Selected Poems of Zheng Min.* She closes the few feet between them to stand next to him at the table. Wright and Rick pause to see what Mai is going to do next.

"We have met! At the university, Mr. Wright, at a poetry reading a couple weeks ago. It was organized by Brown University alum. I remember meeting *you* that night. You *do* remember talking to me, don't you?"

He remembers all right. He had manipulated to get her invited to his Brown alum soiree at Beijing University where he could observe her. An important mission like this one required the painstaking care of preparation for which he is proud. He sat at the coffee bar with his iPhone and watched her ping approach from the GPS on her phone, although it was completely unnecessary. It was obvious when she walked into the coffee shop. She looked just like the surveillance photos. And she was easy to look at. And easy to talk to. They chatted about poetry and China and home and such for a few minutes. They exchanged cards. He forgets which fake identity he gave her. Now Rick and Mai know he was spying on her, too.

Mai continues, "Why do you think I'm here today? I have to trust you. You have to trust me. And that means ZHAO, too. We're all in on this. *Lives* are at stake."

Rick says, "She's right. Lives *are* at stake. My life."

November 1

Interrogation

The North Korean gang arrives at Beijing University before Rick's arrival, just watching. They prefer victims that make it as easy as possible. They are women, frequently, and Asian—small and manageable. Usually they have surprise, training, and numbers on their side. In fact, women and children are a specialty for which they have a variety of ruses and props. They can snatch them right out from under the noses of their families without a hitch. Rick Martin, on the other hand, is a large man. The couple of days before the scheduled interview, they shadow him around campus and off. During the day—during the workweek—Rick ventures into the general neighborhood by himself, but is careful. And he is *big.*

***

Reports of an incoming storm system, with colder than usual temperatures, are predicting snow in Beijing. Commander GAO wants the interview in the morning on November 1, but the Harbin Chief claims he can't arrive until later in the day. Reluctantly, the Commander schedules the meeting for 14:00, sending Maj. TANG to the heliport to get the Harbin team.

Ron ZHAO drives Mai and Rick to the Main Building and parks in the VIP lot, facing the back door where he can watch. Ron has a camera with telephoto lens mounted on his dashboard and trained on the door. He gets out and walks around the parking lot, jotting down license numbers of parked cars and making notes.

Not far away, the Beijing Field Office squad, Wright, Poole, Choy and two Marines, sit in an Embassy vehicle, watching the ping data from a nano-transmitter glued into the seam of his shirt. Earlier today, they ran a series of tests with Rick while Mai was at work, establishing his ping broadcast and adjusting the software controls.

The young guard at the entrance has Rick and Mai on his list and passes them through, calling upstairs to Commander GAO's office. Sgt. WANG meets them in the hall and escorts them into a side room to wait.

"Want tea or coffee?" he asks, estimating that Rick must be twice his weight. *The man is impressive,* he thinks. Rick says *no,* and Sgt. WANG leaves them alone.

In the room, there's nothing much to see, no photographs, nothing on the whitewashed walls, just an empty desk and two chairs.

Looking out the window, he sees ZHAO's Park Avenue below. A few minutes later, he hears a slight knock at the door and the Commander steps in, closing it behind him.

"My name is Commander GAO Bu," putting his hand forward in a friendly gesture. Rick takes it in his big paw, "Rick Martin," is all he says.

Turning to Mai, "*Xiawu hao*, Martin Taitai. The interview will begin in a few minutes. The Harbin District Chief and Institute Director DIANGTI has arrived at the heliport, and I have sent someone to bring him." The Commander sizes Rick up quickly, decides he will not be an easy catch. He must be as big as Capt. LI. Looking up at Rick's steel blue eyes, he says, "I regret the Harbin people are late arriving. Would you like tea or coffee?"

"No, thanks."

"*Haode*, Sgt. WANG will be back to bring you to the conference room when we are ready," says GAO, turning and leaving Rick and Mai in the room.

Again Rick looks out the window at the Park Avenue. He's still looking down when a dark blue Toyota Camry pulls up near the rear entrance and several men get out. He counts four including the driver.

Sgt. WANG knocks on the door. They're ready and follow him down the gloomy hallway to the conference room.

Four men are lined up on one side of the table. Sgt. WANG escorts Rick and Mai to empty chairs next to the interpreter on the other side. Commander GAO sits in the middle and makes introductions through the official translator, a young cadre dressed in uniform.

Rick grimly nods to the men. Next to the Commander, on his right, is Sgt. WANG. To his left is Harbin Director DIANGTI, and next to him is Gen. MA. Two of the men from the blue Camry—Maj. TANG, the driver, and Lt. GUAN, another of the late arrivals—stand at the door, arms crossed over their chests. Chinese cups with blue-and-white porcelain lids are set in front of each place with a small pad of paper and pencil. Curious, Rick lifts the lid and smells a flowery tea fragrance, and then he closes the lid.

Rick looks relaxed while systematically observing each man. The two muscular guys at the door are dressed in civilian clothes: brown pants and windbreakers. Commander GAO's bland Han face reveals nothing; hair graying at the sides, he doesn't dye it; a black sweater under a brown tweed jacket with a tiny gold pin. The Harbin Chief, who made everyone wait, is the only guy in the room wearing a tie. His face is set in a slight, sardonic sneer; his very black hair is obviously dyed. Next to him is Gen. MA, a gentle-looking, older man, short with a pleasant expression. Rick decides to scowl at them all, play tough. Mai sits quietly and observes.

"Well, we're all here?" asks Rick finally.

"Yes, we are, Martin Xiansheng," says DIANGTI, taking control of the meeting. "First, let me thank you for your voluntary participation today at this interview. We have a few questions regarding your internet activities and plans for your visit in Beijing. Can you tell us … how long you have been working for the United States Homeland Security or CIA or for whichever bureau you work?"

"I don't work for anyone, Director."

And so the interview begins. Rick gives up nothing. They ply him with question after question, but he denies most of it. He claims the Wikileaks report is inaccurate—it's someone else.

"Can you answer a question of mine, Director DIANGTI?" asks

Rick. "What's your concern with these rumors?"

"Through a routine background check on your wife, Martin Taitai, we discovered a link to you and your activities. We want to corroborate these reports with your response first hand," answers DIANGTI.

"How is it ... pictures of me and Mrs. Martin are in your data base?" queries Rick.

"We collect information from all sources, Martin Xiansheng, similar to your country, am I right?"

The questions go back and forth, and in the end, both sides have nothing.

After Rick leaves the conference room with Mai, Commander GAO, Chief DIANGTI, and Gen. MA convene a wrap up.

"That was a waste of time," sneers DIANGTI.

"You have nothing on him; there's no proof. He's right."

"What? Are you taking the side of the American?"

"Why are you pursuing this man and his wife so vigorously? I don't see the connection. Show me how this is a threat to PRC."

While the two argue, Gen. MA turns his back to make a call.

***

Ron turns the ignition on and sets the heater to high. Since they arrived at 2PM, twenty-three cars have come and gone in the lot, including Maj. TANG's, delivering the men from the heliport in his blue university Camry.

Ron looks at his watch: 4:15.

Deodar cedars near the back entrance are enormous specimens, creating a premature dusk in the waning afternoon light. Two skinny security guards walk around from the front of the building and stand in the parking lot near the back door smoking.

Ron's phone rings; it's Mai, "We're done, coming down."

A black Buick, same make and model as Ron's Park Avenue, backs out of a space as they exit the glass door. Ron is pulling around the lot to pick them up when the two guards suddenly grab Rick from behind, one on each arm. The trunk pops open. The two men press on the back of Rick's neck, pushing him toward the open trunk. Fast as a pro boxer, Rick slams them into each other, and they fall back limp on his arms for a second. Mai grabs at the man closest to her.

Out of the side door springs a man dressed in a business suit and overcoat. With a Taser in his right hand, he presses Rick in the abdomen, and the big man slumps.

The Koreans snap out of his grip and push him into the trunk. Mai jumps toward the Chinese suit, who swings a wide left punch under her chin, lifting her lightly off the ground. One of her legs kicks up, and her shoe flies off, landing in the trunk with Rick. She falls backward onto the hood of Ron's Park Avenue. He stomps on the brakes. She rolls off onto the street. The trunk slams shut.

The man in the suit, along with who Wright called the KIM brothers, Sang-Bo and Yong-Kyung, leap back into the Buick. They're out of the parking lot before Mai even knows what happened, slipping silently, not even squealing a tire on the cold, damp road. They make a wide left onto the artery up from the traffic light intersection. Dozens of students on bicycles turn to avoid the car, crashing into each other on the slick pavement.

Looking west, following the sight of the look-alike Park Avenue turning left, and back at his lover and client, dripping blood in the street, Ron exclaims, "Mai!—" He opens the door next to her as she struggles to raise herself up to her knees.

"Help me up."

"You're bleeding!"

Fat, hot drops of red blood drop onto the street between her hands, "Help me up, hurry. We have to catch them," pulling herself to standing on one shod foot with Ron's help. She hops around to the passenger side, hanging onto his arm.

"You're missing a shoe."

All she can say is, "*Zouba!*"

He gets back in on his side and, forgetting he's no longer the police, shoves the gear shift into drive and peals out after the other Buick. Fishtailing left onto the avenue of bicycles, he lays on his horn and flashes his emergency blinker: the civilian's lights and sirens.

"Is that them, turning left at the light?" shouts Mai. She has a fierce headache from the punch to her jaw and the lump on her head. And she's starting to shiver. For a moment, her mind fugues, drawing her eyes to the sky. "There's a snowstorm coming," she murmurs, "sometime tonight."

"Mai!" Ron knows the dangers of shock and commands her back to the present. "Call GAO," he says, tossing a little notebook at her. "Look here." He jabs his finger at a notation. "This is the license number of the other Buick."

Looking through her purse, Mai finds Commander GAO's card and punches his number into her phone.

***

Commander GAO's phone rings.

"*Nihao*, Commander."

"Martin Taitai."

"They've taken Rick."

"*Wei*?" He grabs a pencil and writes down the license number and abruptly leaves the room, as Martin Taitai tells him what has occurred right under his nose.

He returns a few minutes later and announces, "Two men dressed as university security guards abducted Martin Xiansheng at the rear entrance just now. ZHAO is pursuing their vehicle. We'll have surveillance tapes to look at in a few minutes." Commander GAO's face is red, he looks like he is about to explode. "I want to know who those guards are. Tell me what you know, DIANGTI!"

"It's not us if that's what you mean, Commander."

"Where's that other man of yours—Lt. GUAN?"

They all turn to look at the door where he was standing. Neither he nor Maj. TANG is there. Instead, Sgt. WANG appears in the doorway, "The tape is ready. Follow me gentlemen."

"Where's Maj. TANG?" GAO asks WANG as they hurry downstairs to the security department on the second floor. "And our guard at the door?"

"I don't know, I'll find TANG. The guard is waiting for you."

The security technician runs the tape. They see Rick and Mai walk out the door and the Buick backing toward them. Two young men dressed as university guards approach him from either side. The security camera inside the entry catches all the action.

"Do we have an ID on the vehicle yet?" GAO wants to know.

JGTS YANG Cai responds, "Same Korean company: Radiant Star."

Commander GAO turns to Chief DIANGTI, "I said, where's your man Lt. GUAN?"

"I called his mobile, but he's not answering."

"Give me your mobile ... and yours," he says to Chief DIANGTI and Gen. MA. It was easy to grab DIANGTI's since he had it in his hand and was waving it around. It was a surprise move for Gen. MA, a small man, no match for the Commander who frisked him and took possession of his mobile.

"Escort these two men to the conference room and secure the door. No one goes in or out. No phone calls. Wait for me." GAO says to his sergeant-at-arms.

"I'll have your head, Director. Your career is over!" promises DIANGTI.

Commander GAO walks away without acknowledging his peer from Harbin. He hands the phones to Cai, "Strip these, get everything you can find. Especially locate Lt. GUAN."

WANG calls to the Commander, "Hey, here's Maj. TANG and Lt. GUAN on the video feed!" They spot the two men and the guard exiting the building after Rick. They run out of range of the camera followed by Maj. TANG's blue Camry driving past it out of the lot. "He's not answering his mobile."

"At least we know where they are. Start the mobilization implementation. Call up the regiments on standby. *Zouba!*"

Commander GAO is ready with a plan. Sgt. WANG calls out a mass mobilization to Lt. LIU in the university Dongfeng to monitor the route: to the bicycle avenue, down to the traffic light, and east. All gates are closed until additional guards arrive to search cars.

Back in his office, the Commander calls Capt. LI, *"Wei, nihao.* Are you ready? Rick Martin was abducted on the way out of our building just now by two men posing as Beijing University security guards. ZHAO is following their black Buick Park Avenue in his, same make, different plates—we're faxing you the picture and the plate number. My guy TANG and another agent from Harbin are following them. We ran the plate, and it belongs to a Korean import company in Seoul. Same one as before. There's more, but it can wait. Implement your plan. We need you to find that car and get those guys. I'm putting Sgt. WANG on this. You can coordinate with him."

"Haode, your fax is just coming in. Got it. *Zaijian,* Commander."

Commander GAO steps into the corridor and calls to WANG, "Take me to the guard." The detained guard is nervously smoking a cigarette in the same small room where Rick and Mai had waited earlier. He stands when Commander GAO and Sgt. WANG enter and rubs out his cigarette on the floor. The Commander regards the young man, asking WANG, "Well, what have we found?" He sniffs the air. "Open that window; it stinks in here," barks GAO, sitting.

"This is university guard Private First Class KUANG," says WANG. "He has worked here for almost two years."

Commander GAO stops him with a hand sign, "WANG, go find profiles on Chief DIANGTI and Gen. MA." Sgt. WANG leaves.

"Tell me what happened today, Private. Start at the beginning of your shift."

The young man stands in front of the Commander. "My shift is from 08:00 to 17:00, with one hour off for lunch. Today, when I came back from lunch, the relief guard was not in his post. That was about 13:30. Here is the log book; you can see when the *Meiguorens* [Americans] arrived about 14:05 and out again at 16:20."

Commander GAO glances at the entries.

"Maj. TANG arrived here with the Harbin people at 14:25," continues the guard, pointing at an entry. He says, "I noticed the two other guards in the parking lot about 16:15. As soon as the *Meiguorens* stepped out of the building, the two men grabbed the man from either side, and another man joins them from the getaway car. The fight lasts only a few seconds before Maj. TANG and another man come rushing out the door."

Sgt. WANG steps into the open doorway. "Those guys are making a big fuss, kicking the door. Can you hear them?"

The Commander's face is grim. He starts reading the profiles on DIANGTI and MA. "I called Capt. LI, told him you're in charge of the pursuit."

He looks up a minute at his assistant. Their eyes meet. WANG would go to the bottom of the sea if the Commander asked him. WANG admires the Commander's swift, competent manner in a crisis. Commander GAO counts on Sgt. WANG. They've been through much and work well together under stress.

"We're going to catch these guys, WANG, and find out what's going on." He resumes reading. "Call Cai and tell him to bring me whatever he has on the mobiles to the conference room. Okay, *zouba*, let's go."

When Commander GAO enters the conference room, Chief DIANGTI is standing near the door. His face is red. He has his arms crossed over his chest and holds a cigarette. Gen. MA is seated and calmly gazes out the long windows to the south.

"This room stinks," says GAO.

"You're way out of your authority, holding us here like this!" screams DIANGTI.

"Ah, yes, authority. Well, here I am, and here you are, in my conference room, in my building, on my campus. Here, I am lord." Commander GAO sits in his usual place.

"A guest to my campus, who voluntarily came to answer your questions, has been violently assaulted. So who knew he was here and when he was walking out that door? My men and yours."

"The North Koreans have been tracking him all week, ever since he arrived."

"And how do you know that, DIANGTI? You talking to them?" asks GAO.

"That's right, I told them. That's part of our agreement. If you don't like it, take it up with the Ministry of Foreign Affairs," says DIANGTI.

"Yes, I will, just as soon as we catch them and determine their identities." The Commander reaches over and grabs the cigarette out of the Chief's mouth and stubs it out on the floor. He turns to the seated man. "Gen. MA, may I call you that?" asks GAO.

Gen. MA turns for the first time and regards Commander GAO, "Dui, haode."

"*Hao*, may I ask you some questions, General?"

"Certainly," the older man says softly.

"I see from your profile that you have retired from the military and are currently in the reserve corps. Is that is right?"

"Yes, that's true," he answers.

"And you are Deputy Army Commander of the Harbin Reserve Force Unit. Is that right?" asks GAO.

"Yes."

"May I ask the relationship you have with the Harbin Institute—especially in regard to this investigation?" asks GAO.

"My association is merely as a North Korean specialist for the Director. My career has given me unique background with which I strive to serve my country in any small way," Gen. MA answers with a submissive nod.

Gen. MA's official profile doesn't include many pertinent details. What Commander GAO sees is his date of birth—1951—making him sixty-years old. He graduated from Pyongyang University in chemical engineering in 1976, the same year MAO died. In 1968, when he was only seventeen, Gen. MA joined an elite company cross-training with North Koreans. As such, he was involved in the US Pueblo incident, which was where he acquired his taste for beating and torture. After a decent career in the PLA, he retired two years ago at fifty-eight, when he joined the reserves.

The door opens, and JGTS YANG Cai pokes in his head.

"Excuse me, please," says GAO. He gets up and steps into the corridor with Cai. "Did you find anything useful?"

"Yes sir, we'll be running the ping data through our filters all night. Here are a couple things: a list of the phone calls made from each phone since noon today. We cross-checked and put the caller or who they called in the next column. I've got guys running IDs on all of them. At 16:10, Gen. MA called this number here. We traced it first and activated its GPS—we think he might be one of Martin's attackers. I've got a guy working on a real-time GPS map. We have ZHAO's and Maj. TANG's cars also located with the GPS. But the lead car has jammed theirs. I've sent all this over to BPD."

"Good, this is what I needed. Get back to work." JGTS YANG Cai disappears down the stairs as Commander GAO turns to his sergeant-at-arms. "It's time to process the two men inside. They will be detained by BPD in their Haidian facility. Contact your counterpart there and start the procedure."

Turning to the two guards at the door, GAO says, "It's imperative that these two men don't leave the room. They're very dangerous to our society in spite of their outward appearance. I want you to expect them to trick you or try to escape. Be vigilant! Only one goes to the toilet at a time, with two guards. Always have two guards at this door. Understand?" He turns to the Sergeant, "Understand?"

**

The *Xiao Qiang* [Little Boss] in the getaway car sits in the front seat with the driver. He keeps his eye on his smartphone, waiting for a text from Lt. GUAN. Or Gen. MA. Or somebody! He's not used to working directly against Chinese Security Forces or abducting *Meiguoren*s for that matter. It's usually just private stuff, no one to stir up international attention. The stakes are high with this gambol, and he's loving it. *Where is Lt. GUAN?*

Back in August, Lt. GUAN had recruited SHENG Jianqiang from the Tianjin gang of criminals that Gen. MA was used to using while doing Chaoxian's (North Korea's) bidding. Tianjin, a coastal city near the Koreas, had long ago developed a network of relationships among

North Korean agents and the seacoast gang Triad, providing a portal and resources for illegal trade in UN-sanctioned commodities and WMD. People too. The success of this decades-old syndicate had resulted in straw corporations that provided legitimate cover. One, called Radiant Star, shipped vehicles, equipment, electronics components, computers and phones into Tianjin from the port in Mokpo, South Korea. Recently, a bullet-train line had been built connecting Tianjin with Beijing, with a train leaving every eighteen minutes. At 176 km per hour, it took them less than an hour to get back and forth, putting the Tianjin Triad in the driver's seat for international crime like never before.

Sitting in the other Park Avenue, SHENG glances at the driver, DONG Zhi Wei. He doesn't know the guy very well. A local Beijing gang driver who was also recruited by Lt. GUAN in August. The way he's maneuvering through these wet, near-icy conditions, rife with traffic and oblivious pedestrians ... well, it's impressive.

The driver looks back at SHENG. They both can see it: excitement. DONG grins and gives him a thumbs up.

"Keep your hands on the wheel and your eyes on the road, *Xiaodi* [Little Brother]," barks SHENG. And DONG does as he's told.

***

Ronald ZHOU has Rick's abductors still in sight and turns left. He might just catch them. Suddenly, he's flagged over by a young cadre with a red flashlight.

"*Zhende*! Goddam it!" shout Ron and Mai in unison.

The guard is so intense; he must think he's hit the jackpot, the make and model of the getaway car on his mind ... but not the tag numbers. He listens while Ron tries to explain the mix-up with the look-alike cars.

Lt. LIU had started the day mobilizing Company BU-040 for a training drill leading up to the 14:00 meeting at the Main Building. In the event of gate closures, Lt. LIU practiced moving squads of guards around campus all morning, setting up support and communication networks and testing them.

News that an early snowstorm was approaching filtered through the platoons when they broke for lunch. Long, heavy, wool greatcoats and fur-lined hats were issued from the central laundry-and-sundries building. The company split in half—some went back to barracks to rest, and the rest returned to drill maneuvers on campus.

When Maj. TANG had returned from the heliport with the Harbin agents at 14:25, rumors were already starting among the junior officers about who was on that helicopter and that a mass mobilization was eminent. At 16:30, Lt. LIU received the mass mobilization call from Sgt. WANG, and the gates closed until all squads were in position. Vehicles were being searched and passengers required to show identification. Pedestrians were also asked for ID.

Cars were backing up along the main arteries on both sides of the gates. It was getting darker and colder. An extra platoon was deployed along the route of the getaway car. At the moment when ZHAO's Park Avenue was being flagged by Lt. LIU's guard, Sgt. WANG was just texting the license plate of the real getaway car.

Ron's attention is drawn behind him as Maj. TANG and Lt. GUAN pull up in the blue Camry. Maj. TANG gets out and walks to the rookie cadre at ZHAO's side window. "I am Maj. TANG of the university security office," he tells the cadre. "Let this man go."

"But, Maj. TANG, this is the getaway car!"

"Didn't you get the text with the license plate number? This is not the right car." He turns to ZHAO and sees Mai sitting there, also. "Do you see them?"

"No, we've lost them now. They're somewhere ahead," says Ron.

Maj. TANG checks the ping data on his mobile. "It appears they're heading toward the East Car Gate. Follow me." He carefully turns on the slick street and walks back to his car. He places a flasher on the roof of his Camry and slowly leads the way across campus. Mai's headache has gotten worse, and her jaw is stiff and sore. Blood has stopped running into her blouse and has dried in streaks on her face.

Ahead on the same road, the gang ducks right into a side street, and left, and right into underground parking at the School of Finance. A stolen permit flashes at the parking attendant who raises the bar. They drive to the farthest corner, next to a white Honda Odyssey, the same one Ron noticed outside Mai's apartment more than a week ago.

SHENG supervises KIM Yong-Kyung, who pops the trunk. He hits Rick with another zap of the Taser. They secure him with tape and zip ties in the few seconds it takes for Rick's nerve impulses to return. Yong searches his pockets, powering off Rick's phone before removing the SIM card and handing everything over to SHENG. Next, he finds Rick's wallet, removing money and cards before throwing it back into the trunk. Picking up Mai's apartment keys, he holds them out to SHENG and shuts the trunk. The gang's phones are all powered off, and the car's GPS is jammed.

A nano-device hidden in Rick's shirt seam continues to record and send minute GPS data to BFO Director Lawrence Wright's mobile command post on campus. One of his embassy men, Frank Choy, riding a powerful BMW C-Evolution electric scooter, coasts noiselessly to a stop near the School of Finance above the cave of parking lots.

At the end of the street, Maj. TANG pulls over near the guard shack at the car gate, ZHAO pulls up and parks next to TANG's Camry. They see cars backed up on Shangqing Roadin both directions as guards search every vehicle.

Maj. TANG calls the Commander with his opinion that the gang must be leaving the campus here, at the East Car Gate.

"That's a reasonable conclusion, TANG. Can you see any Beijing PD from where you are? Capt. LI should be swarming the university exits for the gang's Park Avenue."

"*Dui*, there are groups of flashing lights I can see. Cars are backed up to Hualian Shopping Center. I can't see how far the other way."

"What about on our side. How many cars?"

"We passed forty-four vehicles from the main intersection."

It's dark. All black sedans start looking the same. It's getting colder and the black streets are covered with freezing rime.

Inside the Park Avenue, Mai says, "I'm calling Wright."

"*Haode*, I'm going out there and see what I can find out," says Ron, zipping up his parka and leaving Mai alone in the warm car.

ZHAO's face appears at Maj. TANG's window who steps out of his warm Camry into the freezing night air. Lt. GUAN joins them. The three stand together, watching the line of cars slowly snaking out the gate. The flashing amber light on Maj. TANG's Camry illuminates their faces in high relief, exaggerating the dark shadows on their faces, like theatrical masks.

Sitting in the car, Mai punches Lawrence Wright's number and waits for him to answer. The pain from the throbbing in her jaw pushing her past small talk.

He says, "Yeah, who is this?"

"It's Mai Martin, Mr. Wright."

"Mrs. Martin, how are you? What a terrible thing."

"Save it, Wright. Where's Rick?"

"He's fine. We're watching him. Don't panic."

"You're insane. Where are you?"

"I'm here on campus."

"Get your ass over to the Commander's office. I want to talk with you now," snaps Mai. She hobbles out of the car to where the men are standing. Her head hurts, her shoulder is sore, and Wright is the face on the agency responsible for all of this: she's taking it out on him, beyond caring about proprieties.

"Mai, what are you doing out here? It's freezing," protests Ron.

"I just talked with Wright. I know he knows where Rick is." She whispers into his ear, "He said Rick was fine and not to worry." Ron frowns. He looks at her in the faint strobe light and takes a hand wipe out of his pocket, dabbing at the bloody streaks on her cheek. "Wright's on the campus. Take me to Commander GAO's headquarters now. I told him to meet me there."

While they talk, they don't notice Lt. GUAN edge away into the shadows.

Maj. TANG looks at his phone. It's about 16:45. And then it rings.

It's Commander GAO, "Where are you?"

"We're parked just inside the East Car Gate."

"Is ZHAO there?"

"*Dui*, and Martin Taitai."

"So, she can walk and is okay?" inquires GAO.

"Her face looks bad."

"Is Lt. GUAN with you?"

"*Haode*."

Commander GAO lowers his voice to prevent Lt. GUAN from overhearing. "He's in on it. I've got Chief DIANGTI and Gen. MA detained in the conference room, and we took their mobiles. The Haidian PD guys are coming to process the arrest. I can't tell you anymore right now. Stay close to him and don't let on you know. He's very dangerous. Lead him to Capt. LI and let the BPD do the arrest."

"*Haode*, ha-ha." Maj. TANG looks around in the dark for Lt. GUAN.

"I don't see him now."

"Wait for Capt. LI. He's coming to you. Then come back."

"*Dui*."

***

Lt. GUAN steps backwards out of the glare of oncoming headlights, turns and plunges into a stream of people pushing toward the gate. He peels off into darkness and trots toward the School of Finance on the other side of the road. As far as he can see, cars are stopped, waiting to leave campus. He avoids the car entrance, instead entering the lobby and taking the stairs down to the subterranean car park.

No longer paralyzed, Rick writhes helplessly, bound and taped, as Lt. GUAN helps the traffickers lift him out of the Park Avenue's trunk and into the Honda Odyssey in the dimly lit garage.

"Little Brother, you did well today," says Lt. GUAN to SHENG. "Dalaoban MA and DIANGTI are coming tonight. Be ready. I'll meet you later." He closes the door and bangs twice on the side of the vehicle, stepping away from it.

The gang leaves Lt. GUAN behind in the garage. The Odyssey creeps past the parking attendant and turns left, back toward the center of campus, passing the Beijing Field Office agent Frank Choy on his electric scooter and the long row of cars waiting to exit. Crossing the ancient, imperial canal that bisects campus, SHENG tosses Rick's phone into the night.

It starts snowing. Lt. GUAN returns the way he entered and stands outside the brightly lit lobby. At 17:00, students stream by on the broad promenade, heading for the Main Gate at the heart of Wudaokou. He steps into the stream and blends with the traffic. Everyone's head is down, sheltered from the stinging needles of snow. The squads of guards are overwhelmed for a few minutes, while Lt. GUAN floats past the barrier and out onto Chengfu Road.

The rooms the traffickers rented in the *siheyuan* extend east, just inside the wall separating the campus from the new apartments on Chengfu Road. The men struggle to drag Rick's body into and through a train of adjoining rooms to the last one.

This choice of a hideout, near the LiNai Apartments, was perfect for surveilling Rick and Mai. Now that they have the captive, they remove plywood covering another door in the last room, leading to a vacant storage shed on the corner of the hutong directly beneath Mai's apartment and adjacent to the car gate. They throw him on a mattress in the cold room and shut him in alone.

He lies there, not moving, breathing irregularly. A black bag covers his head. His powerful arms are tied behind with zip ties, as are his ankles. His mouth is taped shut.

Poison Pen

Gen. MA and Chief DIANGTI sit staring at each other in the locked room in Commander GAO's domain. DIANGTI says, "We have to get out of here."

"I was thinking the same thing," agrees MA.

"We need to make a distraction to get them to open the door," DIANGTI continues.

"Good idea." Gen. MA holds his wallet, looking inside it for something small. "Fortunately, the respectful Commander failed to deprive us of all our personal items."

As Chief DIANGTI watches, Gen. MA swiftly plunges a sharp object into his neck. "What?" is all he gets out before the toxin paralyzes his throat, spreads to his heart, and ends his miserable life. Gen. MA quickly pats his pockets, taking the Chief's wallet and watch.

Pounding on the door, MA shouts, "Chief DIANGTI is having a heart attack! Hurry, open the door!"

Sgt. WANG knocks on Commander GAO's open door, "Bad news boss." The Commander looks up. "Chief DIANGTI had a heart attack."

In the confusion, Gen. MA easily slips out of the room and down the stairs as the paramedics are coming up with a gurney. Lights on the ambulance are flashing, and a small group of people at the rear entrance makes good cover for him to merge into the dark campus.

***

Lawrence Wright sits fuming in his heated seat after Mai Martin's call. *"She's* not telling me what to do," he mutters to no one in particular. Ed Poole sits behind him in the black, embassy-owned, Ford Expedition EL, staring at the screen of a netbook balanced on his knees. He's watching Rick's ping data. Every few seconds—*beep*—it refreshes the GPS coordinates.

"It's moving again," whispers Poole from the dark behind Wright's head.

They're posted across the street from Commander GAO's building in the Language Department parking. They see the ambulance arrive.

Wright calls Frank Choy out in the field. "Hey, he's moving. Do you seem them?"

"What? No. I'm here at the last location. They haven't come out of the garage that I've seen."

"Call Poole for your new coordinates." Wright pockets his phone, turns around and says, "Keep an eye on this, Ed. I'm going over there," gesturing to the VIP parking. "I want to know what's going on in there with the ambulance. Put eyes and ears inside their operation. You two, come with me," he adds, speaking to the dark behind Poole's seat, where two husky, young Marines sit. The spacious Expedition EL can carry eight passengers. The Beijing Field Office squad numbers five: Wright, Poole, Choy and the two Marines.

Stepping out into the night, Wright buttons his overcoat and pulls a knit cap over his bald head. Two black figures join him. Catlike, they stay close to the poplars lining the street, looking up and down the bicycle avenue before crossing. A slight wind blows against Wright's back; fat snowflakes dance in front of him, against the bright lights Commander GAO has set up on stands outside the door, making it brighter than day.

Gen. MA walks right past them, hunched over against the stinging wind. Heading toward the hutong, he passes students in the cold. He turns the collar up on his jacket and plunges his hands into warm pockets. Head down, he keeps on walking, turning right into the residential section, away from a squad of PLA cadres spaced every fifty meters and the bright lights at the South Gate.

Gen. MA reviews his gang. Connections make them strong. What was this web made of? Last August, Lt. GUAN had scouted SHENG Jianqiang from the Tianjin Triad, where Gen. MA is an affiliate, to be his *xiao qiang* for this operation. SHENG traveled from Tianjin to Beijing to meet him, and as far as Gen. MA knew, together they recruited DONG Zhi Wei through the Beijing circle to be their driver. The KIM brothers had been in his sights since they were just boys. He'd heard that SHENG was like a father to them. No venerable General could be happier. He felt history smiling upon him.

Legendary Chinese monks had formed the first Triad organizations in 1000 BC to protect the peasants from corrupt officials. In the 1800s, they worked with foreign traders bringing opium into China and convened secret societies in opposition to the Manchu Qing dynasty. During the republic, Triads flourished, connected to Chiang Kai Shek and the Kuomintang. In New China, Mao broke the Triads, and they fled to Hong Kong, Taiwan, North America, and Europe. After a crackdown in Hong Kong in the 1970s, the Triads moved across the border into Guangdong and farther. Triad membership had always included all levels and layers of society, from the top to the bottom, following a Confucian code of ethics, respecting their elders.

Rounding the corner by the wall, Gen. MA sees the Odyssey parked under cover of some trees. Looking up at Mai Martin's dark apartment windows, he suddenly feels exposed. He knocks on the door to the shed. SHENG lets him in. Stamping the snow off his shoes, "We're lucky we got here before the storm." Looking around at the bare room, "This is what we get for 6 thousand yuan? Beijing is expensive. These are rich, city peasants."

"Are you hungry, *Dalaoban*?" asks SHENG, bowing in welcome to the legendary warrior.

"*Dui*, are you *xiao qiang*?"

"*Wo shi* SHENG Jianqiang. I am the Tianjin gang man." Gen. MA warmly shakes his hand. "*Zhe shi*, this is DONG Zhi Wei, he's our local driver and all-around helper from the Beijing gang." SHENG gives the local a look, DONG bows and then hurries to the already-set-up makeshift kitchen to prepare something for Gen. MA to eat.

Gen. MA looks over their heads. Lt. GUAN already had briefed him on their identities, but formalities are important. Behind them, he sees the two Korean boys lounging in the door leading to the next shed. "Ah, the KIM brothers. We meet again." The young agent-gangsters are surprised to hear their names and scramble to their feet to show courtesy. "Show me the *Meiguoren*," says MA, and they bow solemnly, turn, and lead him into the back.

The Koreans remove the plywood covering the hidden door. Light from the single bulb hanging in the middle of the last shed shows a bundled figure lying on the floor.

The sounds awaken Rick. He begins to kick and squirm.

Gen. MA steps into the dark room and kicks him in the groin, insulting him in velvety, British-accented English, "Your wife is a whore, you bastard American."

Rick jerks on the mattress, lifting his head toward the sound.

Gen. MA turns to KIM Sang-Bo, snatching the cigarette out of his mouth. Kneeling on the dirty floor, out of range of Rick's powerful legs, he presses the lit end on his prisoner's exposed chest.

Rick stiffens; a muffled noise escapes the tape wrapped around his mouth. Snot blows out of his nose in a loud breath and his head drops to the mattress. Standing, satisfied, MA says, "Drag him out. Dye his hair." The smell of Rick's burnt flesh and hair mingles with the hot pot DONG is steaming in the other room with garlic and meat.

All the while, the ping quietly refreshes the computer screen a laptop balanced on the knees of Ed Poole in the Expedition, and the chip keeps recording, hidden in the seam of Rick's shirt.

Turning to SHENG, Gen. MA orders, "I need your cell. Get us all new phones. We're moving in the morning."

SHENG says to DONG in the middle room, standing over a hotplate and stirring a bubbling pot, "We have to get hair dye and new phones. Here's some money."

SHENG counts out 600 yuan.

"I want the new 4G, *Qiang ge* [Boss]," says DONG.

"Fine, use your own money to upgrade, now go to the campus shopping center."

Gen. MA powers on SHENG's mobile and calls Lt. GUAN, "This is MA. Where are you?"

"I'm on Chengfu Road. Where are you?"

"I'm at the safehouse in the hutong. Come join us. Chief

DIANGTI's dead."

"What happened?"

"Heart attack."

A man roasts chestnuts in a wok on the sidewalk in the snow.

"I'm stuck out here. They're checking IDs on everyone going onto the campus. I'm going to check the gates going north and will come when I can."

Lt. GUAN pockets his phone after powering off and removing the battery. He gets a bag of delicious, hot nuts, eating as he trudges up the sidewalk, looking for a way to enter the campus. A mob of guards at the south and southwest gates keep him moving. The small pedestrian gate near the hutong is open, but the guards there are checking IDs. Turning the corner and walking north, the snow blows past him from the side. He flips the fur-lined hood of his jacket over his head, pushing his shoulder into the wind, and continues up the street to the next gate. Even the shortcut, through the gas station, is swarming with guards, where the road curves away from campus. Strip malls continue beyond. He'll have to make a long detour before getting to the North Gate. Ahead, pink lights on a massage parlor beckon. He enters and decides to stay the night.

Chief DIANGTI's sudden death is a game changer for him. Standing in front of the chestnut roaster, Lt. GUAN knew instantly what had happened, but his loyalty was not to Gen. MA. It *was* to Chief DIANGTI, who had always sheltered his career, and it was *he* who was supposed to be calling the shots in this operation. Lt. GUAN knows he's not interested in leaving the system behind and striking out with mercenaries and gangsters and double agents. Without Chief DIANGTI, there's no connection to Gen. MA. Where is *his* connection now? He needs to think.

***

At the rear entrance to the Main Building, Wright is confronted by a pair of Chinese-style, secret-service agents, all in black and fitted with earpieces, to whom he has to show his embassy ID. Campus security guards collect electronic devices. Wright passes through the recently erected metal detector, but his Marines set it off.

"I'm here from the US Embassy. I want to talk with your commander," Wright communicates in serviceable Mandarin.

Shortly, Commander GAO arrives with a suave apology, "*Duibuqi*, Wright Xiangzheng. What is the problem here?"

"What do you want us to do about the metal detector? Every time my Marines walk through, they set it off."

"Would you like to step into this side room? We can discuss this in private."

Once inside the plain, cold room, GAO offers, "Please remove any items in here and place them in this box with your phones."

The two men stare at each other without blinking.

"Your personal items will be safe while locked in this box," GAO points to the box.

Wright begins, "The netbook … may I?"

Commander GAO takes it from a Marine, "I will carry for you, haode?"

Wright nods to Commander GAO and to the Marines, who comply, depositing their permitted sidearms and several knives.

The Commander confronts Wright, "Why are you here?"

"We're concerned about the American's disappearance."

"Where is he? Do you know?"

"We believe he's still on campus."

Upstairs, Commander GAO ushers them unarmed into the conference room.

"It's an honor to receive your visit tonight, Wright Xiansheng. Please, sit here in my chair," the Commander turns the swivel around for Wright.

"Thanks." Wright gestures to the Marines to stand behind him near the long windows. At that moment the doors open. Two blushing *fuwuyuan*, dressed in red jackets and trousers, push carts ahead of them, loaded with steaming, aromatic dishes and a regiment-sized hot water carafe. "Why was there an ambulance downstairs?"

"We had detained two officials from Harbin we believe were involved in the abduction of Martin Xiansheng. One of them had a heart attack. In the confusion, the other man, Gen. MA, escaped."

Moments later, Maj. TANG, Mai, and Ron pass through the same metal detectors and go up to conference room. Mai is still on one shoe, and her foot is frozen. She has wiped her face, but strands of her hair are stuck with blood, and her blouse is ruined with blood from the cut on her chin from the smack she got. Her jaw throbs, her head aches, and she's angry. Ron drapes her coat over her shoulders and holds her by the elbow up the stairs. The second floor offices are lit and teeming with people. At the top of the stairs on the third floor, she pauses at the open door to the conference room. Maj. TANG brushes past her and hurries over to Commander GAO.

While the Marines focus on the pretty *fuwuyuan* in a savory and spicy halo, Wright leans back in the Commander's swivel executive chair. Mai spots him immediately, reaches him in a few short steps, pushes the chair backward onto the floor, and places her dirty, bare foot on his throat. "Where's my husband? I know you know where he is!"

Wright instinctively grabs Mai's leg and ankle, flipping her onto the floor. She twists and lands on her hands and knees at the feet of the Marines, who reach for the guns in their empty holsters. Instead, they pull her up between them. She strains in their grasp toward Wright, "Tell me where Rick is! Tell me, is he's okay?"

Ron brings his right fist toward his left palm in front of his chest. With a soft, whipping sound, he shifts weight onto one leg and flips the other into a Praying Mantis high kick and strikes the closest Marine hard on the jaw with his booted foot. Feeling him relax his grip on her arm, Mai drops to the burgundy carpet as the second Marine punches Ron. Maj. TANG swings back at the Marine while Mai crawls toward Wright, hissing, "Where's Rick!"

Commander GAO steps between them while reaching into his pocket. He removes the safety on a US M1911 .45 semi-automatic pistol and points it at the ceiling, firing once. Pieces of plaster fall onto the table. In the sudden silence, a shell casing bounces on the table, leaving a dent. A couple dozen guards rush in and stand, two by each person.

"Maj. TANG, secure the door with these two Marines," orders the Director.

"Martin Taitai, how are you?" he asks, with genuine sincerity. "We forgive your disruptive entrance, because of how distraught you are." Commander GAO holds his chair for Mai at the head of the table.

"*Xiexie*, Commander GAO."

Next, the Commander holds a chair for a young female guard, gesturing to her from across the room, where she's been standing with the translator. *"Zhe shi* Sgt. LONG Yandong," he says by way of introduction. "I would like her to be your constant companion until we find your husband, Martin Xiansheng."

LONG Yandong's black, wavy hair is pulled back in a simple ponytail with a pouf over her brow. Tall and angular, she looks more Chinese fashion model than military officer.

Commander GAO taps the top of the table with the barrel of his M1911. "Wright Xiansheng, please sit here," pointing to another comfortable chair at the opposite end of the table from Mai.

Sgt. WANG brings Mai and Wright cups of tea. The jasmine fragrance penetrates Mai's tough exterior, followed by a wave of cold *chi*, drenching her. She shudders, silently sobbing, staring into the bottom of the cup. Embarrassed silence floats on the tea perfume, mingling with the faint odor of mildew from the hole in the ceiling.

"ZHAO Xiansheng, kung fu Master," Commander GAO turns, suppressing a smile, "Please, sit here near Martin Taitai," gesturing with his pistol. Addressing the room, he continues, "What do we know?... Rick Martin was abducted from the parking lot downstairs after a meeting in this room, this afternoon, with myself, members of this team, people from Harbin, and both the Martins."

The double doors open, and Capt. LI from the Beijing PD strides in, shaking snow off his heavy, blue greatcoat with striped cuffs. Following behind, his assistant Lt. WU, wearing a plaid wool coat and running pants under her skirt, takes a seat next to Capt. LI at the table. The Captain nods toward the Commander, slides his glance over to take in Mai's disheveled appearance, then over to Ronald ZHAO, and nods at him. Lt. WU looks shyly at a badly bruised Mai, her own face framed in Italian glasses, women in a building full of men.

Sgt. WANG enters and whispers something to the Commander before passing around images from Ron's car camera and the building's security cameras.

Commander GAO pauses while the images are inspected, observing Wright. "Lt. Col. Chief DIANGTI died, possibly of a heart attack, while in custody in this room. Gen. MA escaped, and Lt. GUAN is a fugitive. Two university guards are missing."

"There is good news about the getaway car. It's been found in the underground parking of the School of Finance. Maj. TANG, please take the US Marines with you to supervise the collection of evidence. Agreeable, Wright Xiansheng?"

Wright nods in the affirmative.

People clump together in small groups—the guards, the fuwuyuans, clerks—standing and quietly conversing. Commander GAO and Sgt. WANG have their heads together. JGTS YANG Cai enters the room and joins them.

"Ron, my god, that kick," starts Mai, sipping tea. "What time is it?"

"It's … six-oh-five PM…. Didn't I tell you, I'm a graduate student of kung fu? Red belt. I'm a Crane-style specialist. Plus kicks." It's hard to look her in the face; those bits of dried blood still sticking to it in the creases of her eyes and in her hair. To his experienced eye, Mai is shook up but not seriously injured. Facial cuts bleed a lot, but hers have stopped. Ron examines her face, holding her chin delicately. "If you were kung fu students, you would be Panther, and Rick would be Tiger-style." He looks away toward Mai's new escort. "This young woman, Sgt. LONG, will take you to the *xishoujian*, the women's wash room, Mai." He speaks to her in Mandarin, explaining what is needed: some first aid. Sgt. LONG replies to him that there is a kit in the *xishoujian*. While Mai is gone, Ron turns to LI, "Captain, how have you been since we last played basketball?"

"It's been too long since I've had the pleasure," starts LI, "This is my assistant, Sgt. WU."

Standing this way, speaking with Capt. LI, Ron can examine Wright on the other side of the table who continuously stares at his netbook screen, briefly breaking to scan the room before returning to gazing.

Capt. LI draws a netbook out of his enormous overcoat, "Is there somewhere I can plug this in?"

Ron gestures toward Wright, "I think there's a plug over there."

"Who's the man?"

"He's from the US Embassy."

Crowding Wright in his corner, Ron helps Capt. LI set up his netbook.

"You missed the action," says Ron, keeping Wright in the corner of his view.

"What?"

"The Commander broke up a fight between Martin Taitai and Wright, and the Marines and TANG and me," says Ron, loud enough that Wright could hear them talking in Mandarin.

LI chokes. "Zhende! A fight?"

"Commander GAO pulled a semi-automatic out of his pocket and shot it at the ceiling." Ron glances at the Commander and the ceiling and then down onto the table where the plaster chips still lay.

"Who won?"

"Guess."

"Two Marines and the embassy guy against you and TANG ... and the American woman? I'd say a draw." He laughs without laughing in a peculiarly Chinese authority way.

"It's not settled," Ron says, standing.

Capt. LI sits next to Wright with a grin in his direction, and powers on his netbook. Sgt. WU joins them with plates of noodles and cups of hot water.

***

Mai follows Sgt. LONG to the ladies room. Spacious but sober in light gray polished stone ... and freezing. For the first time all night, she looks at her face in a proper mirror. *That wretched man, Wright! I know he knows where Rick is this very minute, and he sits there smug, not talking, while everyone around here is trying to find him. That's Homeland Security. They're users.*

First, she removes her suit jacket and then the pink blouse, washing it in the sink. LONG tries scrubbing some blood stains out of the jacket. "Thank you, Sgt...."

"Qing, wo shi Yandong" [please, call me Yandong], the young officer nods with a smile.

"Xiexie," replies Mai, quickly lost in thought again. *Where is he? Is he here on campus? Will he just walk in the door any minute? Laughing and smiling, making a joke. Hilarious!*

Next, Yandong helps Mai clean the dried blood out of her hair. They inspect the lump on her forehead. The cut on her chin has stopped bleeding. Just surface abrasions. Her jaw is stiff and sore, and her head throbs. Out of a hidden closet, Yandong produces a hair dryer. While the soldier fluffs Mai's hair, Mai lifts her foot into the sink of warm water to clean off the dirt and grime. *And Ron. Like a Chinese warrior, flying through the air and kicking the Marine in the head! Why Commander GAO didn't throw us in the brig, I don't understand. And that antique gun! Wow.*

Returning to the conference room, Mai hangs her wet blouse over the back of a chair in front of an electric heater. Even with her jacket buttoned up, the lapel damp from scrubbing, the cleavage between her breasts still shows the lace edge of her brassiere, which she tries covering with a scarf out of the pocket of her overcoat.

The young guards stare. The Marines fix their gaze elsewhere. Commander GAO drags his chair over for her. She sits and props her foot up in front of the heater.

"*Xiexie*, Commander," she murmurs. Ron brings another cup of tea. Sitting there, she glowers at Wright on the other side of the room, but says nothing.

Wright is not forthcoming as to Rick's location and returns her look of hatred. His men know exactly where Rick is and are confident they can sweep in at the last moment if necessary. He doesn't have to reassure her. Who is she? Some English teacher. No one. A muggle.

***

Robert the cabdriver comes home to the hutong after driving all day. A special permit allows him to enter the campus, and he parks in his usual place on the snowy street. After dinner at his favorite canteen, he runs into his landlady coming downstairs from the better restaurant upstairs in the same building. She invites him to escort her home,

"*Zhongguo nanren* [Chinese man] was murdered today by *Meiguoren*. They are searching for the murderer door to door."

"I heard the same story, Auntie, but a little different. The American was taken here on campus—by foreign spies who also murdered the Chinese man. They are hiding somewhere here at the university. Every car leaving campus is being searched. All the gates have double the guards and will be closed tonight at ten PM."

"What about people walking?"

"Bicycles and people can pass, but must show ID."

Three weeks ago, Auntie started buying coal for her hutong heat, piping it throughout the rabbit warren of sheds and rooms illegally subdivided and developed on her siheyuan parcel. She rented three bare rooms to some men from out of the area, charging them two thousand yuan for the same type room Robert pays 800Y.

"Come to my house, Robert; stand here on the porch and watch the snow. Let's drink a toast to good fortune tonight," she says, pouring him a generous glass of baijiu and one for herself, to savor in the snowy courtyard.

Robert looks toward the brightly lit LiNai Apartment for Foreign Experts where his client Mai Martin lives. Her fifth floor windows are dark. *Is Martin Xiansheng the American man in the rumor? He's not the only Meiguoren in the neighborhood, but he is the newcomer.*

***

Maj. TANG and the Marines burst into the quiet conference room with evidence from the getaway car: Rick's phone minus the SIM card, his empty wallet, and Mai's shoe. He opens a zippered gym bag and sets the items on the table. The phone and wallet are individually wrapped in clear, zip bags. Mai stands, hops, and limps over to look at the few items.

"Cai called me with a lead on Martin Xiansheng's phone from ping data. We recovered it from the canal. Here's a list of cars that entered the garage today. They must have switched to another vehicle before driving off campus."

Commander GAO hands the list to Sgt. WANG. "The gang had a van. Compare that license number to this list. And track down Lt. LIU for me."

Sgt. WANG hurries out the door.

"That's the phone I bought for Rick, and that's his wallet," Mai says. Her throat contracts; her chest feels tight. Hot tears sting the corners of her eyes.

The Commander hands her shoe to her, "Good fortune, Martin Taitai." It's been a stressful day and appears to be stretching into a stressful night, but his bland face betrays no thoughts or emotion, but neither does he seem unsympathetic.

Wright picks up the phone.

"Hey, what are you doing?" asks Mai. She grabs it from him. "This doesn't belong to you."

Commander GAO intercedes; his strong, callused hand extends, palm open, "*Qing*, Martin Taitai. Please. This is evidence." JGTS YANG Cai walks in. "Take this phone," says GAO, sliding it to him across the polished surface. Cai hurries into the beehive beyond the doors. Down on the second floor, he and his technicians have already dissected Wright's phone, made photocopies of each layer and dumped all the data they can extract. They reassembled and replaced it in the box with the Marines' gear and locked it.

While JGTS YANG Cai's cyber team continues to work on Gen. MA and Chief DIANGTI's phones, extracting the ping data and cross-referencing for significant clues, Frank Choy is loitering in the dead-end street near the gang's rooms in the hutong. He's standing under the canopy of a tree overhanging the twelve-foot wall, marking the southern perimeter of the university, astride his electric Beamer. He sees light from a doorway halfway up the row of dark sheds, partly obscured by a white Honda Odyssey. He's looking for somewhere he can get out of the worsening storm and still monitor Rick.

Ducking under the bicycle canopy across from the LiNai Apartments entrance, he observes activities in the warm and brightly lit guard shack next to the car gate. Three men inside are smoking and playing cards. He looks up at Mai's fifth-floor apartment, directly above, thinking it would make a great lookout. He silently rides back to Wright's car, their mobile ops center near the Main Building, where Ed Poole waits. The ping data broadcasting from Rick's transmitter has not changed coordinates for more than an hour.

Upstairs in the conference room, GAO says to Mai in English, "Please, Martin Taitai, the storm is harder now. Go home. *Hui jia.*"

To Ron he says, "Take Martin Taitai home now. We have work to do. She needs rest. Assure her: we will not sleep until her husband is found. I will send Sgt. LONG in the morning. She should be safe with you tonight, dui?" Although Commander GAO had intended for Sgt. LONG to be with Mai always, he felt comfortable making adjustments for the human factor, letting LONG sleep with her family, her young husband and infant child, since it seemed clear that Ron would be sleeping over at Mai's.

Ron offers his hand to Mai, who is back on two shoes and ready to go.

Once they're out and the door closes, Maj. TANG and the Marines standing by, Commander GAO turns to Wright and barks, "So, where *is* Martin? Of course you know. You're the American's handler. He's working for you. Don't deny it."

"I'm here as a favor to your department. Representing Americans, that's what embassies do, Commander GAO," Wright's eyes bulging.

"And I am extremely grateful for your collaboration on this distressing situation." The Commander's stocky neck inclines his large head slightly, in a deferential nod. "Please be my guest at the campus hotel. You and your men can take the rooms we reserved for the Harbin men." Gesturing to Maj. TANG, "Major, escort Wright Xiansheng and his men to the LiHua Hotel before the storm forces them to sleep here in my office."

Bright lights beckon at the entrance of LiHua. Behind the double glass doors, a round table of rare hardwood displays a graceful Norfolk pine *penjing,* the original bonsai, in a shallow dish of water and rocks. The ancient art of growing miniature trees on rocks was once the hobby of the entitled. Now, Beijing University greens-works runs a small *penjing* nursery under glass. Young *fuwuyuans*, again in red jackets and trousers, smile at the guests. Wright's rooms are secure, with private bamboo gardens for each suite, quietly extravagant in a Red Chinese sort of way.

Meanwhile, Ron creeps slowly across the silent, deep streets, turning left at the dark alley leading to the LiNai Apartments, driving past Robert's snowy cab. He turns right through the car gate and hunts for a place to park. Mai's shoes are soaking, and her feet are frozen. She stamps up the cold stairs. There's a light on every landing except hers. She turns on the light in the entry and heads to the shower. Ron follows, closing the clumsy iron gate and sturdy door behind them and carrying a duffel over his shoulder. Before anything, he scans the apartment for bugs; finds none.

At University HQ, Commander GAO assesses the situation with his team. Lt. LIU has returned from spending hours on campus traveling from gate to gate, supervising the mobilization and car search. JGTS YANG Cai is presenting a report on the information they have found on the phones, when Maj. TANG returns from getting Wright and his team settled into the LiHua.

Lt. LIU digs into a big plate of food, slivers of meat and peppers spooned over a mound of rice. "The entire Company BU-040 was mobilized. We have fifty-four guards at the five perimeter car gates, double-staffed with six for each of the nine guard shacks. Sixty total, if you include the second checkpoint at the Southwest Gate. Another platoon is deployed at other permeable locations. They will continue until 20:00, when all but the east and south gates will close for car and pedestrian traffic until 07:00. All the pedestrian gates will close at 20:00. At that time, we will revert to our normal staffing."

Sgt. WANG interrupts with an announcement, "We have a lead from the parking garage. The license number for the gang's Tianjin-registered Honda Odyssey was parked there today. Clocked in at 11:30 and clocked out at 17:05."

Capt. LI takes the information, "We're on it. *Xiexie*, Commander."

By 20:00, the staff at the Main Building is at a minimum,

monitoring systems, processing data. Walking down the wide, stone stairs, Commander GAO confides in Sgt. WANG, "We must find the *Meiguoren* soon. Deputy Commander HUANG wants this closed tomorrow."

The metal detector has been pushed to one side. The Commander nods to the one guard huddled next to his electric heater. Snow is driving harder from the east. Car tracks left from the frenzy of activity earlier have started to fill in. The men part in silence and carefully drive home on the now deserted streets.

November 2

Rick wakes. He's freezing from lying on a wet spot on the mattress. Listening for any sound. He tests his feet, raising and lowering them onto the floor; he rolls over onto his stomach, pulls his feet under him and stands. Pain throbs and pounds in his groin, kidneys, and abdomen from being kicked. *At least they avoided hitting me in the face. And I'm alive.* He reaches behind with his bound hands to feel for the wall, leans against a stack of crates, resting, controlling his breathing. One of the boxes falls, glass bottles break.

Gen. MA is in the next room. While the operation is in play, he sleeps poorly. The noise wakes him. He looks through a peep hole at the empty mattress.

"KIM brothers, get here, open this door now."

Rick hops around in the dark, falling over things and making as much noise as possible. He kicks a stack of empty bottles onto the first person through the door. Yong-Kyung shouts in Korean something about Rick's mother and father. The KIM brothers overwhelm him and start the kicking again.

"Stop it. Quiet," hisses Gen. MA, pulling back on Yong's arm, and Tasers Rick.

Down in the hutong, loud noise and muffled shouting wakes Robert, who glances at his mobile: 4:17AM. He sticks out his head into the steadily falling snow. Looking up, he sees a light on in Mai's apartment, the only light in the neighborhood. Freezing, he goes back to bed.

Overnight, a car had parked behind the Odyssey. Now the gang moves everything into the van. Only one way out, straight ahead through the locked gate; so they wait.

Upstairs in the apartment, Mai wakes and heads into the kitchenette. Ron got up before her and has heated the water in the electric teapot.

"Want tea or coffee, Mai?"

Ron, the martial arts master, is ready to search for Rick, dressed in black gabardine trousers tucked into black gum-soled boots, a white, cable stitch, turtleneck sweater, and a swarthy shadow on the cheek he usually keeps shaved. No longer the urban, metrosexual man Mai is accustomed to seeing.

It had been a rough night for Mai and Ron, both dozing in the small office with the heater, in the small bed, hugging each other, not talking. Early, before light, Mai had heard the shower and the on-demand water heater roaring; *Ron's up*. Closing her eyes, she drifted a few minutes longer.

"Tea," she answers, turns and disappears into her cold bedroom, emerging in a few minutes dressed in winter boots and rain pants over her jeans. She throws a matching coat onto a chair. "I think they have started the heat. Feel this." Mai rests her hand on the radiator under the bay window.

In the kitchenette, Ron tests the radiator. "Thanks to Buddha," he says, squinting out the black window. He carries the tea things into the next room where they watch the gloomy dawn arrive, draining the dark out of the sky.

***

Only a few hundred meters away, Rick sits in the first room, strapped to a chair half his size. Gen. MA pulls his head back and drops a temporary blindness tincture into each eye. Next, SHENG holds his head, and Yong-Kyung forces his mouth open while the General pours in strong liquor, *baijiu*. They pull a knit cap over his head, covering the newly dyed black hair and his blind blue eyes, zip his jacket over his bound arms, pull his pants up over the fresh bruises, and stick his unbound and bare feet into his shoes. In a few minutes, Sang-Bo emerges with SHENG, holding Rick between them. Drunk and blind, bound and abused, Rick staggers with his captors out the door into the fresh snow in the lane. Gen. MA follows.

They squeeze past the parked cars and slowly approach the pedestrian gate servicing the hutong neighborhood. More people join them, hurrying to catch a bus once they get to Chengfu Road and get to work. The general commotion at the checkpoint, with everyone having to show ID, overwhelms the PLA cadres who let the drunk, migrant men pass without scrutiny.

Their escape plan involves splitting up. SHENG, Sang-Bo, and Gen. MA will walk the disguised, blind, and drunk *Meiguoren* east, through the hutong to the pedestrian gate. Once on the other side, they'll be picked up by DONG and Yong-Kyung in the van.

The Odyssey was boxed in overnight with another car behind. The last two men will wait until the car gate between the hutong and the LiNai is unlocked at 7AM. Without Rick inside, they plan to go through the search and exit the campus at the double checkpoints at the Southwest Gate. Once out, they'll drive up Chengfu Road to the other side of the pedestrian gate and pick up the others.

***

Lt. GUAN is waiting at the West Gate when the guard shift arrives in the morning. He explains who he is to a surprised young guardsman and his intention to turn himself in. The two troops close the gate and march him across the quiet campus, blanketed in snow. A bus lumbers up Zhongguancun behind them, smashing the fresh snow into gray porridge.

***

Robert's room is toasty from Auntie's coal furnace. He lies in bed as long as possible, enjoying the warmth he has paid for. When he sees black branches outlined against pale gray, it's time to get up. Standing in the alley next to his cab covered with snow, he muses about the possibility of not working today. Looking up, he sees Mai's lighted apartment windows again and calls her.

"*Nihao*, Martin Taitai, is okay to call you?"

"*Dui*, Robert, what can I do for you?"

"Where Martin Xiansheng?"

"He's ... not here, Robert, *weishenme*?"

"Is he the man they look for, Martin Taitai?" asks Robert. He sees her dark form in the bright window. He waves. She waves back.

"*Dui*," she answers.

"Come down here, about your husband."

Mai finishes dressing, selecting a hat and scarf from the commode in the entry. Gloves go in a pocket. *Kuai bao* in another. "I'm going downstairs," she says to Ron who's reading text messages on his mobile. "Take your phone," he calls after her. "I'll be right down."

Mai sees, through the dirty windows at each landing, that the car gate is still locked, although it's after 7AM. A couple cars are backed up on both sides of the gate, and a small knot of people cluster around the pedestrian gate on Robert's side. Talking through the decorative iron, he says, "Look in there, Martin Taitai," pointing to the vacant shed on the corner, adjacent to where they stand. "I heard big noise early morning."

Mai looks in the direction he points. She sees a squat, concrete block building with a sturdy door and one boarded-up window.

"What's going on?" asks Ron, crunching through the crusty snow toward the closed auto gate.

"Ron, this is Robert, our cabdriver. He says he heard something last night."

Ron appraises Robert: a short but tough, tanned man in a thin, blue cotton jacket, zipped up to his neck. Every schoolchild is given an English name, making it easy for introductions with foreigners. They use their Chinese name when talking with each other. Ron nods and introduces himself in Mandarin, adding, "What's your real name?"

"*Wo shi* WEI Junjie. I heard loud noise from this shed last night at 4:17AM. I worry Martin Xiansheng not safe. Look here," urges Robert, pointing again at the shed.

"*Xiexie*, WEI Xiansheng," says Ron to the cabbie, who stands a little taller. "Call the Commander," says Ron to Mai. Turning back to Robert, "Who has the key to the shed?"

"Auntie, my landlady, she is here ..." Robert points to an elderly woman standing in the crowd.

The tardy guard arrives with the gate key and opens the car and pedestrian gates. Ron and Mai push through against the stream of people.

People and vehicles begin creeping through the snow. Most are leaving the hutong and going to work off campus, passing through the Southwest Gate at the other end of the street from Mai's apartment. DONG and Yong-Kyung have been sitting in the Odyssey, waiting for the gate to open. Now, they nose into the slow-motion column of cars driving past Mai as she stands in the street. They snake through the second checkpoint and then the first checkpoint. Guards search the van but don't find a bound victim. The men's IDs are acceptable. They never got the text about the Odyssey, so they let them through.

They leave campus through the Southwest Gate. DONG turns left and left again onto Chengfu Road. At the next intersection, they cross the broad boulevard and park in the mini-mall closest to the pedestrian gate behind the hutong.

Yong-Kyung gets out and walks through the parking behind the apartments and waits, stamping his feet in the cold and blowing on his hands. In a few minutes, the three in front followed by Gen. MA work their way to the checkpoint. Rick's head is bowed. An empty bottle sticks out of his pocket. Laughing, SHENG and Sang-Bo persuade the guard that their friend is drunk, and pass through. Once everyone is stowed, the Honda Odyssey turns right on Chengfu Road and right again on Zhongguancun, heading north. Out of Beijing.

***

Looking up the street at the line of cars waiting to pass, Mai sees Commander GAO slowly moving toward them in an electric university car. Sgt. LONG is riding in the back. A large man in an over-size overcoat drives while the Commander directs, sitting next to him and similarly garbed in ankle-length greatcoat with red stripes on the broad cuffs. Before they come to a silent stop outside the gate, Commander GAO jumps out and hustles forward through the crowd.

"Commander GAO!" cries Mai.

"Martin Taitai, what is the cause of this commotion?" asks GAO. Although snow is rare in Beijing, it can snow every winter, more or less. The car drivers go more slowly than usual, the pedestrians and bicycles are subdued by the beautiful but slippery stuff, delaying the arrival of the morning guard and stopping movement in the lane. Once the gate opened and the workers passed by, the corner clears of traffic in a few minutes.

"The man was late coming with the gate key. But, wait, this man here, Robert, has something to tell you about Rick," says Mai, gesturing to the corner shed where Ron, Robert, and Auntie huddle at the door.

Inside the shed, broken glass and blood are scattered over a dirty mattress in the center of the floor. Beyond, another door opens into the adjacent shed. Commander GAO's driver, Sgt. GU, stands in the doorway, keeping out the curious passersby.

"Hey you, guard!" GU calls to the man in the shack. "Keep people and cars out of this lane. Do you have a barricade?"

While the middle-aged guard drags a portable barricade from behind the bicycle shed, Sgt. GU and Robert direct people away from this end of the street. Commander GAO lays his flashlight on the snowy road; its beam catches the pattern of car treads heading west through the gate.

Returning to the rooms, he looks carefully for evidence. Sliding his thumb down his address book, he calls Maj. TANG first and then Capt. LI. Walking across the road to where Mai waits, he says, "We just missed them. They passed by here through this gate. We'll catch them, Martin Taitai. You can be sure of this. Today." He shows Mai a plastic bag and asks her, "Do you recognize this as your husband's?"

A strangled shriek catches in her throat when she sees Rick's blood-spattered socks and shorts. She turns to the Commander, "Where's Wright?"

"First, Lt. GUAN turned himself in this morning."

"*Zhende*," remarks ZHAO. "Where is he now?"

"We're holding him at the Main Building. I'm going there now to question him. We're looking for two of our guards, missing since yesterday, besides Martin Xiansheng. Lt. GUAN should have information we can use. He says he's willing to negotiate his cooperation for dropping any charges. About Wright ... He's at the LiHua Hotel. I'm stopping there on the way."

Ron concludes, "We're going out to find them. Have someone at your office phone my assistant with the chase coordinates."

"Is Martin Taitai staying here? I'll have Sgt. LONG stay with her," says GAO.

"She's coming with me."

"Stay in touch. Good hunting."

Commander GAO finds Wright in the LiHua dining room, monitoring everything on his netbook while eating breakfast from the buffet. "Join me for coffee or tea, Commander?"

One of the Marines is sitting at the table, playing with his iPhone. He watches the two men over the top of his combat game.

"No time for games, Wright. Anything you want to tell me? We tracked a bloodied Martin Xiansheng to a shed in the hutong, very near to Martin Taitai's apartment—"

Wright looks up from his plate of sautéed vegetables and French pastries. "Good job Commander. You'll doubtless get a promotion for your work today."

"And we lost them!" Commander GAO turns his back and motions for a guard to stay with Wright. Later, he tries to get Wright's smirking face out of his mind while he slowly drives through the slush and crush of students on bicycles.

Upstairs in the Main Building, Lt. GUAN Qinchen sits at a little table at the back of a bare room. It overlooks a grassy hill and a bamboo hedge. He gets up when he sees the Commander.

"Sit," says GAO, taking the chair opposite. For a few minutes, Commander GAO checks his messages. "We haven't found those two guards yet."

Lt. GUAN sits expressionless.

"Do you know where they are?"

Lt. GUAN shakes his head *no*.

"Well, what good are you going to be if I can't get the information I need?"

"The Chinese lead man is named SHENG, from the Tianjin triad. The Koreans are KIM Yong-Kyung and Sang-Bo. The Chinese driver is

DONG and belongs to the Beijing Triad. They report to me or Gen. MA."

"The guards," GAO reminds him.

"All I know is that they needed uniforms."

"Can you tell me what is so important about this man, Rick Martin? What's the purpose of your operation here, *really?*"

Lt. GUAN takes his time answering. "There's a bounty on Martin. Chief DIANGTI was going to split it with me. The North Koreans will pay 120,000 in US dollars for us to deliver Martin alive."

"Why do they care?" asks GAO.

"The Iranians set the bounty. It's a pass-through. They keep some."

"I see...." GAO writes on a pad, rips the last page out, and hands it to an aide, with a one-word order, "Cai," sending the aide quickly out of the room. "I'll talk with my superiors about your cooperation, Lt. GUAN. This has been a useful interview. It might just save the university guards' lives." He puts the empty pad back in his shirt pocket and worries, will it be enough?

***

The gang picks up another tail, besides Frank Choy. A Beijing PD unit prowling Wudaokou sees the license number, make, and model of their van.

While his Park Avenue warms up, Ron thinks about how to keep Mai from panicking, which would endanger everyone all that much more. The sight of Rick's bloody underwear is hard on her. She's withdrawn and morose, staring at nothing. He says, "Hey, Mai, I need a navigator."

"What can I do?"

He retrieves his laptop from the back seat and hands it to her. "Boot up." Ron pulls into the middle of the now-empty street, heading toward the Southwest Gate at the other end. While waiting for the Park Avenue to be searched, Mai gets TSC's proprietary GPS program up and running. "Here, take the phone, Mai. There's a technician on the line who can speak English. She's going to work with you on tracking the Odyssey."

Mai sees a black screen with streets marked by colored lines. A beeping light indicates where the two cars are located. "Where's the power?" she asks.

He reaches behind the screen and pulls her fingers to the place where the cord plugs into the laptop and into the car. "That's neat, is that the Wi-Fi?" she asks, pointing to a device in the USB port.

The blinking light that is Capt. LI's cruiser turns right on the 5th Ring Road Freeway. "They're going to take the Jingzang Expressway," bets Ron.

Mai looks at the corner of the display—only a little after 8:30AM.

Capt. LI passes the Jingzang and continues east toward the immense Olympics Park area. The freeway is crowded, but traffic is still moving at about 60 kilometers per hour or 40 mph. Three police vehicles, lights flashing, enter the freeway at Lincui Bridge, Mai tracks their blinks. Ron's blink catches up at Baiyuan Bridge, where Capt. LI exits, making a wide left turn. Baiyuanlu is jammed with cars, busses, pedestrians, and bicycles.

Mai looks at the time: 9:05AM.

***

The gang in the Odyssey realizes they are being pursued by Beijing PD, exits the expressway and turns onto a major boulevard, looking for a subway opening.

Gen. MA heaps abuse on Rick for the last time, before jumping out of the rear side door, using an approaching bus to cover his movement, and shouting to the others: "Ditch the car. Leave the Meiguoren, unfinished business." And vanishes like a ghost.

***

The front blinking light stops; they are close to catching up. Mai leans forward, peering out the windshield.

"There it is," says Ron. The Odyssey is stopped in the middle of the boulevard.

The doors open, and the occupants abandon their vehicle, running left and right. Mai reaches for her door. "Wait, Mai!" shouts Ron, slamming the car into park; he leaps out after her into the stalled traffic.

SHENG and Yong-Kyung race for the Datunlu East ditie entrance and disappear down the stairs, pushing through peddlers and bus passengers in a queue. Beijing PD follows while more policemen cross the street to the other side to pursue DONG and Sang-Bo. Mai climbs into the back of the Odyssey and rips the tape from Rick's mouth. His head rolls from side to side, straining to see from his blind eyes and hear through the commotion.

"Rick, Rick, it's me, Mai!" Overcome with emotion, Rick

screams like a wounded tiger.

"Mai ... oh Mai," he wails. "I can't see ... my eyes ..." His speech is slurred, and he stinks like alcohol. Standing in the street, Ron watches Mai cover Rick's face with tears and kisses.

Police emerge from the subway entrance with Yong-Kyung and hustle him into a police van.

"Looks like they caught one," says ZHAO. He spots Capt. LI in the crowd and waves his arm.

An ambulance arrives. Officers make way for it, directing morning traffic around the stalled Odyssey. Paramedics approach the back of the van with a gurney as Capt. LI leads a clot of officers toward Rick.

"I have to get out now, Rick. Help is here. I'm here. I'm right here," says Mai as she climbs out and a woman, Lt. WU, climbs in. Mai recognizes her from last night.

First, WU photographs the scene. Then, she cuts the zip ties binding his arms and feet, placing the ties in an evidence bag with an empty liquor bottle. She stuffs his heavy jacket into another evidence bag and climbs out.

"Nihao, ZHAO," says Capt. LI, offering his hand. While the men discuss in Chinese, Ron turns to Mai, "They want us to go downtown to report this."

"I'm going to the hospital with Rick. Can't we do that later?"

Ron turns back to Capt. LI, and they continue to talk.

The paramedics have Rick strapped onto the gurney with his feet sticking out past the end and load him in the back. Over the heads of Capt. LI's officers, Ron watches Mai climb in behind. They close the doors and drive away slowly in the mad congestion on the boulevard.

"Where are they going?"

"Wangjing Hospital. It's close." Standing in the street after the ambulance leaves, Capt. LI says to his assistant, Lt. WU. "I want the identity of the prisoner *today*. Set up to use the medical technicians."

"Certainly, Boss."

"I'm going to the hospital," says LI while Ron continues looking for it on his iPhone. "Follow me, ZHAO. I want to talk to Martin Xiansheng at Wangjing."

Wangjing Hospital

Riding in the back of the ambulance with the attendants, Mai watches them wipe his face. She extends her hand toward the moist towel. They let her pat him while they inspect his head and neck. He growls when the cigarette burns are touched. Rick opens his eyes and looks toward the paramedic without seeing. On the way to Wangjing Hospital he wants to sit up, but they have him strapped down. He turns to the sound of Mai's voice. She's cleaning his face, saying, "Rick, your hair's dyed black." There's a bloody bruise on his mouth; an attendant covers it with a bulky bandage. They offer him something to drink from a straw. He's suddenly very thirsty and grateful for the kindness.

At the hospital, Mai waits in the lobby with groups of families. She realizes she doesn't have her phone; left it in Ron's car. Just then, Capt. LI walks through the big glass doors and engages a hospital staff in conversation while Ron walks in behind him, bringing Mai's phone and carrying a duffel bag over his shoulder. She jumps up and runs toward them.

"I want to see Rick," she says following Capt. LI.

Ron says, "Wait Mai. Capt. LI goes in first."

"What …?"

"Mai," is all he can say. The agony on her face stops him. This is not the US. They're both thinking it. He walks her back to the waiting area and sits beside her; they wait together. A nurse leads Capt. LI out of the lobby into the interior of the monumental facility, double doors swing closed behind them. Mai remembers something—"I'm calling Wright."

"Nihao, Mrs. Martin," greets Wright. "Where are you?" He's been lounging in the LiHua suite, monitoring Rick's movements since the Odyssey started moving this morning. Frank Choy on his Beamer lost sight of the Odyssey when they entered the Fifth Ring Road, but caught up as they passed the Jingzang Expressway.

"I'm at Wangjing Hospital, you puke."

He hangs up on her.

Ron stands, "I'm going to find Rick."

"I'm going with you."

"Stay here. Let me find out where he is. I'll come get you." Shouldering the duffel, he pushes past the double doors, muttering what a lousy mess this is.

The ER nurse approaches. "ZHAO Xiansheng?" she asks.

"Yes?" says Ron.

"You can come in here and speak with Martin Xiansheng now."

"Martin Taitai is anxious to see her husband. Will you bring her here?" flashing his brightest smile. The young woman turns and disappears around a corridor. Ron steps into a large ward filled with beds separated by flimsy white curtains. All the beds in the ward are occupied.

Rick lies exhausted on the narrow bed, looking like a giant: his big feet stick out over the end, wrapped in soft, white sheets. Capt. LI sits to the side, but stands when he sees Ron enter.

"I'm just leaving," he says.

"Good job, LI, catching that one."

"We're going to get identities of the gang today if it kills me, or him. *Ha-ha.*" Turning to Rick he says, "*Xiexie* for your help, Martin Xiansheng. Come to the station when you're able to make a formal report."

Rick mumbles a reply. Ron claps Capt. LI on the shoulder as he passes, "Good luck finding the guards."

The tall Captain slips through a curtain drawn around Rick's bed. A nurse is ushering Mai in as he leaves. They nod.

"Where's Mai?" Rick whispers toward the side where Ron stands. "I can't see you, ZHAO. My eyes ..." Bandages cover half his face. Where he isn't bandaged, ugly bruises mottle his pale skin.

"I'm here, baby," she says, brushing the curtain aside. Rick rustles under the sheets, and one paw reaches for her. "I can't see you ..."

"Shush," her small hand, looking even smaller, resting in his red, swollen mitt, the skin tight over his fat fingers. Deep, purplish-red gouges surround his wrist.

"Help me sit up."

A calm, female voice coming from the doorway says in American accented English, "I'm Dr. CHOW. Does Martin Xiansheng want to sit up already?" She calls to her attendants, who float in to raise the mechanism on the bed so Rick can sit.

Mai turns to look at a tall, handsome Chinese woman in a white coat.

"Martin Xiansheng has suffered numerous traumas to his body. In addition, he's in a state of intoxication and demonstrates a fleeting blindness." Dr. Chow lifts the sheets covering his abdomen, revealing a bandage on his chest and significant discoloration from bruising. "He has a deep burn here," gesturing to his chest, "and there are underlying, small bone fractures which will take several months to completely heal." The doctor makes notations in Rick's file. An attendant brings a small jar of pills, pours out two and helps Rick swallow them. "He'll experience a limited range of motion in his legs until the deep trauma is healed.

"I want to check out, go home," Rick croaks.

"I'm not recommending it," says CHOW.

"Where are my clothes?" he persists.

The attendant retrieves a plastic shopping bag from under the bed with his shirt and pants. A second bag holds his size thirteen shoes. Ron ZHAO puts them into his duffel. Rick swings his legs over to the side and sits there, resting until the pain in his groin subsides. He turns a little so he can face toward the doctor's voice.

"Show me you can stand and walk, and I'll sign your discharge form."

"Come here, ZHAO, help me," Rick reaches toward Ron and slides off the bed onto his feet, still resting his butt on the edge.

"Take your time, Rick; this is not a contest," interjects Mai, trying to get out of his way in the narrow enclosure.

Rick takes a few feeble steps and starts to sway. He sits down hard, stifling a moan, as Mai pushes a chair under him. "Can we get a wheelchair to take him to the car?" she wants to know.

Dr. CHOW signs Rick's discharge form and orders a chair.

"*Deng yixia*, let me pay Rick's bill. You know, healthcare isn't free here," says Ron, pulling a pair of sweat pants and a zippered jacket out of the duffel. "These might fit." He shoulders the bag, pressing past the curtain as he goes. Walking the halls back to the cashier's office, Ron curses himself and the North Korean gang.

Alone with Mai, Rick gropes for her hand, "Mai, darling, please come here. Don't be mad."

"Wright is insane. What you two do is insane."

Beijing Police Department

Using sodium pentothal injections to obtain information from recalcitrant prisoners doesn't always work. Yong-Kyung has been trained and conditioned in North Korea. Usually these agents are difficult to crack, but not impossible.

After his initial booking they move him to the infirmary. He's strapped to a bed and injected with a light dose, which acts on the small man's brain within seconds after asking him some easy questions. The drug suppresses Yong-Kyung's higher cortical functions and renders him chatty and cooperative with the specially trained interrogator working with Capt. LI.

The questions quickly move from what he had for breakfast to what he did yesterday. Soon, Yong-Kyung is relaying details about the gang's activities. Skillfully, the interrogator suggests, and soon Yong is talking. His name is KIM Yong-Kyung, and the other man is his brother, KIM Sang-Bo. Gen. MA is the *dalaoban*. This data is immediately relayed to the technicians developing ID profiles on the gang. He tells about tricking the university guards with a delivery, taking them bound and naked to a gang safehouse near Wudaokou in Haidian District, where they were traded to a trafficking faction of the gang.

Unexpectedly, he starts crying and calling out "Bo, Bo, *zai nar?* [where are you?] The interrogator continues following Yong's recall of his own abduction six years ago. He and his brother Sang-Bo were vacationing in the Philippines with his Chinese family when they were 12 and 13 years old. Their father was a wealthy Taiwanese businessman who traded heavily with partners there. They were snorkel-diving in a beautiful bay while their parents were relaxing at the resort. They met some boys who offered to take them in their boat. Before they knew what was happening, they were going farther and farther away from the beach toward another boat beyond the reef, where they were transferred to a motor launch and taken by stages to an encampment with other young Chinese and Japanese men and boys being taken to North Korea where they were inducted into service to the KIM family as translators, language instructors, or paramilitary assassins. Abductees with no talent were sent to labor camps.

The drug gradually wears off, and Yong sleeps for a couple hours before recovering consciousness. Work immediately begins on finding the missing guards. Lt. WU calls Capt. LI at the hospital with the news.

"Nihao, WU … Was the drug interrogation fruitful?… Contact the gang unit. I want them at my office immediately. I'm leaving now. Be there in twenty minutes."

At the Sanlitun Police Station, Lt. WU greets Capt. LI at the elevator.

"Tell me about the interrogation," starts LI.

"The *kid* Yong-Kyung, it turns out, was abducted as a child, six years ago off a beach in the Philippines vacationing with his Taiwanese parents. The other kid, Bo, is his brother. If you believe the story, they're 18 and 19 years old."

Capt. LI's eyes widen with surprise. He's Chinese, and a victim himself!

"He gave us a lot of information, and it needs to be corroborated."

"You're right. It's not always helpful, what we get from the drug interrogation, but it's somewhere to start. Did he tell what happened to the guards?"

"Yes, we have to hurry if we want to save them. They've been traded to a gang trafficking in human misery. That was yesterday. They could be anywhere by now. According to the kid, they grabbed the guards at Beijing University and drove to a gang safehouse in the Wudaokou area, where they were transferred."

Before she finishes talking, he reaches for his mobile. WU turns to go.

"*Deng yixia*! Wait! One more thing—send someone in here who can report to me about the image-recognition search for the other gang members."

"When do you want to start the meeting with the gang unit?"

"Fifteen minutes.... Good work, WU." Capt. LI regards WU, quietly standing in the doorway.

She has worked with Capt. LI for three years, starting when she graduated from college. Unlike many young women, she wants a career in law enforcement, but she knows her sex and small stature are negatives that are hard to overcome. Taking an administrative job is an opening, scoring highest on the qualifying test. Capt. LI is open-minded and observes, she works twice as hard as the men and never complains.

Capt. LI begins plans for an assault on the safehouse. "Wei, nihao Capt. CONG, his counterpart at the Wudaokou PSB, Capt. LI here, Sanlitun, Chaoyang District," he says to his counterpart at the

Wudaokou, Haidian Police Station. "Can you mobilize for an attack on a gang safehouse in your district?"

"Where is it?"

"The Qinglinyuan neighborhood near the Shangqing Bridge interchanges in Wudaokou. This is the gang related to the incident yesterday at Beijing University. We should be ready to roll tonight. Did you hear about the missing guards?"

"Dui, everyone is talking about it. Do you think the guards are being held at the safehouse?" asks CONG.

"Dui," answered LI. "We have to move as soon as possible if we want to save them. Can you get a gang unit at your station?"

"Yes. I'll call district HQ now."

"*Haode*, it's 15:00. I'll call you in one hour. *Zaijian*," concludes LI and hangs up.

He looks up to see two computer technicians standing outside his door. "Do you have information for me about the gang members?"

"*Wei, nihao*, Captain, *dui, dui*," they answer in unison.

"Follow me," the Captain leads the way toward a conference room.

This room is smaller than Commander GAO's imposing, Soviet-era hall at Beijing University. Red PRC and CPP party flags are the only adornments. Plain tables and folding chairs have been pushed together to make one large table surrounded by the seats. Lt. WU is setting an electric carafe of hot water down when Capt. LI enters with the two technicians. He points to the table, on which the technicians lay their reports for his review: ID profiles and pictures on each one, Gen. MA, SHENG, DONG, Yong-Kyung and Sang-Bo.

"We need to get on the road to Haidian. Where's our gang unit?"

"You better call Sergeant FANG. I'll text you his number," says WU.

Many of the men in the department refuse to acknowledge her, even if she *is* acting on Capt. LI's orders; they prefer to work only with men.

"*Wei, nihao*, Capt. LI here," to the gang unit's Sergeant FANG.... We're staging an attack on a gang safehouse in Haidian this evening.... We're convening the prep meeting now.... When Lt. WU contacts you, it is not a request; it is a command from me—do you understand, Sergeant?... *Ha, ha*, we meet now."

***

After arguing and gambling all night, the Qinglinyuan Gang in Wudaokou, Haidian District, decides to harvest the organs of the young and healthy guards. This requires transporting them to a nearby hospital alive. A corrupt doctor will perform euthanasia and remove all the useful tissue. Other hospitals in the district then accept the organs in the usual way; the certification of death by natural causes allowing the third-party recipients to be innocent of the actual crime of murder. The gang waits until the last hospital shift to start at 22:00.

Shortly after 16:00, Capt. LI and Sgt. FANG's vehicles drive into the underground parking at the Haidian Zhongguancun Main Police Station. The Qinglinyuan Gang's safehouse is located in the farthest northeast corner of the Wudaokou Police Station jurisdiction bounded by the Xiaoyue River and the expressway.

In the assembly hall, Capt. CONG has units taking form as officers arrive from the field and off-duty officers come in for the special assignment. Additional units of street control officers are assembled in the parking area. The two gang units take a conference room adjacent to the assembly hall to compare information and develop strategies. Lt. WU disappears into the computer department.

The Haidian District houses most of the universities in the Wudaokou neighborhood and also boasts its version of Silicon Valley in the Zhongguancun neighborhood. The Qinglinyuan neighborhood is an old abandoned industrial zone hidden in the neck of the 5th Ring Road and Jingzang Expressway interchange called Shangqing Bridge.

Two miles or about four kilometers separates the gang safehouse from the university, if you could fly like a magpie, up out of the forest of poplars at the campus, to the desolate post-industrial neighborhood of Qinglinyuan. But by car, the zigzag route is 6.7 kilometers and takes half an hour to drive to the East Gate of Beijing University.

Shangqing and Xueqing Roads lead to it from Wudaokou where numerous warehouses and apartment buildings are crowded together. This is where the Qinglinyuan Gang has its western safehouse, housing an itinerant group of criminals, overseen by a cadre of permanent members. The university guards are locked in a storage room here, within an interconnected maze of lockers, shops, and vacant buildings.

Neither Capt. LI nor Capt. CONG know whether the guards are still there, if they've been moved to another Beijing location or out of the city. They *do* know they must act quickly before the trail is cold and they lose any chance to find them alive. Choke points are identified at Houbajia Road and the connector roads under the freeways. Starting at the outer edges, police barricades are set in place. Capt.'s LI and CONG move their units quickly into the inner section, blocking exits as they go.

The iron gates of the industrial complex are rusted wide open.

Inside the entrance at the back of a vacant factory building, a yellow dog sits by the office door. Several new cars are parked around the side, out of sight from the street. The BPD units move to secure all exits and begin to open and search the facility. The gang sentries are gambling and fail to notice the BPD approaching.

The police brigade breaks into companies and platoons, each unit with their objective. They breach the possible entry points and systematically search the connected buildings. The entire operation lasts until past 24:00. Eight gang members are apprehended alive; four are killed in the raid; and the two university guards are eventually found alive. Cataloging and removing to the evidence vault all the contraband, drugs, weapons, phones, and computers will occupy several days following the raid.

Capt. LI puts into motion a data-base search for the gang boys KIM Yong-Kyung and Sang-Bo's identities through a national bureau for missing persons, including official databases for missing Chinese children dating 2004–2006 in the Philippines.

CHAPTER 4
Abducted

In the afternoon of November 2, Commander GAO's driver Sgt. GU Fan and Sgt. LONG Yandong are waiting at the entrance to the LiNai Apartments when Mai and Rick arrive by taxi. GU is about the same stature as Rick; he pulls on Rick's arm and lifts him up with his shoulder. Yandong, on the other side, hugs Rick around the waist. Mai follows them up the five flights of stairs, carrying the duffel.

Ron had offered to drive them back to Haidian, but Mai objected, feeling she had pressed him beyond what his good nature could tolerate. He called them a cab instead and got them headed back to Beijing University before driving straight to the office. They could have waited for Sgt. GU to get them, but Rick was anxious to get home.

The apartment is warm and welcoming when she unlocks the double gate and door. Winded, GU pants a minute on the landing before shouldering Rick and carrying him into the bedroom.

Mai looks at her phone ringing in a call, "*Wei, nihao*, Commander ... GU and Yandong are here, *dui, xiexie* ... Rick is sleeping now ... Can you please, *keyi*, call my boss, ZHANG Hong, and make an excuse for me not showing for work today? I don't know what to tell my office about all this ... Oh, she already knows? ..." Mai turns to Yandong and hands her the phone.

When Yandong returns the phone, Mai notices for the first time she's carrying a travel bag. Commander GAO booms on the phone, "Sgt. LONG will be staying at your apartment tonight, Martin Taitai, *haoma*?"

"I'm okay. No need."

"You flatter me, that you think you are safe at Beijing campus."

"Aren't I?"

"Is more convenient than staying at guest house, *dui*?"

"Well, alright, *xiexie*. I welcome Sgt. LONG's protection," concedes Mai.

"Haode ha-ha bye-bye," concludes GAO.

Mai shows Yandong where she can leave her bag and where she'll be sleeping, in the spare office.

Booting up *Pépe*, Mai carries the netbook into the sitting room to read messages. While it connects, she fills the electric tea kettle and fixes tuna sandwiches on a toasted bun for her and Yandong. Last week, she had planned a party for Saturday for her friends to meet Rick. Now, she sends a cancellation email to the guest list. Listening to a San Diego jazz station, she cleans up the kitchenette and picks up the disarray in the apartment. Emptying the duffel, Rick's clothes are tossed onto the floor in the bathroom near the washer. His shoes go into the office with the rest of his clothes.

Ron's things are in every room, last night's stay seeming to expose their last several months together. She gathers and places the items into the duffel: razor and toothbrush from the bathroom, a pair of shoes from the sitting room, and a complete set of clothes hanging off the bookcase in the office. Her phone needs charging. The pile of clothes on the floor grows. Sgt. LONG hangs a few things on the back of the office door where she finds a couple hangers.

Without making a sound, Mai opens the bedroom door to check on Rick. The only feature she can see is his mouth, puffy and pained-looking, his breathing in shallow, regular gasps. Mai selects clothes for tomorrow from the armoire and tiptoes out. *Rick can rest here while I go to work in the morning.*

The sunny sky, following the snow, betrays the cold breath of November. Afternoon sun hits the top windows in new apartments east of Mai's, reflecting icily on the wall over the Chinese table. Yellow and brown poplar leaves drop into hutong lanes where residents sweep them into piles. Blue patches of snow show in shadows on the north side of buildings. Magpies swoop through bare poplar branches. Clouds of steam and smoke roil out of a tall smokestack glimpsed between the trees.

Looking down into the street, Mai sees people hurry back and forth, holding scarves to their faces; hands plunged into pockets or pulling children behind, bundled up so tightly only their bright eyes show. The gate at her door rattles, followed by loud pounding. Checking through the peephole, she sees two men standing on the landing and doesn't recognize either of them. One man is a tall American, and the other is a sturdy Chinese.

"Who are you?" she wants to know.

"Ed Poole from the US Embassy, Mrs. Martin. Please, let us in."

"Show me some ID," answers Mai, alarmed, remembering the loathsome Mr. Wright. "Under the door, I can't see it in the dark out there."

Mai and Sgt. LONG examine them. The ID cards look official. Mai lets them in while Yandong steps backwards into the doorway of the office, holding her pistol in ready position, pointing up.

"Where's your husband, Mrs. Martin?" asks Poole, first in the door, and surprised to see Sgt. LONG staring at him over the pistol barrel. "Who's this?" he wants to know, gesturing to the young soldier in a gray uniform covering him at close range.

"That's Sgt. LONG. Rick's sleeping. What do you want?"

"We want the shirt he was wearing."

"You mean this?" asks Mai, stooping to scoop up Rick's filthy dress shirt and holding it out. Ed Poole reaches for it, but Mai snatches it back. "What do you want it for?"

Rick's voice cracks from the bedroom, "Mai, come here." Putting her head in the door, he says to her, "Give them the shirt, Mai. I need to talk to them ... privately."

She holds the bedroom door open for the embassy men, disapproval on her face.

"Can you go out, Mai—go shopping or something? Leave us alone," gasps Rick.

Mai glowers at him—*"Don't be mad,"* he says—shakes her head, and expels an exasperated breath. Then she does as he asks, rides her bike to the shopping center with Sgt. LONG by her side. Obviously, Rick has his own alliances. She needs to go to the bank and get food anyway. Coming back an hour later, dusk is overtaking the day. Icy wind blows in gusts on the ride back to the apartment. The stairwell lights are now out on every floor. Only half-light from the dirty windows casts a pale glow on the frigid, concrete stairs. Cheerful light and warmth await her inside. She double-locks the door behind them. The embassy men are gone, and Rick is sleeping.

Yandong says goodnight and disappears into the guest room studio, reminding Mai to call if anything unusual occurs. Mai thanks her and sighs. Sitting in in the dark, in her favorite chair, looking into the Wudaokou skyline, she meditates on the possibility that the ordeal is over ... or not. Rick is back. *Rest and quiet, and he'll be okay. He's tough. A Tiger.* But ... is it over? Will they try again? Where's Homeland Security now? Are they still nearby? She thinks about sending a text to Wright but changes her mind, texting the Commander instead, but GAO's mailbox is full.

Around 9PM, Mai's phone rings with a text from Ron: can u tak? She calls him back, "*Wei, nihao*."

"*Nihao*, indeed, and how are you, *Tangzi?*"

"Okay, I guess. It's quiet. Rick's sleeping. He took half a bottle of pills and is out of it."

"Want me to come over tonight?" Ron asks.

"Yandong is here. The guard from GAO's unit."

"Oh, right. Good."

"Some guys from the embassy came over today."

"What did they want?"

"His shirt."

"*Zhende? Weishenme?*"

"I don't know. Then Rick kicked me out while he talked to them. He was barely conscious. When I came back from shopping, they were gone and Rick was asleep."

A few seconds pass.

"When can I see you?" he asks in a husky whisper.

"Want to join us for dinner tomorrow? I'm going to work in the morning and let Rick rest here."

If he wants to see her, he'll have to include her husband. For now. "I'll bring *jiaozi*."

"I have your bag here full of your things."

"Yeah, *duibuqi*, sorry for the mess."

"I cancelled my party."

"I know."

"I wanted Rick to meet my friends. Now ..." Mai mumbles into the phone with a sob.

"Yeah, it's sure different now," agrees Ron.

They talk like that for a while. Mai cries. Ron consoles. They continue until there's nothing left they haven't discussed ... well maybe one or two things ... and hang up. Without discussing their plans for the future or how Rick's arrival has changed *things*.

She tiptoes into the office where Yandong sleeps to plug her phone into the charger. Padding through the dark apartment, she climbs into bed next to Rick and listens to his breath, soft and regular. The last thing she remembers is the sound of the night guard closing the car and pedestrian gates below in the street, separating the LiNai Apartments from the hutong and the rest of the campus.

***

Once Rick had been found, everyone's attention refocused on the missing guards. The gang had evacuated their hideout in the hutong after Rick's clamor, but left plenty of information. They were able to capture one, and another turned himself in.

Capt. LI continues the manhunt for MA and his crew until just before daylight. The exhausted troops return to barracks. Wright's squad checks out of the guesthouse on campus, eluding observation by the guard assigned to watch them through a simple distraction technique.

The security office takes a break to rest. Lying in bed at last, GAO's arms around his sleeping wife, he thinks he must see Martin Taitai first thing tomorrow, before sleep claims another victim.

***

Gen. MA's gang knows the neighborhood of the rendezvous hotel: it's several blocks south of where they abandoned the Odyssey. The Chosun Beijing Hotel is one of many in the Embassy District. Each man, by his own route, heads to the hotel. The first one to arrive is Gen. MA. While waiting for the others, he tries Lt. GUAN's number: no connection.

He orders a big Korean meal from room service and a couple massage girls from the spa. Looking at Chief DIANGTI's watch, it's 1:20PM.

Later, over *kim chee* soup, Gen. MA and SHENG work out the next step.

"We need another car and more men," says SHENG.

"I'm going to contact the people in Tianjin to send us a new car," says MA. "Enjoy yourselves, men; we leave tonight." He tosses Mai's apartment key into the air and catches it, laughing.

November 3

Early morning, a silvery Chevy Tiggo SUV stops at the entrance to the LiNai Apartments. Four black figures ascend the stairs in darkness. The clunky gate lock clicks, then creaks. The door lock succumbs the same way. A pillow presses to the wife's face while a heavy hand grasps her through the duvet.

Mai struggles wildly for a few seconds before passing out. She's shoved to the side, off the bed onto the stone floor. *Thud.* A pillow to the face and a Taser shot to the groin takes care of Rick, already sedated from pain medication.

Sgt. LONG wakes instantly at the sound of the clunking gate. Holding her breath, she counts four dark figures pass her open door. She slides out from under the duvet where she's been sleeping in panda-themed bra and panties. She hears a thud from Mai's bedroom as she pushes the bedroom door wide open and says, *"Ai, bendan!"* [Hey, asshole!]

A kick from the side knocks her gun into the air and a punch lands her in the sitting room, one of the armchairs breaking her fall.

The black figures roll Rick in the duvet, tape him round and round, and easily carry him downstairs to the waiting Tiggo.

When people are asked if they heard anything as the investigation gets underway, some said they heard the gusty wind blowing and rattling their doors.

*** *

Mai wakes on the cold floor moments later. Rick is gone. Yandong lies on the floor in the sitting room. The apartment door wide open, *her* key in the lock. She runs barefoot down the stairs while looking down the stairwell to the first floor. She glimpses a shadow of a figure, a leg really, leaving the building. Looking out the dirty windows in passing, a red taillight winks out of sight. A swirl of wind blows into the entry. Covering her face, she runs out into the amber glow of the streetlight on an empty road, under a moonless sky. "Rick!!" she screams at the red taillight at the far end of the block, blinking into black.

Mai, a pale ghost in pink pajamas, runs back into the entry and up the stairs. Panting and gasping, hands shaking, she powers on her phone.

Sobbing, "Ron! Ooh Ron!"

"Mai, is that you?"

"They had my key! They got Rick. Again. And they're gone. Help me! Help me! Please, Ron!" More keening sobbing.

Sgt. LONG's figure appears in the entry. She's found her gun and stands, holding her head with one hand, leaning against the doorjamb. She flips the light switch and scans the studio for her mobile.

By the time Ron arrives from across town, Mai's apartment has become a crime investigation scene. Guards stop him at the second checkpoint, and he has to call the Commander.

"*Wei, nihao*, Commander, ZHAO ... Can you let me in your scene?"

"Martin Taitai is sitting in my Toyota Royal Crown," answers GAO. "It's parked next to the bicycle shed. You can come up. Tell the guard at the entry to call Sgt. WANG for your pass."

At 4:15AM, the campus is dead quiet. Bright lights at the end of the street near the locked car gate cast harsh, greenish-blue shadows on the frozen tableau. Commander GAO's black, luxury sedan takes on a greenish glow, squatting with authority. Ron knocks on the car window. Mai's face, gray in the night light, turns to look.

"Get in," she says. Wrapped in a fleece robe with lace-flower appliqués over her pajama top and jeans, she sighs, "You're here." Pink, fuzzy arms encircle his shoulders; her cold face presses against his neck.

Petting her hair, Ron says, "*Tangzi*, sweet baby, I'm here. It's okay now."

Sitting in the dark, back seat of the Commander's Royal Crown, neither wants to break the spell of quiet safety. Ron tracks back in his mind to yesterday at this same time … he was showering at Mai's apartment, getting ready to search for Rick. Worried for *her* safety, he couldn't be sure if she would be the next target. Not sure if Rick was part of a US-controlled plot or a DPRK–instigated abduction. Not sure if Mai was in on it. Rick's wounds are real enough. The man is a Tiger, hard and able to take punishment, mental and physical.

Upstairs, Sgt. LONG searches through Mai's clothes, staying out of the way of the detectives. Bright lights in the bedroom for the photographer, bright lights in the hall. She throws some underwear into a Polo bag: shoes, clothes laid out for work, some things out of the bathroom, Mai's netbook, purse, phone charger, things she'll need for a day or two. The Commander's putting her under protective custody at LiHua.

Puffs of condensation surround Sergeants GU and LONG's heads, catching bright backlight from the huge, outdoor lights, attracting Ron's attention. Their dark figures cross the street together, walking toward the Royal Crown, casting long shadows.

At the LiHua Hotel, Mai lies on the bed in the single room; Yandong turns out the lights, pulls closed the curtains, and lies on the bed next to her. Without speaking, each woman thinks her own thoughts in the dark, falling asleep as a cold, red day dawns.

***

Gen. MA and the gang drive to Shijiazhuang and by 7AM get breakfast at a truck stop, leaving the target rolled in a quilt in the back of the Tiggo.

***

The ping tracker transmitting from the nano-device imbedded in the concha of Rick's ear had started recording new coordinates and set off an alarm. Poole was the first to notice and called Wright at his apartment in Chaoyang, waking him about 4AM.

They would need two vehicles to carry Wright and his two men, Ed Poole and Frank Choy, as well as the two Marines they'd used before and a ton of gear, including Frank's BMW C-Evolution electric scooter with an agile, hybrid chassis. The stealthy scooter can go 96km, or about sixty miles on a charge, takes only three hours to re-charge and can do 120 kilometers per hour, or 75mph. Charging stations were redundant in Beijing, making the Beemer an ideal mode of short-track travel.

Although they had prepared for this, things always take longer, especially where the government is concerned. By 9AM, they're pulling past the last Ring Road on G4 Jinggang'ao Expressway, heading roughly southwest in two identical, black Ford Expeditions—one tagged US1041, the other US1042. They cut off onto G5, the new expressway, bypassing Baoding.

***

The gang pushes on to Jinzhong, driving the 523 km from Beijing in seven hours, arriving there by lunchtime. One thousand yuan provides the needed privacy to sneak Rick into the hotel elevator. They take two adjoining rooms for one night only: Gen. MA lets his men rest. They have a long trip ahead of them, going to Weinan and on to Wenzhou to board a freighter and travel to United Arab Emirates, only

2,200 km or 1,400 miles from Iran.

Gen. MA fires up his internet account at a local Korean Wi-Fi club, sending a message to his boss RI Hongyi, General Bureau of Surveillance, Chief to General Staff of Korean People's Army. He attaches a JPEG of Martin, the *trophy*, taken with his iPhone.

***

Stopping in Shijiazhuang at a truck-stop, the Beijing Field Office squad grabs some lunch and pushes on. Tracking Rick is a priority beta test on the prototype nano-chip Ed Poole had embedded yesterday in the cartilage of the natural acoustic receiver that is the human ear. He located it in the concha area where it was hidden from view by a fold in the antihelix. It's communicating directly to a satellite and relaying back to Wright's netbook. Poole has spent the day switching to backup scenarios based on signal interruption, developing new protocols in the field. After long periods of no signal, it would suddenly pop back on, giving him a quick laugh.

Around 4PM at Jinzhong, they run past the signal and turn around at the G55 intersection. A couple hours later, they home in on a hotel near the airport where the coordinates ping: no change.

Staying at another hotel down the street, the BFO waits. In the parking garage, Frank Choy unloads his scooter. It's quiet, battery driven, and powerful. He cruises to the underground parking at the gang's hotel. Upstairs, he systematically walks the corridors on each floor with a handheld receiver, looking for Rick's exact location. Ed Poole sets up laser snooping gear, but the oblique angle isn't promising. Before leaving the hotel, Choy records license plate numbers of all the vehicles. Near the elevators, he dismounts and inspects the vehicles closer. He makes notes in his company BlackBerry, takes more pictures, and returns to the squad.

***

In Beijing, Commander GAO removes Lt. GUAN from custody and begins paperwork to have him transferred to the university regiment. Friday morning, November 4, the Commander calls a Bureau Meeting at 08:00 with the new team member.

Sgt. WANG is busy distributing the new Incident Report around the table as the men arrive.

"Who wants to start the briefing? Sgt. WANG?" asks GAO, walking in with a coffee cup and sitting in his usual place.

The sergeant starts reading:

Last week was unusual for the Beijing University Office. During a cooperative interrogation with the Harbin Institute, an American, voluntarily participating, was abducted by a North Korean gang outside our Main Building; two of our guards were taken captive and traded to a trafficking gang in Haidian; Harbin Institute Director DIANGTI had a simulated heart attack and died while in detention; two members of the Harbin team escaped, one is still at large and suspected of leading the gang as well as being involved with the death of the Harbin Chief, and the other turned himself in.

The men cast curious looks toward Lt. GUAN, but he reveals no emotion, as usual. Dressed the same as the first time he arrived back in August—camouflage tee-shirt and brown trousers, dark blue windbreaker, and black, laced combat boots—Lt. GUAN looks steadily at Commander GAO.

Sgt. WANG continues:

Martin Xiansheng was recovered by Beijing PD the next day, Thursday. BPD captured one of the gang and busted the Haidian safehouse, rescuing the two university guards. That night, the gang returned to Beijing University and seized Martin out of his bed in his wife's apartment. At this time, we have no leads. We suspect the Americans are aware of his location, but have no confirmation of this. Communications with Beijing Field Officer Lawrence Wright have bounced.

"*Haode*, Sgt. WANG. And I want to commend all of you for your swift and capable actions these past days," says GAO. "Several lapses in the security plan leading to the second successful abduction are mine. The fact that Martin Taitai's apartment key was not recovered in the trunk of the getaway car was missed. And the possibility of the gang entering her apartment was not considered. Expecting Sgt. LONG to overcome our errors of judgment, one woman against four assailants, was egregious." He scans the faces of the men. His habitual bland expression twists into a grim frown. "Do we have a coroner's report on the DIANGTI autopsy?"

"We are still waiting for that," answers Lt. LIU. "Informally, a needle or puncture mark was found on the throat of the victim and discoloration on the hands consistent with poisoning. The exact toxin used is still being tested. They don't say when their final report will be completed."

"Sgt. WANG will you give us an update on the political response?" asks GAO. Keeping his *dalaoban* informed is a frightening opportunity to have face-time with the boss: it can backfire, adding an internal political dimension to their actions.

"Well," starts WANG, "since notifying Deputy Commander

HUANG about the Martin assault and subsequent developments, we are receiving daily inquiries. Because the guards were recovered, and because Martin Xiansheng withstood the first abduction, no actual damages have occurred affecting Beijing University. Since the second, successful abduction, the university is mired in this situation. The university president's office has been calling daily, also." WANG takes a breath before continuing.

"On the other hand, the suspicious behavior of the Harbin Chief has triggered an investigation of the Harbin Institute, which is outside the scope of our responsibilities here at the university. It is my understanding that Lt. GUAN has been fully cooperating with the Harbin investigation."

"You are right to wonder about the exact status of Lt. GUAN," responds GAO by way of moving on to a new subject. GUAN shifts almost imperceptibly in his seat. "Lt. GUAN and I have had several conversations. After discussion with my superiors, it has been decided to allow him to remain here at the university for the time being. The Harbin Institute is currently without a leader; all the personnel up there are going through a thorough examination. Lt. GUAN will be subjected to the same level of scrutiny as well. I also have put in a request for the transfer of LAO Zengjin as a Senior-grade Technical Specialist. You may recall his assistance here last August.

"I've found Lt. GUAN to be extremely loyal to the Third Department. He's made grave errors, to be sure—his blind loyalty to his late superior officer being his most egregious, a lesson to us all—and for which he readily accepts responsibility and has righted his thinking. He has tremendous experience and training, which our Office will gain through his addition. His serious demeanor and punctilious attention to detail is exemplary. Now is the time to raise any questions or objections to this arrangement."

No one has any comments. Lt. GUAN bends his head minutely in a mute signal of gratitude toward the Commander.

November 4

The gang drives six hours to Weinan. At the Tongyi Hotel, Gen. MA checks his email.

November 4   To: MA Minho   From: RI Hongyi
Subject: Re: Martin

ENCRYPTED: Contact our pupil EU Sun at Xi'an.

At 8PM, EU Sun, another North Korean agent liaising with Iran, arrives in a new, gold Toyota Land Cruiser, dressed in a silk suit and camel's hair overcoat, tailored in Gangnamu District, Seoul, and accompanied by his personal assistant, LEE Han-Joo, and driver, GONG. He's been nearby in Xi'an working on a deal to trade DPRK WMD—weapons of mass destruction—to the Triad in exchange for relics looted from the Terracotta Warriors Monument.

Gen. MA asks, "You have information for me on this relics-for-*plowshares* deal Dalaoban wants me to focus on?" That's twisted code for weapons. The Koreans are not without a sense of irony or devoid of humor. Even if the humor is submerged. Like laughing without laughing.

"We will combine efforts. I have brought plow ... *samples*. You are undersupplied?" asks EU Sun.

"We won't need them. Unless we have time to trade."

EU Sun's face doesn't react. "Show me the Meiguoren."

Rick Martin has soaked the sheet and shivers while EU Sun inspects him head to toe. "This precious person needs medicine." Looking past the Beijing and Tianjin gang men, DONG and SHENG, EU Sun calls out to the Chinese-Korean agent Sang-Bo, "Go with my driver and bring back a Chinese medicine practitioner. *NOW!*"

Turning back to the Chinese gang men, "*Feichang ganxie ni*, your services have been invaluable to our operation. What is the arrangement for your payment?"

The Triad members SHENG and DONG return to Beijing that night, taking their Tiggo with them, no longer needed now that EU Sun has arrived with his own car, driver, and guns.

***

While the gang conducts business around him, Rick fades in and out. Someone covers him with a soft blanket and presses a cloth to his forehead, wiping the clammy sweat running into his eyes. A faint light, like a blur in a black tube, excites his instincts.

***

The BFO rises before daybreak; when the ping alarm sounds, they rally and follow behind. In Weinan, Qianjin Road is lined with mini-plazas backed by legions of apartment buildings. Wright thinks it looks a lot like Chengfu Road in Beijing. Tongyi Hotel, in the middle of the block, is a big inn catering to Asian businessmen. Across the wide boulevard, he sees two more hotels. They split up and take a room at each—on the top floors where they can look into the front of the Tongyi.

They set up gear at each hotel. A laser receiver, looking like an ear doctor's otoscope, fitted with female threads, screws onto a tripod and is pointed at the windows opposite. All this is guided by software, scanning and recording on quadrants. Choy rolls out his scooter onto the wide boulevard, and parks in the mini-mall next to the Tongyi. As before, he prowls the corridors, searching for Rick's signal, trying not to look suspicious.

November 5

By the next morning, Martin's fever has worsened. EU Sun worries that their prize prisoner might die on them, and sends the men to find Western medicine for Western man. They return in a few hours with an American on a visiting contract with a nearby clinic, Dr. Joshua Braithwaite, a swarthy man with missionary zeal. Those folks are granted visas only if they keep their heads down and don't make news. EU Sun figures he'll fix it and keep quiet.

EU Sun contacts Dalaoban RI Hongyi for further instructions. RI contacts the Iranians for final arrangements, waiting a day to hear back.

***

Wright and his men spend the day in Weinan running the laser software. Choy returns to the Tongyi to surveil the parking lot, recording all the vehicles and taking pictures of those nearest the elevators. Returning to their hotel, he uploads the data packets to the corresponding DHS 104 office in the States for analysis.

By Sunday morning, his US contact, Alice Nolan, replies, "Keep watching."

They check out and into two more hotels that have a view of the back of the Tongyi. Frank Choy has been receiving fugitive signals, obstructed by a hidden barrier in the sectional concrete construction. The hotel is a warren of rooms and annexes going in all directions.

Over lunch on Sunday, November 6, Poole and Choy take a break from the squad and meet in the dining room of the Tongyi. Islands of tropical plants separate groups of booths and tables, creating private corners here and there for business contacts near the international airport. Their favorite booth is in the back next to the kitchen. From there, they can survey the entire room without looking obvious. The tall American with the Asian man attracts no unusual interest in the immense hall as they peruse the menu.

"Hey look, pizza," says Poole.

"You should know better, here?"

"Yeah, you're right. We should find a Pizza Hut in town."

"We're here now, Ed."

"So rational, man, thanks for dialing me in. So, what do you think about the signal? Can we be sure he's here?"

Silence for a minute as they consider the possibility while scanning the color photographs of food in the oversize menu.

"I'm getting a club sandwich and French fries," continues Choy, looking up at the *fuwuyuan*.

"I guess I'll have the hot pot," pointing at the color picture. "*Yige*" [for one], says Poole.

She tallies up their bill, and they pay first.

"I mean, how do we know he isn't dead and we're just getting empty signals from the rubbish?"

"I checked the rubbish," says Choy.

"So rational, I like that. But you know what I mean. He could be dead for all we know," persists Poole.

"I've thought the same thing. The punishment that guy took. My god."

"Yeah, I know."

Their food comes, and they eat for a while in silence, gazing around the room, noticing things, thinking about Rick's signal.

"Let's go over this," starts Choy. "The main ping going into Wright's system has remained constant since day before yesterday. What can that mean? It means Rick Martin is right here, not moving. Is that because this is where they want to end up? I don't think so; they're on the way to Iran to trade him for the reward: to the coast to catch a freighter or overland. So what's stopping their movement? They could have found the chip in his ear."

"Not likely.... He could be sick."

"Yeah, that's my next thought. The guy was in rough shape to begin with. How much more of that do you think it would take?"

"Take to what?" asks Poole.

"Before it's too much, he dies in transit. It's happened, kidnap for ransom. They don't mean to, I'm sure. The Wikileaks cable says they want him alive."

"Okay," continues Poole, "maybe they stop and get him a doctor."

"Totally rational, Poole, I'm proud of you."

"Shut up."

"Just getting the captive in and out of here would be a major deal. Cost them something," muses Choy. "Easier to bring doctor to him."

After lunch, Choy cruises the Tongyi parking structure, taking more pictures which he uploads to Nolan at DHS 104 in Fort Belvoir, Virginia.

November 6   To: DHS104   From: BFO
Subject: 11-06-Data

ENCRYPTED: Looking for vehicle; see anything?

***

Sunday November 6, Rick's fever breaks. Slowly, he focuses on the sound of someone talking or reading. He rolls to one side, closer to the sound of a man speaking English, reading from the Bible. Rick makes a small sound, "Shhh, man."

The hirsute American whispers back "I'm here for you, shhh."

Off and on during the afternoon, between delirious dreams, Rick begs Braithwaite to take a message to Mai and writes it in the book.

The next morning, Monday, November 7, the gang leaves Weinan, without waking the American doctor.

On the road, RI Hongyi calls EU Sun to tell him transportation is being arranged via an oil tanker owned by the Islamic Republic of Iran Shipping Lines (IRISL)—routed from Vladivostok, Russia, with a load of steel to Wenzhou to pick up Rick Martin.

The tanker *Lantana* is prepped to leave, clearing Golden Horn Bay on Monday November 7, scheduled to arrive in Wenzhou on

Sunday, November 13. It will stay in Wenzhou for two days, departing for Abu Dhabi on Tuesday, November 15.

"I don't like this schedule," starts MA.

"It's not our job to question," says EU Sun.

"We should have a fallback." The older, more experienced agent worries about things going wrong and has given up long ago on the idea of perfection.

Gen. MA met EU Sun at Pyongyang Archaeology School where she was a brilliant student on an exchange program from a Chinese university. He had cultivated her, manipulating her loneliness into an attachment to him and the DPRK. Back then, in 2002, she was all female. Now, she dresses and acts like a man. It's beyond his understanding.

"What do you suggest?" asks EU Sun. The younger agent trusts his teacher, but is conflicted about not following orders from Pyongyang.

"The Americans," says MA. "Make them pay."

"We don't talk to Americans. That's for Dalaoban RI and the great leaders," says EU Sun, falling back on policy.

"Call RI, ask him."

Rick has been riding in the boot, listening to but not understanding their talk in Korean.

November 7

November 7   To: BFO   From: DHS104
Subject: RE: 11-06-Data

ENCRYPTED: 2011, Gold Metallic, Toyota Land Cruiser

By morning, Choy has a possible description of the gang's

vehicle. At 7:15AM the ping alarm starts the day; they're optimistic they can home in on Rick. Everyone's eyeballs are on the road.

When the gang abruptly leaves Weinan in the early morning, the BFO squad members are eager for a change in course. The reawakened ping alarm sets juices flowing again, spurring them to silently congratulate themselves for their patience and belief in Rick: that his suffering might be for some greater good.

Wright and Poole take off immediately with one of the Marines driving. The rest catch up after checking out. They travel west toward Xi'an, taking the G40 south, managing the turn without losing them. They immediately climb into foothills dotted with small villages.

Before Shanyang, they take the G70 cut-off around 8AM, where the ping exits the expressway at a truck stop. Wright's group stays at the onramp while Choy's grabs some street food for breakfast, spotting the Land Cruiser at a mini-mall. Choy captures more pictures of the gang exiting a restaurant, but no sight of Martin. The second Marine transfers a case of bottled water into the lead vehicle, hands off their food, and the caravan resumes.

The ping slows down to about sixty kilometers an hour, 40 mph, following the Dan Jiang River through a long valley. Keeping an eye on the gold Land Cruiser, the BFO hangs back behind a row of trucks. It feels like they're crawling. They cut across the river and start climbing again, up and down the Xing Kai Ling ridges separating the Dan Jiang drainage from the greater Han Shui River at the foot of the Wudang Shan Mountains.

By 3PM, at Zhangwan, the ping putters off at G209. Poole follows the Land Cruiser to a Korean hotel, Hanjian Dolo, in an industrial strip. The BFO squad passes it and checks into the next hotel.

That night, they have the gold Land Cruiser staked out and tagged with a beacon. They take shifts all night in the hotel parking garage, sitting in their vehicle across the aisle from the Land Cruiser, a dash-mounted video camera focused on the hatch set to record on a motion sensor.

Wright is on shift at 6:45AM when the elevator doors open and he glimpses Rick for the first time in four days of pursuit. He jumps to action, waking up his netbook and selecting the live feed from the dash-cam.

Rick is in a wheelchair between two Asians, head drooping onto his chest, dressed in a jogging suit and knit cap. Coming down the stairs are three more Asians: Gen. MA, accompanied by a young man and woman. Two men stoop to cut ties on Rick's ankles and wrists. He offers no resistance as they lift and load him into the back, where he curls up like a dog next to the collapsed wheelchair. The elevator doors open again. A man ferries bags into the back with Rick, climbs into the driver's seat, and backs out right in front of Wright.

Poole is already up and scrolling through his emails when the ping goes off. He flips to the dash-cam feed while pulling on his boots. "Look," he calls to the men, "here's Martin." Poole's phone rings.

"Did you catch any of the action?" asks Wright.

"Yeah."

"Okay, they're moving. Let's go," says Wright. He uploads the media to his netbook. When the squad arrives, he's already sending it to Nolan.

The drive through the foothills the next morning is torturously slow, creeping along at 60 kph, up and down and around, crisscrossing the Han Shui River. G70 veers southeast at a well-watered stretch, where dozens of smaller waterways converge farther downstream at the Yangtze and Chang Jiang Rivers. The Land Cruiser stops at a truck stop near Zaoyang for half an hour around lunchtime before moving again.

The scenery is outstanding, but the squad barely notices. Poole continues to work the tracking software while the Marines drive. Wright communicates with the office, reading official emails and sending replies. Choy plays a gladiator game on his personal iPhone.

My Husband Is Coming Back— *Wode Laogong Hui Jia*

On Monday, Mai and Sgt. LONG pedal to the International Building and crowd into ZHANG's office.

"*Feichang ganxie ni*, Ms. ZHANG, the fruit basket was delicious." says Mai.

Ms. ZHANG nods appreciatively, *"Bukeqi."*

"This is Sgt. LONG ... Yandong, *zhe shi wode laoban*, Ms. ZHANG ... They are still looking for Rick. Commander GAO says he spoke with you about all this."

"*Xiexie*, Martin Taitai, I appreciate the update. Do they expect to find him soon?" ZHANG asks.

"Any day, I'm sure, he will come walking back. Commander GAO has committed to finding him, and Martin Xiansheng is a resourceful man. The BPD caught a Korean gang member. And they rescued the two guards."

"What do you know about that?" asks ZHANG, slipping her phone into the top drawer, under her computer keyboard, and leaning closer to Mai.

"It was a Beijing gang in Wudaokou. They were going to sell

their organs to a local hospital."

"*Zhende.*"

Ms. ZHANG gravely regards Mai, "This is very serious, Martin. Have you retained a lawyer?"

"No, do I need one?" asks Mai.

"This is very serious. You should get advice," says Ms. ZHANG.

"*Zhende*! Well … can you recommend anyone?"

"I don't know, but I will make calls for you. Take whatever time you need. We want your husband found as soon as possible and returned to your home."

The next stop is the American Embassy, where Mai has an 11AM appointment, made online over the weekend. In the lobby, Mai checks her mobile at the desk while Sgt. LONG reads a book. A young, Asian man leads her to an interior conference room, equipped with a PC set to a Skype link. Too restless to sit, she inspects a rack of embassy literature.

At 11:10, the door opens and an older woman enters, greeting Mai cheerfully and extending her hand, *"Duibuqi,* Mrs. Martin, for making you wait. I'm Marianne Willits, Homeland Security and Embassy liaison."

"*Bukeqi*, pleased to meet you, Ms. Willits."

"We have a Skype link on standby with your husband's supervisor at Homeland Security. Feel free to ask any questions. We want to help you in every way possible." Turning the monitor toward Mai, another woman's face lights up and begins talking.

"Good day, Mrs. Martin. I'm Alice Nolan." She looks to be about Mai's age, early forties with a plain, businesslike appearance; her long dark hair sweeps into a ponytail above a crisp white shirt, buttoned up to her throat and relieved by a silk foulard tie.

"Yes, hello, Ms. Nolan." It's difficult for Mai to sit still. She's bursting with anger at Homeland Security and looks away from the screen.

"I understand you're angry with us. I get that."

"What do you get?" exclaims Mai.

"It must be agonizing, being left out and lied to."

"Duh," replies Mai adolescently. "Where's my husband?"

"He's in China. We're tracking him."

"How?"

"There's a tracking device in his body," answers Nolan forthrightly.

"No! He's a wreck. I can tell you, I saw his body. The bruises and burns on his groin. He's blind, for God's sake! Has he been trained for this? Brainwashing and torture? Is this a game for you guys? It's real for Rick. And for me. And what are you doing? Sitting on your asses, collecting *ping* data, and *analyzing stuff.*"

"You should retain an attorney, Mrs. Martin. We have a list of attorneys in Beijing."

Ms. Willits slides the list, printed on Embassy letterhead, toward Mai who registers it but asks the screen, "Why do I need a lawyer? That doesn't make sense. I've done nothing wrong."

"The criminal justice system in China is quite different from back home. Have you visited our website? We have a section for victims of crimes. You have to start by making a police report. Have you done this yet?"

"I'm doing this? What are you guys doing?"

Nolan replies without replying, "Having an attorney working for you will allow you timely access to updates and information. Please, we want to help, Mrs. Martin."

"Don't take this personal, but I've never gotten *any* help from Homeland Security. You dragged me into this mess through Rick, using my presence here as a pretext for this insane operation. I had to hire my own security just to protect me from you and your crazy scheme."

"You are a smart, resourceful woman, Mrs. Martin. I can see why your husband is devoted to you."

"Cut the crap, Nolan."

"No, seriously, I know the details of the situation in August. I admire the way you managed things on your end."

Mai makes a disgusted sound, slumping back into her chair, arms crossed over her chest.

Nolan continues, "Once you make an official police report, bring us a copy, please. This is a very complicated crime in which you two are enmeshed. The FBI will be involved. We are interested in following your progress. Please keep us in the loop. Especially if you get an attorney— we can get the FBI in touch with them," concludes Nolan. The connection blanks out.

"How do I get in touch with you?" Mai asks the blue screen.

"Here's a list of lawyers," says Willits. "We don't endorse any of them. And a brochure *Victims of Crimes in China.*"

Mai scans the list and comes upon the name of the man Ron introduced her to at the 798 Art District, Alan Spires.

Waving at Sgt. LONG, Mai says, "*Zouba.*" Blinking in the bright sunshine outside the embassy, Mai hails a cab and calls Ron.

"*Wei, nihao* Mai," answers Ron. "Are you done already?"

"Yeah, I want to come by your office. Can you tell the *shifu* how to find it?"

***

Ron's assistant, Lily, enters the room carrying a tray with coffee things, dressed in a short skirt and improbable shoes. When the American client got off the elevator next to the reception desk, accompanied by a striking Chinese officer, the office staff was seized with curiosity. Lily volunteered to get through the door with the ruse of refreshments.

"*Xiexie*, Lily," says Ron.

Mai says, "*Nihao*, Lily," and gives her a big smile, trying to look into her eyes. The young woman looks down, whispering, "*Hao*," gazing at Mai from behind feathery bangs, inspecting her dress and demeanor before turning her surreptitious gaze to Sgt. LONG, setting down the tray and leaving them. Back in the outer office, she makes her report to the women and they discuss Mai's appearance in detail. They conclude she looks like, so must be, an American movie star traveling with a PLA bodyguard. She's an important client for TSC, and they're gratified to finally get a look at her.

"How old is she? She looks thirteen," says Mai.

"She has a master's degree in law from Haidian University, and is twenty-seven," says Ron matter-of-factly.

"Huh," says Mai. "And what does she do?"

"Today, she's working for you. She's been interfacing with Capt. LI and Sgt. WANG on the investigation. Do you remember tracking Rick with GPS?" Mai nods. "That was her; she was the technician on the other end of the phone." While he and Mai converse in English, Ron's gaze drifts to Sgt. LONG, standing by the door, holding a cup and saucer of coffee. Yandong's English is limited, and she doesn't follow. Her eyes lock on his for a moment, trying to fit Ronald ZHAO into a profile. Ron scans the woman for clues as to her ability to follow their conversation. Mai's voice pulls them both to her. "I need a lawyer, Ron. My boss and the embassy both say so. What about Alan Spires? Your client at 798. He's on their list."

"Yes, he would be a good choice. I'll call him for you. Do you want him to accompany you to the police station today?" While Ron looks up Spires in his address book, Mai turns to the bright cityscape below: windy and clear today. Looking back at him for a minute, her gaze is attracted to a giant credenza covered with memorabilia and photos.

"Sorry Mai, he's not available, but I can accompany you."

"I thought I needed a lawyer for this," she says.

Following her gaze, he picks up an official-looking hat with gold braid and patent leather bill, sets it on his head and strikes a pose, arms out from the elbows.

She can't help but grin, which makes her blush on a day like this. "Oh yes, Police Commissioner ZHAO of Hong Kong …"

"At your service," He smiles. "That was my life for nineteen years."

"Nineteen! Not twenty?"

"Yeah, I joined in 1991," Ron says, putting the hat back on the shelf. "I told you that I retired last year … when I got divorced and moved to Beijing."

"Yes, yes you did. I guess you lost some pension … What is this?" she asks pointing to a group picture of men in black combat suits and holding machine guns. A few in the front row, down on one knee, are holding knives.

"My squad, that's me, right there," he says pointing at one of the men in the back row. Special Forces for two years. Marine Police, here," Ron steps back a pace and holds another framed picture for Mai to see, "five years before I traded it all in for a desk job and a promotion."

"Let's sit here where we can look at the city," he says, changing the subject. He gestures to the other side of the office and a round table with stacks of papers meticulously lined out in a checkerboard. "This is the training project they hired me to do." In front of the big glass windows are a couple comfortable chairs.

Mai sits where directed, closest to his desk, where he sets his cell phone. He swings around to look at Mai, "How did it go at the embassy?"

"Sucked."

He's used to her ... direct but vague speech ... by now and simply follows with specific questions, patient as a seasoned detective should be. "What did they say about Rick?"

"He's here in China, and they're tracking him."

Ron shares her alarm. "How?"

"I'm hungry," Mai announces standing, capriciously plopping his peaked hat on her head. "Can we have lunch now?"

His heart aches for her as much as for himself. "Where do you want to go?" he asks tenderly. "There are a couple really nice restaurants in our building—Chinese, Italian, Japanese ..." He can't help but think she looks adorable in the hat.

"Let's do Italian. I'd love some pasta and a glass of wine," she decides. Looking at Ron, sitting behind his desk with the Beijing skyline wrapping around behind him, he looks executive and competent. *I'm lucky. Rick's strength holds me up and banishes my worries and anguished dreams. Waking up in the night, when I reach out to him, I imagine he's there, snuggling and pulling the duvet close. And Ron's here, working for me.*

Riding in the elevator, feeling secure and safe, Mai clasps him around the waist. "They have a tiny device concealed in his body," says Mai, looking up at his face and finally answering Ron's question.

Sgt. LONG stares at the floor numbers lighting up as they ascend to one of the top levels.

The *fuwuyuan* seats them at a huge round table near tall windows where they can enjoy the view, looking down on the busy metropolis, the Forbidden City complex glimpsed in the distance, between more tall buildings.

Visiting the washroom, the *xishoujian*, with Yandong, Mai is drawn to a tall vase of exotic flowers—ginger, orchids, and bird-of-paradise—on a stone base reflecting in the black tile walls and smoked glass. She inspects her image, touching the lump she still has on her forehead, inspecting the cuts that are still raw on her cheek and chin. She considers the idea that Rick is out there somewhere, being brutalized, while she has tortellini.

The lunch is superb. Ron attends to every detail. Mai is morose and distracted, poking her pasta with the fork. Yandong experiments with Italian cuisine, ordering veal scaloppini at Ron's suggestion.

"Let's try to analyze what happened and where Rick might be," suggests Ron.

"What do you mean?" asks Mai, sipping on a glass of Valpolicella, staring into it like an oracle.

"What do we know? North Koreans want to collect a bounty by delivering Rick to the Iranians. So, how would that look? What route?

What method?" The *fuwuyuan* brings tiramisu with tiny cups of strong, sweet coffee to finish the meal.

"Of course, I'm assuming you want to find him—am I right?"

"Better than the alternative: sitting around doing nothing while Rick kills himself for Homeland Security," answers Mai, staring into the distant horizon.

"So, Homeland Security knew all along?"

"Yes, and that low life, Wright, sat there all night, laughing at us. The whole thing was a big operation of theirs to get intel on Koreans here in Beijing." She remembers the punishing bruising and burns on Rick's body: below his waist and inside his thighs, from cigarettes, boots, and Taser. It was unbelievable. In a low, rasping voice, "Rick was a willing participant." *Unbelievable.*

"*Zhende*.... And you knew, too, all this time?"

"No! Well, I suspected, but I couldn't get it out of him, and then I guessed the rest," she says, looking at Ron's stern and handsome face. *Does he believe me?*

"Are you lying to me, Mai?"

"Ask me anything; I'll tell you anything. I'm hiding nothing. Nothing!"

The one thing he wants to know, he's afraid to ask. He can see she's keyed up to find Rick and angry at Wright. Her adrenaline fired, super-charged feelings look like love to Ron. Love for Rick. All he can do is stand to one side, watch Mai, and worry.

"We have Commander GAO working for us, and Capt. LI. And you have me."

"I'm glad you're here. I need you now more than ever."

"You bet, Mai, I'm in your corner."

She looks at his concerned face a long minute. "I'm going to remember these times we've had together. We had something special."

"We still could," he says.

"Everything is against us," she continues rationally.

***

At the Sanlitun Police Station, Ron accompanies the women to translate and for moral support.

"*Wei, nihao*, LI, this is ZHAO," says Ron by phone to Capt. LI. "Can we park at your place? ... Dui, Martin Taitai is coming in to make an official report ... *Ha-ha, Da-da.*" [Good, good, Yes, yes.]

"He says to go to the information desk on the first floor. They'll direct us to Capt. LI's department."

Capt. LI meets them in a room only big enough for a few chairs and a desk. A lonely window looks out onto the busy East Second Ring Road a couple blocks away from her language school and the police station. Accompanying him is Lt. WU and another officer, bringing six into this meeting. The two female officers recognize each other from the night in the conference room at the university, nod and smile. Ron stays busy translating for everyone, and the meeting proceeds slowly.

Capt. LI starts off saying, "Thank you, Martin Taitai, for coming in so promptly to make your report. We will try to make it as short as possible. Will you write down in your own words the actions of November 1, starting with the meeting at Beijing University? Leave nothing out. We translate your statement into Chinese, and you certify the accuracy." This first part takes about forty-five minutes. Ron and Capt. LI discuss each word. Finally getting a Chinese version Ron approves, he explains it to Mai for her agreement. Once that section is completed they go through the same steps for November 2, the next day, when Rick was abducted again, from her apartment.

"We have collected some evidence from the van on November 2. One of the gang is still in custody. He is not likely to be released before the trial. The prosecutor's office will be looking at all this and making a decision as to whether they will go forward with a sentencing trial in about thirty days or not at all. Has Martin Taitai retained an attorney?"

Ron replies, "Not yet, but she is actively seeking to retain one as soon as possible."

"*Haode*, we are not responsible to notify Martin Taitai about the progress of the case," adds LI.

"In the meantime, is it possible for me to act as her representative?" asks Ron .

"Yes, you may do that. Lt. WU, do you have a contact form that ZHAO Xiansheng can complete?"

"What kind of evidence is there?" Mai wants to know.

"The person MA Minho's prints were found on an empty liquor bottle; from the hutong, we have your husband's bloodstained clothes."

That's all they have?! thinks Mai, alarmed.

"There's one last step: identifying the gang. We can do this by photograph. Lt. WU, can you bring a laptop in here with pictures of the gang?" finishes LI.

Lt. WU has prepared a PowerPoint with the gang pictures arranged like a line-up. Mai identifies Gen. MA, Chief DIANGTI, and Lt. GUAN as the men she saw in the conference room. She recognizes SHENG from the street, but none of the others.

"Thank you for your time, Martin Taitai. Please notify us if you decide to leave the country, although there is no restriction on your movement. The prosecutor's department will not need to call you as a witness as is common in your country," explains Capt. LI.

"What is Beijing PD doing on this case? Are you working with Commander GAO?" Mai wants to know.

"We do not dispense legal information to victims. We urge Martin Taitai to retain a lawyer and direct her questions to him. We know about the bounty on Martin Xiansheng, from Commander GAO at the university. This gang continues to be a problem for us and you, and there is no assurance that they or others won't try to apprehend you, Martin Taitai, whether you remain here in Beijing or return to California."

***

"Is there somewhere we can decompress?" asks Mai in the elevator down to the underground parking.

"I think I know a place nearby," answers Ron.

Mai stares out the window at the street scene as they drive. The late afternoon sun is cold, and a fitful wind stirs up the remaining leaves on the nearly bare poplars. Sgt. LONG quietly texts her husband: "还在市中心" —still dwntwn—from the backseat.

The Park Avenue turns into a small alley, creeping toward a guarded and gated entrance. Ron glances at Mai. "This is my flat. C'mon up."

The guard waves Ron into a courtyard with a yawning opening leading to subterranean parking. The elevator takes them to the 22nd floor, opening onto a stone-tiled lobby.

"*Wei, nihao*, Mama," says Ron into his mobile. "I'm bringing up guests."

First one door and then a second, Ron unlocks them with numerous keys and deadbolts. Mai doesn't notice a pinhole camera fitted into the ornamental molding of the interior fascia adjacent to the entrance.

Ron's mother greets them at the door, curious to meet her son's friends. She recognizes Mai from the theatre and is surprised to see Sgt. LONG. Ron takes the women on a tour of his lavish loft, divided into private and public living spaces. His mother has her own apartment, with her own entry door, connecting to the rest of Ron's flat. The tour ends in the sitting room where overstuffed, contemporary leather armchairs and silk upholstered sofas make conversation nooks overlooking the Beijing sunset.

"Please sit and be comfortable. I'll get us something to drink. I have some new Beaujolais, Mai. Does that interest you?"

"Oh! Beaujolais! Perfect, Ron."

In the spotless black-stone and stainless-steel kitchen, Ron's mother asks, "Is this the same woman you have been seeing, Ronnie?"

"*Dui*, Mama," answers Ron while retrieving leaded-glass goblets from a top cabinet. "Fix us some snacks, please?"

"Is this woman married, Ronnie? And who is the other one, the soldier?"

"It's complicated, Mama," says Ron, giving his mother a quick kiss on the top of her head. "Where are the trays?"

Sighing loudly, she assembles a beautiful assortment of fruit, cookies, and nuts. She makes a flower nosegay out of the elaborate arrangement on the dining room table, a tiny spray of yellow orchids in an antique, blue glass bottle.

The wine takes the edge off the stressful day. Mai unwinds, kicking off her low boots and stretching along one of the brocade couches. Yandong sits stiffly on another opposite. She helps herself to a piece of fruit with one hand while hanging onto the stemmed glass of wine with the other.

"This is *tai haole*, Ron," sighs Mai. From where she sits, opposite a large, gold-marbled mirror, she examines her face from side to side, touching her sore cheek. Digging into her tiny purse, she finds some dark lipstick.

"Mama, this is an important client for TSC. Sit here with us a minute," Ron gives his mother a pleading look.

"Alright, Ronnie, for you," she says in Cantonese, her native tongue from Hong Kong, sitting next to him on a leather couch.

"Wine, Mama?" Ron pours her a goblet and they sit while looking out over the city, side by side. Staring up at Mai's bruised face, over the rim of the glass; she turns to Ron, "Where is her husband?"

"He's been taken by North Koreans."

"Have they contacted her for a ransom?"

"No, they took him right out of their family bed."

Mama ZHAO pats Mai's hand, resting on a brocade cushion, and returns to the kitchen.

"What do you want to do, Mai?" asks Ron, turning in his seat slightly to look at her reclining figure, resting on silk embroidered pillows, her long legs elegantly crossed, sipping the garnet-red wine, her intense eyes focused on him, backlit by the bright sky.

"I dunno," setting the goblet on a low, glass-and-wrought-iron table, stretching her arms behind her head and leaning back into the pillows.

Suddenly, the sun slips into low clouds, and light drains out of the room. Ron reaches for a remote and turns up the recessed lights around the crown molding and wall sconces.

"You need some art on the walls, Ron," says Mai, changing the subject.

"What do you suggest?"

"Let's go art shopping for a distraction."

"Want to stay for dinner? Mama? What's for dinner?" asks Ron.

ZHAO Taitai surprises everyone, turning out a fabulous but simple repast. With Ron's help, Mai gets her talking about orchids. The two disappear after dinner to inspect flower spikes. Ron and Yandong follow them into the mother's apartment. Yandong listens and looks, she's overawed by the luxury of Ron's flat. Ron enjoys seeing Mai in his home. Mama ZHAO is happy to see her son happy. And Mai, well, she's stopped feeling things a few days ago.

Later, Ron takes the women downstairs to the street, and the guard calls a taxi. Standing in the dark, watching the red taillights recede around the corner, Ron zips the collar of his jacket and turns the other way, walking briskly in the cold evening air, thinking about Mai and Rick and wondering about the future.

During the ride back to Wudaokou, the women both fall asleep, leaning together in the back seat.

***

Traffic increases as the BFO approaches Wuhan. The ping travels around the downtown area, finally stopping for the day at the

Blue Sky Hotel right off the expressway near Ezhou. The next closest hotel is about a kilometer away on Jiangbi Road.

***

Rick's mind has been sinking into periods of confused delirium, losing its grip on what is real and not real. Indistinct figures and faces of his captors hover in the blurred vision of his returning sight, but he doesn't trust his own eyes anymore. He doesn't care. He's out of it.

Han-Joo tries to get him to eat, but he is either revolted by the smell or cramping from hunger. She coaxes some sips of soup broth past his lips and wipes away his sweat and grime.

***

Wright's vehicle, moving smoothly at 88kph, or 55mph, leads the way, nosing forward, gradually passing slower traffic through a basin of tributaries and rivulets of the Chang Jiang River on G70, and stopping several hours later in Jiuang at the G56 interchange.

November 8

Mai works the next half day, catching up. She plans to go to Art District 798 with Ron to have a meeting with Alan Spires later. Every day, she's been thinking Rick will come walking into her life again, nightmare over. What else can she do, her calls are being ignored—*don't call us, we'll call you*—and her computer is still being monitored.

Mai has been staying at the LiHua guesthouse on campus under protective custody for the past five days. She dresses in the camel sweater with a deep chiffon ruffle that drapes like a short skirt over pants that Ron bought her in August and goes into the dining room. Sgt. LONG is waiting for her at the bike rack near the front entrance and accompanies her to the office. After a half day working, Sgt. LONG escorts Mai to the *ditie zhan* and waits until the sleek doors enclose Mai who waves *baibai* through the window as the train noiselessly pulls away.

Mai takes the subway to Dongzhimen, the same way as going to language class. When she exits the station, she walks across the valet parking in front of the Ginza mall and texts Ron: "@ ginz."

Ron drives under the canopy, stops, gets halfway out of the driver's side and hails Mai. The valet holds the door for her and she steps into the Buick with Ron. The midday traffic is light, and Ron slips through the Chaoyang neighborhoods, heading east.

Ron distracts himself with a call to Spires's office. "He's made a spot for us at 4PM."

He parks near a cluster of renovated factory buildings surrounding an enormous plaza anchored by a gargantuan brick smokestack. A fashion shoot is being assembled at the foot of the big stack. A black curtain and now the model appear with a camera man and more hands hurrying to catch the late afternoon sun.

Spires's office is on two floors of the building. The ground-floor office is for his mistress/girlfriend Annie, an art dealer, to use. All the upstairs offices have a view of the now-extinguished sunset. Above the covered walkway, leading to the end of the building, a serene, golden moon rises beyond a black smokestack. Where an urn planted with a loquat tree marks the door, Annie stands, welcoming them, "*Kuan Yin cha, Martin Taitai, ZHAO Xiansheng?"*

"*Xiexie,*" murmurs Mai.

Painted canvases are stacked two or three deep against the walls. Pedestals of carved or cast figures and non-objective designs surround Spires's desk. Mai and Ron squeeze into comfortable leather chairs beside the art and artifacts of Spires's uncontrollable habit of buying and selling art.

"What a lovely coincidence you are here after meeting you this summer. Welcome, indeed, Mrs. Martin." Spires greets them, standing, in a crisp, starched dress shirt with cuffs, showing gold cufflinks, and set off by polka-dot suspenders holding up his Armani trousers.

"I've been told by several people, including the US Embassy and the Beijing police, that I need an attorney," starts Mai.

"Yes, things are different here than at home in the US, Mrs. Martin. For one thing, I need you to appoint me as your agent. That allows me to receive communications from the prosecution before the trial."

"What trial? They've only caught one guy, not the leader of the gang. And, they're sending notifications to Mr. ZHAO now."

"It would be better to have Spires involved," says Ron. "I can still receive the notices. But Spires will be able to take actions."

"Like what? And what will this cost me?" asks Mai, always the American, wanting to know price and details up front.

"TSC will take care of the initial retainer, Mai," assures Ron.

"One possible outcome is that the defendants will bargain for their lives by offering compensation to the victims," continues Spires. "This is commonplace in China. Trading execution for life in prison, let's say. Of course, there would be a fee as a percent of the amount. Do you know anything about the other victim's family? He was from Harbin, right?"

"Who are you talking about, the dead man from Harbin, DIANGTI?" Mai asks, confused.

"I have their contact info at the office. I'll have Lily call you," says Ron. "How do you want to structure this deal?"

"Hey, I'm here, answer my question. What deal?"

Alan regards Mai condescendingly, "If I can get the DIANGTI widow's representation, we could assign a split of the fees, Mrs. Martin. This is somewhat speculative at the moment, since they have not concluded the investigation, caught or prosecuted your husband's tormentors."

Annoyed, Mai gets up and looks around at the art. *This business of needing a lawyer is a waste of time and isn't helping find Rick.*

Turning to Ron, Spires continues his discussion. "We can take Mrs. Martin's retainer out of the widow's portion. TSC can locate and pre-negotiate with the widow using your fixer in Harbin."

"You are confident they will catch them?" asks Mai.

"I can try to get the best arrangement for you. And ... the crimes of which you are a victim are of interest to the American FBI."

"Yes, the Embassy wants your contact info for the FBI," interjects Mai again, fed up. "I'm going downstairs to look at Annie's gallery. Do you still need me?"

The inside of Annie's room looks a lot like Spires's, with large, unframed canvases and panels in different styles leaning against the walls. In the middle, a long, felt-covered artist's table is littered with dozens of paintings on paper or calligraphy. She has a corner office with a high-style sofa for clients. It's curved and plush like a blue-green wave in the ocean.

Mai sits on it, "I love this," reclining. "Ooh, so comfortable."

Annie turns to Mai, offering her a thimble of cha hua, "You two look like a couple. Has he asked you to be his mistress?"

Surprised, Mai reacts, "What? No, what does that mean, to be his mistress? You mean *girlfriend?*"

"*Bu dui*. Ron likes you, I can see that. He's going to ask you. He's a Chinese man, isn't he? I know what he's thinking."

"*Zhende*, you know what he thinks?"

"My friend Alan can write a contract for you."

"Like what?"

"Like, how much paid per month, for how long."

"*Zhende* … My husband is coming back," states Mai unequivocally, her own agenda suddenly seen in chiaroscuro.

Mai and Annie regard each other with piqued interest.

Adding hot water to the teapot, Annie continues, "People who disappear, but not for ransom, are prisoners and not likely to return … or maybe after many years of not knowing. That is the Chinese way. You would be a fool not to see it."

The two women sip tea and regard each other.

"Of course, there's always luck," says Annie, without irony, dribbling drops of cold tea on the ceramic tea pet, a terracotta frog with the aged patina of repeated tea applications. It holds a lucky coin in its mouth.

At least, Annie sounds sincere to Mai. *But who knows? At least someone is taking this seriously,* she thinks. "*Xiexie*, Annie, for clueing me in."

Ron finishes with Spires and walks in on the women, who turn to look at him. Things are getting more complicated by the minute in Ron's world. TSC's big client—and his lover—is providing numerous opportunities for the company to grow and seek revenue. He knows it's important to keep expanding in Asia, but his interest is not in money or contracts. Looking at Mai, stretched out on the contemporary piece, gives him an idea.

"Mai likes the sofa, Annie; is for sale?"

"Of course. I can send to your apartment today." She's immediately on her cell, calling the *shifu* with a truck.

Saying *baibai*, they leave Annie wondering and walk hand in hand toward a row of galleries.

"We can have dinner here if you like," starts Ron, standing in front of a chic brasserie and reading the menu board in English. "Why don't they have these things in Chinese?" he wants to know.

"Look, Chicken Tequila Fettuccine, and Pasta Tossed with Brie, Tomatoes and Basil; let's go in here."

Once they're seated, Mai says, "Annie spilled the beans on you."

"What does that mean *beans*, Mai?"

"She tells me, she knows what Chinese men want, and she knows what you are thinking."

"*Zhende*, that's bold," exclaims Ron in mock surprise.

"She told me Alan Spires would be happy to write up a contract for us."

"What else did she tell you, *that lynx;* making trouble?" Ron slides closer to Mai. He gently grasps the scarf around her neck, pulling her lips to his. "I've never been as happy as these past months," confesses Ron. "Is this a dream we live, Mai? Or is there a chance we can live happily together?"

The scarf slips through his fingers as Mai leans away from his kiss. "Rick's coming back."

"I hope so, Mai; truly, I want Rick to come back to you. Then you can choose. You know, most abductions turn out okay. Most are for ransom. We should make an offer."

"How would we do that?" she wants to know.

"Wouldn't your country pay to get him back? The Koreans are only doing it for the money. We do this frequently at TSC. A businessman can be abducted for ransom in some risky places like Africa or Indonesia. Their company carries insurance for that. A payment is made. I say, we should try to barter him back." They stare at each other a minute. Ron adds, "Call Wright now. Do it, Mai, for Rick."

"Okay, but I've been trying. I can't reach him."

Riding home to Wudaokou in a taxi, Mai considers the amount of trouble Rick has gotten her into: that she has to get an attorney and have a personal body guard. *Homeland Security better pay for this. Guess I'll need luck for that too.*

***

At Jingdezhen, the BFO vehicles lose internet and cell phone connectivity, including Rick's ping, all the way up the mountains to Huangshan, where G56 swings north at the intersection with G3.

Huangshan, Yellow Mountain, is a range of mountains, an ancient seabed uplifted for a hundred million years, eroded into stubby humps by glaciers. Granite peaks and twisted Huangshan pine trees catch misty clouds up to 1,800 meters or 6,000 feet at this UNESCO World Heritage Site, a huge tourist destination for some of the millions of Chinese enjoying their newfound leisure time.

For the last fifteen minutes, BFO had re-established contact with the ping. The G56 highway goes straight ahead to Shanghai. Instead, the ping backtracks to an enormous truck stop with several hotels.

***

Every day for a week, Mai thought she would hear something from someone. Stone silence from Alice Nolan. Wright's cell number was no longer in service. Mai, the Panther, tried out-thinking her opponents. Instead of confounding them, she's the one confused, having to play by someone else's rules.

Commander GAO was still working on the case, but had few clues. He couldn't find the embassy man and hadn't the authority to track him down. Finger-pointing had begun. His job was on the line, or maybe worse. At the same time, he felt like an ass, being made fun of by Homeland Security.

She'd noticed a change in the internet that week and corroborated it with her friends, as well as with the Media Department staff. The DAGE firewall had been tightening the filters, especially on news sites. Once clicked onto a media site, trying to select a secondary link to a specific story would be blocked. Every time. Friday, she couldn't get to a cooking site for Chinese dumplings or any English dictionary. The server sites displayed their homepages, when they did at all, without CSS—just text with no graphics. The word-search links were dead. *The Sacramento Bee*, usually working when Sun News wasn't, was totally blocked, also *NY Times* and *LA Times*. Yahoo was working.

She caught herself looking at her inbox ... checking the messages for one from Rick. She kept glancing at her phone ... maybe she missed an incoming text. Communications between her and Ron floated back and forth on the net, brief contacts more for assurance than for what they said.

Work at the office slacked off from last week's deadline for the last edition of the Newsletter for the year. Mai hadn't been much help once Rick arrived. Even so, they managed to get it to the printer on time without her. Sitting around the office with nothing to do emphasized her helplessness, irritating her.

November 9

Preparing files for the next media report, Mai is interrupted by her computer, mutely announcing an incoming email from a friend.

November 9   To: Mai   From: Donna Summerlake
Subject: Your Husband

Where are you? Can you come to my office ASAP?

At the same time, her phone rings. It's a text from Donna Summerlake: "call me asap."

Trembling with anticipation, Mai does so immediately and learns that a man, returning from a missionary project in Weinan, near Xi'an, where he was working at a medical clinic for migrant laborers, has arrived on campus with a message from Rick. She drops everything and races on her bicycle across campus.

Mai remembered the first time she met Donna between

assignments, grabbing a cup of coffee. Jazz clarinet cooled off the work adrenaline, along with a fast-moving spring shower outside the coffee shop near the Mingqing Building. Sitting with a piece of chocolate-mousse cake and a cup of *Americano tang nai*, she noticed an American-looking woman sitting down at the next table and opening her netbook. "Hi, are you an American?" asked Mai.

The petite women, dressed immaculately in a business suit with a purple silk blouse, glanced at Mai, surprised. "Why yes, I'm from Texas. You?"

"California. I work in the Media Communications Office. You?"

"I teach in the Finance School. I'm trying to make an appointment with the embassy. Have you tried to do this?"

"No, don't you just call them?" asked Mai.

"Look at this," the woman said, turning her netbook around so Mai could see. "I'm Donna Summerlake, by the way."

"Mai Martin. *Wo hen gao xing ren shi ni,*" said Mai, flashing her easy smile to punctuate the Mandarin phrase for "Glad to meet you." Squinting at the little screen, Mai saw a form to send an email request for an appointment. Looking up at Donna, she asked, "You can't just go there or call them? You have to do this?" The woman nodded. Shared incredulity.

Mai looked at her watch, "Uh-oh, I've got to be at the Main Building at 3PM. Bye-bye!"

CHAPTER 5
The Chase

Donna Summerlake's fourth-floor office in the School of Finance overlooks the grand promenade, extending from the Main Building in the north, past the School of Law, the School of Architecture, and the National Laboratory, to the main East Gate at Zhongguancun East at the heart of Wudaokou. This Wednesday, at 11AM, relatively few students can be seen from the office where she shares a room with her personal assistant, whom she has hired herself and compensates from her generous salary. Books and binders cover one wall.

She received an email from an American professor at the university, by way of introduction. Today, she connects with the friend-of-a-friend—an ex-pat missionary doctor.

"Thank you, Dr. Summerlake, for agreeing to meet with me. I'm Joshua Braithwaite; we communicated yesterday. I have a most urgent message to get to an American woman working here at Beijing University. Her name is May Martin."

"Would that be *Mai* Martin?" She pronounces it like *my*.

"Yes, possibly, is she married to a large, blue-eyed man?"

"I know a woman who could match this description. You have a message for her?"

When Mai arrives, the bearded man waiting for her is not tall but has ample girth. He extends his hairy hand, "Martin Taitai, I'm Joshua Braithwaite. I saw your husband in Weinan a few days ago. I came as soon as I could."

She nods, trying to catch her breath. "Sorry," she says, rubbing off dirt she's just noticed on the palm of her hand. "I guess I fell off my bike trying to get here so fast," she says.

"Are you all right?" asks her friend, concerned.

"Yeah, I just skidded out in a pile of leaves or something," she smiles half-heartedly.

That's when they all notice she's covered with leafy debris. Donna helps her brush off her legs and back. Pulls a leaf out of her hair.

"I'm good. Really. What about Rick, Mr....?"

"Braithwaite," say the doctor and Donna in unison.

"I have something for you," he continues, opening a zippered pocket inside his satchel. He retrieves a Bible. Flips the back cover open. On it is scrawled, in Rick's unmistakably abominable handwriting, "*H E L P.*"

A shiver shakes her, and her scalp crawls with goose bumps running down her back and out her fingertips.

Braithwaite's story began on Saturday, November 5, when two Asian men arrived at his church-sponsored clinic for migrant men in Weinan, about 1,052 km or 650 miles from Beijing. They drove him to a nearby hotel to treat a beaten and burned American.

"What did you think when you saw him?" asks Mai breathing hard, ears ringing.

"I saw a large man, obviously Anglo, with dyed, black hair and blue eyes. He was delirious from fever. I checked him over and found he'd been previously treated by a medical practitioner, using Western methods such as they use in Chinese hospitals. The bandages needed replacing, and that's when I saw the extent of his burns—like from cigarettes—in his groin and chest area." Braithwaite pauses, looking at the women, resting his gaze on the man's wife. "He appeared to be a captive of a gang. Have they asked you for ransom?"

Mai shakes her head, *no.*

He continues, "I became, effectively, a captive as well. For two days, they kept me in the hotel room with your husband."

"Who was there besides you and Rick?"

"Well, the two men who came to get me, and an older and a younger pair who seemed to be in charge, and a young Korean woman, caring for your husband; that makes five. I speak fluent Mandarin, and it was easy for me to eavesdrop on their unguarded conversations. They also spoke in Korean; three of the five may have been from North Korea."

"And what was the name of the hotel?"

"The Tongyi. Once the antibiotic broke your husband's fever, the gang checked out. I awoke in an empty room, 10 thousand yuan in my medical bag. I let myself out and returned to the clinic. I had to perform several scheduled surgeries before I could come here to Beijing."

"What did you do with the money?" Donna Summerlake demands.

"Yes, the tainted money. I gave it to the men's clinic. It will help many. I took none for myself. My service to your husband was my Christian duty, Mrs. Martin."

"How did you get his message?" Mai wants to know.

"To while away the hours, I read to your husband from this Bible. He gradually recovered lucidity, although he was weak. The Korean girl, Han-Joo, diligently cared for him. I taught her how to change the bandages. She would bathe him and brought us kim chee and rice with pots of tea. Occasionally, one of the others would look in and then leave again. In the few moments of privacy, your husband tried to talk. He told me about you, how to find you. He wrote this message," gesturing to the Bible.

"That's an amazing story, Dr. Braithwaite, and I thank you, *feichang ganxie ni*, for helping Rick ..." Mai falters, tears stream and she chokes. "What was he wearing?"

"A white tee-shirt with a train motif, boxer shorts and socks."

"That's what he was wearing that night ... Could he see?"

"I'm not sure I know what you mean, Mrs. Martin. He was ill and delirious, barely aware of his surroundings. He could hear me, though, and I hope my reading was a comfort. The Korean girl had a narcotic that acted like a painkiller on him. It made him very drowsy, and he would pass out for a while."

Mai looks down into the busy noontime promenade and left, toward Commander GAO's office in the Main Building. "Will you come with me to the campus security office and make a report?"

Braithwaite stands, shouldering his bag. "I must go now, Mrs. Martin. Here's the Bible, for you ... and hope," bouncing abruptly out of the office and down the stairs.

"I'm going to the Security Office now, Donna. Thank you ... for all this," Mai gestures toward the open door and Braithwaite's retreating presence. The friends hug and look into each other's faces. Mai disappears down the same stairs.

The campus is jammed with students off for lunch. Mai fights the mobs of bicycles, parks hers, and trots up the curved driveway to the front of the Main Building, brushing off the last of the dust from her fall. Standing on one foot, she takes off her shoe and something shakes out onto the polished stone floor, rolling away in a half spiral before coming to rest. She shivers for the second time and picks it up. "Heads up," she says, "I'm taking that as sign," and pockets the lucky coin.

Her first lucky break occurs immediately: the Commander is still at his desk. He orders a translator, and they record Braithwaite's story as Mai recalls it. Then she adds, "The man who was here that night—Lawrence Wright from the embassy?" GAO nods. "He's tracking Rick."

"We suspected as much, but haven't been able to contact him since then," says GAO.

"I've had the same experience, the calls bounce," she says.

Mai calls Ron. And the three agree to investigate further together.

"I'll appreciate it if you don't announce our movements to your embassy, Mrs. Martin," says the Commander. "Only two days ago they were in Weinan. If we leave now, we can catch up with them. We leave today."

Commander GAO hits the road with Maj. TANG by 4PM, leaving Lt. LIU in charge at the office in Beijing.

Mai and Ron follow with GPS after gassing up at the petrol station near the South Gate. Mai had cleared it with Ms. ZHANG, convincing her she could work on the media report in the car on the way to Weinan and would send it to her in a day or two.

Ron appropriated from his office a USB internet interface that would connect through TSC's VPN network and a power cord that fit a port on the rear-seat side of the console for her to use. Ron tracks the Commander's GPS location on his laptop sitting open on the passenger seat, while Mai stretches out in the back where she can watch Ron, with *Pépe* open on her lap, searching and clicking through the media outlets. She wearies of this, and resorts to ruminating over the few facts they have and low key discussion with Ron on the long drive.

November 10

The Beijingers start arriving in Weinan around 1AM. Commander GAO and Maj. TANG check in at the CPP (Communist People's Party) favorite, the Guangming in the Linwei District. Mai and Ron check in a little later.

The next morning in Weinan, it's two degrees Celsius or 35 Fahrenheit. Mai stays at the hotel, working on her fourteenth media report for Ms. ZHANG, while Ron goes with the Commander and Maj. TANG. At the men's clinic, they find the administrator in a dingy, cramped office smelling of mildew. He corroborates Braithwaite's story on a tour of the facility. Swarthy men, sitting on long benches, wait for their turn at a variety of posts: X-ray, blood pressure and EKG.

Gesturing to a large group of men huddled together, the administrator says, "These men are going to Abu Dhabi soon to work, during the cool season. Two weeks ago, another group left for Wenzhou to board a freighter to United Arab Emirates, about the same time Reverend Doctor Braithwaite disappeared."

The Tongyi Hotel management obsequiously services the Commander's request for information, but nothing is learned. No one recognizes pictures of Gen. MA or the gang. Riding back to their hotel, Ron texts Mai: "Dun, c u n lob 15 min."

Commander GAO invites Ron and Mai to join him and Maj. TANG at the hotel for a lunch conference. The *fuwuyuan*, dressed as always in red trousers and black jackets, somberly treat the Beijingers to the best Linwei can offer.

The Commander starts, "We're leaving for Wenzhou today," diving into a serving dish of stir-fry shredded pork and bamboo shoots.

"Why Wenzhou?" she asks.

"The clinic administrator thought that might be their destination. It makes sense. Freighters leave that port everyday bound for the United Arab Emirates," explains Ron in English to Mai. Turning to the Commander, he asks in Mandarin, "Wenzhou *li zhe'er you duo yuan*?" [How far is that from here?]

"About 2,600 kilometers." Mentally, Mai calculates that to be around 1,500 miles.

Dishes keep arriving: slivered celery with mushrooms, sliced, sautéed potato and turnip with sugar, *mifan* [rice], noodles, jiaozi [dumplings], Szechuan spicy eggplant, and ginger beef.

Ron has his iPhone out and is calculating the logistics of the journey. "That's like thirty hours. Are you boys up for a road trip?"

Maj. TANG says, "Thirty hours is not so much. We can be there in a day and a half."

"We could fly," suggests Mai.

The men turn to stare at her. *And leave the Dongfeng behind?* Besides driving being a poor decision, they've gotten attached to the luxury SUV and the excitement of the chase.

"Or take the train," suggests Ron objectively, although he has his own attachment issues with the Park Avenue.

TANG is checking train schedules on his smartphone. "There's one train a day. It takes thirty-six hours." He looks up at the group. "Might as well drive and we'll have our own vehicle. We're not far behind."

"You're not counting time sleeping. It will take longer by car," argues Ron.

For several minutes, the men coordinate their next steps. Mai can't pick up enough of the conversation to participate as she'd like, so she looks around the busy, noisy restaurant, packed with people at wide, round tables. The people-watching absorbs her for most of the luncheon: businessmen, wealthy farmer peasants, officials and their wives, children, and mistresses. Glancing back across the table, at the trio of men plotting their next move, Mai concludes things are going well and they don't need her intervention, and she resumes people-watching.

Riding up the elevator to their room before checking out, Mai asks Ron, "What's the plan?"

"Do you want to continue following Commander GAO? He and Maj. TANG are driving to Wenzhou," says Ron. "It's going to be a major trip through farmland and mountains. The road is not very good. We have to share it with big trucks. There are tolls. We can't drive at night; not safe."

"How long will it take?"

"TANG thinks he can get there by Saturday night or Sunday, if we can get on the road ASAP, as you Americans like to say."

"What if we're too late?" she asks.

"We'll find him, Tangzi. The Americans are tracking him. They told you, *haoma*?" Ron tries to console her, but agrees, "You're right, we could be too late."

The elevator door opens at their floor.

"The route crosses mountains and rivers on vast bridges. Mountain mist shrouds the high villages, and the people are very beautiful," says Ron, cataloging the wonders for Mai.

Ron slides the door key through the electronic lock and pushes it open. "Wenzhou, at the end of this road, is a huge port on the southern China coast with close ties to the United Arab Emirates. The Emirates are only a day away from Iran."

"I haven't finished ZHANG's report," Mai says.

"There's no cell service, no internet, Mai."

"Just you and me?"

"*Dui.*"

"*Haode*, I'm ready for a road trip. It's *something* anyway, forward movement. Where do you find petrol out there?"

"The Commander is lining up our route. We'll stay together in a convoy."

"Where's Wright, I'd like to know," starts Mai.

"That's a good question."

Ron is packed in a minute and stands by his bag at the door in skinny jeans and white, cable knit, turtleneck sweater. It's warmed up to 11 degrees Celsius, 51 Fahrenheit, under pale sunlight.

Mai slips her netbook into the outside zippered pouch on her travel bag, pulls out the handle and announces, "Zouba." Throwing her burgundy snow parka over one shoulder, she follows Ron to the lobby and on down to the parking garage.

Commander GAO stows their gear while Maj. TANG studies a map. "I'm aiming at Zhangwan. That's about 300 kilometers," he says.

Traveling west toward Xi'an, they turn south on G40. Ron stays right on the Commander's tail, not trusting the internet or cell service ahead, making the turn without losing sight of the university's black, Dongfeng SUV.

The faint sun disappears, and the sky appears leaden; small snowflakes blot the windshield as they climb into foothills, melting when they hit the ground. Commander GAO slows to a maddening 70 kilometers per hour, 45 mph, sandwiched between big rigs. Before

Shanyang, they take the G70 cut off around 3PM. The storm holds back on the trip down the Dan Jiang River valley and over the mountains. By 8PM, ZHAO and the Commander settle on Xiyu Hotel near Hubei University at the G316 intersection, parking next to each other in the underground garage.

"I'm going to work on my report an hour or two tonight," says Mai, turning to Ron in the dim light.

Fine worry lines crease the corners of his eyes. He's relieved to be off the road at last, leans back into his seat and presses his fingers to his eyes, sighing. Leaning over, Mai kisses him on his cheek, and those almond eyes pop open.

"Tired?" she asks.

"Yeah, what do you say: 'bushed'? What does that mean, Mai? Bushed?"

"Bushwhackers, bushed, beats me. Why don't you have dinner with the guys? I'll order in from room service, let me have some quiet time online for an hour or so? And, thanks, *xiexie*."

"Yeah, okay," he replies, opening the door and stretching in the next, empty parking space.

"Hey, kung fu master," says TANG, "show us something."

"I'm *bushed*," he says.

"What's that?"

"Never mind," Ron answers, crowding into the elevator with the squad.

Downstairs in the hotel restaurant, the three men relax. Travelers coming in stamp snow off their shoes and shake it out of their hair. The hotel fills quickly with stranded motorists reluctant to press on in the dark and worsening weather.

"Here's a new profile of the gang, perhaps you haven't seen," says GAO, sliding a report cover across the table toward Ron, while he and Maj. TANG slurp soup and wrap crepes around green onions and meat slivers in a sauce.

The first profile is MA Minho, b. 1951. In 1968, Ron reads, he joined an elite company, cross-training with North Koreans involved in the US Pueblo incident. He later graduated from Pyongyang University with a master's degree in chemical engineering in 1976. He retired from the PLA in 2009 at fifty-eight, and then joined the reserves. There are pictures from the meeting at the Main Building and more profiles and photographs of the gang, everything in English and Chinese.

"*Xiexie*, Commander. Seems like something's missing from Gen. MA's background here," starts Ron, attacking a serving dish of eggplant with peppers and pork, alternating with *mifan*. Rice.

"What can you guys at TSC dig up?" asks GAO.

"I'll scan this in and send it to the office tonight."

"I've already got it on a PDF. I'll send it to you," says TANG.

The fuwuyuan brings a pot of tea and a liter bottle of *baijiu*.

Commander GAO rips the seal off the bottle and pours three small cups, "*Ganbei*," he says.

They toss the liquor down and resume sampling the regional cuisine—not that much different than Weinan, hot and spicy. The rice is fluffy and hot. The *fuwuyuan* has rosy cheeks and keeps the men stocked with specialties from the kitchen. Once she recognizes Commander GAO as a high-ranking official, there isn't anything she isn't prepared to offer. By 9PM, Maj. TANG has disappeared into the kitchen to instruct the chef on Beijing cuisine methods, a glass of *baijiu* in one hand and the other around the waist of the girl.

"You know, you are one okay Hong Konger," starts GAO.

"*Haode*, and you, Commander, are one okay CPP'er," compliments Ron in return.

"I about laughed out loud when you kicked the Marine," says GAO, holding out the bottle to refresh Ron's glass.

"What about that pistol of yours? I thought you were going to shoot us!" says Ron, tossing down another shooter and lounging back into the padded booth.

Commander GAO pats his leg, "Got it with me, right here."

"Someone should arrest you," says Ron .

"Yeah? Like whom? Ha-ha." He looks arrogantly around the hall. Of all the people here, he was the VIP, more important than any of these hicks assembled.

The kitchen door swings open, and the two men look to see Maj. TANG, his shirt unbuttoned down to his belt, pushing through with a tray of dishes. He strides to their table. The chef has placed his tall, white hat on the Beijinger's head, slightly askew.

While clinging to his shapely bicep, the *fuwuyuan* slides dishes onto the lazy Susan, and the eating begins again. A sharp voice booms from the kitchen, and she reluctantly leaves them alone for a while.

"What's this you bring now, Chef TANG?" asks GAO, pouring another round of drinks.

"A delicate stir-fry of sheep intestine with blood, the way my grandmother used to make ..."

"My grandmother never made anything like that," says Ron.

"That's because your grandmother was a capitalist roader in Hong Kong, eating cake," retorts TANG with a smile. "No offense."

"None taken," replies Ron, "My grandmother was a sixth-level black belt and could kick your grandmother back to Mongolia," exaggerating.

"When can we take on those Marines again? That was awesome," says TANG, fishing delicate rice noodles out of a bowl of spicy broth.

"How about a basketball match with the embassy guys?"

"Ha-ha, I like that. Especially that runt Wright."

"*Xiexie* for taking care of Martin Taitai that night," says Ron, helping himself to a haystack of finely shredded and fried potatoes. "Don't they have jiaozi?"

"She's a lady warrior, that Martin Taitai. The way she knocked him over and had him by the throat ..." says GAO.

"A Panther, that's her!" says Ron.

"She has kung fu training?" asks TANG, looking around for the girl.

"None, she's just a natural, fearless. That's *the American way,*" he adds, smirking.

"And she has a kung fu master to defend her," adds GAO raising his cup, "*Ganbei!*"

"And she has GAO, the Commander," adds Ron, lifting his cup.

The liquor filters into their brains and nervous system, what seemed like good camaraderie sinks into melancholic introspection as they pick through the dishes, keeping their thoughts to themselves. Ron looks at his iPhone, it's past 11PM.

Commander GAO starts, "It's my fault. I'm so sorry, *duibuqi*, please tell Martin Taitai. The night they came and took her husband ... I was asleep in my bed, embracing my sleeping wife ... while the vile creature Gen. MA smothered her face and left her for dead ... taking

Martin Xiansheng right out from under our noses ..." His hands are spread out on the soiled tablecloth, his eyes try focusing on something while looking inward at his failure. A tear drops off his nose onto his plate.

Maj. TANG pats his boss on the shoulder, "Who knew they would come back like that?"

GAO brushes his arm away, "I should have known, me, the Commander, that's who!"

The three men find their way to the elevator and to their rooms.

***

Before going to bed, Mai sends Media Report #14.

Incident Report 20111110

TRIGGER ACTIVITY: MEDIA REPORT 11/10

22—Subject violates accepted-use criteria: uses SunSystems search to access keyword-excluded media. 11/10

SECURITY RESPONSE ACTIVITY:

22—Response: Automatic keyword search Layer 7 Tier III: IP identifier unit
Keyword searches are collected in a live-stream search
Tabulation of violations pushes alert

***

Now, Wright has the Land Cruiser ping to follow besides Rick's signal. On Thursday November 10, during the long, twisting route down to Wenzhou, Poole works out a split-screen display with some elementary programming. By afternoon, he has them superimposed. The ping takes them to the Shachengzhen neighborhood in the suburbs to the Chosun Wenzhou Hotel where the gang checked in to wait for the *Lantana's* arrival.

Parking across the street in a Construction Bank mini-plaza, Choy unloads his scooter, looking for a suitable place to set up a listening post. He's connected by hassle-free ear buds and mic clip. The gang's boxy hotel is crowded by other boxy buildings. The BFO checks into another one down the street.

November 11

The next day in Wenzhou, BFO parks in different locations outside the Chosun Wenzhou Hotel, scanning perspectives of the building with the laser software, trying not to look suspicious. At the front, they park in the mini-plaza. They don't need a window through which to aim the laser. It penetrates the thin metal car shell. The problem is finding a window to bounce off and having it be the room you want to listen to. While they try listening, Choy maps the interior of the hotel with his smartphone and homes in on a group of rooms on the fifth floor most likely to be the target.

***

There is still no word from Dalaoban RI approving the plan change and contacting the Americans about a ransom as a backup. EU Sun makes arrangements with the ship provisioner to construct a crate for Rick's transfer.

The *Lantana* was built in 1995 as an oil products tanker, 114m x 19 m, speed 6 knots, registered in Singapore, IMO: 9110444. Besides picking up Rick, the ship's Captain has ordered CO_2 canisters, rice, cooking oil, fresh vegetables, and meat.

Another ship, a chemical tanker about the same size—106 meters long—in the North Korean merchant fleet but registered to Tuvalu, a Polynesian nation, which is slated to pick up a load of N,N-Diethyl-3-methylbenzamide (DEET) in Wenzhou, is tapped to transport Gen. MA back to Pyongyang. Luxury items such as Perrier water, Martell cognac, Belgium Scabal tailored clothing, and Italian brand Moreschi shoes, restricted by UN sanctions, are assembled and crated for shipment to DPRK—North Korea.

After moving Rick into a pair of adjoining rooms on the fifth floor via wheelchair, they tether him with a couple of looped, extra-long, heavy-duty zip ties between his ankles and wrists. He's so cowed; he's curled himself on the floor between the bed and the wall closest to the bathroom. They throw his filthy-by-now quilt over him for the time being. The two rooms face the side of a new brick office building only twenty meters away. They keep the window curtains closed. The hotel maid is allowed to clean in the adjoining room, shared by EU Sun, Han-Joo, and Gen. MA, but not in Rick's, which is locked with the bolt. During the day, however, they leave the connecting door open.

He's shut down, in survival mode, desperate to guard his core integrity, peering out at the surroundings occasionally before retreating into his inner fortress, enduring much, like a wounded tiger in his cave. He can't reveal his mission: the nano-chip in his ear. Wright's bunch is here ... He knows it ... they'll show up any minute now and pull him out of this hell. The euphoric high, from whatever the pills are Han-Joo feeds him, swirls him into an expansive feeling of well-being, thinking everything's going to be okay. He crawls around the room, to the amusement of Sang-Bo and Gen. MA, in a restless search for something, before returning to his nest and crashing for hours, waking depressed and agitated until the next dose from Han-Joo's golden hand.

Not that all his time is spent in a drug-induced state. There are times of lucidity, and his sight has returned. Gen. MA even tried engaging him in conversation ... once.

"Bastard American," he began, in velvety Brit English, "Why are you so important to the Iranian comrades?"

"Just that Wikileaks thing," Rick replied. "Not me. Mistake."

"You mean they want to pay $120,000 for you, and it's all a big mistake?" the diminutive General asked, incredulous, mocking. "No, you did something to them. What was it?"

"Not me."

Gen. MA rises to strike Rick when EU Sun's voice from the other room halts his arm.

"*Laoshi* ...."

MA, muttering in Korean, "I can make him talk."

"Dalaoban RI said to protect the cargo, remember? Gently, *Laoshi*."

EU Sun is right. Beating the truth out of the Meiguoren isn't in the contract. "They should pay extra for that service."

"Gen. MA, what's your beef with me anyway?" asks Rick, emboldened by the conversation.

"We collect from the Iranians, for helping with balance of payments for Korea."

Rick is familiar with the role DPRK plays with Iran and their murky trade based on exchanging nuclear technology and weapons.

"You're just in it for the money; you don't care what I did, not really," suggests Rick, looking for a wedge to negotiate with his captors.

"Stop talking," says EU Sun from the other room. "Let's go out."

***

Ron wakes to the sound of water running in the shower. He lies there, listening to its muffled shush behind the closed door; the warm, steamy air floats out and suggests something. Desire and covetous wisps of tan twine through the puffs of *yuanfen*. The glass door of the shower opens, and Ron steps into Mai's steamy, soapy embrace.

"*Zao shang hao*," he starts, pushing his head under the hot, streaming water.

"*Hao*, I'm just getting out," says Mai, leaving him unfulfilled and a little hung over.

Later, on the way into the dining room, she finds a week old *China Daily* at the reception desk. At breakfast, the only person with an appetite is Mai, enjoying hong cha and waffles from the breakfast buffet, with sliced dragon fruit and pineapple. Returning from the buffet for the second time with more tea with milk, hong cha nai, Commander GAO catches her eye, waving her over to his table.

Bloodshot eyes under puffy lids, faintly shadowed, sculpt his Han face into a mask of tragedy above a heavy, black turtleneck sweater and camel-hair jacket, a small gold pin in the lapel. Maj. TANG sits opposite with his face buried in a bowl of porridge, thumbing through emails on his smartphone, his foul-weather parka zipped up over brown gabardine trousers tucked into the tops of PLA-issue boots.

"Martin Taitai, *xiexie*, sit with me here for little minute," GAO starts, his usually expressionless eyebrows tilting slightly.

Glancing at Ron at the next table, who's absorbed in his smartphone like Maj. TANG, she slides onto the padded bench next to the Commander. She's wearing her parka over the same gray turtleneck sweater and jeans, ready to go, like they've been doing for the past couple of days, hotel to hotel. Each one different and the same. The hotel restaurants, life on the run, chasing Rick, saving Rick. The message said, "H E L P." *I'm coming honey, here we are, and we're coming. I got the fucking PLA looking for you. Hang on.*

The smokily fragrant tea, a smooth, aromatic balm, flows down her throat as she listens to the Commander saying, "*Duibuqi*, Martin Taitai, this is my entire fault." He grasps her free hand and holds it in his two paws, staring down at how fragile and pale it looks in his.

Is the Commander apologizing? Mai's eyes widen under dark eyebrows and are looking into his face when he raises it to take a peek.

"*Duibuqi*, so much suffering, Martin Taitai ... *duibuqi*, for Martin Xiansheng."

He grips her hand a minute more and then drops it with a sigh, looking away. All this opening up to the Western woman exhausts him immensely, more than he thought it would. The elevated heartbeat pounds his ears, and now he feels so hot he thinks he'll faint in front of her. The stakes are high: he has to capture Gen. MA and free the Meiguoren Martin, save face for himself and his Office. There'll be consequences if he fails. Maj. TANG and Ron pretend not to see his discomfort.

"We'll find him, Commander. And he'll be safe. I know it," says Mai.

She pats him on the hand and resumes breakfast at her table, reading the week-old news. Sometimes she's confident, clinging to small clues. Sometimes despairing, detached from the men and their desperate chase. *Are we too late? What's happening to him now? Where's Wright?* Turning the pages, skimming the articles, like the men, lost in her thoughts.

Ron sets his phone on the tablecloth and turns to the Commander and Maj. TANG, "The road ahead is closed."

"*Zhende*," mutters TANG, scrolling to the weather app. "Ice." He rises and leaves the dining room.

"Are we stuck here, Ron?" asks Mai over the top of the newspaper, folding and stashing it in her Bernini bag on the chair opposite.

"Maj. TANG will find out. Perhaps only for a few hours until it warms up. This is to be expected on this hell road this time of year."

"You look tired this morning. Can I help drive?" offers Mai.

"You?" Ron's eyebrows arch over puffy, almond eyes.

"Yeah, me," she says, fishing around in her purse and sliding a plastic card across the tablecloth toward him.

"What's this?" he asks.

"That's my California Driver License. I can drive here."

Ron inspects it, squinting. He pulls out his reading glasses, "That you?"

"That picture was taken ten years ago, my hair was long then."

"So young and beautiful, Mai, why you color it black?"

"I'm turning Asian now. It's the new me," she answers, fitting the card back into her purse, winking at him. *He's starting to perk up.*

"Aren't you going to eat anything? The buffet is delicious," she says, rising to get another cup of tea.

Ron glances at Commander GAO, sitting immobile in the booth opposite, lost in thought. He stands stiffly, shaking out his legs, and follows her lead.

"What time did you get in last night?" she asks.

"Uh … last night," he holds his forehead and closes his eyes a moment, "Eleven." After hesitating, he fills a mug with coffee and tentatively surveys a display of bread and rolls, waiting for his stomach to respond *yes* or *no* to the idea of food.

"Let me make you some toast, honey," she whispers, dropping two slices of white bread into a commercial toaster. "Go sit, I'll bring it to you. Do you want butter and jelly?"

Maj. TANG strides toward them from the lobby and pours two mugs of coffee, "The road is closed all the way to Wuhan, 450 kilometers. We have to stay here this morning. Why didn't we take the train?"

He turns and carries the coffees to their booth, setting one of the mugs in front of his boss. The Commander offers Maj. TANG a faint smile of gratitude, folding his hands around the hot mug. They talk quietly about the mission and how lucky they are that HUANG hasn't sent them to re-education camp, *laojiao,* yet. Bright sunshine slants through high windows above a garden of silk bamboo, making lemon-colored squares on the opposite wall.

All morning, waiting in Zhangwan, Commander GAO has ample time to check in with Lt. LIU and micromanage him with to-do lists, updates, and reports. The Deputy Commander's office has been calling every day. What to tell him? Justice can be swift and it can be slow, but eventually he'll have to face HUANG. He'll be a hero or a criminal.

***

One thousand seven hundred and forty-two kilometers ahead in Wenzhou, at 10AM, Gen. MA inserts the sim card from Rick's phone into his and selects the names Mai, Wright, Poole, and Choy from the digital address book to send the text: "NEGOTIATE?"

He hasn't heard from RI and he hasn't convinced EU Sun about the plan change, but that doesn't stop him from initiating contact with the Americans, accessing the contacts he needs from the card.

***

The dining room at the Xiyu Hotel is packed with travelers waiting for the road to open. Mai glances at her phone announcing a new text.

"Look at this, Ron," she slides it to where he can see.

"Who's calling you?"

"I don't know. It's a Chinese caller ID."

"That's Gen. MA! Commander, look," Ron passes the phone and turns back to Mai, "Remember talking about this? He's asking for a ransom! Good news for Rick. Text him back: 'YES how much?'"

The call stimulates the squad to have another cup of tea or coffee and discuss the new piece of information.

"What should I do?" asks Mai.

"You need to get in touch with your people at the embassy and get them started on this," says Ron.

Commander GAO gives her a nod, "Okay, Martin Taitai, call Wright Xiansheng. Ask him if they are negotiating."

Like the other times, Mai's call bounces. Wright has been incommunicado.

***

Lawrence Wright, BFO Director, can't answer immediately. He has to talk to Nolan, but he likes the idea of a backup plan. He calls Alice Nolan in Fort Belvoir, Virginia, at 21:00 or 9PM of the previous day, Saturday.

"Nolan, Gen. MA wants to negotiate."

She glances at the time display on the corner of her laptop.

"What time is it there?" she wants to know.

"It's ten hundred hours, Sunday."

"Did he say how much he wants? What are his demands?" she asks, sharpening her consciousness.

"It's just an invitation to negotiate. In a text. It appeared as a message from Rick Martin with a Chinese caller ID. I know we got his phone, but it was minus the sim card."

"Okay, I like the idea. It has merit. We need more details. Start talking with him. Keep the US out of it. You know."

"How do we get the money?" asks Wright.

"I'll work on that in the morning."

"We should have enough data. I'm calling the Chinese to get him out,"

"Anything else?" asks Nolan

"That's all."

"'Kay, bye."

Wright texts back to Gen. MA: "ok to pay. when? where?"

***

EU Sun, Gen. MA, and Han-Joo visit the local museum, studying the thousands of pieces of cultural relics on display.

Gen. MA continues to persuade EU Sun about the backup plan.

"Did I ever tell you the story about the KAL flight?"

"*Dui, Laoshi*, a hundred times."

"It was in 1987. I was a young cadre of thirty-six years old and was one of the field agents who brought the bomb that blew up the airliner."

"*Dui, Laoshi*, you have been like a father to me and have taught me everything."

"And the young woman agent, KIM Hyun Hee, who was captured, and her mentor, KIM Seung Il, who swallowed the poison cigarette?"

"Dui, Laoshi."

"She was only twenty-five years old at the time. Younger than you."

Gen. MA walks a few steps together with his protégé. They stop in front of a case exhibiting fine *huahua* painting on silk.

"We should have had an alternate plan. We made serious mistakes in '87. We need a backup plan now for ourselves. If the Great Ones screw up, I want to be ready to run."

***

By 10:30AM, traffic is allowed back on the expressway. Big-rigs squash the ice into slush and throw up muddy sprays, coating Ron's Park Avenue with a brown glaze that collects in chunks in the wheel wells.

"I'm getting my car washed when we get back to civilization," mutters Ron, peering through grimy streaks left by the windshield wipers.

"Don't follow so close; you won't get that back spray," Mai suggests.

"If I don't, someone will cut in," he defends himself.

"Fine by me. Won't you let me drive a while? You could take a nap," she continues.

"Mei wenti, Mai, I can drive," he says, hunched over the wheel, glaring ahead at the road.

"What does your Driver License look like? Show me yours."

After a short struggle, Ron produces his wallet from his pants pocket and hands it to her. Inside, she finds a photograph of a young man, "Who is this? Your son?"

Ron glances at the school picture of a teenager in a blue uniform and back to the road. "*Dui, ta shi* Jiechi."

"Jiechi ... Handsome, like his father. He has your beautiful eyes." Mai searches through the credit cards, his TSC parking permit and receipts. "This, is this it?"

"*Dui.*"

"Looks new, when did you get it?"

"When I moved to Beijing."

"Do you have a Hong Kong driver's license or does the Beijing license suffice?"

"No, I don't drive there."

"What, you mean you've only been driving for, what ...?" searching the card for a date, "since January of this year?" Mai looks at him, suddenly concerned.

"What about you? How long you drive in *Jalifunia*?" he counters.

"Since I was sixteen years old! Let me drive. These are not conditions for a new driver!"

A loud CRACK! stops their conversation.

"What was that?" he asks, white knuckles gripping the wheel.

"That was a piece of gravel, kicked up by the truck, hitting the windshield—another reason not to follow so closely, Ron," Mai answers, searching the windshield, pressing her finger over a small craze on her side.

"Is broken window?"

"Just a crack, it won't break, the glass is strong. Your insurance should cover the repair when you get home. You have insurance, don't you?"

"Of course, Mai," he answers, insulted.

Ron drops back a few meters, and they drive for several kilometers in silence. Mai gives Ron's ID back and resumes reading the paper, trying not to look at the road.

"So you get your *Jalifunia* license long time ago?" Ron starts again.

"Everyone in the US gets their license at sixteen. Fifteen and a half, if you count the learners permit."

"What year was that, when you were sixteen?" Ron glances sideways at her, admiring her profile and in awe of her life skills.

Counting mentally, "Nineteen eighty-eight."

"*Zhende*, so young."

"What were you doing in nineteen eighty-eight?"

Sun shining on the expressway dries patches of pavement, Ron relaxes his grip slightly and leans back into the seat, "Mmmm ... I was twenty-two. That was the year I was married." Thinking about it, he smiles faintly: He and Claire were in love. His future looked assured. "I joined the Police Training School that same year."

"Sounds like a busy year for you," says Mai. "I was a self-absorbed teenager, eager to grow up and leave home.... Are you going to let me drive sometime?" getting back to the moment. Looking out her window, down into a gorge with a river flowing at the bottom, Mai judges the drop to be about thirty meters, or about one hundred feet. Big trucks lumber up the grade to the right, obscuring the view. Cars are clustered in packs, following a leader, tailgating and driving slowly.

"Yeah, sometime, not today," he answers.

It's clear, Ron isn't relinquishing the wheel to her. In the States, Rick wouldn't keep her from driving. She can't remember not driving or sharing the driving with him when he was tired. She doesn't feel like making a big deal about it. She shrugs, accepting the danger and trusting Ron.

After that, they drive in silence. Mai watches out the window at the passing scenery, thinking about Rick and Wright and Gen. MA, wondering about the Homeland Security group and where they were.

"They aren't going to abandon him, Mai," Ron glances at her and back to the road.

"How do you know what I'm thinking?" she asks, startled from her reverie.

"You look worried," he answers.

"That's what Alice Nolan said. They're *tracking* him."

"Have you tried calling him again?"

"What am I calling him about? The ransom?"

"Tell him the Commander wants a phone appointment. Get a date and time. Can you do that?"

Mai tries sending to Wright. This time she gets a ring tone and a connection to his mailbox and says, "Nihao, Mr. Wright; this is Mai Martin. Commander GAO from Beijing University would like to talk with you. Please call me to set up phone appointment at your earliest convenience.

"That's promising," she says.

At 11:30, Lawrence Wright, BFO Director, receives Mai's message.

Ron calls the Commander with the update. They ride along for a while. Mai picks out the business section of the *China Daily* and settles into pensive waiting.

For the past half hour, G70 crossed a long valley, gleaming with reflections off watery tributaries and lakes hemmed in by brown, muddy rice fields. Mai finds sunglasses in the glove box. Maj. TANG, ahead, picks up speed with the better conditions, turning off at S303 and cruising Gucheng for some place to stop for lunch. He herds them back to their cars by 1PM; the little caravan inserts itself into the stream of trucks heading to Wuhan, 350 kilometers ahead.

Slipping between the Tongbai Shan and Dahong Shan Mountains, they travel through the ancient State of Chu. Mai imagines the Bronze Age: kind of like Xi'an terracotta warriors, wandering bandits, silk merchants and Mandarins.

"Listen to this," starts Mai, reading the paper. "'Vehicles plunge into river after bridge collapses in central China Province of Henan.' This is dated November 5, that's ten days ago. 'At least four vehicles fell into the river after a bridge collapsed in a central Chinese city on Saturday morning, local authorities said. No casualties have been reported so far. A bridge collapsed at around 5 a.m. after an overloaded sand truck drove onto it, said the city's publicity bureau. The bridge was built in the 1970s. Investigation into the cause of the accident is under way.'"

"That's a comforting story to read to me, Tangzi. Here's a bridge coming up, it could be next one."

Sunday night, lights are twinkling on in Wuhan as they cross the Chang Jiang, the Yangtze River, and exit the expressway at the G42/S3 intersection. Hotels galore swarm around the lakes inside the Third Ring Road. Ron thumbs his iPhone and calls Maj. TANG, "*Wei, nihao*, is this Wuhan?"

"*Dui.*"

"Let me pick the hotel tonight, okay? I need a massage."

"I hear you, man. Where do you want to go?"

"Howard Johnson Pearl Plaza."

After a short pause, TANG replies, "Commander GAO says too much, what about Asia Hotel?"

Ron looks it up, "Okay, has spa? I want a massage."

"Yes, spa."

Ron pays 15 yuan to have the parking valet wash and buff his car. It was probably too much, but he wasn't in the mood to haggle, besides, *It's worth it at twice the price.*

After checking in, Mai and Ron head to the spa floor. The *fuwuyuan* in red trousers leads them to a room of comfortable recliner chairs. Steaming cups of hot water are passed around for the guests to drink.

In a few minutes, two men enter, struggling with bamboo vats of hot water, fragrant with herbs. The treatment starts with them sitting, facing away from the *anmoshi* on low, cushioned stools, up to their ankles in the buckets, so hot Mai alternates dipping her feet with resting them on the sides of the tub, her jeans rolled up to her knees. The expert massage technicians work the back and shoulders, out to fingertips and up into the scalp. The hours of strain melt away amid grunts and yelps when fingers find a pressure point, injecting healing pain.

The Commander walks in a few minutes later. "Where's Maj. TANG?" asks Ron.

"He's having a full meridian-balancing treatment," GAO answers, jerking his thumb toward a row of private rooms on the other side of a corridor, glimpsed through the open arch of the foot massage salon.

When the *anmoshi* finishes, Mai is reduced to a semi-coma,

drifting in the mountain mists under sparkling stars of the Road of Heaven, the Milky Way.

The crew is sober around the dinner table tonight, drinking nothing stronger than hot jasmine tea and sticking to depressing assessments of their mission.

"I wanted to stay in Jiujiang tonight," starts TANG.

"How much farther is that?" asks Mai.

"Two hundred fifty kilometers," he replies, smiling meekly at the fuwuyuan setting dishes on the lazy Susan.

"Where are we going, again?" asks Mai pouring tea.

"Wenzhou," says Ron.

"How much farther is that?"

Ron calculates on his travel app, "From here, more than nine hundred kilometers."

Maj. TANG adds, "It would be a long drive, perhaps eleven or twelve hours."

"What's ahead," Mai wants to know, "more mountains, or are we through with them?"

"The most torturous portion is ahead. Very likely we will not have cell or internet service," says TANG.

"We'll leave early tomorrow if possible. If the road ahead is open. First light is about 07:00. By 12:30, where will that get us, TANG?" asks GAO.

Maj. TANG opens the roadmap onto the round table for twelve, making it their command control. Setting cups and glasses on it at Wuhan, Huangshan, and Wenzhou, he points at Jingdezhen with the tip of his chopsticks.

"Jingdezhen to Wenzhou would be another seven or eight hours, depending," he adds without his usual enthusiasm.

Mentally toting it up, that would make a twelve-hour day. He's never driven that many hours in a stretch. This whole trip has been a new experience for him, driving such a long distance and for so many days. It was like nothing he could compare. And he found it stimulating. He felt smarter. He felt like he was part of a grand effort. His admiration elevated the Commander to god-like status, incapable of fault. Maybe little faults. He appeared so much greater than everyone else. The first night out, staying in Weinan, Maj. TANG saw the automatic pistol under his pillow. After that, TANG noticed a pronounced bulge in Commander GAO's right pants pocket and wondered if he should be carrying something, too.

Ron gets up to go to the men's room, and TANG follows him, through the lobby with a karaoke bar raging at one end.

"Hey, Ron," starts TANG.

"Yeah?"

Maj. TANG walks around the men's room, checking that they are alone. "Do you carry a gun?"

"Weishenme? *Bu dui*. I'm a kung fu master, remember, not knife or gun guy."

"Ha-ha, haode, I was wondering if I should get one."

"I didn't know they were legal," says Ron.

The door opens, and a group of men interrupt.

Walking back, Maj. TANG says, "They're not. But it's different if you're PLA. With my classification, I might be eligible. With the Commander's approval."

"Would he approve one for me?" asks Ron, curious.

"Maybe, after this, huh?" TANG winks, and they return to the dining room.

Dishes are already ranged round the table. The Commander and Mai have been waiting for them, sipping tea.

"What do you think is going on in Wenzhou with the gang? Can we assume they have preceded us and are already in accommodations somewhere in the harbor district?" starts Commander GAO, invigorated by the rugged scenery and fresh air, stimulated by historical stories he learned in school of Warring States heroes, and everything stirred by cold mountain *chi*.

"Good question, Commander. So you think the harbor," thumbing down his iPhone to check SunSys Maps. Ron looks up at Commander GAO's gaze, "You know, I was Marine Police for five years."

"You know how a harbor works, man; I'm a city cop. Tell us, qing," says GAO sincerely.

Sincere or not, Ron takes him up on the offer. "Is there a naval base nearby?" Ron looks at Maj. TANG for confirmation, setting him busy on his smartphone.

Another hour is spent plotting and discussing before they leave the restaurant. Holding out his hand for Mai to follow, Ron leads her back to their room.

"Sit," he orders, dropping cross-legged onto the carpet and facing her on the edge of the room overlooking the lakes. Lights on both sides of the river burst in brilliant clouds of crystal iridescence in the black velvety night, trailing squiggles of raw color on the river crossed by ships in dark silhouette and running lights. Hotels with ornate crowns, lit in bright colors, poke up through the freezing mist.

"Tonight, I initiate you, Panther Girl, *hei bao nuhai*, into a sworn pact between us." He grasps her hands and holds them prayerfully between his, looking into her face. Finding the affirmation he seeks, he says, "Swear that you will strive with your heart and soul for the perfection which will guide you to your ultimate goal of achievement: the capture of MA Minho and the rescue of Rick, your husband. Nothing will swerve you from your purpose." He releases her hands, "Do you know about meditation, Mai?"

"Yes," she answers, awed by his formality. Growing up in a geodesic dome on a hippie commune in the 1970s, who wouldn't know about meditation?

"Tonight, we meditate. Do whatever style you like, just to relax the mind and begin to focus your special powers."

***

Later that night in Wenzhou, Wright and the BFO squad discuss the wisdom of taking a room on the same corridor where they could surveil up close, get pictures, and perhaps listen. The risk is that they could be recognized, compromising the mission and Martin's safety. After a consultation with Nolan, Choy goes online and reserves two adjoining rooms across the hall from the gang on the fifth floor. He and Poole check into the Chosun Wenzhou that night. Wright and the Marines gradually move in, bringing up gear from the Expeditions. Their view of a new brick apartment building on the other side of the hotel from the gang's rooms is only twenty meters away. They keep their curtains closed.

The squad fully outfits the rooms. The peep hole in both doors is replaced with fish-eye cameras, hooked up through motion-sensor software to automatically record on an external hard drive connected to Poole's laptop. Outputs are arranged on a split-screen for every installed camera; signal boosters are placed in the hallway near the rooms. The men design a schedule that allows them to sleep, work, and take breaks outside the hotel, while avoiding brushing arms with their target in elevators, stairs, or lobby.

Another laptop is set up to receive and process the ping coming from the beacon they installed on EU Sun's gold Land Cruiser in Huangshan two days ago. They park their Ford Expedition across the aisle from where the gang is parking, near the elevator, and rig a camera on it as well.

November 12

Nolan and Wright had determined long ago that the best way to free Rick Martin would be to tip off the Chinese and let them do the extraction. They agree: now's the time to conclude the experiment and bring him in. By 17:00 Virginia time, Nolan calls Wright with details about the money transfer. He's already up at 06:00 the next day, Monday.

"Have you heard from Gen. MA, about the amount?" asks Nolan.

"No, not yet."

"I got the banks lined up today, on Saturday," brags Nolan, "call me awesome."

"That's amazing," says Wright dutifully.

"We're going through the Israel Discount Bank to the Golomt Bank in Mongolia and then to American Express," says Nolan.

"Why don't we use the American woman to pick up the money? Puts another layer of insurance between us and the terrorists," asks Wright. "She's been messaging me."

"Go ahead, get her involved now. And the Chinese. Work up some scenarios and get back to me. Including neutralization. If things go awry, Martin won't survive Tehran."

***

Gen. MA started the day slurping soup Han-Joo brought to their room from the hotel kitchen and persuading EU Sun to his point of view.

"I'm not confident in this operation. I remember things that went wrong with that KAL job, and we weren't authorized to make changes. And the top-level decision makers weren't listening to us down below. This time, we're sitting ducks, waiting for Monday night. Why can't we go now? Too many people know about the plan. I don't trust the people at Compass Marine."

"We cannot deviate," says EU Sun.

"Why haven't we heard from Dalaoban RI? Something could be going wrong. We could be pawns. How would we know?"

"They have a word for what you are, Laoshi, *paranoid*," says EU Sun, disturbed by this line of conversation.

"I'm paranoid. Okay, but I'm alive. I have instincts, not just orders."

Gen. MA waves EU Sun away and texts Wright: "Prepare $100K."

He drops EU Sun off at the museum while he and the driver, GONG, canvass the docks. Pier 40-3 is part of the old harbor on the north side of the Ou Jiang River. Here, docks fringe the mouth of the river, many of them idle shipbuilders. The *Lantana* hasn't arrived yet. Next to the empty bay is a parallel road lined with small warehouses and equipment. Beyond them the dunes gradually slope away from the water, sheltering low trees and a group of about forty Chinese migrant men, waiting to board the *Lantana*. They've erected a communal kitchen under a tarp and sleeping areas between the trees. Behind them are low dunes vegetation and vegetable plots, farther inland. Sitting in a noodle shop in nearby Panshizhen with GONG, Gen. MA pencils out his plan.

***

Returning to the museum every afternoon since they arrived, EU Sun studied the pottery, bronze and lacquer ware, and painted sculptures, taking pictures of examples he thought the Great Leader would like. There were fine *huahua* brush paintings in ink on silk and paper and rooms of calligraphies. It occupied him during the few days before the *Lantana's* arrival, feeding long-dormant memories of life before North Korea, when he was a Chinese archaeology student—before his life changed. He bought a replica of his favorite piece, a terracotta horse.

***

The day dawns cloudy and freezing. Ron wakes first and is in the shower by 5AM. Mai rolls out of bed and into her jeans. He stands at the sink, a white towel around his waist, peering at himself in the fogged mirror, preening his GQ five o'clock shadow. Lost in his image, Ron inspects the job, concludes that it's satisfactory and splashes on sandalwood aftershave, throwing everything back into his ditty bag. He turns toward Mai with a pose, leaning against the sink, one arm casually wrapped across his smooth chest, holding onto his shoulder, those almond eyes smoldering beneath a mop of black hair.

"You are so hot, Ron. I like this new look with the beard."

"*Xiexie, hei bao nuhai.*" He grins and closes the door on her view. A few minutes later, he emerges in the same black gabardine pants and white sweater he's been wearing every day. Sitting on the edge of the bed, he laces up gum-soled boots, "Today I want the Commander to ride with me. Will you go with Maj. TANG?" He straightens up and grabs for her waist, but she wiggles off the bed and trots into the bathroom.

"*Weishenme?*" she asks through a partly closed door while running water in the sink and brushing her teeth.

"Let me drive the car, Mai."

A few more minutes and her toilet is complete, she nudges the door open with her big toe and says, "What?" Scooping up her things from around the sink, she tosses them into a zippered bag that fits into her carryon.

"You let me drive the car, I'm the boss, and I drive the car. Now it's time the Commander and I get real about what's going to happen in Wenzhou, Mai. Me and him, the bosses. I can call you in Maj. TANG's car, not like you're not going to be part of the plan ..." Ron gets up, standing close; he searches her face for a signal of agreement, submission, and validation.

"Yeah, okay," she says, relieved that something proactive is being done. "*Tai haole!*" She makes a touchdown gesture with both arms raised in a V.

Kneeling to zip his bag, Ron hands a report cover to Mai standing by the door with her bag, ready to go. "You might find this interesting. Commander GAO gave it to me: profiles on Gen. MA and the gang, and photos."

Riding down the elevator, she asks, "What did you call me?"

"*Hei bao nuhai,* Panther Girl."

The doors open into the garage. The Commander and Maj. TANG are there already.

Mai had found another *China Daily* in the lobby, only a few days old, to read in the car with Maj. TANG although it's too dark to read this early. She adjusts the back and naps in the heated seat of the Dongfeng. The road is open, and they pull onto the G56 Expressway by 05:45, skirting the lowest-lying areas smothered in freezing fog.

Behind them in the freshly detailed Park Avenue, Ron is saying to the Commander, "My presumption is that they will embark on a UAE-bound freighter, the soonest one they can book passage."

"*Dui,*" comments GAO, "my thought as well. When do you think they arrived?"

"It's possible the gang got to Wenzhou even before we got the tip from Braithwaite on Thursday the tenth. But not any ship will take them. With a captive? As much as they dress him up or dye his hair, it will be impossible to hide Martin Xiansheng when boarding. They'll be charged a high transit fee. Not impossible though," continues Ron.

"Are there shippers that do this?" asks GAO aghast.

"Maybe. But we can find out. Can you call the Port Authority? Find out the inbound ships taking passengers for Abu Dhabi."

Commander GAO rings Sgt. WANG and gets him started finding the proper contact at the PA. While he's at it, he wakes Lt. LIU, too.

Ahead to the west, the rising sun colors the mountain fortress neon pink against a colorless gray-blue sky. Few vehicles are on the road this early. Ron feels in control of his world, sitting high in the driver's seat and directing the Commander.

At 08:00, Maj. TANG exits G56 ten kilometers past the G35 intersection at Fuliang to gas up, get provisions and some street food for breakfast. Ron and Mai stand in a short line at a cart to get *shabing jiaji,* a delicate pan-fried muffin filled with a fried egg, lettuce, and hot sauce.

"Pretty morning," she says, shivering.

"How are you and Maj. TANG getting along?"

"I was asleep until half an hour ago. You?" Puffs of condensation hang between them, making her laugh, making more clouds, making him laugh, and making more clouds.

"Yeah, good. The Commander woke up Sgt. WANG and Lt. LIU with a list of things to do. Mainly, he wants to get in touch with the Port Authority today. We're going all the way to Wenzhou. The road is great. God, I love to drive when there are no trucks and no ice."

Ron gets two cups from a woman at the next cart selling warm soy milk. He walks Mai back to the filthy Dongfeng, handing one of the cups to her, "See you later." To Maj. TANG, behind the wheel, he says, "Mai wants to know about *hei bao fengge de gongfu.* [panther style kung fu] Can you help her?"

The last bits of muffin disappear between her lips before Mai asks, "What did you get for breakfast, Maj. TANG?" sipping the soy milk and hugging the warm cup in her hands.

"Sop Kambing" [mutton soup], he answers, holding up a bag of steamed buns, *"Baozi?"*

"Xiexie," she takes one, pulling it apart delicately, cautious, sampling and then devouring the rice dough bun filled with shredded pork and hot chilies.

Maj. TANG's phone rings in a text from Ron: *"zouba."*

It's warmed up to 35 Fahrenheit or 1 Celsius. As they resume their climb, treacherous freezing fog in the deep valleys clings to crevices of the mossy, humpbacked peaks, breaking into sunny skies once they're in the mountains. Twenty minutes later near Jingdezhen, they lose cell service.

TANG resumes, "Martial arts master ZHAO wants *me* to explain kung fu?" glancing at Mai briefly.

She has the newspaper open on her lap, kicks off her boots and props her feet on the dash. Looking back at TANG over her Italian reading glasses, she says "Tell me about Panther Girl."

"The panther style is special: the panther out-thinks attackers, confuses, bribes, and lies. Panther controls with the mind to win with speed and surprise. It is good style for women."

"What style are you?" she asks.

"Meiyou, not me, I am not kung fu expert," TANG answers.

"You're an expert at something, dui?" she continues.

"Wushu, Chinese boxing."

"And Ron?"

"He is kung fu advanced degree, Crane style: patient, defensive, turns attacker strength to weakness. Martin Xiansheng is Tiger: strong, overcomes attackers and endures much."

Driving in silence, looking out the muddy windows, she thinks it makes sense. An image of Rick swims into her mind, tortured and suffering. Image after image flies by in a montage of mud splatters, mountains, cigarette burns, and bruises. His face eludes her, wrapped in bandages. He roars in pain. She squeezes her eyes shut to stop the sound. It fades to a soft wail merged into the rhythmic drone of the tires on the pavement. She reaches her hand into the pocket of her parka, fingering the lucky coin that fell into her shoe the day Braithwaite gave them their first lead. *When was that? Thursday. What day is this? Monday.*

Maj. TANG looks at her a moment, hunched against the far door, staring at the scenery whizzing by with unseeing eyes, mouth set, without makeup to soften the expression of tension and worry.

Mai's been turning over and over in her mind conflicting feelings and ideas. She remembers the night at the theatre, meeting Ron and his mother. Before she was plunged into the abyss of Homeland Security. She tries keeping Ron's strong and kind face in focus and remembering how he stepped up to help her when she was eluding the Dage ... and his delicious kisses. Something she has been denying herself, ever since Rick arrived.

She's been angry at Rick and Wright. The Commander had called off the investigation, and he kept his word, until Rick decided to come and entangle sovereign nations in a game of hide-and-seek.

She sighs bitterly and grips the *lucky* coin in her pocket so tightly it cuts into her palm, feeling the sharp pain, a reminder of her present predicament.

While Mai ruminates on her problems, BFO Director Wright has been developing the ransom plan. He tries calling her but gets a bounced message while she's out of range of cell service.

***

ZHAO turns on the ignition and starts the heater, while he and the Commander scarf their breakfasts. The altitude and rare air burns carbs, expanding their energy. Commander GAO offers Ron a *baozi* in exchange for a muffin. Gulping down half the warm milk, Ron sets it into the cup holder and texts Maj. TANG: "zuoba." It doesn't matter that they lose cell service a few kilometers up the road; it'll take Sgt. WANG all day to thread his way through the various bureaucracies.

"I don't know why I haven't thought of this before," starts ZHAO, "All this time I've been imagining Martin Xiansheng being carried all the way to Iran by the gang to get their reward. Why wouldn't they simply get him onto an Iranian vessel in Wenzhou? Done deal. They wouldn't have to go any farther in jeopardy of being caught or Martin escaping."

"It should be a simple matter to identify and locate the ship; that work is routinely undertaken at the Wenzhou Naval Base by the Coast Guard, the CCG," says GAO.

"So it would seem, Commander," says ZHAO, "but ownership and registration of ships is murky at best and tedious to determine at worst, if we have to track down shell companies in places like Singapore and Hong Kong."

Near Wuyuan, ZHAO follows Maj. TANG onto S26, and starts climbing again.

"Let's consider the port for a minute. They'll need to transfer Martin to the ship. How would that look?"

"He could be in a crate, delivered to the ship," suggests GAO.

"*Haode*, ha-ha, provisions or such, restrained or drugged or both? So, we need to know the provisioner working with the Iranian fleet. Tomorrow, Mai and I can go into town to the Wenzhou men's clinic for leads and also go to the provisioner location, probably near the harbor. You say you'll be at the naval base? You and Maj. TANG staying there?

"*Dui*, the base is in Wenzhou Bay on a restricted island. I'll call on the Commanding Officer tomorrow. A network will have to be set up to implement our plan. You realize, the PLA controls this operation," says GAO.

"Of course, Commander. Qing, will you allow me to be your advisor? TSC is paying for my expertise; all you have to do is let me into your operation." Ron looks at the Commander, and for a second their eyes lock, before returning his gaze to the road.

"You need a gun. This man Gen. MA is dangerous. I have already processed the necessary applications for you and Maj. TANG. Do you have a preference? Can you fire one, or are you purist kung fu man?" asks GAO.

"Of course, as Hong Kong Police, I have mastered all forms of combat. Spent two years in the Special Forces before joining the career track to Deputy Commissioner. They rotated me through all the departments after graduation from Police Training School."

"*Zhende*," Commander GAO expels a puff of admiration. He's finally getting a lucky break with this case. "I'm putting in for a standard issue QSZ type 92 for Maj. TANG. It's a semi-automatic pistol made in China, takes nineteen millimeter cartridges like a Luger."

"*Haode*, I know the type 92, *xiexie*," says Ron.

"It comes with shoulder holster and ammo. I'll have them make up a kit for you. Radio control ear buds, knives, night goggles."

"I brought my own gear."

"*Haode.*"

Fifteen minutes before arriving in Changshan, they get their connectivity back, and the Commander calls Maj. TANG about stopping for lunch. ZHAO pulls into a mini-plaza and parks next to Maj. TANG's mud beast at the quaintly named village of Xian Linchang, County Forest Farm. Before turning off the ignition, he checks the temperature reading on the rearview mirror display: 17 Celsius, 43 Fahrenheit. Leaning back and sideways, resting one long arm along the steering wheel and the other across the back of his seat, he says "I hope we're not too late getting there."

Commander GAO's attention flickers toward Maj. TANG and Mai standing on the sidewalk in front of a hot pot restaurant. "She's counting on us. We can't fail." Turning back to ZHAO, he says, "You go first. Tell Maj. TANG to order for me. He's an expert in this cuisine. He'll be in the kitchen again if you don't watch him. I'm calling WANG and getting things started."

Mai is dishing out bowls of mifan and pouring tea when the Commander slides into the booth next to Maj. TANG.

"WANG has made a phone appointment for me with the CO at 15:00 today. Turn up the temperature on your wok, TANG, we have to go ASAP."

***

Saturday afternoon, the low sun slants into the Park Avenue; Mai lowers the visor and pulls the report cover out of her bag, while Ron cruises behind Maj. TANG, following the Dongfeng onto G60. He selects a CD and pushes it into the console player.

Gen. MA's profile is on top. She scans the half page of citations. "Not much here on Gen. MA the mystery man. That 1968 Pueblo citation is wild. How old would he have been?" mentally calculating, "Seventeen!"

"TSC is doing some digging. We should get some more intel soon," offers Ron.

"Pyongyang University? I didn't know such a place existed," she continues, turning the page and scanning details on Lt. Col. DIANGTI Yong: Ninth Bureau Section Chief, Director Harbin Institute, Information Security Research Institute (ISRI) and National Information Center (NIC) in Harbin, born 1961, expected retirement age 55. The DOD on the attached autopsy says November 1, 2011. Someone has translated it in a summary stating the cause of death was from a toxin applied with a sharp instrument directly into his jugular vein in his neck. Nothing she hadn't already figured out.

Behind this are some blown-up images of Gen. MA and Chief DIANGTI at the conference table and shots of the whole room from different perspectives, hidden cameras she guesses.

The captured Korean agent KIM Yong-Kyung's profile is next: presumed nineteen years old of ethnic Chinese origin and older brother of KIM Sang-Bo, still at large and possibly ahead in Wenzhou with Rick's captors. "Did you see this part about the captured man, KIM Yong-Kyung?"

"No, what?"

"It says here he was abducted with his brother when a boy and trained to be an assassin by the North Koreans."

"I remember hearing something about that," says Ron.

The image following is of a young Asian man, sitting in a cell block, shirtless and staring vacantly ahead. Behind that are shots of Yong-Kyung and another young Asian, dressed as campus security guards taken from the outside security camera on the building.

The next profile for Lt. GUAN Qinchen details his advancement to Deputy Regiment Commander for Chief DIANGTI's division in Harbin: born 1969, expected retirement age 50. Mai calculates he's about Rick's age being born in 1970.

"Here's something new. SHENG Jianqiang and DONG Zhi Wei were gangsters recruited by Lt. GUAN back in August. Apparently, they've been planning this for some time. SHENG is from a Tianjin Triad and DONG is a Beijing gangster. He was their local driver."

"*Zhende*, that's interesting. Suppose that these men are with Rick's captors. That would be a large contingent to keep hidden, fed, and motivated."

Next in the report is an image looking to Mai like the famous 007 henchman Oddjob, with his steel-brimmed bowler hat and martial arts. "Yeah, I remember this guy, SHENG. He's the one who punched me in the face." More pictures of the scene in the parking lot: she and Rick walking out, the scuffle, and one of her lying on the ground next to the Park Avenue. She gazes at the images for many long minutes.

"What's that picture, Mai?" asks Ron, glancing at her lap.

"That's me lying next to your car."

"Hold it up, let me see," he says.

The last report is on the corporate shell, Radiant Star Company aka Compass Marine Company, South Korea, aka Global International Shippers (GISCO) 28th Floor, Sebang Bldg., 708-8, Yeoksam-dong, Kangnam-Gu, Seoul, Republic of Korea. The Chinese version is quite long. The English translation is merely a summary of facts:

> Owned or controlled by or acting or purporting to act
> for on behalf of IRISL, blacklisted in 2008 by US
> Department of Treasury's Office of Foreign Assets Control
> (OFAC), pursuant to Executive Order 13382, which targets
> proliferators of weapons of mass destruction (WMD) and
> their delivery systems.

A long list of Chinese and Korean names follow: managers, vice-presidents and CEOs, including Faridoun Shafaie Karaji and S.A. Mohensi. Not that she recognizes these names, but that they are Middle Eastern and not Asian. The Radiant Star's Honda Odyssey and getaway car Buick Park Avenue are listed.

"It says here the company Radiant Star, owner of the gang's cars, is connected to Sea Tigers as provisioner for IRISL—Islamic Republic of Iran Shipping Lines. Do you know what the Sea Tigers are?" asks Mai.

"Sure do; they were the navy of Sri Lanka separatists back in the 1980s, before my time. They've been a nuisance in the Bay of Bengal and over that way, east of us, hijacking several vessels outside Sri Lanka, throwing the Chinese crew overboard, that type of thing, stripping the ships bare and setting them loose as phantoms. Supposedly, the Sea Tigers were annihilated in 2009—which was about the time I was leaving the force—by the Sri Lankan army, killing their top leader and depriving them of their bases. It's believed they have found bases in Somalia and Malaysia where they continue to thrive, providing services to outlier nations such as Iran and North Korea."

Mai's phone rings, rousing her from thought. For a moment, she can't focus on the sound; It's been so long since anyone has called her.

"*Nihao*, Mrs. Martin," says Wright.

"*Nihao*, Lawrence," Mai replies sweetly, as she and Ron exchange looks.

"I got your message."

"*Dui*, and I also have an apology for you, for the disgraceful way I greeted you the last time we met."

"Oh, really, well ..." Wright is caught off-guard, something he has little experience with, and forgets what he had prepared to say. "Where are you?"

"I'm driving to Wenzhou."

"Really? With ZHAO?"

"Yes, but I can't tell you more. I urge you to speak with the Commander. He asked me to find a good time for you to connect."

"How about right now?" he suggests.

"I'll call you back, or rather, the Commander will," she says, "One more thing: Rick. Is he okay?"

"We've seen him. He seems okay, Mrs. Martin."

"Are you guys negotiating?"

Wright pauses a few seconds considering the best answer.

Mai realizes what's going on and answers for him. "Oh right, we don't negotiate with terrorists. Is that it?"

"Mrs. Martin, you can count on us," he says. "I look forward to working with Commander GAO toward a suitable solution."

Paging through her address book, she sends a call. "Wei, nihao Commander, Martin Taitai … da-da … Wright says he can talk now. Will you call him? You have his cell number in your phone?… *haode, bai-bai.*"

***

Commander GAO folds down the sun visor against the blinding afternoon light and gets comfortable in his seat, ratcheting back a notch.

His call finds Wright relaxing at the Chosun Wenzhou Hotel, across the hall from Rick Martin. He's clicking through the Chinese television stations while anxiously waiting for the Commander's call.

"*Wei, nihao*, Wright Xiansheng. Where are you? *Ni zai nar?*"

"We've been following the gang since they left Beijing. Now we're at the Chosun Wenzhou Hotel, in rooms across the hall from the gang," offers Wright. He sends the Commander the beacon frequency on the gang's gold Land Cruiser.

"Thank you for this information," says GAO

Wright confides, "The US wants to offer a ransom for Rick Martin, but only if it's initiated by his wife or the PRC."

Commander GAO backs off, saying, "PRC can't be involved, but it's prudent to develop an alternative to interception."

"Or neutralization," adds Wright.

"Under what circumstances?" asks GAO, a little shocked at the possibility.

"Do you have an interception plan?" Wright wants to know.

The Commander invites him, "Come to our planning meeting at the Naval Base. Do you have the money?" GAO wants to know.

"Our money goes from the US to PRC through Israel Discount Bank to the Golomt Bank in Mongolia and then to American Express. "I need help setting up the account for Mrs. Martin at American Express. Can you guys do that?"

"*Dui*, that's possible. There's probably one here in Wenzhou." suggests GAO.

"What about the fees? Can they be waived?" continues Wright, pinning down details. "We do it like this and my boss and yours are shielded."

"I can do that overnight. Send me the registration information you want to use. Only you Americans care about getting caught paying."

Obtaining the criminal Gen. MA for terminal prosecution, vindication of his Office and Deputy Commander HUANG supersedes vague and unenforceable agreements with DPRK. And will save him from uncomfortable reprisals. Commander GAO offers to send a technician to set up a SIGINT listening post at the Chosun Wenzhou.

"I'll be tied up at the Naval Base tomorrow morning. Can you go to the Wenzhou airport to pick our snoop tech up? It's close to your hotel. He's Junior-Grade Technical Specialist YANG Cai, from my Office in Beijing. I'll text you his flight information later tonight."

***

ZHAO turns at Longyou onto S33 south to G25, following Maj. TANG, and jogs at Fuling onto G1513 east. Here the expressway tracks next to the Ou Jiang River, dropping in altitude steadily.

After crossing the river near Yangyixiang, three hours later, around 17:30, 5:30PM, Maj. TANG calls ZHAO and they confer. Pulling the headset off and tossing it onto the console, Ron says to Mai, "They're heading to the Wenzhou Naval Base. I want to stay downtown near the harbor." He heads east where Maj. TANG turns south.

***

At about 16:30, agent Frank Choy is relaxing in his room at the Chosun Wenzhou Hotel, watching the vehicle beacon ping as the Land Cruiser approaches on the GPS monitor. On the other laptop, he sees the video feed of the Land Cruiser pulling into its usual space near the elevator when the motion sensor prompts the camera to start. In a few minutes, the gang walks into view of the fish-eye cameras in the hall. Gen. MA and two Koreans, EU Sun and Han-Joo, and the Chinese driver, GONG, have returned from their excursion to the local museum.

At 17:00, Choy witnesses the Korean man, KIM Sang-Bo, and the Chinese driver, GONG, leaving the room. By 20:00, the last man has returned. Choy rigs up earbuds and mic to sync with his BlackBerry, like a walkie-talkie app. Poole takes his place at the laptop station, looking out for any gangsters approaching the garage, while Choy goes downstairs to install mics and cameras inside the Land Cruiser, using superglue and wireless technology. The whole operation takes only eight minutes, including breaking into the car and getting back into the room.

"I got a good shot of you in the parking garage," says Poole.

"Show me," says Choy, stripping the gear out of his ears and shirt.

"You should send it in to YouTube."

CHAPTER 6
IRISL

The Beijingers arrive in Wenzhou, the night of Saturday November 12. *Are they too late?* Commander GAO and Maj. TANG stay at the Wenzhou Naval Base on an island in the bay buffeted by constant wind, arriving at 20:30.

November 13

It's 06:00, and Lt. GUAN Qinchen and YANG Cai, the Junior-Grade Technical Specialist from Commander GAO's Office, are at the Beijing Airport, boarding a commuter flight to Wenzhou. Wright meets JGTS YANG Cai on his end and brings him back to their listening post at the Chosun Wenzhou Hotel while GUAN transfers to the base chopper shuttle. By 10:00, Cai is listening with them to telephone conversations in real time, collected by the Chinese through SIGINT towers locked onto the gang's and Compass Marine's cell frequencies.

***

Commander GAO is sitting in the officers' mess hall when he gets a call from Ron, after spending all morning connecting with his PLA counterparts at the base, the Wenzhou Public Security Bureau (WPSB) and Port Authority (PA).

"We're here at the men's clinic," starts ZHAO after a brief greeting.

"Anything?" asks GAO.

"We have a lead on a group of men waiting to board a ship to Abu Dhabi on Pier 40-3."

"I'll have the PA check that out. We discovered the name of the closest IRISL freighter, the *Lantana*, owned by Iran and operated by the National Iranian Tanker Company."

"We're lucky the ownership is obvious," says ZHAO. "How did you find this out?"

"Chinese satellite images confirmed its location on Wednesday, November 9—saw the *Lantana* leaving Golden Horn Bay."

"Have you guys determined the possible date of the ship's arrival?" ZHAO asks.

"It arrives today, this afternoon."

"My god," gasps ZHAO.

"Indeed," agrees GAO. "And is scheduled to depart on Tuesday."

"Have you identified their provisioner?"

"*Meiyou*. PA has their entire department working on it. I'll call you when I know. Where are you staying?"

"The New Asia Hotel, a couple blocks from the harbor. Where are you?"

"At the base in the bay. We had to leave our vehicle at the airport and take a chopper shuttle. So, have to go. I'll call you with the address. *Zaijian*."

Ron starts the car's ignition and turns to Mai, "Hungry?"

"Starved," she answers.

"Let's go back to the hotel for lunch. I have work to do."

Back in their suite at the harbor, Ron boots up while ordering tuna sandwiches on toast with sliced tomato and French fries from room service. "I got an email packet from Lily," he says, half turning toward Mai.

Their suite is on the top floor. The bedroom and sitting room both have spectacular views through mullioned French doors off a private balcony extending across both rooms. Bright, marine blue iridescence dissolves her where she sits in an overstuffed armchair. The *fuwuyuan* sets the tray of dishes and a bouquet of tulips on a table next to Mai, who perks up when she sees her favorite sandwich perfectly toasted, with the crusts trimmed and cut into diagonal quarters.

Ron drags his laptop, still connected by its power cord, across the room to sit with Mai by the windows and eat while reading the encrypted and compressed packet of reports from TSC. The full transcript of an interview is attached in PDF and MP3 formats.

"Listen to this, Mai," says Ron. "There was a famous case of international terrorism involving Korean Air Lines flight 858, which exploded in 1987, killing 115 passengers. A young woman traveling with an older man on Japanese passports was determined to have planted the bomb. The man swallowed cyanide disguised in a cigarette and carried as a self-destruct mechanism. He died, but the woman lived, after a bright-eyed airport security staff pulled the cigarette from her mouth.

"This past week, our TSC office in Seoul questioned South Korean authorities about the old case. They always thought there were more people involved in that daring attack, and when asked about Gen. MA, they replied his name was on a short list of conspirators.

"Other instances researched by TSC were abductions of Japanese in the late 1970s and early '80s, but the office didn't approve airfare to Tokyo to follow up."

Ron's phone interrupts with a call from the Commander.

"I've got the address of the provisioner for you: Compass Marine Company on Ou Hai Qu, near the river. We're capturing cell signals from phones at that location. My technician is working with the Americans to gather this in live time. They're across the hall from Martin, in the same hotel."

"*Zhende*. Martin is alright?"

"They haven't seen him for several days."

"How many are there?"

"Gen. MA, three Koreans and one Chinese, plus Martin Xiansheng."

"I have new details about Gen. MA from TSC. I'll send you the data packet before going out."

"*Haode, bai-bai.*"

Ron turns to Mai, "Wright is in the same hotel as Rick."

***

Driving by, Compass Marine looks like any other warehouse-based business: five to six kilometers from the Ou Jiang River on a tributary off the south side of the river. Ron encircles the neighborhood; beyond the clusters of warehouses are patchwork fields of crops dotted with peasant cottages. A housing development of apartments, at least twenty stories each, sprouts between a dry wash and the expressway. In the other direction, immense salt ponds cut swaths along the margin of a substantial creek. Where Compass Marine is situated, at the mouth of a confluence of waterways, their dock offers delivery services to larger vessels anchored outside the harbor without paying the high rent of dock slips on the main river channel.

From the G1513 Expressway, where it crosses the creek, they can look east right down into the operation. Crisscrossing town, Ron picks up another elevated highway, providing a view from a different angle. After an hour and a half of driving, he settles on a finger of land opposite Compass Marine, sharing a canal and boat ramp with it on one side. He captures some data and sends the coordinates to GAO and TSC.

"Stay here."

"I'm coming with you," Mai responds, unclicking her seatbelt.

The day started cool at just a half degree above 0 Celsius, 33 Fahrenheit, and overcast, gradually warming by midday to 7 C, 35 F. She zips her parka up to her chin and steps out of the car. She closes her eyes a moment, inhaling a deep whiff of low tide marine air, redolent with rotting fish and tangy salt. She opens them with a snap and catches up with Ron hiking up the canal, taking pictures and writing notes in his smartphone.

At the top of the boat ramp, they find a bridge wide enough for one car lane, leading into the back of Compass Marine. Hesitating before crossing, Ron carefully looks around at the empty landscape. On the left, along their side, is a high wall with a parking lot behind a chain-link fence, about a half mile beyond where they're standing. The other side of the canal is the back of Compass Marine, obscured by large trees. The boat ramp is empty.

Ron holds Mai by the elbow and propels her across the open bridge into the shelter of the trees on the other side. From this perspective, they see the main entrance is about one hundred meters or three to four hundred feet to the other side of the U-shaped piece of riverfront, surrounded by water on three sides. The operation is huge, comprised of about twenty warehouses cobbled together with additions and covered walkways. The Hong Kong man and the California woman, Crane and Panther to their cores, slip through the trees to a breezeway connecting two buildings. Keeping to the perimeter, they gradually skirt the development.

Employee living quarters in a combination of small apartment buildings and siheyuan-style houses are separated from a parking lot near the front entrance by a couple acres of vegetable gardens. At the narrow neck of the property, where it touches Ou Hai Qu, an old, crumbly wall protects the property with a guard shack and gate.

Shielded from view of the guard by a pump house, Ron takes a few shots before guiding Mai back the way they came. The warehouses sit silently as they sneak past. Only one warehouse seems to be busy; they avoid that one and slip back across the bridge.

Invigorated and sure of herself, Mai pauses walking and stares up at the bright, gray sky while Ron's figure trudges ahead to the car.

Tugs are nudging the *Lantana,* stern first, into its slip at Pier 40-3 in Wenzhou Bay, on the north side of the river and far from Compass Marine, as Ron transfers his images to the Commander and TSC.

***

This afternoon, Sang-Bo has brought a couple weapons upstairs to clean and oil, with the adjoining door closed and out of sight of the captive and his keeper. Han-Joo has been holed up with Rick in their room. They're lounging on the beds watching television when Gen. MA comes back from the harbor. GONG dropped him off before going to fetch EU Sun from the museum. Gen. MA opens the adjoining door, looks blankly at the TV and TV-watchers, closes it and gestures to Sang-Bo to follow him down the stairs, out the front, and down the street.

Pausing at a street vendor selling hot, roasted chestnuts, he says, "We have worked some interesting jobs, haven't we, little brother."

"*Dui, Laoshi,*" replies the teenager, already a junior agent.

"I remember when you first arrived at the boys' camp," continues MA. Digging a nut out for himself, he offers the bag to the young man.

"Don't speak of it, *Laoshi,* I was young and untamed then."

"That is your internal strength, Sang-Bo."

"I worry about my brother. What will they do to him? He's probably already dead!"

They walk together a ways in the cloudy afternoon. The sun burns through for a few glorious moments before another squall approaches the coast. A brisk breeze rustles the palm fronds on the trees lining the boulevard in front of the hotels.

"I'm concerned we haven't heard from Dalaoban RI since Sunday the sixth. Almost two weeks."

"*Dalaoban* RI … ?" Sang-Bo is alarmed. People disappear back home in DPRK. One day they're standing with Dear Leader, and the next day they're gone. *Not RI*, hopes Sang-Bo. "What do we do? I know EU Sun wants to stick with the plan. But, tell me, *Laoshi*, what should we do?"

"I've started talking to the American CIA. As a backup, if something goes wrong, understand. I'm developing a new plan. Be prepared to act quickly and follow your training. No questions, no talking, no slacking."

"What about EU Sun?"

"I will persuade him. If not, we may have to improvise. Remember: no questions, no talking, no slacking."

Later, as night falls, Gen. MA wants to call the Captain of the *Lantana,* but he doesn't have his number. All the arrangements have been made on *Dalaoban* RI's end, and RI is incommunicado these days. Gen. MA searches for the remote, turning the volume up on the televisions in both rooms. He takes EU Sun into the bathroom to discuss the plan, running water in the shower and sink to thwart anyone listening. He expresses fears about them being bugged or followed when they leave with Rick.

"*Laoshi*, why do you persist with this treasonous line of thinking?"

"Is it treasonous to bring this operation to a successful conclusion?"

"Why do you think this?" asks the younger agent.

"Have you noticed anything about the rooms across from ours?"

"They have 'Do Not Disturb' sign on the door."

"Two doors, like us."

He's perched on the edge of the sink while EU Sun stands firmly with arms folded across his chest.

"Have you seen anyone go in or out of the doors?" asks the General.

"*Bu dui*," says EU Sun.

Gen. MA continues, "This could unhinge our plans and make us vulnerable to capture." The General detects a flicker of recognition in the younger agent's expression. "Before we go anywhere, I have to be sure we won't be followed. This is critical, EU Sun, are you listening?"

"*Dui, Laoshi.*"

"We have one chance at surprise … so … So the Land Cruiser has to be abandoned. We need a new car. What about the American himself? They could have planted a tracker in his body, a bionic signal emitter. The Americans are so sophisticated in their mind control; we can learn from them."

"*Dui, Laoshi*, but what is the plan?"

"The tradeoff will be at the parking lot next to the *Lantana* tomorrow, after we arrange things with the Captain. There are some options open to us. And I want him to have a sniper on the ship, or on the dock, these are things we must discuss before the CIA arrive with the money."

"That's not much of a plan, General."

"Trust me, EU Sun, trust your Uncle MA. I have plan."

***

Back at the New Asia, Ron works upstairs while Mai sends her clothes to the laundry and shops for new ones. Finding anything in the gift store that fits the tall *Meiguoren* limits choices to white jeans and a brown, embroidered hoodie sweater, finishing with high-topped cross-trainers. Mai waits for Ron in the vast hotel lobby of polished white stone, crystal chandeliers, and potted exotic palms. A mezzanine runs around one end with its own set of elevators for private meetings. She's gazing at the revolving door while clumps of travelers pass through it, circling in and circling out, when the elevator doors opposite open. Kung fu master ZHAO, the Crane, disguised in a soiled white cable-knit sweater and rumpled jeans tucked into the tops of gum-soled, black leather boots, steps into the modern, polished lobby.

At the hotel restaurant, the hostess in red jacket and black trousers leads them to a table. Ron takes care of ordering, including the local specialty, river crabs. The *fuwuyuan* pours a bottle of Chang-an sparkling wine to accompany plates of fresh oysters. Over a solemn parade of fresh seafood and wild vegetables with noodles and soup, Ron's phone interrupts again.

"*Wei, nihao*, Commander," says ZHAO.

"Maj. TANG is at target practice with his new QSZ type-92," starts GAO.

"Did you get my data packet today?" asks Ron.

"*Dui, xiexie*, very interesting," replies GAO. "We have known about those incidents but never thought to connect them to Gen. MA. And all the while, he worked for us, going back and forth to Pyongyang as a specialist. For you, we hoped to get something from Gen. MA's phone. Sadly, none of the ping analysis from the collected phones led to him. Calls from Lt. GUAN's phone went to a dead account."

"Have you heard anything from the SIGINT post?"

"*Meiyou bangzhu*." [Nothing helpful.]

"Did you have time to look at the shots I took today at Compass?" asks ZHAO.

"I passed the file to the platoon leader," answers GAO.

"When do I get to meet them?"

"Come to target practice with us tomorrow morning at the base. Be prepared to give a briefing at ten hundred hours," says GAO. Chain of command applies to team advisors too, so he makes a point of not asking the civilian, but rather, delegating. "Check out of your hotel in the morning. I'm sending a driver to pick you up. Tell Martin Taitai, she made a good impression on Wright Xiansheng. I make her platoon communications specialist."

Hanging up, Ron turns to Mai with an enigmatic and insane grin, "We're checking out in the morning. Commander GAO wants us at the naval base for target practice. The ship is here. It leaves Tuesday, day after tomorrow."

Ron empties the bottle of wine into their glasses while the *fuwuyuan* clears the table. They relax a few minutes, savoring their meal and considering the wealth of information that they've collected in only one day, since arriving in Wenzhou.

All those days on the road, pushing to get here, and worrying they might be too late, the words: *the ship is here* just don't compute for Mai. Her heart is lodged in her throat, and she can't seem to say anything. Looking at Ron, she doesn't hear what he's saying over a roaring wave of *chi*, choking her in a mist of brackish, low-tide affect blended with sparkling wine. As if coming to, she gropes for meaning in his words.

"... the Commander has started listening into Compass Marine cell communications from SIGINT towers, catching their signals, homing into their location, and using voice-recognition software, searching for the keyword: *Lantana*. That's the name of the ship." He raises his glass saying, "*Ganbei*."

"Have they figured out that Compass Marine is connected to Radiant Star?" asks Mai, her brain connecting dots on its own, reaching up to click her glass with his.

"Dui, they are aware," he says, stopping a moment to think.

Mai's phone rings, muffled inside her purse. It's Wright. She puts him on speaker phone for Ron.

"We've heard from them. The amount has been agreed on. They'll take 100 thousand USD for Rick."

"That's fantastic, Lawrence. When?"

"Soon. Do you have the money?"

"What?! We don't have that kind of money! I expected that you … the US sent ransom money to release missionaries in Africa!"

Wright laughs, cruel to the end. "Don't worry, Mrs. Martin. We got it. But the US cannot be in a position to be in the middle of any of this."

"That's bullshit that we don't negotiate with terrorists."

"That's right. Or North Korea or Iran … So, that brings me to the most important part." Wright sucks his breath. "You have to deliver it."

Whatever chi or prana or yuanfen has ever moved through her stops. No breath, no thought, no sound. Her eyes drift to Ron's grave face. *How did I get in the middle of all this?*

Ron grabs the phone and speaks directly to Wright, "This is insane. I won't allow it."

"Is it up to you, Mr. Zhou?" asks Wright.

Mai shakes her head, resigned and ready to face her destiny.

Defeated, Ron hands the phone to Mai.

"Listen, Mrs. Martin, we're very committed to the safe return of your husband, and the Chinese are fully prepared to go through with this, with your help or not. What are you willing to do?"

She hears herself say, as if from some muffled box, "I'll do it. I'm not afraid. He's my husband. I'll do it for Rick."

"Be prepared for anything."

"Our plan was to check out in the morning and go to Wenzhou Naval Base."

"For the money hand-off, we need you to stay in town. I'll contact you. Keep your phone on."

"What just happened?" asks Mai, tucking the phone away.

"You're in it now."

November 14

Mai stays behind at the New Asia Hotel. Ron is gone by 5AM. A guard takes him to the Maritime Safety Administration (MSA), China's Coast Guard heliport at Yongqiang Airport where he hooks up with Lawrence Wright and a Marine traveling to the base. The trip, in a Texas-made helicopter by Bell, takes twenty minutes, arriving at 05:55. The day starts clear and cold, around minus one Celsius or thirty-one degrees Fahrenheit.

***

At breakfast—mutton soup and *baozi*, fetched from the kitchen by Han-Joo—there is little conversation. When someone begins to talk, a scowl from Gen. MA withers the words in their throat.

"Everyone shower today and pack."

While Gen. MA takes his turn in one of the bathrooms, EU Sun takes Sang-Bo aside in the other.

"Are you prepared to follow the plan?" asks EU Sun.

"I'm prepared to follow our leader."

"Gen. MA has a valid concern: that we could be bugged here and the CIA could follow us when we leave. He wants to be sure," says EU Sun.

"How can he be sure?"

"He has a plan. So ..."

"I know; no questions, no talking, no slacking."

Their bags are packed. The men are sitting around playing cards and watching television. Gen. MA beckons to Sang-Bo and GONG to follow him.

Not thirty feet away, Ed Poole is watching when the three of them leave the hotel room and get into the elevator. But instead of showing up on the Land Cruiser cam, they walk out of the front of the hotel onto the busy street. He loses them.

Stopping at a neighborhood park, they sit and watch the old people exercising in the frigid air.

"We're changing the plan," MA says. "For all the reasons we have discussed before. I suspect the Land Cruiser and our rooms are bugged. The American CIA is close by or they wouldn't be able to make a trade this quickly. Go get us a car and come back. Don't use your phones. Throw them away. Get new ones. Get a new one for me. Here," he says, digging some yuan out of his fat wallet.

He returns to their room in the hotel while the minions set out on their errand. Han-Joo has washed Rick in the shower, something they both seemed to enjoy. She's toweling him off when Gen. MA begins inspecting him carefully for a bug.

"We bought the clothes you've been wearing, dog. So they must be clean. But what about your body? You are wearing some kind of device. Am I right, dog?"

"Wrong. Wasting your time."

Gen. MA stands on the toilet to inspect Rick's head while EU Sun holds him in a lock.

Looking in Rick's ear, he spots a red, tender place. "What's this?"

In a second, Gen. MA has stuffed a hand towel in Rick's mouth and sliced off his ear. Rick nearly chokes on his gagged shriek, instantly quieted as he gasps for air. One crisis averted by another. EU Sun jerks him backwards, controlling Rick's windpipe with a choke hold as he pulls the towel out of his mouth. Han-Joo crowds into the room at the sounds of trouble.

"Put the towel around his head," barks MA. "And keep him shut up."

Gen. MA digs at the offending spot in the dead flesh and discovers a hard pellet under the skin. He folds the ear in a facecloth and puts the mess into his jacket pocket.

***

Downstairs in front of the hotel, Sang-Bo and the Xi'an driver, GONG, hail a cab and ask the driver to take them to Compass Marine, the only address they know. When he stops near the gate, they pull the driver out onto the road. GONG yanks his cap off and shoots him in the head with an automatic pistol similar to Maj. TANG's. The few startled drivers on Ou Hai Qu don't bother to stop. The gangsters pop the trunk and throw the man inside. Farther down the road, they find a good place to throw him into the river. But not before robbing him of the cash he made on fares this morning. Forty-five minutes later, Sang-Bo is calling Gen. MA from the hotel reception desk.

Upstairs, Ed Poole is still watching when Rick emerges from the room, sitting in the wheelchair flanked by Gen. MA and EU Sun. His head appears to be bandaged with a white cloth and tape, his dyed black hair sticking out under a knit cap pulled low. Han-Joo follows, pulling the travel bags.

"Hey, guys, look, they're moving out," shouts Poole to the squad. In their dim room, with the curtains pulled across windows that look out onto another building next to the hotel, the men have been catching up with emails on their smartphones.

Choy and the Marine jump up, and they each stuff in an ear bud. Choy selects Rick's ping app on his BlackBerry, and they take the stairs down, synching up their systems as they go. On his end, Poole is hooking them up with his headset mic while he scans the video displays.

"Where are you, Choy? MA is in the Land Cruiser," he says.

"We're following Martin's ping to the parking level. We see the taillights of the Land Cruiser at the exit. We're following in the Expedition."

Poole has one eye on the netbook with Rick's ping and the other on the interior Land Cruiser cam with audio. MA and Sang-Bo are driving. He can't see into the back, and the men aren't talking.

***

Maj. TANG greets the three men at the base heliport as pale morning sun disappears behind high haze. The grounds are green and muddy.

"*Wei, nihao*, ZHAO," shouts TANG, waving to them from the sideline. The rotor blades whip his dark blue windbreaker with one star on the shoulders as he holds his arm against the downwash. Wright sticks out his hand in a stiff gesture of cooperation. Maj. TANG blinks at it and gives Wright a knuckle-popping squeeze. Maj. TANG and the Marine exchange grips and nod to each other. Walking to the Wenzhou Naval Base (WNB) Jeep, Maj. TANG unzips his jacket to give Ron a conspiratorial glimpse of a QSZ strapped in its holster next to his chest.

"First thing, we go to target practice," he says. "Where is Martin Taitai?"

"She's staying in Wenzhou. Didn't you hear?" asks Ron, turning a black look on Wright following behind. "They tagged her for carrying the ransom money." Ron's angry about this and doesn't mind letting others know about it.

"*Zhende*! There's a ransom now?" asks TANG.

At the firing range, Maj. TANG pulls a bag out of the Jeep's hatch and hands it to ZHAO.

"Here, for you, martial arts man," he says grinning. "*Zouba*," he adds, with upraised arms, herding them into the shelter of the bunker complex as a thunder clap and burst of rainy wind sweeps them ahead.

Once inside, Ron opens the bag and removes a plainly practical-looking, QSZ type-92 semi-automatic pistol and a new, black leather, cross holster.

"It's made in China, takes 19mm cartridges like a Luger," says Maj. TANG, fitting the holster around Ron's torso diagonally where it holds the gun firmly in front of his chest, easy to grasp with his right hand. The leather is stiff and smells new.

Maj. TANG hands around ear-protecting headsets to the men and leads them to the individual bays. ZHAO finds an empty one and begins practice. Maj. TANG disappears farther down the aisle into another free bay. Wright and the Marine have their own hand pieces, find bays and begin, even though they've been practicing at the embassy firing bunker. This will make a great story when they get stateside.

By 07:00, Maj. TANG has exercised his troops on marksmanship and brings them to the CO's compound for a formal greeting. Large, outdoor *penjing*, dripping with moss, adorn the courtyard upon carved-stone stands flecked with lichen.

The CO, Sr. Col. GAN, elegant in black, double-breasted dress uniform with four stars on his epaulets, meets them in a cozy sitting room, warmed by an electric fireplace flickering against one wall. This is the most exciting thing that has transpired in his jurisdiction since the local militia drove the Kuomintang out of the offshore islands in 1945. He eagerly welcomes the visiting official from Beijing and the crack forces he's reputed to have brought.

The platoon leader, Maj. WONG Kaihao, has been modeling strategies with his IT group since dawn. Reluctantly, he allowed Commander GAO to drag him to what he deemed a ritual meeting. To his surprise, the *laoren*, the old man, GAN, engages him in pointed questions about the mission.

Across the room, ZHAO spots a familiar face with two stars on his epaulet, "Lt. GUAN? Who else is here?"

"Cai is embedded with the American running dogs," he answers in his usual deadpan. As far as he's concerned, the CIA is behind this. Not realizing it has been bundled up into the larger and more ominous Department of Homeland Security.

Commander GAO maneuvers ZHAO over to Col. GAN and Platoon Commander WONG.

"This is Ronald ZHAO from TSC Securities, joining us for this mission. He was Special Forces with Hong Kong Police."

At that moment, a hush, as everyone takes in the stranger in rumpled jacket and jeans.

"Where is Martin Taitai?" asks GAO, looking around the room. "Col. GAN wants to meet the American man's wife."

"She has remained in town, sir," says Ron. "In case they need to transport the ransom money." He can't get over being mad about this development.

"At the New Asia Hotel?"

"*Dui.*"

"*Haode.*"

Commander GAO gestures to Wright to step up to GAN. "This is the man from the American Embassy, Commander."

Another hush. Never in his life had GAN imagined he would be welcoming a CIA operative in his cozy study. The two men gravely smile at each other, noting their shared trait of baldness. Wright boldly extends his arm to the Commander, who returns the gesture with a fingertip grip. Maj. TANG and the Marine instinctively stand at the door, surveying the gathering. The Commander can't tell if this is one of the Marines from the brawl in the conference room.

Commander GAO guides Wright to the coffee table where a young Marine in the regulation four-blues-camouflage uniform pours coffee for the Beijingers. They faintly smile at the woman and retreat to a corner to talk.

"The money is at the Wenzhou American Express," starts GAO. "The account has been set up as you specified. One of my staff will accompany Martin Taitai to the bank; I expected him to take her from here, but since you have ordered her to stay behind alone, I will send him immediately. It will take a long time to conclude the transaction, counting and verifying the amount of the withdrawal."

At 09:15 the Commander calls JGTS YANG Cai. "Go directly to the American Express bank near the New Asia Hotel. They're expecting you. Martin Taitai will meet you. Call me when you get there."

Col. GAN declares something in Chinese like "Go kick their asses, men." Then, he turns and leaves the reception, signaling that everyone can go back to working on the operation.

Standing in the empty room with the electric fireplace, the Commander's next call is to Mai.

***

Sitting around the hotel room, Mai stares out at the harbor. *We'll find Rick soon. I'll see him when I give them the money. And then what?* She tucks her chin into the top of her sweater and withdraws into her thoughts. *They better find him soon.... Or what?* She considers her options: *Leave here and be completely on my own in a strange town where I'm barely able to converse because of this crazy southern dialect, get Rick—but how?—and then do what?* She hooks her legs over the arm of the chair and stares out the windows at the approaching squall line out at sea. She closes her eyes and rests her head back. One hand unfastens her jeans and slips into her underpants, stroking the soft hairs. The other hand gropes under her shirt and hugs one breast.

Her morose thoughts are interrupted by Commander GAO's call. She zips her pants and reaches for the mobile.

"*Nihao*, Martin Taitai," he starts.

"Commander," she says.

"*Feichang ganxie ni*, for your invaluable services today."

"Okay," is all she says. "Is it now?"

"*Dui*, go to American Express Bank near to your hotel. The concierge can direct you. You will meet there a member of my staff, YANG Cai, junior-grade technical specialist. Bring your passport."

"What happens next?" Always the nosy American, asking questions.

"*Zouba*. Be safe."

Resigned to not knowing, Mai flips off her phone and prepares to go. She looks around, tucking loose clothing into her travel bag but leaving it open on the bed. Standing there, looking down, she spies the Bible. Impulsively, she stuffs it into a Bernini bag with her passport and a black knit cap, something Ron had given her to wear. Feeling in the pockets of her parka for gloves and a scarf to tie around her neck, she dabs on some dark pink lipstick and says *goodbye* to herself in the mirror.

The foolishness of running away from her problems in Sebastopol comes home in that moment. Instead of needing validation from Rick, here she is bailing his ass out!

Riding down the elevator, she plays with her lucky coin, turning it over and over between her thumb and fingers. If she was looking for adventure, she succeeded. In fact, she figures, Homeland Security and the lies Rick has been feeding her have turned her life upside down. Looking for the good in people and trusting has been working so far. Maybe she can find something good about Homeland Security.

Mai arrives before the bank opens at 10AM and waits outside with a small group of like-minded ex-pats needing money. Not feeling chatty, she covers her head with the parka hood and keeps to herself. At 09:45, JGTS YANG Cai arrives by taxi. She's been scanning the front of the bank for the arrival of Commander GAO's staff. When Cai bounds up the steps two at a time, she doesn't recognize him. But he recognizes her from the many security briefings. He's been watching her life for almost a year now, and he's excited to finally get to meet The Subject.

The bank officials let the queue file in the locked door.

***

GONG waits in the stolen cab, in the dead man's hat and shirt while Sang-Bo goes into the lobby to use a house phone to call Gen. MA. Once notified, Han-Joo opens the door for the General to wheel the *Meiguoren* into the hall. Rick sits passively in the wheelchair with his bandaged head covered by a cap. Han-Joo follows, pulling the travel bags, followed by EU Sun, checking the room one more time for careless clues left behind. The elevator doors open at the lobby, where EU Sun, Rick, and Han-Joo exit to join GONG, waiting for them at the curb in the stolen cab. The hotel doorman helps Rick out of the wheelchair and into the back seat, with EU Sun on one side and Han-Joo on the other. GONG pulls into traffic and turns toward downtown Wenzhou.

Gen. MA and Sang-Bo continue down to the parking level. They get into the Land Cruiser with the dismembered ear in a bundle, luring the Americans away from Rick. No questions, no talking, no slacking.

Frank Choy and one of the Marines follow the Land Cruiser.

Ed Poole remains behind at the hotel to monitor the feeds and keep the inventory of positions. Wright is at the naval base with the other marine and Cai is at the bank getting the ransom money.

Meanwhile, with the Marine in the driver's seat, Choy attends the app for Rick's chip and they follow his ping in the Expedition until they spot the gold Land Cruiser. It's parked near the shore in a field of vegetables. The doors are wide open, and it appears no one is in it.

"We see the vehicle, but no one around. Are you still getting Martin's ping from here?"

"Affirmative. Trace it," says Poole.

Choy and the Marine have barely taken two steps away from the Expedition when Gen. MA and Sang-Bo rise up from the vegetables and gun the two men down, shooting out the tires and the transmission of their vehicle while they're at it. Those assault rifles EU Sun brought from Xi'an came in handy after all. A short jog across the field brings them to a no-name road where the stolen cab waits.

"What was that? Frank? Frank?" Says Ed's voice through Choy's earphone, unharmed in the dirt near his body.

***

After the ritual coffee chat with the CO, everyone adjourns to the Special Forces quad. At 10AM, Commander GAO convenes their planning meeting promptly when more introductions ensue. He shares the front of a classroom arrangement of desks with a whiteboard, an oversize LED video screen, and an array of flags announcing country, party, and battalion loyalties. Unlike GAN, Commander GAO simply asserts his rank with a black turtleneck showing four modest stars on the shoulders over the four-blues camouflage pants, his automatic pistol in a holster around his waist. Most of the seats are taken by a select group of Maj. WONG's regiment.

WONG initiates a PowerPoint on the LED, comprised of images Ron took yesterday at Compass Marine, relinquishing control to Ron.

The excitement of the impending mission is hard to miss. WONG's elite corps checks out Ron before falling under the spell of his presentation. Besides images of Compass Marine, there are new images of the *Lantana* at Pier 40-3 taken by the Port Authority earlier this morning. At the end of the PowerPoint are some images from Wright's group, shots taken in the parking garage at Zhangwan on November eighth, six days ago.

Ron pauses, clicker in hand, gazing at a chilling image of Rick, not seen since the abduction eleven days ago. He's in a wheelchair between two Asians, head drooping onto his chest, in a jogging suit and a knit cap, taken at the moment the elevator doors opened in the parking garage at the Hanjian Dolo Hotel in Zhangwan where the BFO had rigged a motion sensor camera. Another shot of three more Asians coming down the stairs—Gen. MA, a young man, and a woman, taken the same day.

"Can you tell us who these people are?" asks Ron, directing his question to Wright at the back of the room.

"The old man is Gen. MA. The other two haven't been identified."

The next image shows Rick curled in the hatchback of the gold Land Cruiser with various people standing around him.

Recovering himself after a few seconds, the grin wiped off his face, Ron turns to look toward the Commander, sitting in the back of the room. He clicks through the next few images of the gang in Wenzhou taken a few days ago, one inside the Land Cruiser, one at their door, and another at the elevator.

"Here is Gen. MA again, this time with the Chinese Korean agent KIM Sang-Bo, the younger brother of the agent arrested after the first abduction on November 1," continues Wright. "We installed a camera/mic inside their vehicle and a beacon. Besides listening through the walls, we have cameras in the hall. We haven't seen Rick Martin since they checked into their hotel in Wenzhou on November tenth."

Ron clicks the display off, and the room lights up.

Striding toward the front of the classroom, Commander GAO addresses the Special Forces. "Before we go any farther, the SIGINT post has combed the recorded conversations and run them through our digital voice-recognition software, but no significant information has been found. In fact, near silence has gripped their communications, from Compass Marine to the gang's mobiles. The listening post run by the Americans has corroborated this silence from the gang. We expect something will happen soon."

Maj. WONG picks up where the Commander leaves off, "Now we work out the plan: to ambush the Land Cruiser with their human cargo. We have identified pinch points between the hotel and Compass Marine."

"How fast can you get into position?" asks Wright, a little skeptical.

"Maybe forty-five minutes."

"From here?" he presses.

"Dui, from here," Maj. WONG replies.

"What about at the hotel?"

"Only if necessary. Too many people," says WONG impatiently.

"What about if that doesn't work?"

"That's what the ransom is for. Do you have a different idea?" asks WONG.

Wright pretends not to notice the edge creeping into the man's voice. "No, that's reasonable."

At 10:45, Wright looks at his BlackBerry. It's a call back from Gen. MA. Wright takes it and then goes ashen.

"I'm thoroughly aware that you have been following your little tracker," begins the suave, Brit-tinged voice. "That has not gone well for you."

Wright is dumbfounded by this new input; nevertheless, he keeps his cool. "The deal is, we get Rick Martin back alive and well, Mr. MA."

"Mr. Wright, it is you who now have blood on your hands. I doubt the world is aware the United States is at war with China.... This either goes my way or ... well, my way. It's your choice who lives, who dies, and whose career survives ... if that's what it comes down to. No double-cross or else."

Gen. MA follows that with a text: "PIER 40-3 NOW"

Wright thumbs through the phone features, jabbing it with both hands, to locate the recorded call as an MP3 file, and send it to Nolan. When Wright gets Poole's call he steps to the back of the room where he can concentrate on what's being said.

***

When Poole arrived, the sight of the massacre sickened the veteran agent. "Oh Frank ..." is about all he could muster as he approached the bodies beside the Expedition with the US1042 plates. He found Rick's ear wrapped in a towel on the front seat of the gold Land Cruiser, still pinging. He walked off into the vegetable field and stared at the cloudy sky for a few minutes before taking pictures of a scene he would surely have to cover up. This was supposed to be a cushy job, working out of the Beijing office!

He bites back his unexpected grief, fueling feelings of revenge. Is it the executions themselves, the mutilation, or his own thwarted expectations that make this so intense? He swallows back unacceptable tears. *Axis of evil? You bet,* he thinks.

Poole calls Wright at the base.

"Calm down, Ed. I can't hear what you're saying."

"Choy and the Marine have been shot. They shot up our Expedition!"

"Dead?"

"Yes, fucking dead, Larry. We have bodies in China. What do you want me to do?"

"What about Rick Martin?"

"They cut off his ear and left it on the car seat."

"Fucking shit! So, we don't know where he is?"

"Right."

"And the Iranian tanker is in the harbor?"

"Yes."

"Where's Mrs. Martin?"

"She's with the Chinese squaddie, YANG or something, at the American Express downtown, getting the money. Now, you know what to do over there. Make it quick."

"I'll call you back in twenty minutes."

Poole finishes taking pictures. Of the bullet-splattered bodies of Frank Choy and his Marine driver. Of the shot-out vehicle. Of the abandoned Land Cruiser with Martin's bloody ear on the seat. He looks through the emergency supplies in the boot of the Ford Expedition, finding a half-dozen death kits, including two body bags and a heavy-duty car-vac. He goes through the checklist, brushes dirt off his colleagues' skin, collects their personal things in manila envelopes, and bags the bodies separately. He bottles, bags and labels everything from the wreck and transfers it into the second, identical, black Ford Expedition, tagged US1041.

Then he inspects the Land Cruiser, collecting Martin's ear, anything else that has mass, and removing the beacon and cameras. He bags these and thoroughly vacuums the vehicle and removes the debris receptacle. He hasn't left a scrap of dust or hair or lint, not even a Korean booger, behind as he attaches plastic explosives to the gas tanks of both the other SUVs and blows them to smithereens.

***

Wright stands up and shouts to be heard from the back of the classroom. "New intel. The gang is on the move with Martin Xiansheng."

The Commander asks, "Has something changed their plan?"

"They're going to the *Lantana*," says Wright.

"We act now," orders GAO. Get people into squads. Let's ship out. Squadron leaders report in ten minutes."

Diagrams of the pier with each man's position are distributed to the squad leaders and are drilled by Maj. WONG.

"How far is that? I mean, how long will it take to get into position?" asks Wright.

Commander GAO buttonholes WONG, "Have you worked out this scenario?"

"Dui, Commander."

"How long will it take to get into position?"

"I'm taking the advance forces ahead of you now. We leave the helipad and drive to Pier 40-3." WONG looks at his multipurpose watch, calculating, and sets a miniature timer, "The first squad should get there by 12:45."

"What about Mrs. Martin and the hand-off?" Wright wants to know.

"She comes in the last group. With you and Commander GAO," continues WONG. "As soon as we're in place, we send one vehicle with Martin Taitai."

"What if they back out?"

"We have Navy Seals boarding the ship," grins WONG, in spite of himself.

"*Tai haole*, WONG," Wright grins back, "This might work."

***

That morning at American Express, it took them an hour and a half to count the money, an operation with numerous checks and double-checks, initials, and recounts—some kind of speed record for an amount this large. As soon as they had it stacked and locked in an AMEX-supplied travel case, Cai and Mai grabbed a cab and raced to the mainland helipad.

At 11:45, Commander GAO looks at his smartphone. It's a call from Martin Taitai.

"*Wei, nihao. Zai nar?*"

"Cai and I are at the helipad."

The Commander says, "*Deng yixia*. Stay there. We come now."

The squads are assembled in clumps around the classroom; they get their orders and depart, followed by the officers. Ron turns out the lights and disconnects his laptop, winding up the power cord in the dim classroom. He hurries to catch up with the brigade at the island-side helipad. The pale sun is obscured by fast-growing clouds that blot out the sky while the wind kicks up, whipping the palm trees.

The senior officers are the last to transport. Commander GAO wants to get his corps in place as soon as possible. While waiting for the chopper shuttle, Ron calls his mother. They talk a couple minutes about household things.

She wants to know, "Where are you, Ronnie?"

"I'm in Wenzhou, Mama."

"With *her?*"

"*Dui*, Mama; she's delivering the ransom money."

"*Zhende*, a ransom now?" she asks.

"*Dui*, it is fortunate. We go now. Love you, Mama."

"Is dangerous, Ronnie?"

Laughing, "*Meiyou*, Mama. It's just like Hong Kong."

"Call me soon, Ronnie. I stay up all night for your call."

Then he tries his son. It just rings. No voice mail. So he texts: "love you, talk soon?" and clicks off his phone.

By noon, the squads have been transported to the Yongqiang Airport and are immediately re-routed as they arrive via motor transport to a staging area near the pier, outside Panshizhen.

***

Back at the airport restaurant where Mai and the young JGTS YANG Cai wait, he's holding the wheeled suitcase with the $100K between his legs under the table when he gets a call from the Commander telling them to come to the executive lounge.

Local *jingcha* and soldiers are stationed all around the airport. They stand in small clumps or pairs every twenty meters inside the terminal. Cai feels self-conscious, as if every person in the place is staring at the man dragging a carry-on bag obviously packed with ransom money.

The executive lounge in the mezzanine level overlooks the busy terminal. A graceful, curved staircase, cantilevered and appearing to float, swoops past luxury-goods boutiques, terminating at a landing and a pair of double doors. Outside the lounge, Maj. TANG and a Marine hold the doors open for them.

"We have dead bodies in China, Nolan. Wake up." says Wright on the phone as Mai and Cai walk past him into the executive lounge that the Commander is using as a temporary staging area.

In Virginia, it's the night before, Sunday, at 11:10PM. Wright tells his counterpart that Rick has gone missing and his man Choy and the other Marine are dead. Nolan focuses on the red LED display on the digital clock opposite her bed. "What time is it there?" she asks.

"It's 12:10, Monday."

"Call Gen. MA now. Tell him you're ready. Do it now. We have special ops at our base in Yongsan, Korea, that can scramble and get the bodies. Send me the GPS coordinates. Can you get clearance on the air space from your Chinese commander? This is code red."

"Whatever that means," he says by way of closing.

Next, he texts Gen. MA: "Ready 2 go R U ?"

Cai darts over to the Commander with the case of cash and immediately engrosses himself in the hubbub. Wright is on his heels, pushing into the knot of men to converse with GAO. Next, he calls Poole back.

"They're sending an extraction squad from our SOCKOR [Special Operations Command Korea] base at Yongsan, Korea," says Wright.

"How long will that take?" asks Poole.

"They'll be there in a couple hours. They have the GPS location."

"Do I leave these guys here in a ditch or what?"

"Leave them. I'm at Yongqiang Airport; they're transporting the brigade right now and moving troops to Pier 40-3. I need you here."

Ron sees Mai, who is holding her breath, all the whites showing around her eyes. *What dead bodies?* In a flash, he's beside her, urgently whispering something about the money transfer. The two of them zigzag through the contemporary furniture, arranged in conversation groups and overtaken by GAO's command personnel, to sit next to the windows where Mai barely registers that it's raining outside. The overcast sky bursts into a steady downpour, warming up to 4 C 39 F. Squalls roll in waves, alternating gloomy patches of clouds with feeble sunshine. Ron takes an overstuffed armchair across a low table from Mai, where he can survey the entire room and keep Mai in his orbit.

"Who's dead, Ron?" Mai asks, gasping for air, a hysterical edge to her voice.

"What? No one, what are you—"

"Wright said, 'Dead bodies,' just now, on the phone to someone, when I was coming in—"

GAO interrupts with a general announcement. "New intel people. Eyeballs this way."

The Commander explains about the massacre in the vegetable field. But Mai can't follow. She starts to make her way back to Wright, using the backs of the chairs like handrails for support. GAO sees and heads toward her.

"Dead bodies, Commander?" is all she can get out. Then, "Ron!" Because she knows she needs a translator.

The Commander and ZHAO exchange looks. Neither wants to frighten her with the gruesome details.

"Is Rick dead? Tell me now!" she insists, pulling herself fully upright.

"No, Martin Taitai. It is two of Wright's men. Now, we must prepare you for the hand-off."

"Oh." She glances over at a pacing Wright still making calls and slumps back into the bucket chair beside Ron as a couple of technicians materialize and begin fitting her with an ear monitor. Ron promises to be in constant contact.

Ron and the Commander instruct: walk quickly but carefully, remaining aware of each step, not swaying or swerving to the left or the right, keeping Gen. MA's people on one side and keeping in mind a straight shot for us if possible. They tell her to drop the bag, open and show it to them, and not get within arms' length, like about a meter, of anyone.

"This entire operation is too dangerous for Martin Taitai. I can do this part. Let me do it," begs Ron. "Lives are at stake."

"I have a pistol approved for Martin Taitai. Here," GAO gestures to Maj. TANG across the room.

"*Bu dui*, Commander," says Mai.

"*Weishenme*? ZHAO is right, this is dangerous role for you," continues GAO as Maj. TANG arrives with a QSZ type-92, the same model the others have. Maj. TANG hands it toward her, butt forward.

"No, no, I'm not confident carrying such a thing. What if they get it away from me? And shoot me with my own gun? Uh-uh, no gun."

Ron gives her pepper spray. *That* she knows how to use; she puts it in her pocket.

"If anything goes wrong, hit the ground and cover your head," drills Ron.

They drill. Remembering to listen to the monitor was worth practicing, if nothing else. And trying to stay calm. *Just cram the feelings down, shut out everything, focus on the now.* A wad of tears are stuck in her throat, choking her while she fingers the lucky coin in her pocket.

Just as Maj.'s WONG and TANG, Lt. GUAN, and JGTS YANG Cai are collecting their gear to transport ahead, Ed Poole pushes through the lounge door at 12:45.

"Commander GAO," says Wright, interrupting him at a conversation nook near the coffee bar. "I have another man to muster with your troops." He gestures to Poole, standing at the door, to present himself.

The Commander already had received a call from the airport security downstairs that a big American carrying weapons wanted entry. He turns to look. Poole's outfitted himself with gear from the Expedition, bringing his own assault rifle and a backpack of techno gadgetry. At six-foot-six, he towers like a giant over the others, transformed from his geeky previous iteration as squad technician. And he's pissed off.

Maj. TANG buttonholes the tall American to join his group, giving him a robust handshake and steering him to Maj. WONG for introductions. In a few more minutes, WONG's squad departs. The Commander, Mai, and Ron, standing near the wall of glass, look down at the wet tarmac and watch the men boarding a CCG Humvee.

Ron wants Mai out of the equation: protecting his client from unnecessary risk, doing his due diligence, earning his fee.

"Tell me, Commander, why can't I take her place? I have experience."

Wright explains from across the now empty room, "It's the liability thing, ZHAO. Neither China nor the US wants a connection to this transaction." He zips his bag and sets it near the door, before joining the others.

"We moved the money to an American Express Bank in Wenzhou," adds GAO. "A special personal account was set up overnight, as the Americans directed, in Martin Taitai's name."

"It's got to look like the wife came up with the dough herself to ransom her husband," continues Wright.

"So, I'm her agent; let me carry it for her," Ron's exasperated, trying to get the logic of it across to the superpowers.

"You're Chinese," says Wright.

"Not really, I'm an FE from Hong Kong."

"Stop splitting hairs, ZHAO," orders Wright with glaring finality, red sparks in his bulging eyes.

Commander GAO and Wright drift back to where their bags are piled, ready for departure. Subject closed.

"I can do it, Ron," says Mai, turning to him with a crooked smile.

"Sure, Mai," says Ron, trying to reassure her when he's the one needing reassurance. He reaches out his arms and folds her in a teddy bear embrace. "*Mei wenti*, I'll be there, close as your ear."

Pier 40-3

Once the gang is in the taxicab, leaving the massacre in the vegetable field, they head northeast to the G15 Expressway, cross the river, and head to Pier 40-3.

GONG drives. Han-Joo is squeezed between him and EU Sun. In the back seat, Gen. MA is on one side and Sang-Bo on the other side of a tethered and mouth-taped Rick desperately trying to be alert to what's happening. The pain on the side of his head that used to have an ear is so bad he doesn't feel it anymore. Instead, he focuses his attention on his surroundings, floating out of his body and hovering above the gang.

"The drop-off location is a trap. We will not go to Compass Marine," says MA.

"Agreed," starts EU Sun. "We take the *Meiguoren* to the *Lantana*." He turns around to look at Sang-Bo and says, "Gen. MA was right. They were listening to us. It was a trap. And the Land Cruiser, too."

The gang drives in silence, crossing the bridge that spans from one side of the Oujiang River to an island in the middle, and to the other side.

Gen. MA starts again, "We have improved our odds. They have two fewer men and one less vehicle. Their operation has been dealt a crippling blow, but not enough to kill the CIA dogs." Tapping GONG on the shoulder, he says, "Stop here in the village coming up. We eat. I need to check my messages."

It's almost noon when the gang stopped in Panshizhen and Commander GAO's brigade arrived at Yongqiang Airport. While Gen. MA was thumbing through his messages, a text from Wright came in: "Ready 2 go R U ?"

***

The *Lantana* shares a double-bay slip with an empty slot at the end of a row of double piers on the leading edge of land at the mouth of the Oujiang River where it surges into Wenzhou Bay. She's preparing to board a group of migrant men looking for work in Abu Dhabi. The *Lantana's* Iranian Captain is annoyed about being detoured here to Wenzhou to pick up a hostage for the government. Right in the harbor, with the Chinese Coast Guard everywhere. At least he can pick up some cash from *these* men.

Early in the morning, port officials had suddenly become interested in the men and were asking for their paperwork. Two PA Jeeps painted blue and white with a medallion on the doors parked in the road next to a string of warehouses. Six PA officers set up a folding table and chairs for an onsite document inspection. The migrant men dug into their knapsacks for their passports and entry permits from their Abu Dhabi employer and shuffled into lines.

One tank of the older, single-hull petroleum tanker had been repurposed for different cargo. The ship also had a uniquely designed port hull with a square opening at sea level, large enough for a fully loaded rubber dinghy or mini-sub to exit … or enter. Inside the modified tank, the dinghy bay was on one side and the human cargo on the other.

By the time GONG pulls into the pier complex, the PA had finished checking the men's documents, taken some pictures of the general area, and left. The cab slowly motors to the end of the row of piers and parks near the warehouses where the migrant men's camp is located.

"Sang-Bo, take GONG, check these buildings. Find a place to hide the *Meiguoren*. I go talk to the Captain," orders MA. "And give me one of the pistols."

GONG pops the trunk, grabs a bolt cutter, and follows Sang-Bo. The two men cut the lock off a door of the closest building and enter.

Gen. MA leans over the seat to EU Sun, sitting in the front, "Make sure they get a good place, close to this end. Transfer the *Meiguoren* to the hiding place. Keep one man on him: Sang-Bo. The other man, GONG, have him hide the cab pointing for a fast getaway. Give them the guns. Place GONG where he can cover the hiding place. Then, you and Han-Joo come to the ship. *Zouba*." He opens his door and walks across the road, past the empty bay toward the *Lantana*.

At the top of the gangway, Gen. MA strikes up a conversation with the watch commander, and the two disappear into the ship's quarters. After several minutes waiting, the *Lantana* Captain appears. He determines Gen. MA is bringing the American hostage. The head of their Iranian intelligence bureau has made a personal vendetta to get the American and transport him alive to Tehran. Something about the internet and spying. He's not been briefed on the details, but he's been chosen to do the transporting and communicate with the Korean intelligence chief, RI Hongyu.

"How do you plan to defend yourself if there's trouble?" asks MA.

"Are you expecting trouble?" asks the Captain, turning to a galley mate bringing an enameled tray with a pot of hot tea and a plate of fresh pastries. The mate sets a gilded and etched glass in front of each man on a small brass saucer, and a bowl of sugar cubes. He pours the steaming, rich tea into the cups and leaves them alone.

"Always. I always expect things to turn out differently than planned," counters MA.

"We have shooters. We can cover the area around our slip," offers the Captain.

"Who are those men camped over there?" asks MA.

"They're taking passage with us to Abu Dhabi," explains the Captain.

"When do you plan to depart?" MA wants to know.

"Tomorrow at 11:00," answers the Captain.

"There are three of us, besides the Meiguoren, going to the Emirates," says MA.

"What? I only heard one," says the Captain.

"We've been trying to contact Dalaoban RI. Have you been in contact with the DPRK?" asks MA.

"Not for two weeks."

"We changed the plan, and I was not able to call you, Captain, since all arrangements were made between you and RI," says MA.

"It would have been better to follow the plan," mutters the Captain. "When do you want to bring the *Meiguoren* onboard?"

"After dark."

"Why not now?" the Captain wants to know.

"Too dangerous. He's in a safe place. We may have been followed, although precautions have been exercised. We eliminated two CIA dogs today, near our hotel."

***

At the forward staging area near Panshizhen, called Fengshan Park, Commander GAO's advance corps begin arriving, traveling quietly and quickly up Ouhai Avenue to the G15 exchange and north across the Oujiang River in a loose caravan of Dongfeng PLA Humvees painted in camouflage style. A good thirty minutes behind Gen. MA's gang.

Maj. TANG's squad, including Ed Poole, Lt. GUAN, and JGTS YANG Cai, proceed to set up forward command communications in their Hummer hatchback. The Special Forces block off the area and surround it, creeping through the coastal vegetation: tall reeds and low, bushy trees, infiltrating the area adjacent to the *Lantana*. They're on top of the warehouses and the container gantry crane in the empty slip with snipers.

The *Lantana* Captain has positioned his own crack shooters on the gantry crane above his ship, and they immediately spot movement in the adjacent slip.

GONG has wedged himself into a corner of the roof of the

building concealing Rick Martin and Sang-Bo. He can see down inside the building and cover the shed door behind which they hide. He also can see out across the piers to the *Lantana*, and he can see the back of the cab, partially concealed by trees in the migrant men's camp. And he sees black-masked men with guns sliding like shadows in and out of view.

The migrant men passively sit in clumps with their bedrolls, removing themselves from the situation while watching the newcomers carrying AK 47 style rifles and creeping through the trees.

***

The Marine stows the gear and ransom case in the last PLA Humvee waiting for them at the Yongqiang Airport. He wants to drive, but has to ride in the back with Mrs. Martin and Wright. Ron adjusts his ear monitor and the GPS on the dash while Commander GAO gets in on the passenger side. The view up and down the Oujiang River distracts them from their solemn thoughts.

Mai tries looking past the Marine to glimpse the sparkling water of Wenzhou Bay, "Hi, what's your name?" she asks him.

"Russell Gleaves, Mrs. Martin," the young man replies.

"Where are you from?" she continues, as he tucks his chin into his chest, giving her a better look out the window.

"Worcester, Massachusetts, ma'am."

Mai looks into his face, ruddy and handsome, and asks again, "Do I know you? Were you in the conference room at Beijing University?"

"Uh … yes, ma'am."

Mai sits back into the cushioned seat, catching Ron's eye in the rearview mirror.

Turning to Wright, she says, "That was an exciting night, don't you agree, Lawrence?"

Wright's bald head turns bright pink, "Compared to today, it was diddly," he says.

"Try to focus on today, Mai. This is serious business," scolds Ron, turning off the expressway onto Pan Road. "Repeat for me the steps we practiced."

"I'm going to walk straight to the *Lantana*."

"Or to Rick …"

"Which is it?" she asks, peeved.

"We'll see when we get there, okay? It depends where they have him. Stay to one side; give us a straight shot to cover you and Rick. What do you do next?" he continues drilling her as they follow the winding road down to the coast.

"Show 'em the money."

"Bu dui, Mai; *drop the bag,* and then show the money." Ron looks sideways at the Commander's immobile profile.

"Right, right, drop the bag, open the bag, show the money. Then what?" she asks.

Wright interrupts, "Get out of the way. Leave the rest to us professionals."

***

The forward sniper calls the *Lantana* Captain, interrupting him and Gen. MA from their coffee and pastries. "Two people approach."

"Here comes two more of my party now," says MA, gesturing off the rail toward EU Sun and Han-Joo. They're walking on the road past the empty slip on one side and a row of warehouses on the other, toward Pier 40-3.

"Allow them to pass and board," answers the Captain.

"There's movement in the yard," the sniper presses. "Who are they?"

"Can he see our men?" asks MA. "There are two guarding the Meiguoren who is strapped in a wheelchair."

"Where?" asks the Captain.

"Ask my lieutenant, coming now," finishes MA as EU Sun climbs the gangway.

***

At Panshizhen, Commander GAO has the harbormaster call the ship's Captain. The first mate answers, irritated, "Can I help you?"

"*Duibuqi*, we need head count of the crew," says the harbormaster.

"What?"

"*Qing*, assemble your crew top decks for document examination and safety inspection."

Meanwhile, PLN divers approach the ship's exposed bow, knives in their boots, guns zipped in latex pockets.

Again, the Captain is interrupted, this time with a call from his first mate explaining this new request from the PA.

"Do no such thing. This is harassment. Everyone stay in their positions."

Turning to Gen. MA, he asks, "Who is after you? The CIA, you say? What about the Chinese?"

"Don't you have favored status? Like us?" wonders MA aloud.

"We will soon see," is all the Captain says. He leaves the Koreans and goes looking for his officer.

***

As the Iranian crew watches, a camouflage-painted Humvee with CCG insignia on the door creeps toward Pier 40-3, past a ship loaded with blue ISO shipping containers, past two empty slips, past a small, custom petroleum tanker, another empty slip, and the *Lantana,* stopping in the road where Pier 40-3 intersects. After several minutes, the passenger door opens and a woman in white jeans gets out. She walks to the boot, which pops open for her to grasp the handle of a wheeled travel-case. She sets the case on the road and closes the hatch door.

The *Lantana* Captain sees the CCG insignia on the Hummer and sends a mate to bring Gen. MA to the bridge, "What's this?" MA says nothing.

Mai walks from the Humvee to the gangway, dragging the carry-on stuffed with cash behind her on the rugged pier. No Rick, no Gen. MA in sight. Gunmen check sights, shift position, and listen for orders.

***

The Captain gets another call from his sniper on the crane. "Yes, I can see a woman walking this way."

Gen. MA speaks up, "This is the Meiguoren's wife with ransom."

"How much?"

"One hundred thousand US dollars."

"Interesting, and who is driving her? The Coast Guard? She has powerful friends, General."

"Indeed, it has been nothing but difficulties with this operation. We picked up the *Meiguoren* once and were caught once. We got away, and they recovered the *Meiguoren*. The next night we took him again, and they've been following us ever since."

"How do we get the money and keep the *Meiguoren*? Have you thought about that Gen. MA?"

"I have."

***

Standing at the foot of the gangway, Mai looks up at the deck of the ship many meters above her head and calls out, "Rick!"

"Tangzi, listen, turn around," sings Ron soothingly into her ear, thinking, *please stay calm.*

Mai looks toward the Humvee, where Ron is watching her and waiting.

"That's right, come back this way slowly."

Rick's mouth is taped, and he's lashed to the wheelchair, only a few pinholes of light piercing the darkness at sharp angles like white lasers. He hears her calling—S*he's here!*—and attempts a muffled response, "Mmmf!" followed by pistol-whipped silence. Sang-Bo runs from one side of the shed to the other. At the back, through another small opening, he sees a Special Forces squad leap-frogging toward their building, the forward man covering for a man behind to run ahead who then covers for the man behind to pass him. He whistles silently to himself and mutters under his breath, "We're sitting ducks! Where's GONG?"

Ron, waiting in the Humvee, is about six meters beyond where Sang-Bo peers out of a rusted screw hole in the front of the prefab metal shed. The Chinese Korean teenager looks at his mobile, wonders where his mentor, Gen. MA, is and why he doesn't answer his phone. As soon as Sang-Bo sees Mai suddenly come around the back of the Hummer, toward him and within three meters of his position, he panics and slides open the shed door, making a sound like scraping metal in the otherwise quiet afternoon. He gives the wheelchair a kick. The gunmen contract, ready to shoot.

"Hold fire!" orders Maj. WONG from the crane. Out rolls Rick, coming to, blinded by sunshine, and suddenly pissing himself.

"Don't move!" Ron's voice in her ear is all that stops Mai from running toward him.

"Stay where you are and drop the bag."

She drops it, crying out, "Oh Rick, Rick!"

"Stay calm, Mai, open the bag," says Ron in her ear, patiently. He watches her through the rearview mirror, where she stands in the road behind the Hummer. Mai unzips the lid to show rows of hundred dollar bills in bundles.

***

Another call from the sniper interrupts the ship Captain's box seat as the drama unfolds.

"Captain, we're surrounded. I've seen more and more troops coming from the trees."

Speaking in Farsi, the Captain says, "Hold your fire. Don't move." Next, he calls his first mate, "Come to the quarterdeck and arrest the Koreans, now." Waiting for his men to arrive, he looks over the rail at the commotion near the warehouses.

***

Rick is not two meters from her. Just staring at her. Soiled and bloody. "This is my husband!" shouts Mai to the men on the ship, to the empty-looking shed, to anyone listening. Sang-Bo in a dark corner, trembling, terrified, is also pissing himself. The fearful stories of what happens to agents caught in China penetrate his discipline. Chinese policemen are ruthless inquisitors who resort to physical violence to extract confessions from their prisoners. Executions are swift and frequent here. He torments himself with thoughts of his older brother, Yong, probably already dead after being tortured.

With a beloved's rage, Mai keeps hollering, "Here's your goddam money, you fucking cowards! See?" She twists around to look at Ron sitting in the Humvee and back over to Rick. Dropping to her knees, her hands together as though praying for mercy, she sobs, "What do I do now? What do I do now? Somebody tell me what to do!"

Rick is crying too, which is causing him to choke, because of the tape. He starts to panic; Mai can see it in his eyes, bloodshot and vacant holes.

"Rick," says Mai, pulling herself together to calm him and reaching toward him without moving from her spot on the ground, straining to touch him if only with her intention. "Hang on! It's gonna be okay, honey. Just breathe; that's right, it's gonna be all over in a few more minutes."

He nods, his chest heaving, their eyes meeting.

Ron can't stand how helpless and vulnerable they look out there.

"I'm going in," he says into his phone, to JGTS YANG Cai at the command post.

He slyly clicks open his door and slides out to the front left fender, shielding himself at the wheel well. He counts, *"Yi, er, san,…"* scoots around the front of the Hummer, and runs toward the yawning opening in the side of the shed. Maj. TANG snaps his fingers for Lt. GUAN's squad to follow. The others begin to shift forward to their post-drop positions, some on the move, some retrenching. The Commander gets out of the backseat of the Hummer and begins to walk slowly toward the *Lantana* gangway, pushing buttons on his phone.

"Gen. MA? *Ni daodi zai nar?*" [Where the hell are you?] And snaps his phone shut.

Wright remains where he is, seated in the back with Russell Gleaves, the Marine, behind tinted windows. He texts Nolan: "Pkg solo."

Sang-Bo walks out of the shed, his hands up, propelled forward by Ron who has a gun to his back.

Wright lowers the window and shouts, *"Nide xigai!* [On your knees]" Sang-Bo drops to the ground, hands on his head, choking on his fear. "Jesus," says Wright to no one in particular, "What a buncha crybabies we've got here."

***

Gen. MA deduces what the Captain is determining: the Coast Guard has arrived in concert with the CIA and he better run fast if he's going to save himself. He slips back to the captain's quarters.

"EU Sun, Han-Joo, *zouba*, follow me," MA says emphatically, turns and disappears down a ladder. EU Sun pushes Han-Joo in front of him, keeping close to Gen. MA's back. Without too many wrong turns, Gen. MA finds the converted hold, confronting a pair of Seals entering at the waterline port. With a flash, the two Korean agents fire on the men, kick their lifeless bodies into the water, and jump into a fast, attack craft in the bay, pulling Han-Joo behind them. Gen. MA casts them off while EU Sun masters the controls.

MA texts GONG: "现在拍摄"—XIANZAI PAISHE. [Start shooting.]

More Chinese Navy Seals board and search the ship. The Seal platoon leader confronts the Captain, who explains he attempted to arrest the Korean agents who were perpetrating a type of extortion or fraud against his ship. From the hold below, a hatch opens and a fast, attack craft screams out—Gen. MA, EU Sun, and Han-Joo aboard. They head into the bay, toward another ship barely visible in the distance. A Seal fires his rifle. Rat a tat-tat, seven bullets into the air-filled tubes, bringing the craft to a deflating stop. Another Seal blows his whistle long and loud while the shooter calls out, grinning, *"Renwu wancheng!"* [Mission accomplished!] *"Women dedaole tamen!"* [We got 'em!]. Their voices faint but discernible.

A Coast Guard cutter arrives in only a minute or two, churning through the hazy fog, and hauls them out of the drink and into the onboard cage.

***

CCG and PLN swarm the *Lantana* amid shouts and orders. Maj. WONG pushes to the front line. Crew members sink to their knees, hands clasped behind their heads. An ambulance and Port Authority vehicles scream onto the troubled pier. Ron tears the tape off Rick's mouth and cuts the ties lashing him to the chair while Mai wipes the congealed blood from his face. Maj. TANG's squad, with Poole and Lt. GUAN, runs toward the *Lantana* at the sound of machine gun fire.

Gleaves makes a motion to follow them. "Alright, but call me from the ship with a report," says Wright. While Gleaves catches up with the squad, Wright retrieves the bag of cash, still lying open in the road.

Ron pushes the wheelchair, with Mai hanging onto Rick's hand, toward the ambulance. "We knew we'd find you; we knew you'd get out of this, Rick, didn't we Ron?" She's so happy and relieved, yet at the same time, still turned inside out with anxiety.

Rick grunts.

"What? Oh yeah, of course. *Mei wenti*, Mai," says Ron. Hearing something in his voice, she looks at him over Rick's banged-up head.

"Are you okay?" she asks. *He regrets it*, she thinks, frightened by the implications. Her thoughts are cut off by the sight of the Commander approaching them.

"Did you find Gen. MA?" asks Ron.

"*Dui*, he tried to escape the ship in a dingy," answers the elated Commander. "And two more of the gang."

"*Zhende, tai haole*, GAO."

"I offer you and Martin Taitai the opportunity to fly back to Beijing with me tonight. I'll be leaving Wenzhou with my staff and Martin Xiansheng, once they've stabilized his condition," says GAO, looking into the back of the ambulance at the American.

"Stabilized?" queries Mai.

"Your husband will go to a hospital in Beijing."

"What about my car?" asks Ron.

"I can dispatch soldiers to drive your vehicle back. That's how we're getting our Dongfeng to Beijing. There's been enough road trip, *dui*? We rest."

Mai smiles, "I don't mind taking you up on that!" Ron, his mind already moving on, gently moves around Mai to watch the misty blob of a white CCG cutter approaching, with a grim smile. "Ron?"

"*Bu, xiexie*, Commander," says Ron, matter of factly, "I will drive my car. Mai you go, stay with Rick." The ambulance leaves Mai standing in the road, holding onto the empty wheelchair as Ron turns back to the Hummer.

"Can I speak to you a moment?" she asks, needing to connect somewhere, to something.

"No, Mai, not now," he says, walking toward the vehicle, not even looking at her.

She stands there as the men scatter to their squads and vehicles, ill-equipped to know her next move. She hadn't been coached on *after*. She takes the earphone out of her ear. And waits for someone, anyone, to retrieve her.

A shot rings out. Two. Three. Four. And the ear-shattering sound of glass breaking. Metal pinging and clinking. After a puff on the road, a piece of gravel strikes Mai in the face; she yelps and hits the deck, covering her head. Ron springs back beside her, crouching on one knee, blocking access to her with his body, in perfect marksman position: left hand holding his right onto the butt of his smoldering pistol, arm still straight out. His return fire pure instinct, but whether borne of his training or his attachment to Mai, he has no idea.

All eyes turn toward where he appears to be pointing as a limp arm and rifle shaft slide through a broken window on the upper floor of a warehouse not ten meters away, exploding with one more shot when it lands. The remaining troops fan out and tear apart all the warehouses along the alley, finding GONG's body but no additional combatants.

***

The base infirmary is housed in an unimaginative, concrete building with dark bushes on both sides of the entry, behind a massive concrete pour of steps.

The digital clock on the wall above the reception desk says 18:25.

Mai sits up with a jerk. She must have fallen asleep. The noise at the entry helps focus her attention on the Commander walking up to her. He says, "Martin Taitai, would you like to see your husband?"

Mai follows the Commander, who follows a medic to a private room. The locked door has a window through which Mai can see Rick, lying in a hospital bed and hooked up to an IV. Commander GAO gestures to the medic to let them in. He enters a password on the digital door lock and opens the door for them.

Rick has been cleaned up and is connected to a slew of monitors. He looks asleep to Mai as she approaches the bed looking at him, after all this, face to face. The fresh ear wound is bound with bandages all around his head. The medic lets her pull the sheets down and inspect Rick's old wounds. Actually, they've healed some since the last time she saw him, in her apartment the night of the second abduction. New burn sores spot his arms and neck.

The medic removes a blood-soaked bandage on Rick's head. While he swabs the swollen and misshapen orifice with alcohol and then sprays it with an atomizer, Mai sees Rick's ear wound for the first time. The medic tapes a fresh bandage over the ruptured flesh and oozing fluids.

Mai waits for him to finish before turning and leaving the room. When the Commander comes out later, she's sitting, waiting for him.

"*Feichang ganxie ni*, Commander GAO," starts Mai, impulsively grabbing his arm.

He pats her hand before removing it and folding his arms across his chest. Looking across the small, poorly lit reception room, through an ornate, puzzle-style window into blackness, focusing on a pinpoint of light, he says nothing for several minutes. The rustic ice-ray lattice design perfectly fits his mood, with its irregularity and lack of symmetry. He's absorbing the meditative moment, replenishing his drained psychic battery. He closes his puffy eyes and lets his head rest against the wall.

The two of them sit like that in silence, each exhausted and running on adrenaline. For a little longer, they can push themselves.

He breaks the mood. "As soon as the chief medic approves, Martin Xiansheng will be transported to the PLA hospital at the First Bureau facility in Xianghongqi outside of Beijing. You won't be able to visit him there. As soon as possible, we arrange with Wright to send him back to US."

"I see, the same flight I am going on, with you?"

"The same. We leave at a moment's notice. I suggest you eat now. We don't have food service on the transport."

"All right. Now I've seen Rick. He seems better. But, what happened to his ear?"

"We think he was disfigured by the gang, but don't know why. We caught them all, and they will be prosecuted. The truth will come out."

"How long is the flight?"

"Five or so hours. Be prepared to go ... *ASAP*, as you say," says GAO. She nods and gets up to go, but before she is even halfway up, he grasps *her* arm this time and pulls her back into her seat. "Your husband ... he might seem okay, but might be *not* okay. Understand? It's drugs that make him look like sleeping."

***

The Beijingers are anxious to go. Behind them, the moon rises out of a fogbank sitting offshore, crystalline and sugary. The turbo-prop Harbin Y-12 only holds a crew and seventeen passengers maximum. Rick has been pre-boarded and is being held, sitting upright, by his seat harness. Otherwise, he's still passed out. The others are strategically seated around the cabin to balance the weight. They've seated her one row forward of Rick where she can turn around and look at him. A medic has the aisle seat next to him. JGTS YANG Cai and Maj. TANG sit together in the back, trading stories about the arrests. Lt. GUAN sits by himself in the front. Commander GAO and the base chief medic share aisle seats. Mai's tired and falls asleep as soon as they attain cruising speed, around 21:00 or 9PM.

November 15

Rick's body is battered, and his mind is blown. Flying back to Beijing, he gradually regains a kind of drug-addled consciousness. An ambulance greets the military transport plane where they land at the Beijing PLA Air Force headquarters at Nanyuan airport at 01:00 or 1AM, Tuesday morning. Mai's standing on the tarmac, hoping to see Rick for a minute before they whisk him away.

A clattering sound brings her attention to the plane as the medics struggle to get Rick Martin down the ramp stairs while strapped in a gurney. Mai reaches into her Bernini bag and withdraws the Bible Joshua Braithwaite gave her. It seems like a million years ago, but actually only a week has passed. In it, on the inside back cover, was their first solid clue: "H E L P," written by Rick while captive in Weinan.

They get the gurney on the tarmac, and before they can roll it into the ambulance, Mai runs over to him, "Rick, are you okay?"

He turns his head to look at her. His eyes are wild, his face flushed. His powerful arms struggle against the straps, "It's your entire fault!"

"What? I ... uh ... brought this for you," she says, tucking the Bible into the side of the gurney. "Remember? The Bible with the message?"

"What did you do to Han-Joo? Jealous bitch!" Rick growls. With a wrench of his shoulder, he pushes the Bible onto the ground and screams, "Don't kill me!"

The medics push Mai to one side, load Rick into the ambulance, and slam the doors. Lights on the roof rack twirl, sending red and blue rays into the night as they slowly drive away.

***

Mai climbs the five flights of stairs to her LiNai apartment, aching in every bone. Someone has replaced the broken lights in the stairwell. The door and gate clangs shut behind her.

In the morning, she carries a mug of tea to the window and looks down at the street. The morning traffic, passing back and forth on foot and bicycle, streams around a car slowly turning at the auto gate. *Wonder if I still have a job to go to*, she muses, staring up at the cold morning sky. The nearby smokestack is billowing gorgeous clouds of condensation. The edges catch the light of sunrise. *Beautiful*, she thinks. It's not the greatest homecoming, but it's what she's got welcoming her back.

Resting her head against the glass, she's overwhelmed with emotion. It's been held back for days and days. Now she's alone, it comes tumbling out. At first a little gasping moan in her throat when she breathes; it swells and chokes her until she spits it out and starts bawling in the kitchenette, sliding down the wall onto the warm floor tile, and hanging her head between her knees.

Instead of going to the office, she rides to the Main Building and finds Commander GAO on the third floor. The Beijing University Security Office is prepping for a Bureau Meeting tomorrow, November 16, being attended by the Commander's *dalaoban*, Deputy Commander HUANG. He can give her a few minutes.

"What can I do for you, Martin Taitai?"

"I want to see Rick," she says.

"*Meiyou*, Martin Taitai."

"*Weishenme?*"

"This is PLA matter now. I have no jurisdiction," he answers.

"I insist," she says. "Can't you call someone for me?"

Rick Martin's lunatic behavior on the tarmac is fresh in his memory. "He's not well enough for visitors. I promise I will do what I can to get a visit for you. *Mei wenti.*"

When he has a chance to ask the Deputy Commander, he says "The *Meiguoren*'s wife wants to see him before we send him back. Can you arrange that? I've tried asking but they've declined my requests."

Deputy Commander HUANG replies, "They're still examining him. And treating him for drug reaction. I want to see him myself. I'll get back to you. *Ha-haode*, Commander, you're a good man."

***

During Mai's interview with Ms. ZHANG at her boss's office in the International Building, Mai tries to pin her down about her contract.

"Ms. ZHANG, I'm worried about whether I have a job here

anymore."

"What? Why you worry, Martin?" counters ZHANG.

"When I come back from Spring Festival, will I still have a job here?" persists Mai.

"Of course, *mei wenti*, Martin Taitai."

"You would tell me, wouldn't you? If there was a problem with my visa?"

"If there was a problem with your visa, as you say, I would know, Martin; I'm your sponsor," declares ZHANG with a finality that ends the conversation.

One more thing she has to do is go shopping for a toothbrush. She has to replace the things she left behind at the New Asia Hotel when she went to American Express on Wednesday. Ron hasn't called, and she's feeling too guilty and ashamed to call him.

All the lies of omission, not being honest with Ron about Rick and hiding his involvement with Homeland Security ate away at their intimacy. She's ashamed of being petty at the pier, attributing selfish, low motives to Ron at the end. *He risked his life for me and saved me from the shooter, and I didn't even thank him for that.* Instead, they went in different directions.

More guilt and shame for not choosing him over Rick—or at least for making any choice at all—for hiding from her feelings and letting events and circumstances smother their love. She dragged it out and entangled him when Rick arrived. *Why can't I run to him now and declare myself?*

November 20

Five days after the operation in Wenzhou, on Sunday morning,

November 20, Mai is picked up by GAO's driver, Sgt. GU. Commander GAO is sitting up front for the long drive to the PLA hospital in northwestern Haidian. Mai passes the time sitting in the backseat catching up in her blog diary. It's been ages since she posted one. *Certainly can't say anything about the past few weeks. What am I going to write?*

They meet Deputy Commander HUANG in the lobby of the plain, concrete monolith of the First Bureau facility in Xianghongqi. At the hospital, they're led through the maze to a private room, similar to Rick's room at the Coast Guard infirmary, with a window in the door and a keypad security lock. First thing she notices is he's off the IV. He's dressed in a dark red nylon track suit and expecting them.

Jumping off the bed when he sees her, Rick says, "Mai, so glad to see you. Where have you been?"

Their embrace in the middle of the room is like electricity; it charges out to the corners and bounces around, catching everyone. He hides his face in her hair and holds her close, breathing in her essence like a healing tonic. She feels his skinny ribs, *Never seen him so thin.* She sees the stump of his ear, stitched in black thread. He lets her go and looks at the men.

"I am Commander GAO from Beijing University. Do you remember meeting me?"

Rick has gone over the events of the past few weeks, as well as he knows them, with the interrogators at the hospital, every day. He's learned the names of the players while the doctors did their best to minimize the damage to his severed ear.

"Yeah, sure do, thanks man, for getting me," Rick gives the Commander as firm a handshake as he can manage, just a little shaky.

"This is Maj. Gen. HUANG," says GAO. Rick stares at the two men dressed in black military coats with insignia on the shoulders. Commander GAO's uniform has four small stars on the epaulets. There's one big star with a laurel on the other man's. They stare back.

"I brought things for you, Martin Xiansheng." Out of a report cover, the Commander produces a brief on the gang. Rick pauses at the shot of Mai lying on the street next to Ron ZHAO's Park Avenue, after SHENG had punched her. He pauses again at the image of himself in a wheelchair in the elevator.

"Your embassy man, Lawrence Wright, cooperated with us on your extraction. It is regrettable the loss of life in his squad," confides GAO. "Two of our own Navy Seals were shot by the gang trying to escape from the ship."

Rick looks up at the Commander's face. "When can I talk with him? You can't keep me here like this."

"I know: you're an American citizen. Tomorrow, you fly home to the US. Your embassy has been notified, and they'll meet you at the airport. After that, you're their concern. We have no interest in detaining you, Martin Xiansheng. Your or your wife's presence is not required for the prosecution of Gen. MA and the gang. The doctors here have been treating you for a narcotic addiction you picked up these past three weeks. I hope you agree, your care here has been excellent," finishes GAO.

He and HUANG leave Mai alone with Rick. Down the hall, they

join a group of people watching the several video feeds from Rick's room.

"I've been wretched to you, Mai," starts Rick.

"How would you know?" she asks without irony. He doesn't answer. She's always forgiven him. "You ruined my China trip, you know. How can I go on here, the American woman married to a US spy? They're never going to renew my contract."

"They love you here, Mai. You've got them wrapped around your finger. Like ZHAO." Rick gives her a sideways glance while she looks in her bag and pulls out the Bible.

"Want this now? You dumped it on the tarmac when you were being a paranoid jerk."

"Look at me, Mai," he says, pulling at her hands, feeling the roughness of his skin against hers. The red wounds around his wrists are an angry reminder of his pain. "What about ZHAO?"

"He loves me and doesn't put me in the cross hairs." She hopes it's still true, but she hasn't heard from him. And she doesn't mention that to Rick.

"That's fair. I've been worse than a jerk." Rick drops her hands and starts picking at his fingernails, finding a shred and chewing on it while watching her. His blue eyes are watering and feel like they're liquid fire. "I need you."

"You have Homeland Security."

"What if I told you I was quitting?"

"I wouldn't believe you."

A noise at the door attracts their attention. Commander GAO has returned to say, "Martin Taitai, your husband may stay tonight at your apartment. In the morning, a driver will take Martin Xiansheng to the airport."

"*Feichang ganxie ni*, Commander, I am forever indebted to you for your kindness," says Mai, staring into the man's inscrutable eyes. For all the differences, deep at their core, they recognize a fellow traveler.

"Yeah, thanks, Commander," echoes Rick, surprised by the man's unexpected compassion.

"You ride with us ... back to the university. We go now," concludes GAO, who turns and gives instructions to the medic.

"Great, you can come home with me—" starts Mai.

"Is Beijing home, Mai?" asks Rick.

"It is now," she says, shoving the Bible back into the black, Bernini bag.

The medic gives Rick one last shot before they leave and hands GAO a bulky envelope as he passes out the door.

Back in GAO's Crown Royale, Rick feels drowsy and falls asleep for the ride. Mai looks at him again. The ear wound is on his right side, next to her, where she can inspect the bandage and the skin around it, puffy and pink. They've got him dressed in a casual, athletic styled suit: nylon trousers with zippers at the ankles and matching zippered, hooded jacket in a dark wine red color. *Where did they find something big enough?* Mai wonders, noticing the snug fit and the way the pants hang on his hips, below the jacket, on Rick's new slim physique. The red gouges encircling his wrists have simmered down to dark red marks, not deep, swollen grooves like before.

Commander GAO turns in his seat to see her and says, "The medic gave him a narcotic sleeping preparation. It should blunt the cravings he experiences."

"How long will he be like this?"

"*Wo bu zhidao*, he will need observation," he answers.

"Oh …."

"You will be okay with him tonight?" he asks.

Mai says, "Sure, of course…."

"I will have guards all night, parked in front of your LiNai apartment. In case," he says.

"In case what?" she wants to know.

"Here," he hands her the bulky envelope.

Inside, she finds a bottle of pills labeled dextroamphetamine, a tube called Complex Polymyxin B Ointment and several documents in English: his hospital discharge papers, instructions for the medications, and his passport, which they had impounded from Mai before the rescue operation. Scanning the documents, she sees—no more than two pills every six hours. She shakes a bottle containing a couple dozen red-and-white gel capsules.

A campus patrol car is waiting for them when they arrive. While Sgt. GU walks over to ask the officers to help him carry Rick to her apartment, he surprises everyone by waking and walking upstairs without assistance.

Once inside, he says, "Hey Mai, when did they turn on the heater?

"A couple weeks ago.... Do you want a shower or anything?"

"No, took one already today," he answers, walking around the apartment, looking at her things.

"Your bag is here if you want anything," says Mai from the studio as she drops the Bible into his travel bag lying open on the floor.

"I'm just a little tired still ..."

When Rick wakes alone in Mai's dim bedroom, it's past dinner time. He pushes the bedroom door open and plops into Mai's favorite chair, looking out over the sparkling night lights of Wudaokou.

"Hungry?"

"Yeah," he says.

"I've got rice, stir-fry veggies, and dumplings I can heat up in the microwave."

"Not more Chinese food!" he says emphatically. "Don't you have anything American?"

"Like what?" she asks.

"Dunno. McDonald's?"

"I could make you a tuna sandwich ..." she offers.

"Yeah, okay."

While Mai gets busy in the kitchenette, she says to him sitting in the other room, "They gave me some pills for you—every six hours."

"Let me see."

Rick studies the documents, chuckling and talking to himself. Mai brings him a glass of water and watches while he takes two pills and slips the bottle into his jacket pocket.

Mai pushes past Rick to get the mayonnaise, tuna and tomato out of the fridge. He spies a bottle of beer and grabs it before she closes the door.

"What happened to your ear?" she asks, returning to the kitchenette.

"The Generalissimo cut it off," answers Rick, taking a quaff. "Boy, I like Chinese beer."

"Why'd he do that?"

"He thought I had a tracker or eavesdropping device in my body. He was right," Rick says before taking another quaff. "The guy was clever and scary."

Mai's wondering, *Was it worth it?* "Want to tell me about it?"

"No, not really … except to say it seemed to go on forever. What day is this? I kept expecting our guys to show up and get me out of there. What took you so long?"

"For one thing," she says, "We didn't know where you were. Though Lawrence Wright and those guys were following you the whole time."

"No shit."

"Had a room across the hall, taking pictures and listening," she adds.

Rick reaches in his pocket and feels for the pill bottle. "Where's my sandwich, Mai? I'm starving here." Two more pills disappear down his throat.

She sets the sandwich on a plastic plate in front of him. "Watch it with those pills, Rick, only every six hours. And you shouldn't drink with them. They're powerful narcotics."

"What pills?"

"Didn't you just take another dose?"

"No."

She knows he's lying, but what the heck? He's been lying to her for years. *Why should he change now?* "Fine, just watch it." She smiles and gently reaches for the beer bottle. But he snatches it back.

"Are you calling me a liar?"

"No!"

"Then what are you ragging on me about the pills?" He knows he's pushing her buttons, but he finds he enjoys it. Pulling the bottle out of his pocket, he shakes it and, on impulse, pops the cap and shakes out two more into his hand.

"Please don't do that," she urges him.

"What? This?" And he swallows what she figures must now be an overdose. Rick slams the little glass, painted with autumn leaves, into the corner of the room. And takes another pull of his beer.

Mai is already edging out the front door. She's grabbing her purse off the hutch when Rick spins her around, shouting, "Where are you going? Sneaking off to see ZHAO? Where is he?" Rick bounds down the stairs, leaving Mai perplexed and frightened, standing in the open doorway. She locks it and follows him down.

Since their return from Wenzhou, it's been colder, down to the 40s F, 4 C, at night, and sunny and nice during the day—if it's not windy—high of 65 F or 18 C. Now, at 9PM, it's plenty cold standing in the street and watching Rick argue with the officers. She zips the parka up around her neck and digs her hands into the warm pockets. She had forgotten about her lucky coin and is happy to find it tonight.

The men from the guard shack are standing outside in the cold, smoking and watching Rick and the officers. Puffs of condensed air float around their heads. One of the officers notices Mai and gestures to her to stay back. Helpless to do anything else, Mai sees Rick break away from the men and start walking toward the other end of the street, toward the Southwest Gate, while the officers follow at a safe distance. They disappear into the gloomy shadows, reappear farther down the street and walk further into shadow.

When they haven't returned after fifteen minutes, Mai is frozen and goes back upstairs to her warm apartment, and locks herself in. She wishes she could talk to Ron. Her phone is finished charging, so she disconnects and carries it into the sitting room. She selects Ron's number from her address book and sends a text: "can u tak?" It bounces, giving her a message: "Number is out of range." She cleans up the broken glass, dumps the uneaten tuna sandwich in a plastic shopping bag, and carries the rubbish down to the trash barrels in the street before falling into bed and a black, friendless sleep. In the morning, she feels guilty for locking her husband out.

A loud banging at the door disturbs her while she's dressing for work. It's Sgt. GU, Commander GAO's driver.

"He's not here." she says.

GU nods and points past her at Rick's travel bag on the floor in the studio. His English is limited, but he manages to communicate by saying, "*Zouba*," as he deftly brushes past Mai and bends over the bag, zipping it. "*Huzhao*, passport," he says.

Mai finds it on the table and stuffs it into the envelope with the medical documents and tucks it into a side pocket of Rick's bag.

GU gestures again at Mai and repeats, "*Zouba*," pointing down the stairs. Mai grabs her purse and locks the apartment, again, and follows the man down to the street.

GAO leans out of the passenger-side window of his Crown Royale to greet her, "Martin Taitai."

Mai looks over his shoulder and sees Rick sitting in the back between two soldiers.

"I'm sorry, Mai. I'm a fucking asshole, and I'm a no-good jerk. I'm sorry. God, I'm sorry ..."

"You're a wreck, Rick. Clean yourself up."

"You're right, Mai. I'm starting right now. Please forgive me. Say you do. Say it."

"I'm not talking to you till you get straight."

GAO starts edging the window up one inch at a time. "We go now, Martin Taitai."

"*Xiexie*, Commander."

CHAPTER 7
Good-Bye

November 21

Rick is transferred to the United States.

Mai stops checking her phone for a message from Ron.

Her internet goes out for a day and a half at the apartment. She's sure she's lost her job. At last, a couple of tech guys arrive and determine it had been accidently switched off at the Internet Office. The job is still hers.

November 24

The night after the operation's dramatic and disappointing conclusion in Wenzhou, Ron went back to the New Asia Hotel alone, called the spa, and paid for two girls to come to his room and stay all night. He zipped Mai's bag and threw it into the back of the closet and closed the sliding doors. In the morning, he retrieved it and stepped out of the room, ready to check out. In the hall, he found a package of her laundry leaning against the door.

Driving back to Beijing the slow way, along the coast, staying at smaller hostels, he didn't get home until a week later. His eyes sought out couples to watch, voyeuristically, pretending they were him and Mai. Twenty times a day he wanted to text her. Twenty times he fought the urge. Feeling like a fool.

Back in Beijing a week later was no different, except that he could go to work and crowd her out of his head for hours at a time. He exercised at his club before and after work. There was almost no time for her.

***

Feeling funky, Mai turns down an invitation to go to the movies with Yunling over the weekend. Instead, she sits around the apartment trying to figure out what she should be doing.

And in what direction should she be going?

Back to the United States, Rick and Homeland Security?

She would run straight into Ronald ZHAO's arms, but she doesn't know where he is. He's been out of range of her calling plan. *Maybe he went to Hong Kong,* she thinks. But she admits, she manipulated him, right from the beginning. Lied to him about Rick and Homeland Security. Lied to GAO about it, too … but he knew anyway. They read her every email and followed every link.

Ron didn't know. She kept him in the dark until the last possible moment. *He deserves better than that. What does that make me?*

She imagines the conversation she wants to have with Ron over and over:

—I have to go back and take care of him.

—I know, Tangzi, you love him.

—I love you, I do, it's just impossible. Right now.

—Come back.

—I promise, I'll come as soon as I can.

But she can't bring herself to call him again. And he's not calling her.

***

Saturday morning, while still lying in bed willing herself to rise, she gets a text from Wright: "R U up?"

She calls him back, "Yeah, Wright, what?"

"Can I come over this morning?"

"What for"

"News about Rick."

"I guess so. When?"

"In fifteen minutes?"

"Where are you?"

"I'm at the Starbucks in Wudaokou. I can bring coffee …" he offers.

"Yeah, Americano with milk and sugar," she says, wondering, *WTF?!*

Mai pulls on some jeans and runs a brush through her hair. The woman she sees looking back at her in the mirror over the big, square, Soviet-style sink, has dark circles under her eyes. Her skin sags and looks pasty. She runs the hot water and splashes her face, breathing in the steamy *chi*. A dab of cream and a bit of makeup, finishing with a stab at lipstick: she looks a million dollars better. Or maybe $100,000 better, she thinks, sardonically.

Sitting with Wright, hugging the Starbucks cup, and sipping, Mai listens to his update.

"Your husband was flown to the US on Monday. He's in an intensive-care facility," starts Wright.

The sun is rising through the forest of buildings surrounding the campus. Bright rays catch the edges of humongous clouds of condensation billowing hypnotically from a black smokestack.

"What does that mean?"

"A lot of doctors are looking at him and giving him the best care, Mrs. Martin. He's getting the best care."

"If you say so," replies Mai, taking a thoughtful gulp.

"Give me your bank routing number; we want to send you a payment."

"What?" asks Mai, startled from her self-recriminations. "Why? I don't work for you."

"I have to remind you that the events of the past several weeks are highly classified," he says, "way above your level."

"Which means what?"

"Have you got a cover story about where you've been?" he quizzes her. "And I don't mean for a magazine."

"My boss knows the whole story," says Mai.

"Besides the Red Chinese, other people—like your colleagues."

"I was with Donna Summerlake, in her office, when I met the man with the Bible, Joshua Braithwaite. Where were *you* that day?"

"We were in Wenzhou. You caught up fast," he says.

"I'm really sorry about your men," she thinks to say, changing the subject.

Wright inclines his bald head slightly, a mute thank-you, "Where will you be going? You're not staying here, are you?"

"I've started packing to go home during the university's break for Spring Festival holiday."

"When are you leaving?" he asks.

"January twenty-third," she answers. "And I'm coming back February twelfth."

"Why? He needs you, Mrs. Martin, now more than ever," begs Wright.

"I have a job here, Wright, which Homeland Security has nearly jeopardized. The Media Office has work to complete before the holiday closes the university. The penalties for unapproved absences are extreme."

"Like what?" he asks.

"Like they dock you two days for every unauthorized day," she explains.

"Under the circumstances, wouldn't they let you go?"

"That's assuming I want to."

"You *want* to come back here? But you're an American."

They watch a magpie eating a persimmon hanging high in a tree in the brightening day.

***

Ron doesn't remember how it happened that he called her. He was driving with the phone in his hand when it almost dialed itself and sent the text.

Mai is at her computer working on the Media Reports Catalog, when a text message comes in from Ron: "can I see u ?"

She writes back: "call 62797987"

"Wei, nihao, what phone is this, Mai" asks Ron, his voice worried and husky.

"It's my office phone. My mobile is acting up. Suddenly the

screen goes blank. So, don't call it."

"I have your things. Your bag. From the hotel," he says. "Duibuqi, Mai, sorry."

A wave of chi sweeps Mai into a maelstrom of emotions.

"Can you bring it over?"

"Just tell me when, Tangzi," he says, full of hope, riding his own torrent of emotions into unchartered territory.

***

That night, in front of her LiNai apartment, he parks and pops the trunk to get her bag, where it's been sitting since the day he checked out of the New Asia.

Upstairs, she smiles at him and holds the door open. It clangs shut with a familiar sound. Her apartment is warm and cozy, enveloping him, possessing him, and he surrenders to it.

Mai's arms are around him before he can release the bag. Her mouth is on his, and he's kissing back, furious, desperate kisses, until he pulls back, and they stare for a moment, trying keep up with the spinning emotions and thoughts that have spiraled out of their breathless passion.

Mai takes his hand and leads him into the sitting room. She's set a romantic dinner for two with take-out sushi from Koreatown and a chilled bottle of plum wine.

"I wanted to call you," she starts lamely, pouring hot jasmine tea, *hua cha*, into small cups.

"Every day, I thought about you," he confesses, opening a shopping bag and setting a to-go box of *jiaozi* on the table.

"I never thanked you. You saved my life," bowing her head

slightly, hiding her shame. She hands him a corkscrew and the wine to open.

He accepts her acknowledgement gratefully, tries looking into her eyes and is confused by her sudden shyness.

Fighting back tears, she ducks into the kitchenette for soy sauce and wasabi, where she splashes water on her face and blots it with a dish towel while looking out the window into the hutong. Although it's dark, people are in the street, coming home from work, carrying groceries or bottles of beer from the mini-mart. Children in school uniforms are coming home from late tutoring sessions. Men in the guard shack are smoking and playing cards. She turns to stand in the doorway, hanging onto the jamb.

"Can you forgive me?" she asks, her chin trembling.

"For what, Tangzi?" he asks. He pops the cork and pours some wine into the little cherry-blossom glasses.

"For lying to you ... about Rick ... and things. I wasn't honest," she blurts out, feeling slightly better.

He hands a glass to her, "Drink, ganbei. Don't be so serious."

She smiles crookedly and takes a gulp.

Later, lying in bed, plum wine forgetfulness seeps into her chi, wafting through a hazy fantasy: sun shining on bare breasts with the fragrance of ripe, juicy pear, and blue sky.

"So, you're not angry with me?" she asks between kisses.

"*Bushi fengle*, not mad, Tangzi," he whispers, his lips brushing her cheek.

Martial arts master ZHAO, the Crane, patient and elegant, practices the finer combat arts. From Ron's throat, a deep, soft sigh, like a moan, escapes. Suddenly hot, he throws the duvet onto the floor, pushing her legs into Grasping the Gate of Heaven, rolling her hot, sweet labia with his tongue, kneading and sucking them. At that moment, she stiffens, swooning.

He slips on a condom, sliding his spear into her velvet chamber. Overcome, they fall irresistibly deeper into the mesh of twining desire. He whispers, *"Wo ai ni."* She answers the same, *"Wo ye ai ni."* Withdrawing, he rolls off the bed and pads into the bathroom.

Over Chinese porridge and *hong cha* the next morning, Mai can't think of anything to say.

Ron starts, "I have to go to Taiwan tomorrow, this time with Alan Spires."

"When are you coming back?"

"Next week. Are you going home for Spring Festival?"

"Dui," she answers, providing him with the dates. Feeling a knot in her stomach. *Here it comes!*

"Who do you choose, Mai?"

The question pierces and lodges in a deep place in her heart, like a narrow shard of glass. Outside, billowing clouds from the smokestack form into Rick's face, dissolve and reform as Ron's, and dissolve again.

"Why can't you just break it off with him?" he wants to know.

***

December 1   To: Mai Martin From: Ronald ZHAO
Subject: ☺

Taiwan is cold and rainy nothing like the road to Wenzhou

***

Mai completes and sends Media Report #15 12/2/2011.

Incident Report 20111202

TRIGGER ACTIVITY: MEDIA REPORT 12/2

23—Subject violates accepted-use criteria: uses SunSystems search to access keyword-excluded media. 12/2

SECURITY RESPONSE ACTIVITY:

23—Response: Automatic keyword search Layer 7 Tier III: IP identifier unit
Keyword searches are collected in a live-stream search
Tabulation of violations pushes alert.

December 5

After two weeks of intensive care stateside, detox, and plastic surgery, Rick Martin is sent to a twenty-eight-day government-rehabilitation program. It's designed for high-value government personnel who get into trouble with booze or drugs. Among the other patients, Rick is a celebrity. Not only is he younger than most of the officers, but he was addicted through espionage and had his ear severed. The new ear is almost as good as his old one. Better, actually, since it has built-in amplified-listening technology.

The treatment center, in Arizona, is bordered on one side by a nine-hole golf course. With a lot of time to fill, Rick takes up the sport with intense competitiveness, playing in the 90s on his first trip to the center. For the entire time, he's cut off from the outside world: no phone, no internet.

***

December 8   To: Mai Martin From: Ronald ZHAO
Subject: still traveling

In Seoul now. More work at branch office. Wo xiang ni ☹

December 8   To: Ronald ZHAO   From: Mai   Martin
Subject: Re: still traveling

When are you coming back? Wo ye xiang ni

December 10   To: Mai Martin From: Ronald   ZHAO
Subject: Re: still traveling

See you next week ☺

December 13   To: Ronald ZHAO   From: Mai   Martin
Subject: smog

The air is so bad today. Airport closed since Sunday. US Embassy air quality reading was 'scary bad' 'basically off the chart.'

December 15   To: Mai Martin From: Ronald   ZHAO
Subject: Re: smog

I am in Pakistan. For sure coming back soon.

A loud rattling at her door jerks Mai to the present. She gets up from reading Ron's email to look through the peep hole and sees Wright standing there.

"Lawrence Wright, what can I do for you?" asks Mai, unlocking the gate.

"Ask me in?"

"Come in," she says, standing to one side as he enters. She notices he's not bringing her coffee this time. "What can I do for you?" she asks.

Wright shrugs out of his coat and lays it over the back of one of the two Craftsman-style armchairs with cushions the color and texture of rhinoceros hide in Mai's sitting room. "Warm in here," he says.

"Tea?" she asks, disappearing into the kitchenette and switching on the electric tea kettle.

"What happened to your phone?"

"It died. Did you try to call me?" she asks.

"Yeah. Anyway, I wanted you to know, not on a phone, that Rick is better. We've got him enrolled in a rehab program for drug abuse."

"What abuse? What kind of program? Where is this?" The hand holding her tea cup starts to shake with shock and fear. How long has *this* been going on? She holds it still in her lap with the other hand. But then she starts shivering. *Get it together, girl. Why are you surprised? Your whole life with Rick has been a big lie....*

"It's government-run. Not for the public. He's getting the best care, Mrs. Martin. Like a spa."

Mai screws up her face and tries to look at Wright. She's having the worst time focusing on him. The muscles in her ears contract, leaving a high-pitched buzz in her head. She sees his mouth forming words. After a few minutes, she realizes that Wright is holding a wet cloth to her forehead and is trying to revive her.

"What ... what were you saying?" she stammers.

"Are you all right, Mrs. Martin?" he asks. "I was wondering when we were going to hit your saturation level."

"No. Not all right, Lawrence Wright." She pounds the carved armrest with a balled up fist. "He was a whole, animated being a month ago. Now he's damaged, and you're bragging how great his care is?... I'm going to be sick." She stands up and dashes to the bathroom, slamming shut the door behind her.

Wright lets himself out.

***

Mai completes and sends Media Report #16 12/16/2011.

Incident Report 20111216

TRIGGER ACTIVITY: MEDIA REPORT 12/16

24—Subject violates accepted-use criteria: uses SunSystems search to access keyword-excluded media. 12/16

SECURITY RESPONSE ACTIVITY:

24—Response: Automatic keyword search Layer 7 Tier III: IP identifier unit
Keyword searches are collected in a live-stream search
Tabulation of violations pushes alert.

The past several media reports had triggered violations from a filter set up to catch them. When the automated scan comes up empty, with no forbidden keywords, it still is registered as an incident. Consequently, Mai continues to accumulate violations in spite of her connections with the Commander in the Main Building.

Sunday, December 18, KIM Jong-Il, supreme leader of DPRK, dies.

On her day off, Mai visits the campus mobile shop and buys a new Samsung smartphone, 3-G. The salesman doesn't speak any English, which limits the dialog to pointing and a few words in Mandarin. The intervention of a kind, Chinese post-doctoral researcher, a beautiful, petite woman with animated eyes, moves the dialog forward. It still takes another half an hour to crunch through the torture of three-way communication with total strangers met on the fly. In the end, it costs RMB 600 or $100 and includes five years of free phone calls, renewed monthly with 30-yuan deposits into her phone account by the manufacturer. It seems almost too good to be true, so she makes them go over it a couple of times. *And* it has the new, cool technology synched up with the internet. Finally, Mai counts out the bills while the salesman packages it for her in a fancy box and bag. She has to show her passport.

***

In the last days before the university closes for the Spring Festival, Mai packs boxes, sorting out her life in piles of clothes, books, electronic pieces, and trash. This past year, living in Beijing on her own without Rick opened up new possibilities and gave her the validation she was missing at home. When things piled up and got difficult, new friends arrived to help. She learned about the covert work her husband had been doing for Homeland Security—all the way back to 9/11. Lying to her for ten years! That partially explained why he had become distant, as he buried himself in his new project: hacking the Iranian intranet. But it didn't explain why she had let the distance grow.

On the other hand, Rick's infernal intrigues with the Department tangled her up in crossfire between US Homeland Security and DPRK agents. Some kind of experiment they were running. She'd had to find her own protection from a security firm! Thinking about it still angered her. But she had to wonder: if she hadn't been so attracted to Ron, would she have hired TSC Security or would she have just gone home when things got weird?

Since their meeting a couple weeks ago, Mai hasn't seen or heard from Ron. What she doesn't know is that it's because Ron's boss at TSC thinks it best if Ron gets his mind off the American woman, now the contract is completed. And there's work to be done in the branch offices. Ron's been traveling around Asia servicing the new TSC branches: monitoring them for communications, training the staff, and supervising their methods for compliance. Two new offices are opening in Taiwan and Pakistan, and he still has the training manual to complete.

Mai obsesses about the impossibility of their love: the truth is, there's nothing promising about her contract for next spring either, especially now the Iranian ambassadors have been ejected over the scandal and the DPRK leader, KIM Jong-Il, has died.

***

While Rick is in rehab, Mai gets a break from the drama of Homeland Security. Beijing has adopted the Western custom of going overboard with Christmas decorations, and she goes shopping with Yunling, finishing with a leisurely visit at a tea shop. All the while missing Ron.

December 22 To: Mai Martin From: Ronald   ZHAO
Subject: at last

Coming home tomorrow. Christmas at my flat?

Mai texts Ron from the subway stop before Chaoyangmen Station, where he is double-parked in the red zone. He paid the parking monitor, the cadre assigned to collect money, to let him wait for her there.

Smog obscures the tops of the tallest buildings and has settled into the distance, the first thing she notices emerging from the mouth of the *ditie zhan.* First, she spots his car and then he spots her, waving. If he weren't double-parked on one of the most traveled boulevards in Beijing, surrounded by crowds of people, he would have embraced her in the street. Instead, he holds the door, standing there like a grinning idiot.

"Look in the back," he says, pulling into the first lane of traffic on Chaoyangmenlu Street.

Behind the seat is a shopping bag. Inside, is a large box. The lid slides open, revealing a tissue-wrapped, faux leopard fur, silk velvet, reversible, short coat with a wide, black, elasticized waistband, circular skirt, and matching pillbox hat. A pin of white jade and cloisonné enamel on gold is fastened to the collar.

"Merry Christmas, Mai," he says. "I bought for you in Hong Kong."

"I love the coat, Ron."

"Take it out of the box, Mai. Let me see it."

"What is this beautiful pin?"

"That's a phoenix. A regal bird, the mate to the imperial dragon. Of course, completely magical. It is our culture."

Mai inspects the amazing coat inside and out as they cut through back streets to the parking entrance at Ron's apartment building.

In the dim light of the garage, she leans toward him, "I thought about you every day."

When they get out of the elevator, Mai's flushed and mussed from passionate necking. With her around the waist with one arm and the huge shopping bag in the other, Ron steers her through the lobby hung with a mural-sized, abstract oil painting and a crystal chandelier above an enormous arrangement of fresh, white, fragrant lilies. Strains of Christmas carols with oboe and strings blend into "The Way You Look Tonight." This is not the first time she notices the fondness Chinese have for Christmas carols. But at least it's seasonal this time.

Ron is happy, his dream love affair has resumed now Rick has left. He flirts with the idea that he has finally met his soul mate and the true love of his life, something every person hopes for, but the Chinese person perhaps most ardently.

Mai is happy, her dream lover is showering her with expensive gifts, sheltering her in his fabulous loft, yet not suffocating in his attentions since she can return to her own apartment during the week. For a while, it's possible to ignore the rest of the world and wrap herself in a cocoon.

Mama ZHAO is happy as long as her darling son is happy. If that means admitting a *Meiguoren* into her home, shopping and cooking for her, then fine.

After dinner, Mai and Ron retire to his apartment. He shows her around: the nighttime, wraparound view and enormous walk-in closets. The massive Chinese bed, with dragon-and-phoenix–carved bedposts like an emperor would possess, is covered with a black silk duvet and white pillows embroidered with animals: a black panther on one, an orange-and-black tiger on another. He opens a door off the bedroom to a spacious bathroom with a large Jacuzzi; the Beijing moonlight reflects off the white-and-gold alabaster tile while the still water glows bright blue from underwater lights. He turns off the switch, closes the door and gently pushes her backward onto his hard bed.

"Your work schedule is amazing. Do you take trips like this often?" she asks, stroking the back of his head, feeling his hair with her fingertips.

"It comes in spurts. I knew there would be travel involved. My Hong Kong passport makes it easy," he says, leaning on his arms, his face centimeters from hers, going over every feature of it, remembering, memorizing, wondering if he ever knew her at all before … before her husband came, before the superpowers took over everyone's lives.

On Sunday, Christmas day, they go to Art District 798 after brunch with Mama ZHAO at the Grand Millennium Hotel a few blocks over on Dongsanyuanlu Road. There, the holiday decorations achieve a pinnacle of fantasy and luxury, combining laser optics with nature and copies of nature, wrapped in gold lamé swag twined with velvet ribbons and jeweled butterflies.

They drop off Mama at his apartment's valet parking turnaround and head toward the outer edge of Chaoyang District.

"Whatever happened to Rick?" asks Ron finally.

"Oh yeah, Rick. Well … mmm …" She's wearing the amazing coat over black jeans. The luscious fabrics beg to be touched, and she touches, stroking unconsciously between conversational cues. "He's in rehab."

"What is *rehab*, Mai?" he asks, dodging a peddler on a bicycle contraption in the roadway.

"Are you going to ever let me drive your car?" she asks, laughing at his red face. But then, thinking about Rick's treatment robs her of the joy of the moment, and she explains, "Rehab is short for rehabilitation. Recovery. Recovering your good health, your virtuous life."

"Yes, I know rehab now," he says. "Why is Rick in rehab? This is a long time?"

"He gets out next month. Right after New Year's. Our New Years, on the first."

They park as usual, near Alan Spire's office and Annie's gallery, but today, on Christmas, they have to park farther away. The crowds are the biggest Mai has seen. The Christmas holiday is like an aperitif for the full-course meal of Chinese New Year coming up in a few weeks. The Bauhaus-style brick factory buildings are mostly tastefully lit up and decorated. The passersby, like themselves, are happy to have a season to celebrate, wear their best clothes, finish old business, and connect with loved ones.

At Annie's gallery, they're greeted warmly with Ceylon tea sweetened by rock sugar.

"Beautiful coat, Mai," murmurs Annie with approval.

The two women look long into each other's faces, remembering the last time they met: when they were in this same place and Annie was giving Mai advice about ransoms and contracts. Mai tries to remember when that was, more than a month ago she guesses. *Prehistoric.*

"*Xiexie*, Ron bought it in Hong Kong!"

Annie leads them around the room, showing them pieces she has selected for his flat. After discussing their various merits, Ron selects one large and one small painting in traditional style, and Mai picks a contemporary one.

"Alan and I invite you to Christmas with us today. Can you come now? We go now?" asks Annie.

Ron looks down into Mai's shining face and says, "*Dui*, we can come. But not for long."

"*Xiexie*, ZHAO Xiansheng, Alan is enjoying his holiday with UK ex-pats and will be overjoyed you join us."

"On one condition," objects Ron with a twinkle in his eye, like any indulgent Santa might have.

"What's that?" ask the women in tandem, smiling at his game.

"This *Meiguoren*," he looks at Mai and back to Annie, "has been too busy to find the right shoes to complement the most amazing coat in Beijing."

Annie looks down at Mai's big feet, skipping over the common jeans—knock-off designer label, not the real thing,—and landing at the low boots Mai wore with everything.

"Come with me," she says, grabbing her purse—not a copy but the real thing—and locking the door behind them. "When do you want the paintings delivered, Ron?"

"I want to be there," he says as they press through the mobs of people to a shoe store in the back of the next building.

"Of course," she says, "next Saturday?"

"Perfect," he says as Annie pushes them ahead of her into an Italian boutique.

December 31

Breakfasting in the dining room of his Sanlitun flat, overlooking the city, Mai and Ron discuss where the paintings they bought last week should go.

One side of the room is a glass wall, overlooking the Dongcheng district and Dongyue Temple. An antique Chinese chest stretches most of the length of the back wall. A heavy, beveled mirror reflects the western sky into the room, making it dim in the morning and bright in the afternoon. An arched doorway leads to the kitchen at the rear corner, leaving the two unobstructed walls available for decoration.

"Where should the big painting go, Mai?"

"In this room?"

"I want to see out the windows and look at my new art while I enjoy my family."

"If you move the table around ..."

"You see how I need you?" he asks, his eyes sparkling.

What she sees is how different his need is from Rick's. But she just smiles.

After their leisurely breakfast, they go downstairs to enjoy the neighborhood, down on the ground level with the people.

She helps him pick out fancy fish from the corner florist and tropical fish store, a gift for his mother. At April's Kitchen, they get sandwiches on pumpernickel bread, Belgium beer, a big pickle, and apple strudel cheesecake *to go*.

Back upstairs, Mama ZHAO pounces on the perfect sandwiches, crusts trimmed and cut into pointy quarters—braunschweiger, cheese, and egg salad—arranging them like a pagoda, and sets the plate in the center of the heavy, carved and inlaid dining table. Ron saws at the pickle and offers some to Mai.

The guard downstairs calls, interrupting their casual lunch with the announcement that Annie, the art dealer, is here. She arrives with workmen to install the three pieces. "Here, Ron, for you and Mai," holding out a bottle of rare *baijiu* wrapped in blue cellophane with a small red-and-gold envelope tucked in the fancy bow.

Annie and Ron walk around his apartment, as she assesses the possibilities for artistic display. Mai trails behind with Mama ZHAO. Then Ron consults with Mama while Mai and Annie lean against the back of a leather couch, where they can watch Ron and his mother deciding on the locations.

By 4PM, Annie's *shifu* have installed the three pieces and departed. In the dining room they installed a large, traditional *huahua* mounted on a scroll and hung horizontally, depicting a crane on one end and a tiger on the other creeping through tall grass. A contemporary *huahua* of lotuses, lots of black, masculine strokes and ink spatters brightens the far corner of the sitting room above a baby grand piano. Calligraphy jumps from the wall in Ron's apartment: an emblem of his kung fu school.

Next, the florist shop delivers a shell-shaped aquarium and several beautiful fish, carrying everything into Mama ZHAO's apartment. They set it up, get the water filter bubbling, drop the colorful, striped, and spotted fish in, clean up, and leave.

"I'm cooking dinner," announces Ron, wrapping a kitchen towel around his waist and twirling a mean knife in the air. He's joined by Mama; they efficiently work around each other, like people who have cooked together frequently. Mai sits on a tall stool at the bar end, sipping on *hua cha* and nibbling pistachio nuts. She plays with her camera, taking pictures of the meal preparation while asking questions about the food. Wiping his hands on the towel, Ron exits the kitchen and brings the tea and snacks into the living room.

Finished in the kitchen, Mama ZHAO has programmed the piano to a familiar waltz. In the shadowy corner of the flat, she dances by herself, crisply holding out her arms as if in the grasp of a dream partner.

"Annie warned me—the last time we were there—she said political prisoners don't come back in China, and I should get realistic.... But he came back, so ... Look at your mother, dancing by herself."

"She's dreaming that she's dancing with my father."

"That is so sweet, Ron."

"When you find out what you want with me, that's the day we dance together. Until that time, I'm a wraith, a ghost from the underworld, not alive, not dead, roaming the spirit world in agony for you." He bends over, pressing into her lap, holding onto her around her hips and grinding his face into her Gateway to Heaven.

"So, dance with me," she says, ready to leap into the future with Ron.

Sunday afternoon, they walk around the neighborhood, shopping, before Mai goes back to Haidian and her own LiNai apartment for the week. Wind is coming in gusts, stirring up the last of the dead leaves. Zigzagging through the back alleys of the fashionable neighborhood, they cut into a bakery.

"Rick gets out of rehab tomorrow," she says, grabbing a tray.

"*Zhende*, that is very good, Mai," says Ron, following her with tongs, selecting the sweet or savory pastries she points to.

Sipping *kaffei nai he tang*, Mai leans into the corner of their booth and asks, "How patient are you?"

"What do you mean, Mai?"

"Just … well … I don't see any of this working out for us."

"I know the same feeling. Times I lay in bed at night and say, 'Ron, you idiot, this American woman, she will go back to US with husband.'"

"That's not it; I mean, how can I expect Beijing University to renew my contract next year, after Spring Festival? I'm married to a spy!"

At the thought of her married, Ron takes pause.

"We will hire you to work at TSC."

It's Mai's turn to take pause.

When he doesn't get a reaction, he continues, "I have to finish the training manual by New Year. Plus, we close accounts. I still have to hand in my hours for last month."

"Who's paying for that?"

"It's on your contract."

"I know, but, Homeland Security should be paying."

"*Mei wenti*, Mai," he says, cuddling her sideways. "The US is rich; they can pay."

January 2

At the Media Office, there's a quickening of pace. Mai catches glances from her colleague's faces, bright with anticipation of the biggest holiday of the year. Most people in the West think of it as Chinese New Year, but the PRC changed the name to Spring Festival in a rupture from pre-revolution feudal customs. In New China, the leaders wanted to make an uncompromising break with the corrupt past, including banning the old holidays and instituting new ones. Ms. ZHANG and Ms. HAN organize mass mailings of brochures and magazines to global universities.

January 2   To: Mai   From: Rick
Subject: Freedom

Flying back to Santa Rosa today. Sitting in LAX on layover. I need you. Come please?

January 3   To: Rick   From: Mai
Subject: Re: Freedom

Coming Jan 23 to Feb 12. Are you better?

January 5   To: Mai   From: Rick
Subject: Re: Freedom

Skype?

While Mai dresses for work, she logs in to see if Rick is online. He is, so she makes the connection.

"Hey, Mai, great to see you," he says. "What time is it there?"

"7:30AM, I'm going to work, but I have a few minutes ... for you," she says, carrying Pépe into the bathroom and setting her netbook on the washing machine where she can see Rick while getting ready.

"I've started a new hobby, golf," says Rick.

"You golf now?" she asks, surprised.

"Picked it up at the rehab place. It's real plush with a nine-hole course. I was hanging with majors and generals and stuff. Nothing to do except golf. Or swim. They had a gym. Played a little basketball. It's in Arizona. Great weather for December. It was sunny every day."

"Did they give you a new ear?" she asks. The last time she saw him, his ear wound, where Gen. MA had cut it off, was stitched in black thread.

"Oh, yeah, is that cool or what?" he asks, displaying his ears for her, turning his head around to compare them.

"Which one is the new one?" she asks, amazed.

"This one on the right," he says, giving her a close-up.

"I can't tell them apart. That's great Rick. Totally amazing."

"I just got back from hitting a few buckets of balls at the Sonoma County Golf Course in Santa Rosa. And a Narcotics Anonymous chapter meeting for a couple hours at a church."

"What's that about?" she asks, finishing up with blush and lipstick.

"You look great, Mai, really," he says beating around the bush.

"Are you an addict?" she presses, carrying Pépe into the sitting room and relaxing for a few minutes in her favorite chair, watching the white, puffy smokestack clouds.

"They say so, I guess so, it's been hard to cope … with the new … uh … situation," he starts. "But, at least I'm off the pills or anything and am doing okay."

"Are you back to work?"

"No, I'm on furlough until Nolan says I can come back. My clearance has been suspended. Have to go to these AA-type meetings every day. I'll be seeing a psychiatrist in a few days," he confides, hanging his head and struggling with defeat for a few moments.

He looks pitiful, and her heart twists in sympathy. "You're looking better," she says cheerfully.

"Thanks," he says, glancing quickly at her face in the screen. "I've got to go now."

"Okay," she says, "see you."

"Can't you come? I need you!" he blurts out suddenly.

"I've got my ticket, Rick. I'll be there soon."

"'K, bye," and the screen goes from black to blue, leaving her unsettled and worried.

***

The next day, Mai awakes, surprised to find the hutong under a blanket of white. The sky is also white, though the snow seems to have stopped. She dresses in foul-weather cycling gear over her work clothes. At the bicycle shed, she runs into Dr. Rebecca, whose stylish gear invites her envy for a moment.

"That cycle suit is so cool," says Mai.

"I have a suitcase full of this stuff," Dr. Rebecca answers, amused. "In Vancouver where I was completing my PhD, I rode my bicycle every day. In the winter, it rains a ton."

"Are you going anywhere for the holiday?" asks Mai,

"I'm staying. I just went to see my family this summer. What about you?" asks the doctor, fastening a chin strap holding her hood snug against her head.

"I'm leaving in a couple days. January twenty-third to February twelfth."

"Whatever happened to your husband, Mai? Can you talk about it?" her friend asks.

Mai doesn't know how to answer that one. "It's a long story. Maybe later."

She rides through an inch of snow to the Qingming Building. By the time she completes and sends Media Report #1 for 2012, later today on 1/6, it has melted.

Incident Report 20120106

TRIGGER ACTIVITY: MEDIA REPORT 1/6

1—Subject violates accepted–use criteria: uses
SunSystems search to access keyword–excluded media.
1/6

SECURITY RESPONSE ACTIVITY:

1—Response: Automatic keyword search Layer 7 Tier III:
IP identifier unit
Keyword searches are collected in a live–stream search
Tabulation of violations pushes alert.

The new calendar year starts a new cycle of data collection. Every day that passes, more people are leaving campus and joining their families in their hometowns all over China. Fewer network monitors every day means the machines just watch other machines.

The workdays pass. The snow that quickly melted in the roads remains on the roofs and in the out-of-the-way places. Every weekend, Mai spends with Ron at his flat.

January 18   To: Mai Martin   From: Ronald ZHAO
Subject: see you

I take you to airport bring your suitcase ready to go.

***

After the snow, the sky remains clear until Mai completes and sends Media Report #2 1/20.

Incident Report 20120120

TRIGGER ACTIVITY: MEDIA REPORT 1/20

2—Subject violates accepted-use criteria: uses SunSystems search to access keyword-excluded media. 1/20

SECURITY RESPONSE ACTIVITY:

2—Response: Automatic keyword search Layer 7 Tier III: IP identifier unit
Keyword searches are collected in a live-stream search
Tabulation of violations pushes alert.

Once Mai sends the media report, she says her good-byes to Ms. HAN and Dandan and bikes back to her apartment. She calls Robert, the cabdriver, who drives her to Sanlitun with her bags packed for a visit to the United States of America.

Ron's mom has already left for the holiday, returning to her flat in Hong Kong, leaving the two love birds alone. And leaving Ron with the responsibility of caring for the fish and her orchids.

"I have special weekend planned for you, Tangzi," starts Ron.

"Does it start with lunch? I'm starved," she says, arranging her bags in his vast bedroom.

In the dining room, Mai finds a gift box at her place. In it is a pair of lover's padlocks in the shape of hearts with a tiny key on a gold chain.

"What's this, Ron?" she asks, looking up at him bringing a tray of sandwiches and a pot of tea through the door.

"Ancient Chinese custom, lovers lock their love at special places, to symbolize enduring love. Maybe hope for love to last long time." Ron pulls at the collar of his shirt to reveal he's wearing a similar key around his neck.

Mai holds her chain up to look at the beautiful craftsmanship and examine the little steel key. He takes it from her and fastens it around her neck.

"What do we do with these locks, then?" she asks.

"Tomorrow, we go to Great Wall, hang them there. It's a custom with lovers, to go there and lock them on fence with others. They say, if one lover stops loving, breaks up, then they unlock their lock and take it away, leaving the other lock still there, faithful forever."

"Darling custom, Ron. A trip to the wall—how fun is that?" she asks, grabbing his hand across the corner of the table and kissing it, "*Xiexie*."

Ron says, "I'll be here for you when you come back from the holiday," holding his key to his lips and kissing it.

"I have something special for you, too," she says, getting up and going into his bedroom. She had wrapped her lucky coin in tissue and stuffed it into a silk brocade sack with tasseled ties, a lucky talisman for him. She finds the little package in her suitcase, breathes, *Good luck!* and returns to the other room.

***

January twenty-third arrives; Ron stands with Mai, waiting to check her bags and get her boarding pass.

"We'll be together again ... sometime soon ..." they promise, their heads bent together, whispering in the crowded room.

"You had better go; you still have to take the shuttle to the boarding area."

At a point, travelers show their boarding pass to leave the main terminal. Airport security checks everyone, and passengers have to leave carts behind to take escalators to the tram level. Soon ZHAO can't see her in the hundreds of travelers passing through the queue. Mai turns and can't make out Ron's figure from others, backlit by a glass wall in the world's largest airport.

***

Their last night together, how they clung to each other and cried. Their tender lovemaking, instead of buoying her, increased her feelings of dejection and defeat by the superpowers, letting them separate her from China and the life and the man she loves, and she gives into hopelessness. It feels like she's going back to where she started, sinking from the inertia like a person drowning.

Except nothing will *ever* be normal again.

And the Commander? Of course, he's there to shelter her.

And Ms. ZHANG did say they would keep her job through the end of the contract. So. At least, that's something.

Her plane flies across the frozen tundra of Manchuria toward

Seattle International Airport. She leans back into the economy seat, resting her head in a doughnut pillow, covering her eyes with a black-silk mask, Pulling the airline blanket up around her chin, she tries to sleep. Soft, ephemeral tendrils brush her cheek in dreams like feathers; they sigh in her *yuanfen*, drawing her back to visions of China. She remembers Ron's hands and the ways they felt.

Changing planes in Seattle, actually walking onto the tarmac to board the small twin-turboprop plane manufactured in Brazil and fittingly called a Brasilia, she begins telescoping into her other self. The American one who lives in California in a town of thousands, not millions, of native English speakers. She watches the wrinkled terrain below on her interconnecting flight to Santa Rosa Airport. Already looking like another foreign country.

APPENDIX : Who's Who?

Chapter 1

1. Mai Martin, American in Beijing

2. Rick Martin, Mai's husband

3. Ms. ZHANG Hong, Director of Media Communications Office

4. SUN Yunling, co-worker at Media Communications Office in International Building

5. Sr. Col. GAO Bu, Deputy Division Commander, First Bureau Office Director, Beijing University Security Office.

6. Specialized Sergeant 1st Class WANG Tao, Assistant to Commander GAO

7. Lt. Col. DIANGTI Yong, Ninth Bureau Section Chief, Director Harbin Institute, Information Security Research Institute (ISRI) and National Information Center (NIC) in Harbin

8. Capt. LI Pei, Supervisor, Class 2, Beijing Municipal Public Security Bureau (BMPSB), Sanlitun Police Station (Beijing Police Department)

9. XU Dandan, Dandan Xiaojie, co-worker Media Communications Office in Mingqiang Building

10. Maj. Gen. HUANG Fuhui, First Bureau Chief, Deputy Army Commander of the Beijing Military Region and Commander GAO's boss, *dalaoban*

11. YANG Cai, Junior-Grade Technical Specialist (JGTS) Beijing University Office

12. Lieutenant Col. LIU Fengshou, Deputy Brigade Commander, Beijing University Security Office

13. Ms. HAN Liying, Mai's supervisor at Media Communications Office in Mingqiang Building

14. Maj. TANG Xiaobei, Battalion Commander, Beijing University Security Office

15. Robert, WEI Junjie, cabdriver

16. Lt. Col. GUAN Qinchen, Deputy Regiment Commander for Diangti's division in Harbin

17. Ronald ZHAO, Partner at TSC Security Consultants Ltd. Beijing

18. EU Sun, DPRK Department of Surveillance assassin

Chapter 2

19. Alan Spires, attorney and client of TSC Security

20. Annie, friend of Alan Spires and art dealer

21. Donna Summerlake, PhD, American from Texas, teaches in Finance School and lives in the LiNai Apartments building.

22. Dr. Rebecca Blackstone, Canadian researcher in National Laboratory, friend of Mai Martin who lives in the LiNai Apartments .

Chapter 3

23. Ed Poole, Homeland Security agent under Lawrence Wright at the Beijing Field Office

24. Frank Choy, Homeland Security agent under Lawrence Wright borrowed from Homeland Security Honolulu Field Office

25. Maj. Gen. MA Minho, Ninth Bureau, Deputy Army Commander Harbin Reserve Force and North Korean specialist

26. Private 1st Class KUANG, Beijing University guard

27. Lt. WU Hong, Police Constable, Class 1 Assistant to Capt. LI, Beijing Police Department

28. SHENG Jianqiang, Tianjin xiao qiang [little gang boss]

29. DONG Zhi Wei, Beijing gang driver

30. KIM Yong-Kyung, DPRK Department of Surveillance agent, 19 years old

31. KIM Sang-Bo, DPRK Department of Surveillance agent, 18 years old

32. Sgt. GU Fan, Beijing University security, Commander GAO's driver

33. Sgt. LONG Yandong, Beijing University security, Mai Martin's escort

34. Lily, Assistant to Ronald ZHAO

35. Mr. Lawrence Wright, Homeland Security USCIS Beijing Field Office (BFO) Director, US Embassy, Beijing

36. Capt. CONG, Supervisor, Class 2 Beijing Municipal Public Security Bureau (BMPSB) Haidian Wudaokou Police Station (Beijing Police Department)

37. Dr. CHOW, doctor at Wangjing Hospital

38. GONG Ho, EU Sun's driver from the Xi'an Triad.

Chapter 4

Chapter 6

Author's Bio

ShaLi is a pseudonym to protect the identities of people who inspired characters in this fast paced and gorgeously patterned international spy thriller. Names have been changed. For more details go to BeijingAbduction.com.

Made in the USA
San Bernardino, CA
05 April 2014